# GIL LEFEBVRE

*Obsessing Rufina*

*Unto Caesar Unto God*

*Not Too Far to Have Never Been*

*Catalina Summer*

# Obsessing RUFINA

a novel by

*Gil Lefebvre*

Library of Congress Control Number: 2014958210

ISBN 978-0-9672172-9-1

*To my parents*
*Ben and Virginia Lefebvre*

# CONTENTS

## PART IV **Intrigue**

## PART V **Providence**

## PROLOGUE

In 1944, Allied forces climbed the treacherous cliffs of Normandy, breeched German lines and took out her coastal defense. This military advance would be recalled in history books as the beginning of the end of Hitler's Third Reich.

Years of battles had worn down the mighty German army, and the Luftwaffe, the pride of Hermann Göring, was almost nonexistent. Germany found herself in an unenviable position, exposed geographically on both sides. The quagmire was reminiscent of preceding conflicts, the Napoleonic Wars and the First World War. The outcome appeared predictable. However, believing providence was on his side, Hitler hung on to his illusion while the disgruntled Wehrmacht pressed on, reluctantly fighting until the last man. Yet, in clandestine corridors, plans began to plot a Germany without the leadership of der Führer.

As the war prodded on, bad news slowly found its way into Germany. She was retreating from the Russian front, and the Allies advanced in the south. The German populace, who once lined the streets, filled the arenas, inhaled Hitler's every word and shared his vision at each victory, now slowly, with defeat at hand, gave way to despair. They too began to wonder what Germany would look like after the war. Now, what started as a creeping blush became a blemish that wandered into her collective psychic.

Resistance began to ferment throughout cross sections of German society. Those openly defiant Germans were rounded up by Hitler's Gestapo and summarily eradicated by firing squad.

Nevertheless, a shocking murmur of dissent continued to form in the military corps and among German intellectuals. Even the University of Munich, which years before was at the forefront of the Nazi movement, now became the home base of the White Rose, a student resistance organization.

Hitler replied, "Up and down the country the devil of subversion strides. All the cowards are seeking a way out or, as they call it, a political solution. They say that we must negotiate while there is still something in hand! The resistance has turned into plots."

The conspirators hoped to end it all, Hitler's dream and his history. Both, they said, had run its course. Taking destiny into their hands culminated in the attempted coup of July 20, 1944. It was a desperate act, a bomb planted under Hitler's table at Wolfsschanze at Rastenburg in an attaché left by Colonel Claus von Stauffenberg. It did its job, killing some of the Nazi elites around the table. But, miraculously, Hitler survived relatively unscathed.

The Führer's broadcast that night echoed throughout the nation: "To my German comrades, the circle of usurpers had nothing in common with the Wehrmacht and above all none with the German people. This time we shall settle accounts with them in a manner in which we national socialists are accustomed."

Hitler then gave orders to purge all sectors of the society that protested his policies, leaving none a reprieve from his vengeance. Seven thousand or more were abused, tortured, tried and hanged slowly from dangling meat hooks, taken from German butcher shops and slaughterhouses.

The implicated German generals were given the option of taking their own lives rather than accepting public humiliation. Even the families of the conspirators were not immune from his wrath. They were ordered disposed of in concentration camps.

Prominent Germans who lost their lives in the resistance became many, and a few became legends. These included student activists Hans and Sophie Scholl, Professor Kurt Huber and, from the cloth, Dietrich Bonhoeffer. Causalities of Hitler's vengeance in the Wehrmacht are too numerous to mention, but two stand out among the rest: Field Marshal Erwin Rommel and Colonel Stauffenberg.

Nevertheless, reality had set in. Hitler's Third Reich was going down in shambles. The rats began to abandon ship and plan their escape. Hitler evaded justice and the gallows by taking his own life. The Nuremberg Trials, by implicating high-profile individuals, placated the international community and gave them some distance from their responsibly for the atrocities that had occurred.

Many Nazis escaped prosecution altogether. Endowed by years of looting and raping, they found like-kinds in profaned countries, which saw the Nazi plunder as just another business venture. Those countries took them in, gave them safe haven from prosecution and hid them under the cover of a new identity, making them immune from extradition and allowing them to live out the rest of their lives as if they were unleavened bread.

PART I

# Prelude

*Heidelberg, Germany*

CHAPTER 1

# Coming Home

The tour guide barked out instructions while passengers began picking out their luggage making its way around the Frankfort Airport baggage carousel. It was the beginning of what promised to be a wonderful guided tour through central Germany. The monotone voice of the guide was heard over the noise of the busy airport.

"Please take your baggage to the bus waiting out those doors, and we'll be on our way."

A group of about 40 adults of varying ages secured their bags as requested, then took them to the waiting porter, who packed them neatly into the side compartment of the bus. The eager passengers climbed aboard and searched out a comfortable seat. The doors shut with a swish, and off they went.

The short, neatly dressed man formerly introduced himself as Karl Heinrich and let everyone know he would be their guide for the next seven days.

"First stop will be charming Heidelberg," he said, continuing with his obviously rehearsed narrative. "After that, we will travel up to Nuremberg. Our final destination will be Munich, historically the epicenter of German art, culture and politics. So, for now, folks, sit back, relax and, in a little more than an hour, we'll be in Heidelberg. There at our hotel, you'll get a short reprieve, have a delicious breakfast and then it's off to sightsee."

The guide turned off the speaker, and many of the passengers slipped into a welcomed sleep while the smooth roar of the bus moved them on. One middle-aged woman who sat next to the window was clearly wrestling against any such inclination. While the bus rolled on, at each passing of a house, a tree, a church, a street, she seemed intent to strain and stare, as if in a trance, as if she'd been there before and was now coming back from a long vacation. She intently looked out the window as the window looked into her.

After about 45 minutes, the speaker crackled on, and the guide began addressing the passengers with a cheerful smile.

"For those of you who are awake and those of you who are waking, we will soon be arriving in Germany's city of romance, beautiful Heidelberg. It is located in the Rhine Rift Valley on the left bank of the lower Neckar. Early Heidelberg can be traced back to the 5th century Celts. They built a fortress and a place of worship on Heiligenberg, the Mountain of Saints. Later the Romans pillaged through the south of this Germanic region, building camps and wooden bridges to pass over the Neckar River. They remained until around 260 A.D.

"Modern Heidelberg was first documented around 769 A.D. as a small village known as Bergheim, meaning mountain home, that now lies in the middle of today's city. The people were a spiritual lot. They converted to Christianity and built the Monastery of St. Michael atop Heiligenberg and then the Neuburg Monastery in the Neckar Valley.

"The first reference to Heidelberg was in documents recovered in the Schonau Abbey and dated 1196.

"The famous Heidelberg Castle was the creation of German kings dating back to the 13th century. A mix of Gothic and Renaissance architecture, it is considered the most unique medieval structure north of the Alps.

"The city, systematically structured, followed Baroque style and is a lasting imprint of earlier Roman encampment. Heidelberg University, established in 1386, is one of Europe's oldest institutions, with a library that was one of Europe's finest for the time period. It was here, after posting his Ninety-Five Theses, that Martin Luther was received to defend them.

"There were many celebrities of academic prominence who attended or taught at the university. Unfortunately, by 1939 an estimated 33 percent of the university's faculty and the city's citizens were sent to work camps.

"We will visit the Church of the Holy Spirit, the Church of the Jesuits and St. Peter's Church, all beautifully designed to reach up toward the heavens. We will also tour Heidelberg Castle, which endured invasions and lightning, and now stands as a testament to past religious struggles throughout Europe.

"During World War II, Heidelberg was a stronghold for the Nazis. In the 1933 election, 45.9 percent of the city's electorate voted for the Nazi Party, helping Adolf Hitler establish his Third Reich in place of the Weimar Republic.

"The huge Thingstätte Amphitheatre was built for the Nazi youth rallies. Later they built the Ehrenfriedhof Memorial Cemetery that honors the fallen Wehrmacht soldiers.

"Heidelberg went relatively untouched by the war. After it was over, the U.S. government used the Grossdeutschland-Kaserne, the Wehrmacht installation, for its headquarters, renaming it Campbell Barracks.

"And, for those of you who are interested in U.S. history, Heidelberg is the city where General George S. Patton died following a car accident near Mannheim. You might get the feeling that you are in America due to the large U.S. military presence. English is spoken more freely here than in other parts of Germany. That's a lot to remember for now. We'll be visiting most of the sites in the next two days."

The bus turned the corner on to Hauptstrasse, the main road crossing Heidelberg, and came to a stop. The guests were instructed to find their luggage then proceed to the registration desk inside the hotel. The dining room was set for breakfast, and in an un-German like fashion, scrambled eggs, bacon and pancakes blessed the plates.

The entire group, rebounding from the flight and bus ride, was now ready to take on the day. However, the woman who earlier clutched at the bus window and seemed engrossed at each passing mile from Frankfurt to Heidelberg sat alone in a corner and looked out toward the street, failing to even peck at her food. It seemed as if she was searching for someone, someone to see or maybe a familiar face to say, "Hi. Where've you been all these years?"

The guide suddenly reappeared and announced, "Okay, the first part of the tour is going to be a walk through Old Town. You will enjoy delightful shops and architecture at the Marktplatz, a plaza that rivals anything you've ever seen in a Disneyland theme park. But, here it's the real thing. Some of Heidelberg's cafés have been in operation for centuries. The same family has run the Zum Roten Ochsen or Red Oxen Inn for 170 years."

At this, the lady turned from the window as if she'd seen or heard the voice of an old friend. For the first time, a noticeable smile came across her face.

Prompted by the guide, they all moved toward the lobby and waited while some of the guests came back from their rooms wearing appropriate footwear for the walk. Once assembled, they went off with cameras and backpacks strapped over their shoulders, some stuffed cold cuts, bread and bottles of water.

The lady, now pressed by the light of day, showed her age. Wrinkles of time lined her face, and a pale texture covered her skin. Her hair was beginning to whiten yet was well kept. The skirt she wore was rather ordinary, flushed to the ground, not sweeping it, but just a little beyond the drip of the other ladies'. The color, a subdued brown floral print, blended well with Heidelberg's forest green background. It made her almost anonymous compared to the rest of the crowd. But, as the group of tourists traversed the narrow streets and Baroque-style buildings, it was the blouse she wore that gave her away. Bright yellow and pleasant for this spring day, it suggested she must have been here before. She fit in so well.

This fractured creature began to transform and become animated, strutting now out ahead of the crowd, knowing where she was going. The guide suggested she stay close to the group, fearing she would be lost down some unknown street. But no, she would have none of that. She'd come too far to have patience now. There was just too much ahead of her.

After reaching the Marktplatz, she veered off from the pack, found the Zum Roten Ochsen and quickly walked inside. Once in, she abruptly stopped and, as if gasping for air at the highest peak of the Alps, stood there, not believing she was back. Had she ever left? Dizzy now, for her mind and body wouldn't let her take it all in so suddenly, she grabbed at a table to hold on and then sat down. Each wall, each picture, each table talked. They had so much to say.

"Oh so long ago I sat here. I sat here so long ago," she said in a low cry. "They are gone, but it is still here."

A soft voice interrupted and asked, "Miss, may I get you something?"

She jumped at the request. "Of course, a pilsner. Yes, a beer. Please pour me one."

The waitress looked concerned and asked, "Are you all right?"

"Of course," the lady answered. "Better than in years. Would you please speak to me in German?"

"German you speak?"

"Yes, I do. I almost… I did, but I do still."

The conversation quietly continued. Then, after some time had passed, the lady stood up and paused as if building up the courage to walk out.

The waitress asked, "Where do you go now?"

"Maybe the library."

"Do you know the way?"

"Every day, I know. It all started there in the library. I will be… Thanks for the German lesson."

The waitress smiled. "Please come back again."

"Oh, I will," she replied as she left the inn and began to trace her way around the cobblestones.

The familiar scent of the wienermart and the baker's fresh pretzels filled her senses. The sound of her shoes clinking against the stone-covered street seemed to drum a song. Peering inside the shop windows, she could see that the many different trinkets and styles for sale had changed over the years but the storefronts were the same.

All this consumed her as she continued beyond Hauptstrasse and searched until she found a familiar lonely street, not for the tourists and certainly not on the itinerary. She walked on, stopping at a building. Oh the colors, they hadn't changed.

Someone squeezed around the bicycle-crowded door and stepped out. Yes. It was here. She brought her hand up to her face and quickly brushed away the hair that floated around her eyes. It was the ocean breeze. "Yes, the ocean," she thought to herself, smiling. It amazingly found its way across the continent and rested in the valley. She remembered conversations of days gone by, but was talking to ghosts of the past. Only in Heidelberg could she do this. Only here, for once in a very long time, did she feel good.

She began again, now knowing exactly where she was going. It was by habit from many times before. As she walked on, her steps quickened, not to get away from the crowd as she had done earlier in the day but to get there. Finally, as she turned the corner, it stood waiting for her. The bell tower of the Church of the Jesuits reached to the sky, like everything else in Heidelberg. It wasn't heaven, but she was certain angels could whisper softly to you from there.

Rushing to greet the steps that graced the church, she began to take them on. Climbing them one by one, she finally reached the top, passed through the open doors and stepped inside. She quickly dabbed a finger into the holy water, signed in and, as if in a procession, walked between rows of vacant seats. The colors of the stained glass spilled out across her face and pulled her toward the altar. She arrived, genuflected, then moved to the front and stood tall, posturing herself as if to say, "Here I am God. I've come home."

She knelt in prayer, silently. There was no need for words. God knew why she was there.

She longed for the peace that had for so many years escaped her. Maybe it would be here at the steps of heaven. But, time passed, and it wouldn't come.

A voice from the back of the church abruptly broke the silence.

"My child."

A chill prickled her body. It couldn't be. Then again, it said, "Welcome my child."

She turned in fright. But of what? This man, whose face was hidden by the shadows? She waited, wondering if her time had come.

"My dear," he started again as he saw her struggling to catch a glimpse of him.

Seeing her in distress he said, "I am Father James. I'm so sorry. Did I startle you?" He waited a few seconds then asked, "Is there something I can do for you?"

She knew it was time. "Yes, father, confession."

"Confession," he echoed back, then turned and walked toward the confessional.

Once she heard its door softly close, she moved to follow, stepping tenderly as if not to wake up the saints. Time was now an eternity. Would it last? She turned the knob, stepped in and closed the door behind her. Sliding onto the seat, she reached for a rosary that had been left behind and began to run her fingers across its familiar beads. A window slid open, and his warm, inviting voice asked, "Are you here to confess your sins, my child?"

"Yes, father." Trying to pitch her voice to rally enough courage, she cleared her throat. Her heart began to overtake her thoughts as history was about to be replayed, with God's help.

"Father, I am Lina Ritter, and this is my confession," she said.

CHAPTER 2
# Heidelberg

T here's no other city in the world quite like Heidelberg in the summertime. The swollen Neckar River meanders toward the Rhine as a gentle westerly ocean breeze sways the trees along its path. The town is a mosaic of history. Along with picturesque mountain terrain, its beautiful Baroque-style churches, shops, cafés and the Marktplatz greet delighted tourists.

But for me, it was our renowned Heidelberg University that put us on the post-war map. The university's summer session had just begun. My lifelong best friend, Helen, and I shared an apartment just outside of Old Town. My days were busy as I traveled through town to the university and pondered my way through their expansive collection of books. Those amazing volumes of emotion and expression were my windows to the outside world. As I read, I could see it all, and my mind was free to venture out with the stories.

It was here in June of 1969, at the back shelves of the university library, that once again I found myself overloading my arms with books. While tiptoeing back toward my seat, I somehow managed to trip over a chair leg. Those precious books and I went flying, eventually crashing to the floor. Out of nowhere help was on its way. An outstretched hand appeared, offering me a lifeline out of the embarrassing predicament. Along with the hand came a deep voice. "You need a little help here, don't you?"

"Yes," I replied. After reaching out we pulled together as I stood. "Danka," I added softly.

He scrubbed about the floor, rounding up my cache and walked me over to my chair. After neatly stacking the books he inquired, "Are you okay?"

"Yes, of course," I replied in a library whisper. I thanked him again, and he went on his way. After a few hours of study, I returned some of the books to the stacks, kept two, then went to check them out.

"I'll take these, Erin."

Erin smiled and, now playing with me, said, "I saw you needed some help today."

"What's that smile suppose to mean?" I asked.

"Not a bad looking American," she said, grinning.

"What are you talking about?"

"You mean you didn't even look at the guy?"

"Of course not, Erin," I said while chuckling under my breath. "No, Erin, I didn't."

"It's about time you did. You're missing the roses," she continued, admonishing me in jest. "There's more to this world than books you know."

"Okay. I get it, Erin. I know where you're taking this. But don't worry. I'll meet the right guy somewhere, maybe some other time, but certainly not in the library."

Erin stamped the books with a flourish, and I pushed away from the counter.

"See you Thursday, as usual," I announced with a smile.

I felt a sense of joy as I walked under the library rotunda and out the large doors into the warm summer air. I strolled on down toward the Marktplatz, a large open-air plaza in the center of town where at anytime you'll find people relaxing, eating, listening to music or coming together for festive occasions.

As usual, today people gathered, lunching their way through sandwiches, wedges of cheese and salted pretzels while occasionally flushing it all down with a tall mug of warm beer. My appetite grew as I strolled to a nearby shop, bought a slice of liverwurst and cheese and sat down among the crowd to enjoy watching the people going about their busy days. Suddenly, a voice broke my routine, and I looked up. The bright sun blurred my vision, but I could hear him say, "May I sit down here?"

Before replying my usual 'no,' I put up my hand to shade my eyes.

"Oh, it's you," I said.

"Yes, it's me again." He smiled. "Do you mind if I share the table with you?"

"Of course not, please. So what have you come to save me from this time?" I asked, smiling.

He stumbled about as if searching for the right answer. "Actually, I felt sorry for you, eating lunch alone."

I laughed. "I choose to do that here most every day. It's quiet and relaxing."

"So, do you go to the library every day too?" he asked.

"No, not every day. More like three times a week."

"With all of those books in your arms, you must be working on something important."

"Yes. A paper for my Art Culture class."

"But it's summer break, isn't it?"

"That's right. I always take a few summer classes."

"Going somewhere fast?" he asked.

"No, it's just that college life has so much for me to enjoy."

"May I ask, do you have a name?"

"Yes." I smiled back. "My name is Lina. And, does your hand belong to a person with a name?"

"It's Thomas."

"And does Thomas have a last name?"

I laughed, as we seemed to be playing a childish game.

"Yes, it does. My name is Thomas Werner," he replied with a formal tone. "And do you have a last name as well?"

"Ritter. I am Lina Ritter."

"My, what a good German name."

"Yes, I think so."

"What are you majoring in, here at the university?"

"I don't really know yet, maybe law. Law, yes, law. I'm specializing in international law while my minor is in art literature, but that's just for pleasure. So, Mr. Werner, it's my turn to ask a few questions."

"Please. Go right ahead."

"What has you coming all the way here to Heidelberg? Is it the castles, the cafés or the romance?"

"Why do you say that?"

"Well, usually American males fit somewhere in there."

"No, no. I've been assigned to Campbell Barracks."

"You don't look military."

"Now, Lina, what does military look like?"

"A uniform."

"No, not today. I'm on my own time."

I finished my liverwurst and cheese, then a silence dampened our conversation. He gave a stunning smile while looking at me with those deep blue eyes, slowing things down. I had just a dose in my glass to wash down what remained of the liverwurst when he jumped in with a suggestion.

"Look, Lena."

"It's Lina," I corrected.

"Well, what's in a name anyway?" he quipped back, hoping to get a cozy response.

He seemed surprised when I responded, "Every thing's in a name. It's who you are and where you come from!"

"Okay. Sorry," Thomas shot back, holding up his hands as if to defend himself. "Well, Frau Lina, since I'm new around these parts, could there be a time when you're free to show me around?"

For whatever reason, I found that humorous. So he asked, "What's so funny? I can see it on your face."

"Well, it's the way you said it. It's like you're from Tombstone or somewhere out west."

"Tombstone? You've heard about that place?" He chuckled. "And the shootout at the O.K. Corral?"

"Of course, Thomas. We do have movies over here. I saw the one about the Earps."

This brought Thomas to an uncontrollable laughter as he said, "I'm halfway around the world, chatting with a pretty German girl and we're talking about the old west."

"Yes. We German girls sometimes come out of the black forest."

He laughed again. "No. I didn't mean that. "

"I know. Just making conversation."

"So, what about it? A tour with you around Germany?"

"I'm not a personal tour guide, and I'm a very busy girl, fending on my own. I don't think that will be possible." Hoping to change the subject, I asked, "How long have you been stationed here at Campbell Barracks?"

"Just about a week."

"Where did you come from? I mean, what state?"

"California."

"Oh, a surfer. That's you?"

"Well, yeah. It's just something we do out there on a hot day at the beach," he explained.

"College?"

"Yes, Stanford."

"Impressive. Well then, Mr. College Student, I must be moving on. I've got this whole world waiting for me out there."

"So, 'no' it is?"

"No."

"You mean 'yes' don't you?" he pleaded.

"No," I said. "No meaning 'no'." And with that I stood to leave. I could see from his posturing and smug smile that my rejection didn't really dent his confidence. "So it's farewell my American military friend. I'll see you around."

"When?" he shot back.

"Heidelberg is a small town."

I walked over to my bike, its basket stacked high with books. I could feel his eyes piercing my back and a teasing thought entered my mind that maybe he'd have a more favorable view from there. Still not giving in, I made sure not to look back. I wouldn't give that flamboyant Yankee anything to hang his ego on. I sensed he didn't need it. I pedaled on my way, leaving Mr. Thomas Werner alone, in the middle of the plaza, sipping away on his last remnant of lager.

I continued riding through town on the Hauptstrasse, then stopped at the baker to pick up some brotchen and tomorrow's breakfast rolls. I carefully placed them on top of my overloaded basket and moved on down the street. Eventually I entered the residential area of Heidelberg, to where tourists rarely found their way. After turning up a narrow street, I finally arrived at my apartment among the rows of freshly painted buildings, built who knows how many years or centuries before.

After leaning my bike against the wall, grabbing the books and pastries, I rushed up three flights of stairs to unlock the door. I almost had it opened when my roommate Helen appeared and said, "Here let me help you in, Lina."

While she took some of the books and brotchen I asked, "So, how was your day?"

"The usual," she answered as she sat back down at the table and continued to eat her sandwich.

"Just the usual?"

"Yes, work and all. And you?"

"Well, I met this American."

"What? Where?"

"In the library."

"Oh, so now you go to the library to meet guys?" Helen chided.

"No, no, no, Helen! It wasn't like that. I tripped, and he helped me up."

"Yeah, sure you did. Old story, Lina."

"No, it wasn't that way, Helen," I insisted, trying to defend my virtue. "It just happened."

"So tell me. What did he look like, handsome?"

"Helen, I don't survey every person I meet, like you do."

She laughed. "Okay. So, really, what was this American like?"

"He seemed nice, intelligent, about 6 feet tall, light brown hair, neatly dressed and, oh, he has blue eyes."

"And did this guy, who concerned you so very little, have a name?"

"Yes, he did, Helen."

"And a place to hibernate?"

"Okay, it's Thomas Werner, Californian, stationed at Campbell Barracks."

"Very good, Lina, especially for not really showing much of an interest in the guy. So, are you going to see him again?"

"Actually, Helen, he asked me to show him around."

"And you said?" Helen inquired between sandwich bites.

"I said 'no.'"

"No? Why?"

"Because I don't work that way. I'm dialed in differently. Plus, it's not proper."

"Oh, Lina, you sound like you're still back at the abbey."

"Helen, I may live here in town, but I'll always be back at the abbey. You know that. A nun, no, but the sisters are family, and Reverend Mother has taken care of us since I can remember."

"All right, Lina. I've got to get back to the travel agency. Got two tours set up for today. One is coming in from Japan."

"That should be fun."

"It's easy. All I do is point at something and they take pictures of it," Helen called back as she left.

Later that afternoon, I bicycled back to the university, then headed on to Heidelberg Castle. Passing the Church of the Jesuits, I stopped in to say "hi" to Father Tobias. As usual, we had a few laughs before I left for my afternoon job as a guide at the castle.

When dusk arrived, I rode my bike across the Neckar Bridge toward the north side where centuries of Heidelberg's philosophers, proctors and students had strolled discussing the relevance of great thinkers. It was here at the Philosopher's Walk that I always got off my bike to walk.

The city lights illuminated Heidelberg across the river and gave a scenic view of Old Town and the castle nestled into the mountain. I could see the lights of the Monastery of St. Michael and the smaller Monastery of St. Stephen, along with the Nazi-era amphitheater and the remains of an eastern Celtic hill fortress from the 5th century B.C. I'd taken in those lovely views so many times. However, somehow something was in the air tonight. Maybe it was intuition or the changing climate, but this time something was telling me my life was about to be turned upside down.

This was not at all disconcerting, not by any means. For, I was always at peace with God in all of this. Would it be love? A new vocation, a cherished term in the abbey? Or was it God preparing me, tapping me on my shoulder, to let me know His divine providence was about to take me on a journey. That was what Reverend Mother always preached when I got these subtle notions. Of course I believed in God's omnipotence, but the compelling question was, where was I going? And why?

Now, for the first time in my life, standing there looking out across the river, an anxious tension filled my mind. I couldn't help but think that maybe, just maybe, I was headed someplace to where I'd already been.

CHAPTER 3

# Trite Dose of Charm

It would be a few weeks later that he came back into my life. I was sitting up front and, like many of the other students, struggling to keep my mind on the lecture—what a great imposition that was. Sensing our discontent, Professor Mueller attempted to tweak his presentation. He posited a provocative question.

"Art literature is but a mirror of history, is it not, therefore a reflection of culture and technology, the zeitgeist of a period? Net result, it's inevitably changing, so how does it relate to morality? And, what is morality? Where is its proper place? Does it not create a predicament to Kant's imperatives? As he did say, 'To know it has been assumed that all our cognition must conform to the objects.' But, let us once try whether we do not get further with the problems of metaphysics by assuming that the objects must conform to our cognition. To put it simply, does not the zeitgeist complicate his philosophical position? Anybody like to join me in this conversation?" he asked in a sarcastic fashion, obviously trying to bring us back out of our slumber.

None took the opportunity, so he challenged us again. "Anyone? Anyone?"

Awkward silence followed. Then finally, from the back of the classroom, a hand rose.

"Yes, yes, you Mr. Werner. Would you like to take this on?"

"Yes, Dr. Mueller. I'll have a try at it."

"Okay, then."

"Isn't history but the byproduct of the human condition, where man finds himself the essence of his morality? If so, may I give you an example?"

"Yes. Of course, Mr. Werner, continue."

A silence now alerted the class. The students became inert and keenly attentive to the discourse that was about to take place.

Mr. Werner rose to respond. "Yes, professor. Well, if I put a man in danger, I have a moral imperative. That is, I am morally responsible to attempt to help him out of danger. However, if a foolish lad wishes to show off and thereby puts himself into a dangerous situation, the morality equation stays unchallenged, but the circumstance implicates the moral response. Does it not?"

The professor asked, "So, Mr. Werner, what then can we presume from this hypothetical?"

"Professor Mueller, it is precisely this. Circumstance does dictate the response, but moral imperative, as prescribed by Kant, remains universal. And, if the stupid lad, wishing to cause his own calamity, then attempts to defend and justify his actions by some absurd rationalization as a moral imperative, well...in the end, I suggest, that his claim will not only be an offense to reason but will indict him as a co-conspirator to his own suicidal demise."

The class burst into laughter, and the professor smiled when he said, "Mr. Werner, I must say, a welcoming proposition. But your reply has given you away. You must be one of those conspiring American law students."

The class broke into another collective laugh. I turned back to make sure it was the very same. His eyes met mine as he sat back down in his seat and tapped his pencil on the table as if to say, "Yes, it's me."

Eventually the class broke. I picked up my books, stepped out to the corridor and pressed on. A voice called out, "Leena."

This was different from the last meeting. The situation was now more reassuring. I kind of wanted to tarry with this intriguing American. So I slowed, letting him catch up.

"So what about it?" he asked.

"What about what?" I asked back.

"The tour, of course."

"Well, Mr. Werner, I am not sure you are in need of a tour guide. You sounded as though you have it all together in Dr. Mueller's class. Besides, how did you get him to allow you a late entry to his class?"

"My dear Frau Leena, may I call you that?"

"Of course not. It's with an 'i 'and not an 'e'," I said, smiling now to encourage him to stay in the conversation.

"Sorry about the name. I've been watching too many American movies back at the barracks. It would be nice if you could or would share an afternoon with me."

"Share what?"

"I'm sure you know a lot about this place," he shot back.

I got the notion that he was hoping I would see him as an unpretentious, uneducated stray cat, which his classroom antics clearly displayed wasn't the case. I knew that, but it was his big smile and the way he asked that kept me on.

"Actually, you picked a good day for me. All right, I will spend a few hours with you out of pity. That is, if you accept my terms, Mr. American Student."

"Sure, anything."

"Nothing."

"Nothing?"

"Yes, nothing." I explained. "Nothing personal will come

from this. Okay?" I asked while pointing my finger in order to make my point.

"Okay, it's a deal." he assured.

"Let's begin with some lunch. I'm famished. How about you?"

"Sure, anything beats sitting alone in the officers' mess, crunching on something that you can't identify if it's vegetable, fruit or dairy, accompanied by an animal that must have been dug up from an archaeological site."

"Well, I'm sure we can beat that." I smiled.

The crowds had left The Marktplatz so finding my favorite table was easy. I gestured for Mr. Werner to sit. The sun was bright and music came from somewhere but it didn't matter. I became aware of how fine things were out here, and it seemed more intense and fresh than ever before.

After lunch was served, I watched as he juggled around a pretzel. Between sips of beer I said, "You see, Mr. Werner, unlike in America, lunch is a big occasion in Germany. And dinners, well, they're more like snacks."

He smiled, raised his stein of beer and asked, "And, do you go on with the day afterward?"

"Of course we do. You see, we drink beer from an early age. That's why we can handle it."

A few awkward minutes passed as he sat there looking at me, obviously trying to size me up. I didn't want that, so I jumped in.

"How is it that you got Professor Mueller to let you in his class so late?"

"Rank has its benefits," he grinned.

"Oh, that is how you Americans play it then?"

"No, no, don't get me wrong. I have a friend who is a friend of someone whom the good professor knows. That's all."

"So, what really brings you here to Heidelberg, Mr. Werner?"

"The military."

"But, why Heidelberg?"

"Well, let me go back a little, Lena. Or is it with an 'i' or…"

I jumped in, saying "Liiiinnnnna will do."

"Okay, Lina it is. I was finishing off my education at Stanford University—it's in California. That's on the West Coast of the U.S."

Not wanting to be patronized, I jumped in again. "I know. It's around San Francisco. I know about Stanford."

"Okay, then. So, since we have this war going on and we have a draft, I decided it would be best to join the officer ranks, pick my spot for duty. Especially since Southeast Asia has never been one of my top 10 places to visit."

Now, as if reading from the tourist guide, he said, "Heidelberg is a city of romance and thousands of miles from Asia. It was an easy decision. So here I am. And what about you? Have you lived here all of your life?"

"Yes. You see, Mr. Werner…"

"Okay, okay, enough of this 'Mr. Werner.' It's Thomas."

"Thomas, then, as you prefer." I began stumbling a bit, careful to not overexpose my past. But it came out anyway. "You can say I'm a product of the war."

"What do you mean? That was over a long time ago."

"Well, you see, um, um, I was brought up in an abbey."

"An abbey? Oh no. Are you a nun?"

"No, no," I laughed. "It's like a monastery. Actually, it is a monastery. You see, Thomas, my parents were executed after they protested the Nazis. Near the end of the war, in Munich, they were hanged. Anyway, that's the way the story goes."

A somber atmosphere came over the conversation.

"That was before I could remember. I was taken into hiding by the Sisters of Neuburg."

After looking into his eyes and seeing his brashness turn to compassion, I continued.

"They raised and cared for me ever since. I'm attending classes here at the university now. I've had a variety of jobs over the past few years and even worked as a secretary at Campbell Barracks."

"Really, at Campbell?"

"Yes, and let's see, I've also been a cook and nurse and now a tour guide at the castle. So here I am."

"Do you miss them?"

"My parents? Well, yes, in theory, but I was so young I can't remember them, even if I try hard. There's just Reverend Mother and the sisters. Oh, and my best friend, Helen, she's like my sister. We came to the abbey around the same time, but we are so different, Helen and I. Well, that's it. That's all of the family I have. We wonder about the war, the past, Hitler. The pain in Germany still is there. It will always be problematic to our lives," I rambled on feeling like I was pricking at my soul with a needle.

He asked gently, "Do you think the German people brought this on themselves?"

I shot back defensively, "How do I know? What was all that nationalist socialist stuff to me? I was too young."

This time he was sarcastic when he said, "But you now know what happened, the Holocaust and all?"

I rebounded. "It seems that you Americans, even to this day, know more about that time in history than we Germans who live here. You are taught in your history classes, and your books divulge all the details. Many of those things are hidden in German curriculums as mere footnotes. We know there were camps out there and that the Nazis did awful things, but it wasn't us who did them."

I found myself taking the offense. "Look at what you're doing in Vietnam. Thousands of innocent lives being burnt by napalm. Are you doing it? No, of course not!" I said, answering my own question and relieving him of having to answer.

"Of course not," I continued. So what do you do? You come all the way over here to Heidelberg, to Campbell Barracks to avoid it all. Should that be blamed on you, the war? Can you stop it?"

Sensing I'd strayed too far with my emotions and tongue, I scrambled out an apology.

"I'm so sorry, Thomas. I get caught up, and my temper gets the best of me."

Sensing our conversation must have run out of lines, I stood to leave and said, "I must go now."

"No, no. You must not go," he said as a smile broke out across his beautifully tanned face, flashing a dashboard of straight white teeth. Those blue eyes looked deep into mine, pleading with my soul to stay just a little longer. There was more to him than I thought, and, against my better impulse, I sat back down.

Thomas broke the silence. "Okay, let's start over."

"All right, sounds like a good idea."

"That was then, now is now."

Somehow that made me laugh. Seeing he had me in a more pleasant mood, he asked, "How about that tour? The military is paying me to get to know Germany better."

"Oh, so that's it?" I asked, still stalling my answer. "So, Thomas, what do you do for the U.S. government back at the barracks?"

"Legal."

"Meaning what?"

"Whatever they come up with. It's really not law related. I just cool down the confrontation." He smiled.

"You mean like you just did with me?"

"No, no, Lina. You've got me all wrong here. I just want to see more of Heidelberg from someone who lives here. That's all."

"That's all?"

"Yes, that's all," he answered.

"Okay then, Thomas, we'll start the tour by walking through Old Town. I'll probably bore you with its history, then on to the churches, some of the most beautiful in the world. We'll take a look at the charming architecture and then on to my specialty, Heidelberg Castle. We'll finish by biking across the bridge and going over some early history of Heidelberg. From the other side, you'll be treated to the mythical seduction of this city."

"Seduction?"

"No, Thomas, after that you'll go back to the barracks, and I will carry on." I grinned.

Off we went, talking and forgetting any differences we had, just soaking up the charm of the city. I paused to notice a rather unique locket on display in the Auerbach Jewelry Store window.

"You really like it?"

"Yes," I replied.

"Well, then let's go in and see what it costs."

"No. Let's not."

"Why not?" he asked.

"You see, Thomas, I've found that life is about options. You take one, you must give up another."

He shrugged his shoulders and said, "Okay."

When we walked by the bakery, he wanted to sit down and

indulge in something sweet. I suggested we wait.

After window shopping Old Town, I took him to my favorite outdoor bistro, where we snacked on roasted meat with schnitzel, potatoes, dumplings and a side dish of veggies and noodles, called spätzle.

"Different from the menu at the barracks?"

He laughed then said, "Very different."

"Well, we have a long day ahead of us, and I don't want you to hold us back by stopping to eat because you're hungry again."

We enjoyed discussing more comfortable topics. I attempted to help with the bill, but he insisted.

"No, no, you're my tour guide. Besides, remember the U.S. government is paying for it."

On we went, seeing sights and stopping off at the Church of the Jesuits. I introduced Thomas as my stray dog to Father Tobias, who said, "You're a lucky man. You are in good hands with Lina, but I warn you, do not get on her wrong side. She is long on passion but short on temper."

Thomas laughed and said, "I think I already know a little about that."

We waved goodbye and moved on up to the castle tram. Once on top we sat to enjoy the view, and Thomas asked, "You actually work here?"

"Yes, I do. Three days a week."

As we got up and walked inside, I began to realize that I was starting to like him. He seemed truly inquisitive, obviously smart, and he was trying so hard to understand my world. At least the parts I let him in on.

Later, I rounded up two bikes, and we wheeled our way across the Neckar Bridge, laid them down and strolled up the Philosopher's Walk. It was a familiar journey, except now, for the first time, I had someone with me. I was not alone. I continued my tour.

"Did I tell you? One of your famous generals died right here in Heidelberg, General Patton."

The sun began its finale, dropping behind the mountains. The lights from Heidelberg Castle, Old Town and the cluster of buildings hanging onto the hillside began to flicker in the night sky. The mythical side of the city now took over.

I told him, "This is where dreams can be made and your heart escapes the earth. It happens every day at this time. You can see, Thomas, why these young socialists came under the spell. For, the night brings something you can't see but you can definitely feel. You can believe anything, and you will. That's why they call Heidelberg the City of Romance."

While the sun collapsed from a long day, and the lights of the city alone kept guard, that familiar feeling came over me, one of belonging. Thomas reached out and took my hand. I took his. He squeezed ever so gently to let me know that there was a bond between us.

We walked back, picked up our bikes and rode to the Hauptstrasse, where we attempted to say our goodnights.

"Where do you live? I can ride with you, you know, for protection," he offered.

"No, thanks. I assure you I can protect myself." I laughed. There was no need to know where I lived, not now anyway.

"So when will I see you again?"

"In class, watching you match it out with Professor Mueller. Oh, did you know next weekend the class is going on a fieldtrip and will be bused to Paris? Have you been to Paris?"

"No," he answered.

"Well you must go then. The university has a hostel there, and it should be fun."

"Lots of good things in Paris?"

"Yes, at least that's what I've read. Do try and make it," I said in a commanding voice.

"Of course I will."

He took my hand again, but this time I let it slide out of mine while looking into his eyes. I pulled back, got on my bike and rode home in the dark. When I came into my apartment, I saw that Helen had waited up.

"Tell me about your day, Lina," she said.

"Let's see. I stopped by and talked with Father Tobias."

"Aah, aah! Father said you found a new friend."

"Now, Helen," I said trying to defend myself and keep my composure.

She rushed in. "Is he the same guy you met in the library?"

"Yes, Helen, and also in Professor Mueller's Art Culture class. He said a friend of a friend got him into the class."

"So, Lina, do you like him?"

"Interesting fellow, good smile, but there's something that keeps me pushing away."

"Oh, Lina, you've always been that way."

"I know. Somehow our past won't let us just go on."

"But that has to change now, doesn't it, Lina?"

"I don't know, Helen. So how's the good friar?" I asked hoping to change the discussion to neutral terms.

"Fine. But you know we both talked to the good friar today and every day since we've left the abbey. You just wanted to change the subject."

"Oops," I said while we both laughed. "Well, I'm going to bed. Good night, Helen, and thanks for waiting up for me."

I went into my room, sat down and pulled opened my bedside drawer. Like most every night, I took out my small ragged notebook and began to record the day's events.

*Dear Diary: Had a wonderful day. Still something doesn't seem right. I hope and pray that I'm wrong. Looking forward to Paris next week, with extreme anticipation.*

CHAPTER 4
## The Abbey

Helen and I soaked in the warmth from the beautiful summer day as we rode our bikes across the Neckar Bridge. The river bustled with boats full of sightseers snapping postcard-worthy shots of breathtaking views. A jubilant mood prevailed as we dodged rows of grapevines on one side and fig and olive trees on the other. Helen pointed out several African rose-ringed parakeets and Siberian swan geese, shoveling about in nearby streams. We found our favorite picnic spot then stopped for a quick snack of cheese and cold cuts. As usual, the ocean breeze making its way into the valley was refreshing.

We were going home, and home was Neuburg Abbey. You see, Helen and I were born out of a war we never witnessed. All we knew about our youth was that we were conceived in love but then history and the war did the rest. Things got so shuffled that we both ended up as mere homeless immigrants taken in by the Benedictine Sisters of the Catholic Church and eventually orphaned at the abbey.

Their strict, compassionate yet loving guidance brought us close to God, and with His help they provided all our earthly needs. Reverend Mother would remind us often that, "It was

God's providence that brought us all together."

Helen and I clung tightly to the only support we had, and the sisters of Neuburg Abbey became our only family. We thought of ourselves as the fortunate ones. Yes, orphaned by our parents' fate at the hands of the Nazis but given a second chance at life in the abbey. We felt blessed, except whatever happened to the hundreds of others? Where did they go? It was far too overwhelming to dwell upon.

Riding alongside Helen, I thought about what a wonderful companion she'd been. She was this petite, cheerful, sparkling ball of life and very attractive, I might add. Her stylish clothes fit her well, and that's not just me saying so, but the many gentlemen whose heads turned to take a second look said the same thing. I'm sure she knew that she passed the test just fine.

I sometimes worried about her though. Far more open to the world than I, Helen liked keeping up with the latest trends and jetsetters. But, she never strayed too far. For, there were always the abbey, the sisters and Reverend Mother Johanna Maria ever present, even as we attended the university.

Yes, there was always Reverend Mother. We knew she loved us beyond the universe, and we were the stars in her galaxy. She said she'd come from Passau, a city high up in the Bavarian Alps. It was there, many years ago, she became convinced God had prepared her for something important.

Reverend Mother said she'd been sheltered from worldly things. However, she had a peculiar intuitive knowledge about the world. It was this dichotomy that made her particularly interesting. Her features, though full of age and not cared for, were beautiful, so noble and discreet. What passion she must have for God, to give it all up for Him.

If you wanted to find her, if she didn't find you first, she'd usually be in the abbey chapel, kneeling and talking to God. She was there so often that I once asked her, "Reverend Mother, God knows all your thoughts. Can't you spend your time doing other things?"

She replied, "My child, God has done so much for us. All He desires in return is for us to seek Him in all that we do." Then she smiled and added, "And it seems we always have something to ask of Him, don't we, Lina?"

On that day, I once again found her in the chapel. She turned to ask, "What have you on your mind child?"

But she always knew what was on my mind, because Father Tobias always let her know what Helen and I were doing in town. He was like the town crier, Friar Tuck and Santa Claus all in one.

She beckoned me into her study, where she often cloistered among tall shelves of books and a few pictures of the saints. A big oak desk with a large familiar Bible and clutters of paper sat in the middle of the room. Behind where she sat was a grand window that looked out toward the mountains. She would, from time to time, stand while talking and gaze out. You knew her mind wandered up there to some other day in those beautiful Bavarian Alps.

She motioned, as usual, for me to sit in the soft oversized leather chair on the other side of her desk. Then the interrogation began.

"So, child, let's have it."

I looked down at the Bible and knew that, when we finished today, it would somehow miraculously be opened to just the right verse to address the situation. Most of the time, she would start with, "How are you doing and are you eating and sleeping enough?" But today she went right to her concern. "You met a new friend?"

"I meet a lot of friends at school and as a tour guide," I

replied. But I knew what she was after, so I thought I might as well get to it. "Reverend Mother, I met a young man at the university library."

"Well, that's a preferable place to me a gentleman. He is one, isn't he, Lina?"

"I think so, Reverend Mother. I showed him around Heidelberg and took him with me on my favorite walk across the river. It was fun, and I enjoyed his company," I said, knowing she wanted more. "He's an American officer stationed at Campbell. Just been here a couple of months and is enrolled in my Art Culture class."

"With Dr. Mueller? Is he smart and handsome, I suppose?"

Blushing, I continued, "Yes, he dresses well, is polite and many of the students have taken to him. He's most helpful with them in their studies and went to a prestigious American university. He said he picked the military before they picked him, so that he could find his own way as he met his obligation."

"This Vietnam is a complication in a young man's life, I suppose," she added.

"Well, there you have it, Reverend Mother."

"I hear you and Helen are planning to go to Paris and stay in the student hostel next week."

"Yes, Reverend Mother."

"This will be your first time to Paris. Seems like a good fieldtrip for your class. It is a city with important art and history, but it is also a city notorious for temptation." After a pause Reverend Mother added, "Make sure you go to the Notre Dame Cathedral to pray. Be reminded of Mathew 6:21."

"Yes, I know it well, Reverend Mother."

"Shall we pray together then?"

I nodded, and she began, alternately praying and reading from the Bible, just to teach me where to find relevant passages in God's own words. We ended with "Our Father who art in heaven...."

On our ride home, I said to Helen, "You say too much to Father Tobias. Like always that little old cherubim of a man goes straight to the Reverend Mother with all the details."

"It's about the handsome fellow, isn't it, Lina?" We both broke out in laughter before she added, "Well, Lina, it's about time for you to meet someone."

"No, it's not Helen. I don't need a man to cheer me up like you, and you have way too many."

"You have friends, Lina."

"But not that kind."

"What do mean?"

"You know what I mean, Helen."

"Well then, are we going to Paris or not? Did Reverend Mother okay it?"

"Yes, but as always in her own way. Yes, we have Reverend Mother's blessing. And, Helen, I'll be watching you with Hans."

"And, Lina, I'll be watching you with Thomas," she smirked. "Agreed?"

"Agreed."

We rode on into Heidelberg just before the sun passed behind the mountain. Later that evening, as I pulled out my diary and began to write, I felt something special was about to happen. I could feel it. God wanted me out there. He would show the way. But what made me so anxious was I didn't have any idea what the way would be. Certainly not romance, I couldn't be pulled into that now. No, something less fleeting, like Reverend Mother said, and certainly not Paris. It would never overtake me. I would not let it, with God's help of course.

## CHAPTER 5
## Paris

Befour sunrise, I climbed aboard the chartered bus and quickly found a window seat. Right on my heels, Helen rushed to plop down beside me. The 337-mile ride from Heidelberg to Paris would take us almost five hours. I pressed my face against the window while we rolled along the autobahn. Eventually the sun came up, and I finally got a view of Germany's magnificent countryside.

When we crossed the Rhine into France, my heart skipped from the excitement of finally visiting Europe's most world-renowned city. I thumbed through the travel brochure and set out a strategy, making sure not to miss an inch. Most of the information was familiar.

"The world looks to Paris, Europe's fashion center, not only for art, culture and clothing design but for cosmetics and perfumes as well," I read.

The city's character was inspirational, especially during the Louis XIV and Napoleonic periods. Then there were the amazing must-see locations: the Eiffel Tower, the Arch de Triomphe, Champs-Élysées, Notre Dame and the Palace of Versailles, with its sprawling, smartly manicured gardens. Of course we couldn't miss the many art galleries found along the narrow streets that gave Paris its charm.

I wondered if we might even get the chance to visit the Moulin Rouge, where painters such as Henri Toulouse-Lautrec sketched the wanton and sinister aspects of the city. Oh, so much to see and so little time. Noticeably absent was Thomas Werner, but I wouldn't let that bother me. I refused to give up an ounce of optimism. I was going to Paris!

It was still early when we pulled up to the hostel. After unloading and dragging our baggage to our various rooms, we gathered in the conference area. Professor Mueller walked in with a big grin and a surprise.

"Did you think I'd just let you wander all around the city without a purpose? Of course not, so break yourselves into groups of no more than four. I've arranged a scavenger hunt."

Some students rolled their eyes but most were delighted at the adventure. The professor continued, "Clues will lead your group to many cultural sites throughout the city. Think of it as a kind of guided tour, without a guide, leaving just enough time for you to take lunch at a sidewalk café. At each point of reference you must provide evidence you were physically there. I also have a questionnaire for you to complete along the way."

Smiling he added, "You see. I know all the tricks you students play. I've been through them all. So here are a map and your first clue. Go ahead and get started. See you folks later, and, remember, I'll be out there somewhere keeping watch, just to keep you honest. Tomorrow morning, you'll turn in your team notes. Then the rest of the day will be yours to spend in whatever way you want. But, it must have a cultural significance, because that's what you'll be writing your term paper on."

After Helen, Hans and I gathered as a team, we rushed to our respective rooms, filled our backpacks to the brim with snacks and then met on the front steps. Out of nowhere, Thomas casually strolled up and tapped me on the shoulder. It seemed as if he were some kind of magician, popping up when I least expected him.

He noticed my surprise and said, "Hey, I had to make quite a few changes to get leave. I also relieved the carpool of this fine automobile, filled with petro. So what's going on here?"

I told him of Dr. Mueller's plot to make sure we visited the city's important cultural sites and asked him to join us, then made the introductions.

"This is Helen, my friend and roommate," I began.

Thomas eyed her for an uncomfortable few seconds, taking her in. She did that to men.

I broke in. "And this is her friend, Hans."

"Lucky man," Thomas witted as the two shook hands.

Hans replied, "Yes I am." That brought laughter all around.

So there we were, the four of us evenly matched with a car and about to plunder Paris. The first clue was easy, and we all shouted together, "Eiffel Tower!"

Thomas jockeyed around the horrible traffic circles until we turned onto the Champ de Mars, and there she was. We jested that the second clue would probably be at the very top.

We took the elevator, avoiding the queue for the tower climb, no need to waste time or energy in the Paris summer heat. That was our excuse, anyway.

When we finally arrived and stepped out onto the upper platform, you could hear a collective gasp. Now, I'd been at the top of Heidelberg Castle, but this was incredible. I flipped out the map of Paris, and we began pointing and guessing at each important site in the distance. The arch, the buildings, churches and amazing architecture could be seen for miles.

Not wanting to leave the solace of the height and panorama, we stayed while penciling in answers to the professor's questions. The tower rises 300 meters above the ground. It was named after engineer Gustave Eiffel, whose company designed and built the tower for the 1889 World's Fair that celebrated the centennial of the French Revolution.

Thomas mentioned that many of the locals considered it an eyesore, but today most people can't imagine Paris without it.

"Okay, now where's the second clue?" Helen wondered aloud.

As if on cue a young lady stepped out of the shadows and asked, "Professor Mueller's students?"

"Yes," I said, and she handed over the next clue. I read the card: *"It was a passion to grow where kings have set."*

"Oh, that's easy. The Versailles gardens," Hans announced.

Helen reminded us to hold on to our lift tickets as proof of the visit and off we went, checking the map and stopping the car a few times to confirm with a local that we were on the right track.

As the day progressed into the afternoon, we wandered through the Versailles halls, taking notes on its remarkable history. Just 10 miles outside of Paris and built by Louis XIV, Versailles was designed to make a statement to the world: France would be a leader of modern fashion and architecture.

We raced back to mainstream Paris, keeping on with the hunt, and drove past the Sacré-Coeur. The cathedral stood as a stark contrast to the mostly Romanesque style of Paris. It was built as an imposing Basilica true to Christian traditions.

Next it was on to the Avenue des Champs-Élysées, a remarkable promenade that stretches from Place de la Concorde to Place Charles de Gaulle and is punctuated by the Arc de Triomphe at its west end.

Unique cafés, luxury shops and theaters bordered by neatly arranged fountains and gardens surrounded the historical sites. This provided a dramatic backdrop to the city's most famous avenue. After parking the car on a side street, we strolled out onto the sidewalk.

Thomas found a shaded, outdoor café and invited us to sit down, talk and take in something cool to dampen the flaming heat. The temperature had been rising ever since we left Heidelberg's cool morning air.

We enjoyed a grand front row seat of people trafficking about, setting in motion all of the unique sounds and smells of Paris. A waitress moved quickly to take our order, but, true to Parisians, it would be on her terms.

Helen jumped in to display her French but got caught up accenting a word in the wrong place. That caused us all to laugh. Her spin on the French language sounded more like a Germanic invasion.

The French waitress, impervious to our jovial mood, stepped in as if to say, "Enough!"

She asked, "What is you order?" in a rather contemptuous tone.

Since all of us were quite aware of French mannerisms, it caused even more laughter.

Helen broke in, "Well, let's see, do you have a Riesling?"

And of course, that gave us away. Poor Thomas was left somewhat outside of our inside jokes about the French.

"Yes, a Riesling would be perfect. Do you have one?" I asked as well.

Standing on her last nerve, the waitress said dryly, "Yes, of course we do."

Helen continued, "But is it sweet and full grape or dry?"

"I can assure you it is very sweet," the waitress responded dryly.

"Oh, and please can the glass be chilled?"

At that, the waitress looked distressed. "No, miss. A chilled wine? No."

Helen pressed on. "A cube of ice will do."

After the waitress took off to fill our order, we chuckled among ourselves. Thomas seemed to catch on that the German and French people were at odds when it came to taste, culture and manners. Somehow history hadn't helped appease the differences.

After a few minutes of comfortable silence while we took in the view, the waitress returned with four goblets of wine and placed them on the table, as if saying, "Viva la France!" Before leaving, she pointed to the one cube of ice floating in Helen's Riesling.

"Are we cheating here?" I said.

"What do you mean, Lina?" Helen asked.

"Thomas gave us a great advantage over the other students. We have the car, but they must use public transportation or a taxi. I bet that's tough with all the traffic of Paris seeming to run without any particular pattern, kind of like a grand prix without direction."

Helen easily brushed my concerns aside.
She always saw the world and its disparity as something worthy of a smile, and she was willing to take it all on with a positive manner.

"Life is God's playground," she would say.

He made it that way for her enjoyment, and enjoy it she did.

When we finished our wine, Helen suggested to Hans, "Let's walk down to one of the fountains and put our feet in to cool down."

"We've got the Louvre next on the list. Only a few minutes, Helen," I called out to her as she floated away.

"Have another?" Thomas asked.

"Yes, I think I will. After all, this is Paris. Right?"

He nodded in agreement and took command as only

Americans do. He politely pointed at the waitress and said, "Please, two more over here."

She arrived with two of the same and, when Thomas smiled at her, it seemed to work out her disposition. For the first time, I saw Thomas not as someone just trying to make it in this world, but one who could command the moment with manners and a keen sense of timing.

"How is it, Thomas, that you can get your way with women?"

"Now, Lina, don't take that too far. At Stanford we used to say, 'we must learn to step on shoes without scuffing the shine.'"

"Really? You really said that?" I laughed. We sipped some more and I said, "Tell me about yourself."

"I thought we already covered me. There's not much more to tell... college, military."

"No, no, what do you do that allows such benefits?"

"Being an officer and a JAG, I always have someone who owes me a favor. It's called networking, Lina. That's all. The art of networking."

"Well, let's see, so far we have the Louvre and Notre Dame left on today's list of discoveries. So, Thomas, up to now, what do you find most intriguing about Paris?"

After a long pause, he became sincere and looked at me, not just at me but deep into my eyes, hoping to get beyond them as he slid out a line. "You. I find you most intriguing."

"Ha. Sorry, Thomas, I don't blush that easily. Okay, then, I'll play. Why do you find me most intriguing out of all we've seen of Paris?"

Acting as a lawyer in need of a good defense he said, "Lina, one, you're a free spirit. I think you see things that others miss. Two, unlike most free spirits, you're going somewhere."

"Really? Now where's that?"

"I don't know, but I'm sure once you find out where it is, you'll get there. And, three, you have an undercurrent."

"An undercurrent? What's that?"

"Something out there from your past that's pulling on your life today. And you must search it out before you can go forward."

"And, I'm sure you will be the one to help me on my way," I said smiling but with heavy sarcasm.

He laughed. "You see, Lina, you're also not very trusting. For instance, this chaperone business, do you always have Helen at your side? Is it that you're not very sure of yourself?"

"No, it's just Paris and I'm protecting Helen."

"Maybe so."

"Thomas, let me tell you how I see it. Helen and I are very close. We've ventured out and have come a long way from the security of the abbey." I smiled and explained, "Thomas, I have no need to grow new branches nor do I have the time. I've got more vertical growth to do before that."

As I began to carry on with that thought, Helen and Hans came back.

"You should have seen her, Lina!" Hans said proudly. "She hiked her skirt up, stepped right in the fountain and danced around while the tourists snapped photos as if she were some sort of celebrity. When she did some kind of jig they actually clapped!"

"Where to now?" asked Helen, clearly pleased with Hans' admiration.

"Let's see. The clues lead toward the Louvre or Notre Dame. So which first?" I asked.

Thomas jumped at the chance to decide. "The Louvre! We'll need to spend some time there. There's so much to see. I had an art class at the Farm so…."

"You were a farmer?"

Thomas laughed. "No, Helen. The Farm is what we call Stanford University." And with a raised glass he announced, "It's on to the Louvre!"

The Louvre had its beginnings in the 12th century. It's one of the world's most renowned and prestigious privately run museums. It's gone through many stages while accumulating such impressive artworks as the Venus de Milo, the Nike of Samothrace, the Dying Slave by Michelangelo and, of course, its signature painting, Leonardo de Vinci's Mona Lisa.

The museum has collected more than a million works of art, and 35,000 are on display at any one time, covering three large wings. The Sully Wing not only contains famous drawings and prints but also antiquated art from all over the world. Another is the Richelieu Wing. There you can view paintings from the middle ages up to the 19th century. Works include the Virgin Madonna of Chancellor Rolin by Flemish painter Anthony van Dyck and The Lacemaker from Johannes Vermeer. Decorative art and furniture are skillfully arranged to give the feel of a castle setting.

The Denon Wing is most well known and best received by tourists. Here you'll find the Mona Lisa, the Wedding Feast at Cana and far too many other valuable paintings, artifacts and art pieces than you can possibly take in just in one day or even a week. For the most part, people pass through the Louvre searching out the most notorious pieces of art while traveling through the enormity of the place.

We entered via the Carrousel du Louvre. The line of sightseers slowed us down and allowed us to browse through the Sully Wing. We passed hundreds of works and commented on a few.

At some of the more impressive pieces, we'd try to stop, but the crowd pressed on, pulling us along like magnets gravitating toward the cherry at the top of this delightful adventure. It would be in the Denon Wing where we would be treated to the famous Mona Lisa. So much had been written about her. Songs of praise and movies carried her name. The world may recognize names like Elvis Presley, Coca-Cola or Walt Disney. But none transgressed across cultural lines like the Mona Lisa.

So, as we slowly moved closer to her, we spread out and began to browse about, finding something we liked. It resembled a holy mass as we contemplated the importance of the art and how it reached us personally. Some pieces deserved a casual glance while others reflected historical episodes and displayed the civility of the time, from royalty to the peasantry scenes of the artist Pieter Bruegel.

However, once in a while one artwork would elicit unguarded soul searching. There and then, it happened to me..

There while I was strolling about the Denon Wing, browsing the pictures, looking forward to the Mona Lisa. I stopped to let the crowd empty their film on her, thinking it would be better to buy a postcard since flash pictures are forbidden, and, with that in mind, a stolen snapshot is but a soiled reflection.

I stood a few hundred feet from her now, just passing time, waiting for the line to move, when I become aware of a piece of art. The picture pulled me in, and, as I leaned against the railing for a better look, I saw a lovely peasant girl holding what looked like a chaff of wheat and a pottery vase. Encouraged to keep moving, I quickly caught the inscription: "Saint Rufina by Bartolomé Esteban Murillo."

What? Who?

That stunned my senses, causing me to push others aside to get a second look. I was now searching for something. It was if there were a voice in my head encouraging me to grab hold of the railing as others pushed around me. The girl in the picture was looking right at me. Was it her voice I heard?

I panicked as my mind began to shut out the distractions around me and focus in on her voice. It became louder, begging me to remember.

Had I been here before? Had I seen this painting hanging here another time? No, of course not. I had never been to Paris. But, as I looked deeply into her eyes, it happened. Flashes of faces began to appear. Some seemed like drawings and some were photos. What was happening?

Beads of perspiration percolated from my soul and surfaced, tormenting my face and trickling down. Was I sick...maybe something from the café? I leaned even closer. Wasn't this just a painting? Maybe... No, it was the painting. And, I could feel it was telling me something. Something from the past that had been locked away and jailed and was trying now to reach out to me, to gain its freedom. I mumbled under my breath, trying to save my sanity from embarrassment, "Talk, lady. Please talk to me." And again undulating flashes of men and paintings swished by. Then, as I struggled for survival, attempting to regain the surface from the depths of the sea, a hand came out of nowhere, reaching out and pulling me to safety.

"Lina, are you all right?"

"All right? What do you mean?"

"Your face is dripping with sweat," said Thomas, pulling out a handkerchief to wipe my forehead and moving me over to an empty bench. "Let me get you some water."

Just then Helen and Hans found me. "Oh my god, Lina. What has happened to you? You look sick!"

"No, no, no, it was that picture there. I was looking at the painting of the girl and something came over to me."

I couldn't let on that she was pleading with me. Give up my

sanity? Not quite. I wouldn't let that happen. Now the worried group started in on my prognosis. It was the bus ride, No, it must have been the hot weather. Maybe lack of sleep?

"Let's go back to the hostel for some rest," Helen insisted.

It was the collaborative remedy, so I gave in. Yes, it must be so. I needed rest. What else was I to do, believe the picture was talking to me? I pretended to accept the alibis.

Once back at the hostel, Helen walked with me up to our room.

"Rest some, Lina. Tonight we're going to the Moulin Rouge to see Paris as she comes out to dance. A little champagne and romance will do you good."

"Now, Helen..."

"No, no, Lina. This time trust me. Get some rest and all will change."

After she left the room, I laid back and pulled out my notebook to write down what had happened to me there in the Louvre. I described the picture and the people I saw.

"It will all go away with a little sleep," I thought. "Maybe it was something I ate."

But I couldn't entirely convince myself that this would be so easy to shake. Something had happened, and, though I didn't know it yet, it would never let me go. It would forever change my life, like the trailhead to a journey that never ends.

Where it would take me, I wasn't sure. But each step would be a peeling, a tearing, a thrashing of my soul, until it became an all-consuming compulsion, an obsession, driving me to find the truth of the life I had lived.

CHAPTER 6

# The Moulin Rouge

I woke just as the sun began to rest over Paris. Looking out from the hostel's fourth floor, I saw a trickling of lights begin to flicker. It was as if Paris were letting everyone know more life was out there, begging tourists to carry on through to the next phase. Yes, it was the night shift coming on. I wondered about the many times throughout history that this contrast of day and night had given the city its true character, something to remember it by. I sat there fascinated by the changing of the guard when the sound of Helen's voice caught my attention.

"Lina! It's time to get going. It's on to the infamous Moulin Rouge!"

Still groggy, I was slow to respond. I needed time to tune in clearly.

Again Helen urged, "It's time to get up, sleepy eyes."

"Okay, okay! So what's Thomas planned for tonight?"

"He's insisted we need to get going, especially you. You need to get something to eat and see the Paris nightlife."

"A little entertainment?" I asked as I quickly combed my hair.

"Yes. It will be good for you. And, according to the travel guide, the best place for both is the opulence of the Moulin Rouge. It's where history was made, can-can girls, the cabaret and more," Helen said while kicking up her legs and twirling on the bed.

"Helen, you're going to have a heart attack or break something. Okay. Okay. I'm going!"

The excitement glowed on her face. She turned to leave and said, "Thomas will pick us up in about an hour out front, so get a move on."

"Go ahead and get on your dancing shoes," I said, "but first, I need a shower."

Clearly a Germanic trait, a shower, but also a therapeutic exercise for me. I slid out of my wrinkled dress, unclipped my bra and stepped out of my panties. I took a step toward the shower and caught a glimpse of my naked body in the bathroom mirror. Those shapely curves that were so often hidden under the cover of stylish outfits were now in full view, and just for a moment I felt like a peeping Tom. I had to steal a second look.

My eyes stalled on my supple breast and its perks. They followed the reflection and traversed down bare skin, over a flat firm stomach, curved around soft, toned hips to discover just below, nestled there, my blonde hair so neatly tailored, cuddling my body. Then downward they leapt to the end of me, to the sight of my firm yet shapely legs.

Now warm passions began to grow in me, but it was more than that. It was a sense of an offering, something worth sharing with someone and being comforted in return. But, yet, how was I to know? I'd never revealed this side of me to any man. And what would his eyes tell me when I did? I smiled with assurance and walked into the shower and let its warmth gently drip down my body. What a pleasure to feel the water caress and massage each part of me. To let it roam freely about, taking its own course cleansing my body and soul on its way down the drain. I became lost in the revealing and intimate images I was creating. They were taking control of me. No, I couldn't let this happen. I grabbed at a towel, to recover, to hide from them. I dried off until they were gone, then quickly dressed.

Helen came in to rush me out the door. It wasn't just the Moulin Rouge that waited for her in Paris that night, but Hans too. Oh how lucky to have a companion to hold close and look for more.

Off we went into the middle of Paris' giant metropolis, the spectacle of lit corners, circles and crossings.

"Stop we're here!" Helen shouted when she recognized the iconic windmill out front. "It's just as the brochure said. 'Since the 1890s, the rich and spoiled have come to dine and let their hair down . They leave the kids, the cares and the values at home and just exploit the night.'"

We all had a good laugh at her excitement.

I assumed somewhere in Thomas' rank came a good American paycheck when he announced, "Ladies and gents, this night's on me!"

"It better be," I thought, after looking at the menu and the cover charge. The total would be well beyond my monthly wages from the castle tours.

The evening went on with a little wine, though champagne hadn't yet gotten involved. While our group sat wide-eyed, I peered over to Thomas, who surprisingly seemed to have other things on his mind. Certainly not the bare-breasted chorus dancers, or me. What was it?

Moments later, the host announced to the crowd that it was time to get out on the floor and dance. "After all. This is Paris!" he said in a distinctly true but overstated French accent.

Helen and Hans jumped at the suggestion, but Thomas, the smooth talking extrovert, for the first time, seemed distracted. This made me wonder. Who was this uncommon man who magically ventured into my life? I began to test him a little, or should I say pry into him, trying to find something more.

As Helen and Hans slipped from the table to get lost in the crowd, I raised my voice over the noise and asked, "So Thomas, tell me again what you do at the barracks? I know it's about all kinds of legal situations, but could you be more specific?"

He leaned in to answer. "Well, let's see. I move from department to department, depending on which one needs my help. Sometimes it's a soldier finding himself in trouble with local authorities, but most of the time I find myself working out legal issues with intelligence gatherings."

"And what would that be?"

"Obviously, I can't go into detail, for confidential reasons. We do have a war going on, and a lot of the problems pass through the barracks."

Clearly wanting to change the subject, he reached over and took my hand. I gave him my other and he laid them on the table, placing his over mine and squeezing them ever so lightly. I could feel the heat all the way to my toes. He looked into my eyes as if to ask permission for something without actually knowing what he was asking for.

I smiled, feeling comfortable in the wine, and said softly, "No Thomas. We need more time. This is so new. I want it to feel right."

Somehow he liked my answer. I think he was assured that his time was not wasted, that there was something more to look forward to, something worth committing himself to.

Sensing that Hans and Helen had escaped somewhere with each other, I said, "Thomas, please go and find them. The wine and the day have gotten to me and this noise, well, it doesn't help. Hate for us to leave so early but…."

"No problem, Lina." Thomas stood when he noticed I'd suddenly become distressed. "Be right back," he added and disappeared into the crowd.

Just then a plump elderly man with an overexposed, large busted brunette draped over him came close to falling on our table. I chuckled under my breath thinking she looked like her price tags were showing and smiled to myself thinking of Reverend Mother's caution.

While attempting to sit down in their stupefied state, the girl's glass of champagne spilled and splashed onto my shoes. The man hurriedly grabbed a napkin.

"Sorry miss," he slurred as he handed it to me. "So sorry," he repeated. I wiped off my shoes while he forced a conversation.

"You're German?"

"Yes."

"It's your blond hair and blue eyes that gave you away. You're from Nuremberg?"

"No. Heidelberg."

"Oh, such nice place, Heidelberg. Do you like Paris?"

"Not sure yet. It's still foreign to me," I said and turned away.

He wasn't finished.

"Well, let me tell you, it's been a long time since I was here."

"Oh, yes, and when was that?" I asked just to be courteous.

"During the war."

"The war?" I echoed.

"Yes of course! The Second World War," he laughed.

I smiled politely trying to breach the conversation, but he swaggered on.

"Well then, you know, when we occupied this city they called it the 'Free Zone,' but it was really ours."

Now my ears perked up. This was all new to me. Most Germans found it unpleasant to revisit this bit of history.

"You've got to see this," he said and quickly retrieved a well-worn photo from his bulging wallet. The booze and the women loosened him because his discretion was entirely oblique. "Look!" he insisted. "That's me and my buddies here in 1944."

I looked at the photo of four men in full German military attire, smiling broadly. One soldier held up a stein of beer, as they stood proudly in front of the familiar windmill. The photo had been shot from the sidewalk facing the Moulin Rouge. It staggered me.

Seeing me stressed, he added, "Yes, we may have lost the battle, but not the war...not the war! We're still here!" Then he put a finger to his lips and whispered, "They just don't know we're still in business. We'll come again."

I was about to flee this man when Thomas suddenly appeared.

"Hans and Helen will be here in a few minutes. They need to work something out...lovebird issues." Realizing he'd interrupted a conversation he apologized. "Oh, I'm sorry."

"No. It's quite all right." Still holding the man's photo I said, "Look here, Thomas," and offered the picture, just to appease the situation.

Thomas took a glimpse then handed it quickly back to the man. "Thanks for sharing," he added when the drunken couple abruptly left to go on with their evening. Thomas reached over and whispered to me, "Well, that was certainly an eye-full."

Now cheering up I said, "We have girls like that back home."

"No. No, Lina. Not her. The Nazi officers in the photograph."

"Really? How do you know that? I knew there was something about him that gave me a chill."

Thomas' expression soured as he moved his chair closer. "In the photo, the insignia on their uniforms, right there on their shoulders. You did see them of course?"

"What did they mean, Thomas?"

"They were SS officers."

"Oh my god," I thought. I knew very little about our recent past. And like other students around Heidelberg, I really didn't want to know. The SS stories always carried sordid information.

"What do you do, Thomas?"

"Well, there's still so much going on around Germany, so just let it go. It's been a long time." But as he looked out into the crowd he added, "I'll take notes and pass it on."

Somehow the whole atmosphere had now changed. The festivity was diminishing by the moment. A place of dining and dancing began to show itself for what it was. The can-can and cabaret were just illusions, a pretense to shield a debauched lifestyle. As each minute passed, what presumed to be romantic had transformed itself into ugly shadows—drunken, wanton orgies and brothels with high-rolling clientele.

I could see now how Toulouse-Lautrec saw Paris. Depressed by excess and realizing its meaninglessness, he was destined to purge his own life. When Helen and Hans finally found their way back to the table, we rushed out the back.

Thomas took note of my demeanor and said, "So sorry."

"It's okay, Thomas. We need sometimes to know the difference between what we do and what others do."

After driving around awhile, Thomas parked aside the Champs Élysées. All of us engaged in some French pastries and strolled about the stores, which easily recovered the night.

Later, as I lie in bed, I took out my journal and wrote: *Wonderful time in Paris with lots of insights, but my experience at the Moulin Rouge exposed a darker side of the city. Certainly not the one I'd read about or saw in movies. But the one that, at times, nurtured perversions, hid monsters, appeased their tastes and made them comfortable with their exploits.*

However, my mind quickly forgot all that. It was taking my emotions way too deep. I closed my eyes, but instead of sleep, the picture from the Louvre flashed before my eyes. The girl began to speak. Her voice was so soft I couldn't make out what she was saying. More voices flooded my mind. Were they haunting me? Was that even the right word?

I just couldn't let it go. I knew, for whatever reason, that this wouldn't be just a fading feeling. It was the girl, so vivid in the picture. Yes, she wanted to tell me more. I needed to press on, strain myself to listen. But I feared she would take me to a place so well deceived, it was hidden from my soul.

PART II

# The Quest

*Eiffel Tower, Paris France*

CHAPTER 7

## Surveying The Terrain

After returning to Heidelberg the next night, tired from the travel, I tried to get in a good night's sleep. But that proved to be impossible, for I feared the girl would take over my dreams again. I slept lightly, if at all, and when, morning began to show, I got up, showered, made coffee and gobbled down a stale pastry.

I raced across town, quickly parked my bike and ran up the college library stairs. On my way past the front desk, Erin whispered loudly, "So how was the weekend in Paris?"

"Intriguing," I whispered in return and started toward the back.

"Okay, Lina, I'll let you go. But you must tell me more soon."

"Will do, Erin, but I've got work to do."

I began in the card catalogue, selecting anything that could possibly be a painting hanging in the Louvre. Looking for what? The girl in the painting, of course. I had to know what she was trying to reveal. What was this thing I needed to know? It was like having an unknown disease that needed a remedy. Actually, it was more than that. I'd become obsessed with the picture, those eyes. What was it that compelled this mystery?

After spending more than an hour looking through painting after painting, there it was in the art history book, St. Rufina by the Spanish artist Bartolomé Esteban Murillo. He lived from

1617 to 1682. Many of his paintings were donated to the Louvre after 1882. But what about the girl?

I read on. *"In the 3rd century AD, two sisters of Seville, living in the Triana neighborhood with their poor but pious Christian family, were known for crafting fine earthenware pottery. The townsfolk sought to buy some pottery for use in a pagan festival, but the sisters, named Justa and Rufina, refused. For this, the townsfolk destroyed their many dishes and pots, and the sisters retaliated by smashing a likeness of the Roman goddess of love, Venus. Demanding that the sisters denounce their faith, the city's prefect, Diogenianus, imprisoned them and, when, they refused, tortured them on the rack and with iron hooks. They held their resolve, even when denied food and water and forced to walk barefoot across the Sierra Morena mountains. It was Justa who succumbed first, and her body was thrown into a well. Afterword, Rufina continued to cling to her faith, further infuriating Diogenianus, who arranged for a lion to maul her to death in an amphitheatre. However, the lion never attacked, and Diogenianus had her beheaded and her body burned. Bishop Sabinus of Seville, having recovered both bodies, buried them alongside one another to rest side-by-side for eternity.*

And that was the legend of Justa and Rufina, now known as Saints Justa and Rufina, patrons of Seville, I learned. The sisters-turned-saints protect the city's Giralda and the Cathedral of Seville.

I also learned that Murillo was not the only artist to honor the two martyrs on canvas, though his works are extremely valuable. I read on that many of the paintings depicting the sisters were once owned by the Rothschild family of France but later looted by the Nazis during the French occupation.

After the war, some of the Rothschild collection was donated to the Louvre, though a cloud of uncertainty about their true ownership still remains. Many of the priceless Murillo works simply disappeared and never resurfaced after the 1945 Nazi defeat.

I continued flipping through books, now looking for only St. Rufina paintings. I turned a page, and there she was. Actually there were many, but the Murillo was the only one that took my breath away.

She seemed to be pleading with me, trying again to tell me something important. It was as if we were old friends and she was begging me to remember. I knew I'd seen her before my encounter at the Louvre, but where and when? I looked at the footnote. The Murillo was one of the pieces that had never been recovered! But, how could that be, when I had just seen her hanging in the museum?

Maybe that was it. Maybe she was trying to tell me that something was wrong, that she wasn't supposed to be at the Louvre at all.

"Find me, and I will tell you my secrets," she pleaded.

I pushed back my chair. Here within the hushed library, I could still hear her—so loud that I even looked around the room to see if she was disturbing anyone else. No, they hadn't heard a word. It was all in my mind. Yes, that was it. I was imagining it all. But, why this piece of art? How could this be?

Suddenly, I knew what I must do. I had to see her again. Let her tell me her story. It might, after all, be connected to me. Of course, this was an intuitive thought, but my physical response to the idea felt all too real.

I sat there and began to calculate what needed to be done in order to move on, up the discovery trail. "How am I going to do this?" I asked myself.

By now, in the late 1960s, there are thousands of looted paintings that have been sold and resold throughout the world.

I started copying as much information as I could for now and packed up to leave the library, with really no direction to go forward.

Erin stopped me on the way out.

"Okay, Lina, what happened in Paris?"

"Erin, would you believe me if I told you that all the romance I came back with I'm holding in my hands?"

"No major breakthrough with the American?" She laughed.

"Well, maybe more than I let on, Erin."

"Lina, it's love!"

"No, no, Erin, just friendship, although it may be beginning to travel that way."

Now shifting the conversation to a more serious mood, I said, "Erin, I'm in need of some help here. You see, I'm researching, um more like investigating, some lost art but I don't really know how to go about it."

"Lost from where?"

"Well, it has to do with Nazi looted treasure. There's one piece of artwork, this Rufina piece. Any advice?"

She laughed. "As to the painting or guys? Because I'm not sure I would be that great at the guy thing. I still can't figure out why my last boyfriend just disappeared into thin air."

"Ha ha Erin, I mean…"

"I know what you mean, Lina. I have a name for you, Pieter Neumann."

"Pieter Neumann? The one from our psychology class?

"Yes, that's him."

"Really? The one who always raised his hand to ask a question just before class was over, prompting the professor to go on and on? Yeah, I remember him. His arrogance and smirk infuriated me."

"Well, there are a few girls around the university who would give their left whatever to spend some time with him."

"Well, not me, Erin."

"You'd better reconsider that thought. His major is journalism, and he is editor of the university newspaper. So, I suggest you put your claws away. He's into investigating this kind of stuff and spends as many hours in the library as you."

"Really? I've never seen him here."

"Probably because you never look for him. Besides, he doesn't hustle here. He works."

"Really?"

"Yeah, really, Lina. Let me talk to him about your project. If he shows any interest, he might be able to help."

"But with so many girlfriends, does he have the time?" I asked sarcastically. "Come on, Erin, I'm not that desperate."

"When you get to know the guy, his reputation doesn't match who he really is. He's one of the good guys," she said sincerely.

"Sounds as if you have something going on here, and I would hate to break up our friendship." I smiled.

"No such luck, Lina. He's too cerebral for me. You'll see."

"Okay, then. I guess there's no harm in trying. How do I get in touch with this Mr. Neumann?"

"He comes into the library a lot, so I'll give him your number. If he's interested, he can call you."

"Sounds great, Erin. Thanks."

I left the library hoping the matter was settled. I really needed someone like this guy. There was no way I could do this on my own.

Three days later, as I was darting out the door on my way to work, Helen said, "Wait, Pieter Neumann called and said he'd love to get together with you at the Red Ochsen sometime today, maybe after work, around 4 pm?"

"How did he know my schedule, Helen? Did you tell him?"

"No, must have been Erin. New boyfriend?" Helen asked.

"Why does it always have to be about boyfriends? Is that all you and Erin ever talk about?"

"So is it about a boyfriend?"

"No. It's about that painting in the Louvre."

"The one that freaked you out?"

"Yeah, I'm hoping Pieter can help me."

"How could he do that?"

"With research. And, Helen, please don't say anything about this to Father Tobias. You know where that will end up!"

"Okay, okay, Lina, but why?"

"Because, I'm still having strange dreams about the picture."

"Like what?"

"In the dream, a man steps in, grabs the painting and then walks away with it. I say, 'Hey mister what are you doing here?' He turns, and I see his face, but just a little, not enough to make it out before I jump awake perspiring and my heart racing out of control. It's happened several times now, but I'm getting a better look at the man each time. It's driving me crazy, Helen."

"Lina, don't do this to yourself. I know how you get onto something and won't let it go. Remember when you had that late-night chocolate craving and wouldn't let us sleep until we went out and got some?"

"This is not like that at all, Helen. It's something different, something very different."

"Lina, I worry about you."

"Nothing ever gets finished in these conversations, so let's get out of here. We've both got places to go."

Later that day I called Pieter's phone number and left a message with his roommate that the 4 pm meeting would be great. I arrived on time, ordered a beer and sat in a back corner to look over my notes. A shadow appeared over my papers, and I heard a voice ask, "Lina, yes?"

The late summer sun hindered my eyes as I looked up and answered, "Yes, that's me."

"Good, you made it on time," he said, and I was immediately reminded of the arrogant flair that preceded him. As his hand reached out to me, I received it just as his smiling face came out of the shadow. I shook his hand as a formality as his eyes pierced into mine. Why do men do that? What are they looking for? I immediately drew a comparison, thinking back to Thomas. His eyes were the dreamer, hoping to somehow warm my heart. Pieter, no. His look was to let me know I could trust him. He obviously hoped to give a first impression that would dispel any untamed rumors. And, that's what I got. The playboy image that shadowed him was noticeably missing. I would think back on this first meeting much later, and it was true.

Dressed in a tailored suit and sporting a tie, his manner was well and proper, no slight hint of exploitation, and his facial expression was strong. Not as sensitive as Thomas' and not as flashing, but more honest. So much so that I was sure he could make a girl believe anything he wanted her to.

"Okay to sit here? The sun is not in your eyes?"

"No. I mean, yes, it's okay," I mumbled.

He sat down and immediately called over a waitress, whom he obviously knew and chatted with on a first-name basis. Then he asked, "Lina, would you like one, a lager?

"Yes, that would be fine."

"Two, Bridget," he ordered, and she quickly left.

"So you've been sitting over there, watching me?" I asked.

"For just a moment, yes. I like to get an edge on the people I interview."

"So what did you see from way over there, Mr. Neumann?"

"No, please, it's just Pieter. And, to answer your question, well, let's just say I'm very interested."

We both laughed. Dispensing with further introductions and in true Germanic fashion, he jumped right in and on to the point. "So Lina, what's this all about? What am I here for? Erin just told me some of the highlights."

After two hours of detailed conversation and with Pieter now entirely engrossed in the subject, I said, "So my problem is, I don't really know where to start. I've got some research, but what's the next step? Erin says all you do is investigate."

"That's mostly all I do, Lina, and 'yes' is my answer if that's what you're looking for. I'd love to dig into this story. Don't know how far it will take us or whether it will be a dead end."

I looked confused.

"Journalism talk." He chuckled and then cautioned, "But, who knows where this will lead."

"What do you mean?"

"Well, it's going to take us back through German history and lead to some very unpleasant facts. And you know the sentiment around here. Nobody knew anything about what Hitler's Nazis were doing, and this art stuff, this looting, was all rooted out at Nuremberg, during the trials, especially with the testimony of Alfred Rosenberg."

"Really?" I asked while thinking I was not aware of any of this. No, that's not entirely true. I was aware of some stories, but the Germans discredited most as post war propaganda. Anyway, it had nothing to do with me, so why play with it?

"It's just that war crimes are not all that popular around here."

"I hear what you're saying, Pieter."

"But I say, 'so what!' Lina, that's what we do in journalism. We follow the story. At least that's my approach. Search out the truth. Write it for the people to read, then it's up to them to decide."

"Yeah, yeah, I know." I laughed nervously and added, "The truth will set us free!"

"What?"

"Reverend Mother's advice."

"Who is she?"

"Never mind, Pieter. Let's do it!"

"Okay, but one thing, one condition, Lina. After we review our findings, you must consent to let me publish the information."

"Where would you publish it?"

"Hmm, probably first the Kilikilik editorial page.

"The campus newspaper? Why would you do that?"

"You're still a student here, aren't you?"

"Yes, of course."

"Then I can write about your story and maybe other papers, like the Heidelberg Daily, would pick it up after that."

"Not a problem with me," I said.

"Okay, then, it's done. Come hell or high water!" Then he raised his mug and gestured for me to do the same. We clashed our glasses together, and it was settled.

That night, a curious feeling began to creep in, much like clouds at the end of a hot summer day. A mysterious climate settled over my head, as if pulling me into the center of a storm. I'd been living on the perimeter of world events all my life. That's all I wanted or needed. It was comfortable there on the edge. I kept going over what Pieter had cautioned, that heading up the path could lead to unpleasant places. Little did I know how truly unpleasant and repugnant they would be.

I ended the night by writing in my journal that I somehow knew, while searching for Rufina, I just might find myself.

CHAPTER 8

# The Trail Head

There was a growing enthusiasm for both of us, but it was Pieter who became totally immersed and even named our investigation "Project Rufina." *"Come hell or high water"* was the mantra to which we committed.

Pieter became all business when he directed the action plan. I'd spend time researching looted pieces of art while Pieter would interview and write articles for publication. Maybe he'd start with a simple short editorial about my quest, and that would be enough to shake the tree, let the apples fall. Then we'd start picking them up and looking for ideas about what to do and where to go next. Also, it would reveal how much interest there actually was on the subject. The Red Ochsen became our home base of operations, and we agreed to meet there on the following Tuesday.

At that meeting, after ordering a beer, Pieter wasted no time getting right to it.

"Okay, Lina, what have you got for me?"

"Let's see, in general, here it goes," I started in while taking out notes stored in my backpack.

Pieter quickly interrupted. "'In general' will not do it here. We must be specific! Too much has gone on since the end of the war. We don't want to spin our wheels on generalities that will get us nowhere. Some of the big players have changed their IDs and moved to other countries. There are anonymous bank accounts out there. You must keep your eye on the ball and keep the facts straight. Just as important, we need to know the ins and outs of the art industry. Then, follow the money trail. Sorry if I sound stern, but this is dangerous business here." He nodded for me to go on.

I gave a big sigh and continued. "Hitler considered himself a connoisseur of art and dreamt of creating a world-class museum like no other, putting classical art and culture on display in Linz, Austria in what would be known as the Führermuseum. He sought works by Albrecht Dürer, Hans Holbein and Christopher Pearse Cranch. However, his favorite artists were Salomon van Ruysdael, Rembrandt, Frans Hals, Van Dyck and Vermeer.

"Hitler, along with Hermann Göring, devised a plan to confiscate art, books and artifacts from the countries they invaded. They put together a group of artists, curators and art dealers to determine which pieces they wanted—either for the museum or to sell off to fund the war.

"Hitler's official photographer, Heinrich Hoffmann, and his favorite German painter, Adolf Ziegler, would systematically select which pieces to acquire. Before an invasion, Alfred Rosenberg would send in an advanced group of specialized men, referred to as the ERR, for the Einsatzstab Reichsleiter Rosenberg or the Reichsleiter Rosenberg Taskforce, to secure the pieces by way of confiscation or forced sale. By the way, Rosenberg was one of the early Nazi party recruits. Then Kajetan Mühlmann, a former art commissioner now on special assignment from the Reich, was responsible for protecting it all.

"As the war progressed, thousands of pieces of art were acquired, and church cathedrals and monuments were stripped of valuables. Hitler kept the pieces he considered classics. But the others, the undesirable paintings, were designated as degenerate' art and set aside to be sold by international art dealers."

I took a long breath and a sip of beer, then went on.

"Now that's where France, meaning the Louvre, came in. You see, the Louvre went through a series of internal transformations. It was always the world's leader of art trade—the place where art dealers, private parties and investors would come to bid and take home priceless treasures. The art market had plummeted during the rough economic time between the wars, however. But during WWII, the art industry flourished again and now pieces of degenerate art by the likes of Pablo Picasso and thousands of other impressionist and modern artists were sold by Nazi dealers at rock-bottom prices.

"Dealers from all over the world could take them back to their countries and sell them for a hundred times the purchase price. Now, that's where Switzerland came in. They facilitated the transactions by conveniently claiming their neutrality, as they'd always done.

"That allowed them to continue to bank freely, protecting the bounty of warring countries through an 'ask no questions' policy. They accepted secret Jewish accounts, knowing that soon these trusting new accountholders would be in death camps, their assets never retrieved.

"Thousands of transactions in art sales, most stolen, were allowed to continue. Later, some were exposed during the Nuremberg Trials as crimes against humanity. However, at this early stage of the war, not many cared about the Jews. They were despised all over the world, and even the self-proclaimed noblest of the world's countries, the United States and Great Britain, refused Jewish immigrants as undesirables. Switzerland later closed its borders to Jews as well.

"But Swiss bankers, those unscrupulous tarts, went further. They made the trading of stolen art even easier when they pushed the Swiss government to institute laws that gave the buyer prima facie evidence of clear title. Even if it could be proven beyond a reasonable doubt that the art was stolen, looted or confiscated by the Germans, the original and rightful owner must reimburse the new owner for the price at which the art in question was purchased. Though, of course in most cases, the rightful owner wasn't easy to prove, because most were dead in the camps. And the Germans, who kept meticulous records about most everything else, attempted to remove evidence of their dastardly deeds in the death camps.

"So, Nazis set up offices in Switzerland and sold degenerate art at the infamous Fischer auctions in Lucerne, Switzerland, making it the main hub for confiscated art sales. Later, when Germany occupied France, the Louvre became the center of such art sales, still banked by the Swiss.

"At the end of the war, it was every SS man for himself, and, to finance their escape, they used gold, diamonds and artwork. They could easily be turned into currency, and the Swiss banks were only happy to assist. That's how they financed their new identities. Now listen to this Pieter, with the help of the Red Cross and the Vatican, who preferred the Nazis to the godless communists, literally thousands of Nazis found safe haven and disappeared into foreign countries, such as Argentina, Venezuela and Chile, where they were immune from extradition."

"The Vatican?"

"Yes Pieter, the Vatican."

"Okay, okay Lina, good stuff. But where does this take us?"

"Well, I think we're back to France. France's Vichy Government, established after Germans took over most of the country in 1940, not only helped send more than 15,000 Jews to death camps but also allowed the Germans to take control of the world's largest art market, via the Louvre.

"The Louvre was once recognized as the leader of

impressionist art, but, under Nazi occupation, it was stripped and emptied of its most valuable pieces. The art was taken to the Jeu de Paume warehouse in France for accounting, where each piece was recorded by marking a number on the back of the frame. St. Rufina was designated 'hr 1172,' meaning it was from the Rothschild collection, art piece number 1,172. The classics or desirable paintings were sent off to a warehouse in Germany for consideration by Hans Posse. He would decide if it was worthy enough for Hitler's prospective museum.

"The art labeled degenerate was sent back to the Louvre and dealers throughout the world came running to buy this now insurmountable supply of low-priced modern art. Much of those proceeds left France to finance the German war machine.

"After the war, the Allies' Monuments Men recovered some of the best-looted collections, but, for the most part, many of these art pieces were never retrieved. Some collectors were the lucky ones, they survived the Holocaust. But, for many private owners, their fates were sealed in the gas chambers.

"Today, literally every corner of the world's art industry is suspected of trading looted art. Pieces submerge then simply disappear. If you ask curators who is buying and selling the looted art, they will employ the common defense. 'I cannot tell you. This is not a transparent industry'. That's it, Pieter. That's about all I have. Now, where do we go from here?"

"Remember, focus on the painting, Lina, the St. Rufina painting. Let's not get lost in all the other information. What do we know about this particular painting?"

"It's a Murillo. The painting is of St. Rufina. There's a sister painting of St. Justa by the same artist. Both of them are 'status unknown, despite the fact that I just saw the St. Rufina hanging in the Louvre."

"And they are both from the Rothschild collection?"

"Yes, and both very valuable pieces. Some of the Rothschild collection has been displayed in the Louvre recently, but the French government will not recant their claim to these paintings. Oh, I came across something else of interest. During the occupation, the Germans employed a certain Rose Valland. And, while other French women flirted with the Germans, hoping to get special favors, this surprisingly unassuming Valland was madly meticulously recording what artwork was stored in the Jeu de Paume warehouse and where the Germans were sending them. After the war, to the Germans chagrin, she was found to be a member of the French resistance.

"Also, I've heard of a classified document referred to as the Schenker Papers. They detail business transactions of some looted art pieces, and it all came out at the Nuremberg Trials. The papers cover a period between March of 1942 to 1945 and record the actual dates that dealers and buyers acquired the art from the Jeu de Paume. But, listen to this! It is still classified material."

"By whom?"

"The U.S. government. The papers are now located in the U.S. National Archives!"

"What?" asked Pieter, now taking notes frantically. "What do you mean 'classified material'?"

"Just what I said, classified by the United States government! Who else orchestrated the war crime trials?"

"How did you get this information?"

"Well, I have this friend at the barracks, and…"

Pieter looked at me quizzically and asked, "Is he a very close friend?"

"Yes, Pieter." I laughed. "But not that close. When you get to know me better, you'll know that's not my character."

"I'm sorry at the suggestion, Lina, but what kind of a fellow would give classified info to a casual friend? I had to ask."

"No, no, it's okay. I understand."

"Okay, so then I think we need to prepare some questions and have a talk with the Louvre's curator, Dr. Lemans."

"Why?" I asked.

"Because that's where the painting is now—where you saw it and where this all started. Besides, the Louvre has other Rothschild's in its gallery. And, like you said, every corner of the art world is suspect, and the Louvre is the center of international art sales."

"So how do you suggest we set up this interview?"

"Simple, my campus journalism advisor is a good friend of Lemans'. He speaks of him often, and I think he'll be open to interceding on behalf of his inspiring talented protégée." He laughed. "Yes, I can do that. What we get out of that goes to print. Okay?" he asked while staring intently, begging me to answer 'yes.'

His intense enthusiasm was written all over his face, and I couldn't resist.

"Okay, I guess."

"And then we'll see where those apples fall."

"Sounds like a scary proposition," I added.

"It just might be, possibly more so than you think. The war was a little more than 20 years ago, but many people still feel the pain. What you've researched, few Germans probably care to know. And those who do know probably want to forget."

"Forget what?"

"The guilt, Lina, the national guilt. I don't know how long or how many generations it will take to rid us of it. But, I do know we can't turn our backs on history. And remember…"

"Yes, I know. 'Those who cannot remember the past are condemned to repeat it.' Santayana."

"Yes. There you are." Pieter smiled, letting me know he was glad we were on the same page. "It's on to the curator!"

I wrote in my journal that night that I hoped Pieter knew what he was doing and where we should go with it all. However, my only purpose at that time was to sort out the painting and the girl in my dreams with her constant begging for me to do something so strange I refused to talk about it to anyone, lest they think I was about to break down.

And, yes, why would he be so free with classified documents?

## Chapter 9
# The Curator

Less than a week later, Pieter and I were on our way to Paris for a morning appointment with Dr. Henri Lemans, one of the Louvre's curators. Pieter set up the interview under the pretense of a simple community interest story about how the inside of the art industry worked. How do they select pieces, and who were some of the current buyers and key competitors?

Pieter was all business when he explained, "I've got enough harmless questions for him to answer so let's not let on to the ruse. Let him talk his way through. Keep him at ease. Then if something comes up, be calm about it, question around it. Nothing should sound preconceived. And, if there is something he wishes not to address, then we know we have a story. However, let's always remember, he's a good friend of my professor's."

After a nice rest, I opened my eyes when we came to the outskirts of Paris. Pieter stopped the car when he found a particular café he liked. It was quite popular, so we waited a while to finally order some pastries and a cup of dark coffee.

"Been here before, Pieter?"

"Oh, yes. Many times when I was younger. I had an aunt who loved music and dreamt of becoming a professional singer. She performed in practically every venue throughout Paris."

"Did she continue to do well?"

"Yes and no. The 'yes' part was she got to know Paris and

the entertainment business, but the 'no,' well' she never cut a successful record. She now works in Munich and sings in a church choir."

"Is she happy with that?"

"Yes, I think so."

"How about you, Pieter?"

He began to mutter something, then asked, "What about me?" His sinister grin gave him away. He was obviously open to more conversation about that topic.

"You know what I mean."

"Girlfriend or career?"

"Okay, both," I said.

"Yeah…. Well, well, let's see…."

"Let's jump the girlfriend question," I joked.

"Why do say that, Lina?"

"Because you stuttered."

"No, I didn't."

"Yes, you did when you said 'well' twice."

"Nah, nah, Lina."

"You're a popular man on campus. There must be a story there."

He smiled. "Maybe so, but being popular only opens up a few more doors. Sometimes what you see is pleasant but other times, not so pleasant. So, it can be useful, though I've learned not to lean entirely on it and tried never to be consumed by it. That can get in your way. It's a façade I like to hide behind, concealing what I'm really after."

"And that is?"

"The story, Lina, just the story."

"And that is?"

"Oh, usually to find some truth, I guess. Letting people know what's up the road, keeping them informed. That's what drives me on as a journalist, keeps me moving. Enough about me, Lina! See what you've done? Now you can write a storyline about Pieter the journalist. Let's get going before we are late. Don't want to keep Dr. Lemans waiting."

We drove a short distance then turned into an underground parking lot. Once parked, we trudged up a flight of stairs to the main floor then went through a series of security checks. I carried a small briefcase I'd taken from Helen's closet, for what I didn't know, to look important, maybe. Pieter cautioned to say and write very little.

"Not too much, just record what he says in your mind and then jot it down later. That way he'll be at ease and speak more freely."

Finally we were directed toward an office and warmly greeted by a secretary. Pieter introduced himself and then said, "I have an appointment with the curator, Dr. Lemans."

"Yes, you must be Pieter. Do you know Professor Bader well?"

"Yes, of course. He's my sponsor at the university."

"How is he?"

"Fine."

"That is nice to hear. You may go on in, Pieter. He's expecting you."

We walked through an open door then were met by an exquisitely dressed, gray-haired man.

"Good to see you, Pieter. The professor has relayed good things about you. He tells me you're one of his more polished students."

"That's nice to hear, especially coming from him." Pieter turned to me. "This is Frau Lina Ritter, a colleague of mine and a student of literature and the arts."

He greeted me with an extended hand and held mine for

a moment while working through his next question. In an amiable tone he said, "Frau Lina it is. What's your pursuit at the university?"

"Hoping to become a legal counsel." I answered.

He released my hand and pointed his finger into the air. "How is it said? Each man should have a proficient doctor, an accurate accountant, a pious pastor…and a loquacious attorney to amuse them all." He smiled proudly at his attempted humor.

"Well done, Dr. Lemans," I flattered.

"So what can I do for you today? What would you like from me? I've put some time aside for you."

"Dr. Lemans, we want to get a behind-the-scenes story of the art industry."

"Well then, I think it would be best to get out of this office. Let me give you my personal tour of the gallery while you fire away with whatever questions you like. Shall we?" As he stood and flamboyantly gestured toward the door, he said, "This way, folks."

We proceeded through the main office, and, while passing his secretary, he said, "Margaret, give me a half hour. I am doing a walkthrough of the gallery."

"Only half an hour?" I thought to myself. "Sure hope Pieter has his questions in order."

We were led through thick large doors when Pieter began his interview.

"So, Dr. Lemans, I can see that the Louvre is a very secure gallery."

"Yes, it is. I don't have to tell you that these painting and artifacts are literally worth billions."

"But, let's say, Dr. Lemans, if one were stolen, for whatever purpose, where would one find a buyer?"

"Pieter, the art market is all over the world, truly international.

However, if one knows the right place and buyer, one could trade or sell any of the pieces in a minute."

"And how would the money and title be transferred?"

"Oh, that would be easy. Our French banks could do the job very well, but, if I were a thief and stole a painting, let's say hypothetically..."

"Yes. of course. Hypothetically." Pieter said with a smile.

"Switzerland has a banking and legal system that..." He paused to look over toward me, hoping to see if he'd surprised us with his candor. "Well, let's just say they can handle any situation discreetly—you can bank on it." He laughed then continued. "Pieter, think about it. Why would a country ever attack friendly Switzerland, when they know their plunder is banked there?"

"Really?" Pieter asked, leading the curator on.

"Of course. Switzerland is the international banker for all countries. Just think of the political figures that have run off with millions from their countries' treasury and put them is Swiss banks."

"Getting back to the gallery, Dr. Lemans, who are your competitors?"

"What do you mean?" the curator asked while leading us just outside the Denon Wing.

"It's just this. Obviously the art you display here, some other gallery would also like to display. How does that work?"

"By reputation. The Louvre is the number one art gallery in the world, and we buy, sell and trade far more paintings than the others. There are new metropolitan museums in practically every country. They have large galleries, many, many galleries, and, along with Sotheby's and Christie's auction houses, there are huge markets with millions, no billions of dollars of art." The curator's passion culminated into a crescendo. "However, the most prestigious paintings and art, like the priceless, invaluable

Mona Lisa, is here! The icon of the art market! She keeps buyers, artists and all kinds of powerful industrial investors, such as Emil Bührle, arms manufacturer of Germany, and others like him, coming back to the Louvre, looking for quality buys. We also have larger-than-life collectors and art dealers, like the Wildensteins. So many of them, they are stepping over each other to own a rare piece of art. But to answer your question, our local competition is the Galerie nationale du Jeu de Paume, just a ways from here, though lately we do share a few different artworks."

Dr. Lemans' expression dramatically changed when Pieter asked him, "What about the period of occupation and the ERR?"

"What? You mean the Einsatzstab Reichsleiter Rosenberg?" The curator now began to adapt to the line of questioning. "Well Pieter, as you must know, Alfred Rosenberg came clean at the Nuremberg Trials. That period of history is over."

"But what about all the missing art from the Schloss, Rothenberg and Rothschild collections, just to name a few? The national recovery register shows that thousands of these paintings have just disappeared."

"Yes, I've heard that, too. Who knows in what direction they went. That's the nature of war; it can do that."

Pieter took over the conservation. "Isn't it a fact, Dr. Lemans, during the war, the Louvre was stripped of her art, and those pieces were sent up the road to the Jeu de Paume and carefully inventoried by the Nazi ERR? And is it not true that some went to Verwaltungsbau and were warehoused in northern Germany for future placement in Hitler's museum? All carefully orchestrated by the Nazis?"

"Yes. And carefully protected," Dr. Lemans added.

Pieter wouldn't be cut short and continued. "Stories have it that many pieces classified by the Nazis as degenerate art never left this region. I've also read that some paintings were sent to Switzerland in the infamous Fischer auctions, but some still remain in vaults, chalets or warehouses right here in Paris."

"Just rumor!" Dr. Lemans interrupted.

"But, is there any truth to those rumors?"

"Well now, Pieter, you've covered a lot of territory in that question." His tone of speech betrayed him as he became obviously perturbed and defensive. "You see, young man, that is all history. Today, today, the world is looking at our industry far more intently. All that unscrupulous behavior is gone! At one time maybe, but after the war, it all changed. I am sure you know the history of the Vichy collaborators, a bad lot. You see, we usually buy and sell paintings in private. In fact, most all of our transactions are done in private. We do this to protect the buyers. If they purchased a painting in good faith, well, we honor that. If we come across a piece of looted art, whatever the value, we back away. You see, things are very different now," the curator assured.

Knowing instinctively the curator was clearly on the defense, Pieter spit out another question. "Is it true the art pieces that were confiscated during that period by ERR were inventoried by the Nazis, then marked with codes on the backs of the frames to indentify the picture and the collection from which it came?"

"That is true," the curator agreed.

"So even if a dealer bought or sold the picture, he should have known whether or not it was a looted painting?"

"Well, yes, that is an issue, isn't it, Pieter?"

Pieter slowed down, trying to calm the conversation by asking about specific paintings. After being evasive, the curator was clearly relieved to change the subject when we came to the next painting.

With his hands open wide, he announced dramatically, "Here she is. I'm happy to give you a private viewing of history's most prominent and recognized painting ever, the Mona Lisa."

I was reminding myself of the queue that was waiting to see her the last time I was here, when it hit me. There was the bench that Thomas led me to in order to console and help me recover. It was then that I looked up to once again to take in the St. Rufina by Murillo, except that she was no longer there.

"That's not it." I whispered to Pieter.

"What?" Pieter asked.

I approached a painting of two girls with bonnets sitting in a field.

"An impressionist?" I asked.

"Yes. That is called Two Young Women in the Field by Henri Lebasque," the curator explained while pointing to the inscription. "He was a French artist, a post-impressionist painter from 1865 to 1937."

Trying not to show my alarm, I asked calmly, "How often do you change the paintings on display, Dr. Lemans?"

"Well, my dear Frau Lina, paintings are usually displayed for at least six months." The curator continued while admiring the painting, "This Lebasque has been here for at least that amount of time."

"But, Dr. Lemans, I was here, standing right in this very spot, just a week ago and saw a Murillo. To be specific it was St. Rufina by Murillo."

"Oh, but you must be mistaken, Frau Ritter! I walk this wing practically every day. The painting you are talking about is quite valuable, but we have never been fortunate enough to have her here, I assure you. You must be mistaken, my dear."

"Do you have any other Murillos, possibly in another location here at the Louvre?"

"We had one, but it has been loaned out to another gallery, months ago."

"Which one?"

"Oh, Frau Ritter, we cannot, for security reasons, give you that information."

Pieter looked over at me with wide eyes, as if to say "enough," so I said, "You must be right, Dr. Lemans, it was a long hot day, and I was exhausted. I must be mistaken. Sorry for the confusion."

Pieter seemed pleased at how I ended it, and, as we moved on, he asked the curator, "How many paintings do you exhibit here at the Louvre?

"Thousands."

"Where are the ones that are not on display stored?"

"Here, below and in warehouses about town. However, the high valued assets are stored in the vault."

"Is there an accurate inventory taken as to which paintings are in the vault?"

"Yes, most certainly! We can't lose or misplace those pieces of art."

"Has the government ever asked to see inside the vault, for tax purposes?"

"I don't know the answer to that, Pieter. That is not part of my job description. But, you must remember, there is a certain amount of trust in these art transactions, where privacy is an issue, for these types of international traders. Again, let me state, this is not a very transparent business."

"What do you mean by that, Dr. Lemans?"

"Well." The curator paused as if to choose his words carefully and looked directly at me when he said, "These powerful people have legal counsel that takes care of those matters." It was obvious he had had enough of this line of questioning and promptly cut us short when he turned and herded us back to his office, without any further conversation. Upon reaching his office, he asked, "So Pieter, tell me, is my good friend the professor providing his students with the right stuff to become journalists?"

"Yes, I believe so, Dr. Lemans. He is a dedicated instructor, well liked by his students. He gives us a wide range of opportunities to write—just enough to keep us and the university out of trouble." Pieter laughed.

The curator rushed us out by shaking Pieter's hand then mine while showing us the door. "Please come again, when I have more time," he said unconvincingly.

A sense of urgency came over Pieter as we walked quickly down to the car. He opened my door, rushed to the other side, started the car, then sped off. He didn't say a word while rubbing his head, as if trying to figure things out. We crossed back into Germany in silence with Pieter alternating hands to continue rubbing his head while keeping one on the wheel. I couldn't make him out. But, his intentions became apparent when he broke the silence and asked, "Lina, are you sure the painting was changed?"

"Yes."

"You could not have been mistaken?"

"No. That picture on the wall, when I was with Thomas, Hans and Helen, was a Murillo, the painting of St. Rufina. I know this! And, when I researched it in the library, there it was. That led me to the other picture of St. Justa. I knew I'd seen them before, but where? Both paintings were classified, 'location unknown.'"

"And, they were both from the looted collection of the Rothschild's?"

"Yes, Pieter. And listen to this, it's been rumored giants in the art world like George Wildenstein & Company, by one witness' account, came into the so-called Free France soon after

France collapsed and made an offer to buy all of the Schloss and Rothschild collections. They were willing to place an extremely large amount in a Switzerland bank as proof of their intent to purchase the degenerate art. While the Jews...."

"Okay, okay, Lina. I got it!" Pieter interrupted, sounding impatient with my babbling. "You're sure the painting was a Murillo not... what was the guy's name? Lebasque, Henri Lebasque the French impressionist? The painting of the two women in the field?"

Now, I could see what Pieter was doing. All those questions and all that prompting the curator to talk, he was fishing for a story to tell to his readers. He was setting up, in his mind, a storyline for publication. He needed enough to put in ink, but this was leading somewhere he hadn't counted on.

"So, Pieter, when do you think you will get the story in print?" I asked.

Aware I'd caught him at his game, he laughed then said, "You know me too well, Lina, and too soon. Let's see, if I get home and stay up late, it could be in the paper by tomorrow afternoon. I hope that it will be picked up and syndicated. This could be a big story, Lina."

"Gosh, never thought the Louvre would make such a crucial mistake. And, how did they know I was... we were on to something?"

"You might have given it away when you almost fainted at the sight of the Murillo—maybe someone at the museum took note. Maybe someone thought you knew something."

"Maybe. But I couldn't help myself. It seemed as if she were actually talking to me and that I'd seen the painting somewhere before, but where, I don't know." For some reason, I had to let Pieter know how personal it had become. "It haunts me at night, off and on, in my dreams. I don't know what...."

Pieter interrupted. "You do know, Lina, we are taking on a lot of big people with this. Let's light the fire. One thing's for sure, going public will tell us if there is really something going on here."

Pieter dropped me off at the university library, and I rode my bike back to my apartment. Helen was waiting up again.

"Lina, where have you been?"

"Paris again."

"Paris? You didn't tell me."

"No, this was a quick, nonstop trip."

"Really, with whom?"

"Pieter Neumann."

"About the picture thing again? I thought you and Thomas were doing so well?"

"No, Helen. This has nothing to do with that!"

Now playing with me she said, "Well, Pieter is a very fine looking guy and popular on campus."

"No, Helen, this has to do with… Oh, never mind. Just read the university paper tomorrow, and you'll get it."

After a quick shower, I flopped onto my bed and asked, "Helen, what's your day been like?"

"About the same. Oh, before I forget, Reverend Mother would like you to come by and see her soon."

"Oh no. You've been talking to Father Tobias again?"

"Of course. You know he's like the father I never had. I love that jolly, funny old priest. I always bring him a bottle of his favorite schnapps. He never turns me down. He says a few jerks from that bottle, and he sees God more clearly."

"I bet he does, and gets you to jabber on," I said, and we laughed together.

I rolled over and slipped out my journal, hidden under the bed. I was beginning to learn not to trust everybody.

I wrote: *Long day. I thought I needed to go, leave, travel, see the world. But, I believe the world may just be coming to me... faster than I wanted. As Pieter goes fishing for us tomorrow, wonder what he will catch. Now, how did they know I'd seen the Murillo? Why did they replace it? Wow, the curator of the grand Louvre...strange coincidence. Scary. Maybe not, but please, Rufina, I've done my best for you today, let me get some rest.*

CHAPTER 10

## The Publication

Martin Luther's Ninety-Five Theses, published on the Wittenberg Castle Church door, would dramatically change the world. What Pieter had in mind wouldn't provide such a universal shock. It would, however, likely create a small quake in my corner of the world. It was sure to raise the eyebrows of many Germans, conscious of the misdeeds of the past. Some needed no reminders, while others would rather let the past be just that.

But, that wasn't the objective of his publication, to thrash the Germans entirely. No, no. It was much broader than that. It was to take on the rest of the world as profiteers of the war, as co-conspirators of war crimes against humanity.

I awoke about 9:30 the morning of the article's publication, feeling fresh for a change. I'd finally slept through the night. I must have done something to placate the voices in my dreams, for their haunting had stopped, at least for one night. I rushed about my room, dressed anxiously and then hurried to grab some food from the refrigerator. On my way out, I picked up a note stuck on the door that simply said, *Go to the abbey. Love, H.*

"Okay," I said to myself. "After class, I will do that."

I scrambled down the stairs, found my bike and off I went. My excitement mounted the closer I got to the university. What would Pieter actually write in today's newspaper?

Once I got to the library, there was no need to look further, for there was Thomas sitting on the steps, newspaper in hand, reading. When he saw me rushing up the stairs he said, "Is this what you're looking for?"

Without waiting for the obvious reply, he handed me the paper already folded to expose the editor's comment. In bold type, the lead was, *Heidelberg student on the trail of Nazis' looted art.*

Pieter lost no time in getting into the story. "Just like him," I thought, now knowing him better, so direct and impulsive. The first paragraph opened with, *Lina Ritter, Art Literature student, while touring the Louvre…*it went on detailing my worst suspicions, in ink for a half page, then left off by saying, *Stay tuned, more to come.*

"Wow! What a story." Thomas exclaimed.

"Really, you think so?"

"Just wait for the response. You'll see why, Lina. Wow, they really changed the painting?"

"Yes. Do you remember, Thomas? It said 'Murillo' on it. I saw a picture of a woman holding pottery and a strand of wheat. They replaced it with a picture of two girls in a field wearing bonnets."

"The painting, the Rufina, was it there?"

"No, no. That's just it, Thomas. They changed the painting! Did you read the article? It's all true! In fact, I'm going to cut my morning class today to research where the last showing of Henri Lebasque's Two Young Women in the Field took place. That was the painting they replaced the Rufina with.

"So, Lina, do you believe you're on to something big?"

"You tell me, Thomas! When I first saw the Rufina, it was with you, Helen and Hans. You saw my reaction in the Louvre that day. I knew I'd seen that painting before. It's been in my dreams for the last few nights, and there is a man in the dream each time, each night I see more. Either I am on to something, or I am losing my mind."

Thomas was about to put his arm around me, as if to ease my stress, but I stepped back and said, "I've got to get to work."

"See you a little later? We can talk some more about it then?" Thomas called out while I rushed off.

"Yes, but not today. I'm going to leave our afternoon class early. Can you take notes for me?"

"Yes, of course. But why, Lina?"

"I've got to run over to see Reverend Mother, but tomorrow after work, let's. Okay? Bye," I said and then pressed on into the library. Erin stopped me.

"What is this, Lina? Pieter's got some headline in the school paper, and you're out there sitting on the steps with Mr. Werner. Provocative." She smiled.

"What, the article or Thomas?"

"Both. You're getting to be the gossip around here, Lina."

"Gosh, I hope not!"

"So, what's next, Lina? Give me clue," Erin begged with a friendly grin.

I shot back, "Research. Back to the art section. See yah."

I walked into the library and began pulling out art books, finally finding the Henri Lebasque collection. I easily traced down where it had been on exhibit lately. Yes, confirming my suspicion, it was at the Galerie nationale du Jeu de Paume, just a short distance from the Louvre. I recollected the conversation between Pieter and Dr. Lemans, coincidence, no. It looked like more than that.

"Did you get what you were looking for?" Erin asked as I rushed by on my way out.

I waved some papers in the air and answered, "Yes, I got it! Remember, you're the one that got me in contact with Pieter. Ha.

See you later."

I crept into the classroom late and sat down discreetly next to Thomas, who for once was madly taking notes. I smiled when he looked over, hoping he wouldn't give me away. Professor Mueller moved about the class undisturbed as he lectured on. I saw an opening to show my presence and raised my hand noticeably to join in on his lecture, but he seemed to resent it. I didn't know why, though I got a feeling it was definitely me. A second chance came to answer a question posited by the professor. Again, he distinctly and purposely overlooked my eagerness to respond. Then, it hit me. Of course, the article, something in it must have hit a nerve.

Half an hour later, I got up to leave, as planned. The class, sensing the tension, attempted to pay tribute to my early departure by giving me a subtle applause on my way out. The professor stopped, then looked noticeably distressed as I left. Behind me, I heard him say, "Okay class, fun's over. Let's get back to work!"

I jumped on my bike and pedaled my way across the bridge, now heading for the abbey. I usually loved getting on my bike and enjoying the ride. But, today all kinds of questions buzzed in my mind. Why would they change the painting? What were they hiding from me? It was personal now.

Okay, I began to reason, they must have been tipped off when Pieter set up the interview. But, who knew that I'd seen the picture and would make an issue of it? Who was there? Helen. No way. Maybe she talks a lot around town, but she wasn't behind this. Hans? No, he's too into Helen. Thomas? Well, he did come out of nowhere to help me in the library, then ended up in my class, saying he's the friend of a friend of the professor's... a likely story.

Then he arrives in France with a car, taken from the barracks carpool, and I really don't know for sure what he's working on. Oh, I don't know. But what I do know is that I'm getting this feeling that somebody is aware of what I am doing. And Pieter, well, he came after the fact and disclosed all of the happenings in the newspaper. No, not him. But, one thing's for sure, the painting was changed, replaced by a picture that had hung in the Jeu de Paume recently.

I arrived at the entrance to the abbey and continued up the main road. Even though I had done this hundreds of times before, it was always a heartwarming feeling to ride up the road, each side guarded by trees, as if going through a tunnel. This was home. All of my life was spent here. When I was young, the abbey was all I had, and it was more than enough.

Once in front, I grounded my bike against a wall and charged up the two flights of stairs to Reverend Mother's office.

Reverend Mother ran the abbey in a punctual, rigid fashion. Life there was always a daily routine. But, for us, she was more lenient. We were exempt from the formalities to which she so dearly clung. It was our privilege. She often referred to Helen, me and a few of the other girls as her "survivors." She'd make jokes on that fact, because, as she said, unlike the sisters, "God delivered you here to be nurtured in His ways, then set free, like a bird from a cage and from the chastity of becoming a nun."

So, to surprise her, I opened the door to her office wide while chirping away at a beloved song. But, she was not there. I looked over at the big Bible that always lay open on the center of her desk. I always thought it was her dictionary for life, which God had written entirely for her.

I walked out of the office, and one of the sisters passed me.

"Lina! Reverend Mother will be so pleased to see you. How are you?"

"Fine, Sister Grace, and you?"

"Well, thank you. Looking for Reverend Mother?"

"Yes."

"I saw her going into the chapel."

"Thank you, Sister."

I walked down the staircase, across lush green grass and up the chapel steps. As I entered, light attempted to break through the wonderfully colored mosaic windows. The serenity of it all came over me as I witnessed this heavenly picture. I stopped, dipped my fingers in the holy water and made the sign of the cross, to the Father, Son and Holy Ghost.

There, up in the front, was the kneeling silhouette of Reverend Mother. I slowly crept up to the altar. Sensing me, without turning, she said, "Pray with me, my child."

I knelt down beside her in silent prayer. After some time she made the sign of the cross, kissed her rosary and stood, then motioned for me to follow. We walked out of the chapel and across the lawn, where she began commenting on what a wonderful day it was. Then on to, "How was your ride here? Lina, have you been eating well? You look on the slight side."

But I sensed she had something more on her mind, beyond this small talk.

"Probably just waiting until she gets me in the privacy of her office," I thought.

Once we made it to the second floor and entered her office, I needed no formal invitation. I plopped myself down in the large overstuffed leather chair in front of her desk, while she casually went about putting this away, then that. After a few moments of silence and muttering about, she finally sat down in her chair and looked across the desk at me.

"So, Lina, since the last time you visited, you've been in Paris not once but twice and in the Louvre itself. And, now, what's this about the publication?"

"You've read it, Reverend Mother?"

"Of course. Hasn't everybody in Heidelberg?"

"But, it was just a local school publication, in the editor's section."

"Lina, Heidelberg is a university town, and word spreads very quickly here. So, you tell me, what's this about a painting—in your words, child."

I held my breath for a moment then, before I could reply, Reverend Mother smiled and said, "Lina, don't you think I know everything about what you and Helen do? Not just every minute of the day, but every second of the day."

"Father Tobias?" I asked.

That only made Reverend Mother laugh and say, "Yes, and there are others."

"I keep telling Helen not to talk too much to him—it always gets back to you. I don't want you to worry, Reverend Mother."

"It doesn't work that way, Lina. So, go on about the painting."

She listened intently as I told her about the painting, the dreams and, finally, about the picture change in the Louvre.

"Now I'm about to question my sanity," I finished.

"I doubt that to be an issue," she assured. "So what will you do, Lina?"

"I really don't know, Reverend Mother. Pieter believes that it has something to do with paintings that were looted from the Jews during the war and never recovered."

"And you?"

"Well, when I saw the Murillo, something told me I'd seen it before. But how could I have? And then, the dreams started, and the man and… and when I looked up the pictures in the library, I found the one of St. Rufina, and that hit home. I knew it, but I couldn't place it. But, the changing of the pictures made me want to find the answers, stop the dreams."

"And Pieter?" she broke in. "How did he come in to this?"

"Well, I had the research and didn't know where to go from there. You know Erin, at the library, how helpful she is. She suggested I talk to Pieter. He's a graduate student and a journalist. Investigation is something he does well. He became very interested. He's a good person, Reverend Mother. So, we're working on this together."

"So, what became of Thomas Werner?"

"Oh, he's still around."

"But, what have you learned about him?"

"The same as I told you before."

"Lina, you need to know more about these people you are trusting, because the questions you're asking are going to cause a lot of problems for you. There are people around Heidelberg who don't want to be reminded about their past or what happened in Nuremberg. The abbey survived by being non-political. Yes, unfortunate and probably not the moral thing to do, but what other choice did we have?"

She stopped, got up and walked toward the large window that distracted her thoughts. Then, she turned back to me and said, "So what now, Lina? How far will you go with this?"

"I don't know, Reverend Mother. We're waiting for the response from the publication. Pieter says that will decide where we take it from here. I don't know. I know I'm repeating myself. All I know is I must find out..."

"What is it you want to find?"

"The truth, Reverend Mother, the truth."

"Oh, Lina." Reverend Mother smiled back at me. "You were always far more stubborn then Helen. Yes, you were. You must have gotten it from your father. You most certainly didn't get it from us here at the abbey. Well, my child, it looks as if the world may just drop into your lap. These things can become dangerous. So you must be very careful. Remember that you are in the hands of God. So pray more, for His guidance and wisdom. For, in the end, as I've told you many times, it is within His divine providence and in His time that you will find an answer. Maybe not the one you're looking for, but, if it's truth you seek, the Bible tells us, in God you will find it, and it will make you free. Now, enough of this! What is this thing with Helen and her new boyfriend?"

I smiled. "I don't know, Reverend Mother. She is so fickle. Once she has him eating out of her hand, she says he's smothering her, and then she moves on."

That brought out a big laugh from Reverend Mother. "Yes, that is true. Oh, poor dear. Do you remember, Lina, how she always loved vanilla ice cream? So, the sisters gave her a steady diet of it. Then one day, she said she couldn't stand vanilla and all she wanted was chocolate?"

"Yes, Reverend Mother, I do. That's her."

We laughed together awhile, then she opened the big Bible on her desk and, as always, gave me a verse. This time it was Matthew 6:33.

"Yes, I know it well, Reverend Mother," I said, knowing this always made her happy. "It says, 'Seek ye first the kingdom of God and His righteousness, and all these things shall be added unto you.'"

"Yes, yes' it does say that." She smiled proudly and said, "On your way, child."

On my ride back to into Heidelberg, I felt a great sense of relief, joy and comfort knowing Reverend Mother, the sisters and the abbey would always be there for me. But, as the day went on, it was Reverend Mother's caution that lingered in my mind, now causing me to worry more.

CHAPTER 11

# A Message From Another Time

You've probably heard the story about the person who found a bottle brought to shore by prevailing winds and tides. Inside was a scribbled, corked-up message by some soul hoping that, through the elements of time, it would wander ashore and into the hands of someone who cared. As letters began to arrive by bundles at Pieter's campus office, I kind of felt that way.

Pieter and I were thumbing through the letters, when he said, "One thing is certain, it isn't for lack of interest we've received all these."

"That's for sure."

"But, remember, our purpose wasn't merely to create an issue or to sell papers was it?"

"No, it wasn't."

"Then, Lina, we need to read every one of them. We're looking for something, maybe a clue."

"A clue to what?" I asked.

"You'll know it when you see it. We shook that tree, now let's see what we've got here in this grab bag of mail. I hope after reading all these letters, we'll know where to go from here. But, our next step is to box them up and get them out of my office. I don't want Professor Bader wandering in on us."

"Why?"

"I just don't, Lina. That's a good enough reason for now.

Take them over to your apartment. Ask Helen to go buy us some sandwiches, cheese and pilsner. I think it's going to be a long night."

We set out on the marathon task of reading all the first day's letters, neatly sticking them in piles: Supportive, Negative and Interesting. After reading a few, Pieter said, "I think we should consider the possibility that we might just be kicked out of Heidelberg U for this. Well, I guess we can always go to Munich."

There was some truth to his statement, and he seemed to enjoy floundering around with it in humor while we continued to open and sort. "Not that bad of a college is it? Hey, with this publication, we might even be accepted to Stanford. Wow! Now that will make all this worthwhile."

I asked Helen to get Hans over here to give us a hand. She answered, "No. He's starting to rub me the wrong way."

"And how might that be Helen?"

"Too consuming."

"Meaning what?" I laughed when she shrugged her shoulders and said, "Well, there you go again, Helen."

The night stretched on for hours as we tore open one envelope after another, not really knowing what we were looking for. The comments were not so much about the present situation with the painting but mostly about the horrors of the past. There were cries and pleas of discomfort caused by the opening of old wounds. And, frankly, by our early tab, there was very little in the way of support for our cause and few reasons given for us to press on. Nothing seemed connected to the painting.

I began to wonder why we ever wanted to shed light on something that so many people wanted to forget in the first place. As we read on, I was reminded of yesterday's conversation with Reverend Mother. She had said the very same thing. The German people would attempt to disclaim their guilt, and they did so in various ways in the many letters.

*We were not all Nazis. 'Why don't you write about that?*

*The French were the real collaborators. Let them explain why the art industry was thriving in France during the war.*

*What about the Swiss financed sales?*

*Don't forget the Holy See of the Catholic Church. They were the ones that allowed for the ratlines, the escape routes for the Nazis.*

*What about the Vatican? Let them open the holy vaults, and we can all see what god sees. They were the Jew haters. They gave Nazis phony passports to go South America, with the blessings of the Peronistas and Chile.*

*What about the American industrialists who refused Jewish immigrates? All of them bare responsibility along with Germany!*

That was precisely the big picture that Pieter was trying to get across to the reader. However, with blinders on as they read, they got only so far as extricating themselves from the issue and from any responsibility and instead focused on blaming others.

We read on into the early morning hours, but nothing stood out. Then Pieter handed me a letter.

"What do you make of this?

I looked at the precise, neatly handwritten note.

*They know. Cui bono. Be very careful. Trust no one, except me. —Sonnenschein*

Sonnenschein? That looked familiar. I've seen that before. Was it some code, maybe something to do with a painting?

Now lowering my voice, as if to adhere to the caution in the letter, I said to Pieter, "I've seen that word before."

"Lina, it's in songs, movies and poetry. It's commonly used. Are you certain? It's probably just a way to remain anonymous."

"No, it means something to me… something more."

"Not just someone trying to scare you?"

I plunged into my memory, but I couldn't find it. I knew it was there, but where? Sonnenschein, Sonnenschein.

"Pieter, call it intuition, instinct or a good guess, but I think this is it. I think this is the connection we were looking for." I looked at the postmark: Berlin. "A Berliner reading the Heidelberg University paper? Wow, can you see it? We have a more extensive reach than you thought, no?" Now looking at the humor of it, I whispered, "We better be careful what we say and to whom we say it."

We finished a little while later, and Pieter said, "Let's shut this thing down for now. I need to get to the university early tomorrow. Professor Bader, I fear, will be asking a lot of questions about this project in the morning. So, keep the majority of letters here for a while. I'll take a couple of them and try to persuade him that we have some support and should continue on."

"Yeah, just two out of what, 400?"

Pieter laughed and said, "I guarantee he won't read but two or three." He thanked Helen for her help and said while going out the door, "Sorry about the Hans thing. I'm sure there will be someone out there less consuming." He smiled and gave me a wink. "Tomorrow then."

Tomorrow came early because I couldn't sleep at all that night. Too many words played in my mind. Turning and resetting my pillow didn't help. No matter which way I tried to position myself, they kept me awake. I got up, showered, then went back to the journal. But, as I wrote, everything came back to *Sonnenschein* and *cui bono*. I wrote, telling my journal how much I still didn't know. Maybe just writing it out would give me a clue and offer some rest. That was it. I needed rest, to get away from it all.

When the sun came up, I rushed out of the apartment before Helen and, to my dismay, found my bike tires were flat, both of them. I looked closely to find they had been slashed. Slashed? Why me? I pushed my bike into town, left it at the bicycle shop and bought a fresh roll and dark coffee at the bakery. I picked up a local paper. There it was. The story of the painting! It had found its way into the Heidelberg Daily News. This was like a grass fire spreading out of control. One small article led to this? I almost wanted to hide myself as I looked out at the early morning sunrise, knowing that, in about a half hour, the town would wake up and read this. I must admit, from then on I became paranoid.

The painting in the Louvre, the missing Nazi looted art, the switching of the picture, the publication, then the Sonnenschein letter...and now my slashed bike tires? I really needed some time to think this over. I scrambled over to the library, which usually was a casual affair, but now it seemed someone was watching me with every step I took.

"It's all in my imagination," I thought. "Calm down. You're just making this up. It's not really happening."

Good, the library light was on, and I rushed up the steps to greet Erin, who was in the process of unlocking and opening the large doors.

"Lina? It's way too early for you."

"I know, Erin."

"You're all over the news."

"I know that too, thanks to Pieter." She tried to stop me and pry a bit. "No time, Erin. I've got to hide myself back in the stacks. Okay if I take my coffee with me?"

She nodded her approval.

I knew what I wanted, just a simple dictionary. I found one, rushed to the back table and sat. I turned to the letter C, and there it was, *cui bono.*

*A Latin adage alluding to a hidden motive or implying that the responsible party may not be obvious at first, possibly due to attempts to pin the crime on a scapegoat. The common usage of the phrase is to relay that the guilty person or people likely had something to gain, particularly financially, in committing the crime*

I just sat there going over and over the definition. *May not be obvious at first.* Someone was on to me, but who and why? Why not Pieter? I really didn't know anything. It just happened. It all started with the painting, there in the Louvre.

I went back into the stacks and grabbed some art books to go over the details again, just to be sure I was right. I turned to the Murillo section, and there she was. The St. Rufina, the painting that had been on display in the Louvre and was now mysteriously missing.

Why had she become my friend? Why did she call out to me? What was the connection to Sonnenschein? Would the person in the letter tell me where she was or who had an interest in her? I sat there with my head in my hands for an hour or so when someone tapped me on my shoulder. I jumped. It was Pieter toting a big attaché case.

"Lina, I knew I'd find you here." He quickly sat down next to me and leaned in close to say, "Listen to this. Remember Dr. Lemans, the curator? Dr. Bader told me he resigned from the Louvre! The professor said he took off on sabbatical to America for a while, or so they say. Little odd, don't you think?"

"So what's that mean?"

"Maybe nothing, alone. But when you put the switch of the painting, the publication and now the missing curator together, it sounds like a little more than nothing."

"Okay, I agree. It's something.  You've seen the local

Heidelberg news?"

"Yes, I saw that. They just grabbed the story from my article."

We both jumped when we looked up to see Thomas standing beside the table. He said, "Hi, there. I thought you both would be here."

There was an awkward silence when I realized they hadn't met.

"Thomas, meet Pieter."

"You're the editor of the university newspaper."

"Yes, that's me." Pieter stood to shake hands and asked, "Word got around?"

"You bet it has. Do you mind if I sit with you? I don't want to barge in, but I have something that may interest you both."

"Yes, of course. Take a seat," Pieter said politely.

"Thanks. Well, as you know, Lina, I work at JAG. Military intelligence is mostly what I do at the barracks. They've picked up your article and pieced it together with something they've been working on."

"And that is?" Pieter asked.

"As we like to say, 'close the ratline, and you'll find the rats.' The thousands of Nazis who fled Germany after the war…"

Pieter jumped back in. "So what does this article have to do with that?"

"As you already know, the Nazis got through the ratlines with looted gold, diamonds and art. Like your publication suggested, many pieces of the looted art are still here and in various other places around Europe. So be very careful…"

"What about the art?" Pieter asked.

Thomas leaned in and whispered, "It seems that one of the missing links to finding the ratlines is by following art trades… looted art trades to be specific. You find them, you'll find a Nazi at the other end."

"Okay, so why tell us?"

Thomas looked directly at me when he said, "Not knowing it, Lina may have walked into a minefield. There are very dangerous people out there who are trying to prevent discovery of their trail. Some of them have diverse interests in the millions of dollars worth of stolen art. From the Mossad to major collectors with powerful friends, such as Wildenstein & Company, who financed presidents into power, to organizations protecting Hitler's lost friends, such as the Organisation der Ehemaligen SS-Angehorigen (ODESSA)—aka the Organization of Former SS Members. Some of these members have the idea that, when the time is right, they will reclaim the cause and rise again."

"And the CIA?"

"Yes, Pieter, them, too. Then there are large insurance companies that want to reclaim their losses and, of course, governments like Switzerland that have millions stored in undiscovered Holocaust victim accounts. Who knows what they'll do to keep them or prevent you from getting at them."

"Okay, okay. Now that you've scared us to death, where do we come in?" Pieter asked.

"Well, obliviously, you come in because you brought up the issue. And, they must believe you know something."

"Know what? Just that someone changed the picture!"

"Yes, Lina, that may be true, but it's important enough that our agents are picking up a lot of movement in the art world, enough to make their ears perk up. So why do I tell you this? Because, I can give you classified information into the art world to help you find out who's involved, and that will help us in return. And most importantly, Lina, you need to let us monitor you. Who knows what danger lies ahead."

"You mean for my protection?"

"Yes, for both of your protection."

Pieter and I looked at each other and nodded in agreement.

Thomas appeared pleased and said, "Okay, just go on as usual. Don't change your routine. Don't let on to anybody what we've talked about here this morning. The Nuremberg Trials produced leads for us to follow, especially from Alfred Rosenberg. His information is what we call the 'Schenker Papers.'"

I jumped in. "Yes, we know something about that already."

"Okay. Let's get right to Wildenstein & Company. They've acquired many of the lost pieces of art. You can interview them, then move up, see what happens."

"Why us and not you?" I asked.

"Because they'll think you are just concerned locals on the trail of a story. They'll be more open, at least that's the theory. Okay? We'll give you the info to set up interviews. But again, for now, say nothing to anyone."

"All right."

"Pieter, may I have a few moments alone with Lina?"

Pieter looked at me and, when I nodded my okay he left us.

"So, Thomas, you're really not a student are you? You're just a plant and what happened between us was just to get me on board?"

"No, Lina. Believe me, I was working on something else, like I told you, and I was interested in getting off the base and into the local community, just to get out of the barracks. I met you and, yes, used my position to get into your class. But, for personal reasons…you… I had no way of knowing this would happen, no more then you did. When I got back to the barracks yesterday, I had orders to see the commanding intelligence officer. I had no idea what was up. At that meeting, he passed a photo across the table to me. It was a photo of you. He asked, 'What do you know about this girl?'

"When I took a look, I thought, 'oh my God, what have I done?' They detailed their interests and asked if I was too close to you to take on this detail. And, at that moment, it came to me. I'd rather be at your side then to just disappear. Something very good was happening between us. I couldn't just let it go. So there you are."

There was an uneasy moment of silence, and then he added, "Let me stay around just for a little while, and you'll see. I'll make you believe."

He took my hand and looked deeply into my eyes. Damn those eyes. Why were they always interfering with my best judgment?

"All right, Thomas. For awhile."

He squeezed my hand, and we agreed with a handshake.

"It's a deal," I said, holding tightly to the hand I'd once held under the pretense of love, while walking along the banks of the Neckar. But, now I held that same hand in partnership to clandestine intrigue. It would no doubt be a precarious undertaking, one that could lead to a world so unlike this peaceful one to which I was accustomed.

CHAPTER 12
# Art Collectors

When I was young and moving about the abbey, we had hobbies, such as collecting stamps and coins, even bottle caps for a while. I suppose they had their value. But, it was more a reflection of what was contemporary and our point of play. Even though we didn't know it then, it was art, something to save, hold on to and find meaning in. It was part of who we were and how we saw things, a feeble attempt to express ourselves, in terms of what we were familiar with, for prosperity's sake. And, there were a few time capsules, efforts to create and capture those early moments in our lives. In essence, they were the symbols, artifacts, timelines and benchmarks that proved our existence and told the world we had lived.

Throughout history, art and other objects were handed down from generation to generation. And, with each epoch, there were new producers of the contemporary. Artists, painters, sculptors, muralists, quilters, pottery makers, pastry bakers, mosaic masonries, musicians and composers all had one thing in common: attempts to offer their interpretation toward a lasting impression of the world in which they found themselves. This was art. And, on it went, until in came those solicitous collectors, miscreants of society, who saw such efforts only in terms of profit. And, why not? The wealthy of the world adorned their homes, cathedrals were graced and public buildings were brandished with art formed by the hands of the masters. Art would be something more than just an ornament of taste. It became an ingredient of culture.

The Nazi revolution, Hitler's vision, his quest for Germany, was more about redeeming its long lost culture, rather than politics or economics. Lessons were given on how ruthless, contemptuous and diabolical the Nazis could be in possessing and protecting such things as art. After France fell to Germany, they moved in and immediately the ERR confiscated art from French galleries. The most prestigious and famous of their thievery was the Louvre.

Wrestling art from private collectors was simply a matter of formality. With the complicity of the French government, anti-Semitic legislation passed that not only showed disdain for Jewish art but also Jewish religious institutions. Their nationality was revoked, retroactive to 1927, stripping them of any legal status or claims to personal property, including art. The dispossessed found little ability to appeal in French and German courts. Their fate had all but been determined, and many were already rotting and dying in concentration camps.

No doubt the French art industry flourished during the war. Art dealers came in droves to France and specifically to the Louvre, which unloaded artwork at bargain prices. Who were these vile merchants who scrambled like vultures into France and the Louvre, between 1940 and 1944, to gobble up every piece of looted art they could? They, like so many other profiteers, saw war as simply a good business opportunity. Greed, as always, sheds people of their standards quite easily.

By now, Pieter and I were given a steady stream of information, courtesy of U.S. military intelligence, via Lieutenant Thomas Werner. Much of it came from classified documents gathered during the Nuremberg Trials. We received names, dates and times of classified art transactions, plus even a condensed list, secretly kept by a French partisan named Rose Valland.

So, it was with this kind of information that we set out to find the St. Rufina, along with several other paintings from the Rothschild collection. With a full head of steam, we were on the right trail and started with the giant of world art, Wildenstein & Company.

A meeting was set up under false pretence and again disguised as an interview for a local college newspaper. It was to be a series about the world art trade. Apparently, we were not as clever as we thought.

Just before our scheduled meeting with one of the Wildenstein heirs, we were instead met by a cadre of corporate attorneys—but not before we were left standing for over an hour in the company's sterile lobby. Finally rewarding our patience, an indignant secretary escorted us up to an oversized conference room and asked us to sit at the end of a long massive table. Another wait, then men in expensive suits slowly filed in and arranged themselves toward the front.

After looking down at his notes, one of the impeccably dressed men made some introductions ending with, "My name is Mr. Keller. I am the corporate attorney for Wildenstein & Company."

Pieter made our introductions as well. Now disposed with the formalities and incensed by what was happening, he quickly got right into it.

"Gentleman, Mr. Keller, you obviously know why we are here but for those who don't, we are attempting to track down confiscated art hidden here in France and other countries. We have a specific interest in one of the pieces taken from a private collection. As you know, many of those items have been purchased and sold by dealers such as yourself and buyers your company represents."

Mr. Keller responded firmly, "You have come to the wrong place. I can assure you that Wildenstein & Company has never knowingly been complicit in or condoned such transactions, during or after the war."

Undeterred, Pieter said, "All right, then. Are you familiar with a painting by Murillo titled 'St. Rufina?'"

"Of course. However, we have never traded any of Murillo's work."

"Is that a fact, Mr. Keller?"

"Yes."

"Have you ever had the privilege to view his work?"

"I do not recall. Though, I can assure you we have never had any transactions with that artist's work."

"Are you aware that, as of this moment, the location of many Murillo paintings is unknown and that a large amount of money has been paid to the previous owners for the loss?"

"Yes, of course."

"You see the concern then?"

"Let me repeat myself, Mr. Neumann, Wildenstein & Company never deals in that kind of art."

"What do you mean, Mr. Keller—that is a British name, is it not?" Pieter, asked sarcastically.

"Yes, it is."

"So, Mr. Keller, what do you mean, 'that kind of art?'"

"You know very well what I mean. That art is considered looted and claims have been made that it was stolen from Jews, during the war. We are all quite aware of that art in this business."

"Then, Mr. Keller, would you recognize this art, if it crossed your desk or the desk of one of your agents?"

"Yes."

"How, Mr. Keller? How would you know it was one of the

stolen pieces?"

He seemed to squirm a little before answering, "Well, there are markings on the backs of the frames, a number designating what collection they were taken from."

"Yes, precisely. So what you're telling me, Mr. Keller, is that if one of the art pieces in question were to pass through this company, you would most certainly know it was a tainted painting."

Obviously annoyed, he replied, "Look, Mr. Neumann, I know what you are inferring. But you see, we have never dealt with any of the Rothschild collection. And, as I have said..."

Pieter cut in. "So you know the missing Murillo paintings are from the Rothschild collection."

"Yes, of course we do."

"Okay! Now we are getting somewhere." I could tell Pieter was about to throw down his ace when he said, "So now, how about the French collector Adolphe Schloss? Did you ever trade, possess or sell any of his works before or after 1939?"

"Not to my knowledge."

"What does that mean? 'Not to your knowledge?'"

About to sizzle at Pieter's impertinent persistence yet attempting to embrace a stoic presence, he said, "Listen, Mr. Neumann, we have literally hundreds of art vaults here and around the world."

"Even in the United States and Great Britain?"

"Yes, there too. How could we possibly know what's in all of them? This is a very fast and fluid industry. And, I might add, privacy is not just a convenience, it is the creed of the industry."

"Mr. Keller, you have stated your company is able to recognize looted art and also claim that you have no interest in such works, due to morality issues. Yet, we have in our possession affidavits confirming a representative from Wildenstein & Company approached the Louvre and other private dealers with the proposition that if they came across any of the Schloss or Rothschild pieces, your company would be very interested in their acquisition."

"How did you come by this information, Mr. Neumann?"

"Relentless, tireless research." Pieter smiled knowing Mr. Keller must have realized by now we had access to classified information. Information the French and U.S. governments had hidden for years as secret and confidential.

Mr. Keller strained to keep from getting pulled further into the quagmire. Defiantly, he said, "Mr. Neumann, maybe you would be better served by interviewing the grand master of this type of art business."

"And whom might that be?" Pieter asked.

"Theodore Fischer, of course. I am confident you have come across his name in your relentless and tireless research."

"Yes, we are familiar with the infamous Fischer and his degenerate and looted art auctions held in Switzerland. Quite an unscrupulous man."

"Go interview him. He would love to talk about such things. He has no regrets and no conscience, some would say."

Mr. Keller, with his arrogant, wrinkled smile, seemed pleased at himself for moving the blame off his corporate client and added, "Mr. Neumann, you are making a big mistake with your accusations against Wildenstein & Company. Misinformation will get you no closer to your St. Rufina. Go see Mr. Fischer. But, remember, we have not made any accusations…"

"You certainly implied as much, didn't you, Mr. Keller?"

"Enough…enough of this nonsense," he said with a raised voice and pointed finger. "We will destroy you in the courts. Whatever your interest is, we will destroy you."

"No, you won't, Mr. Keller. And, let me tell you why. None of you want to see this come to light in the press, bad PR and all that. Plus, need I remind you, counselor, that truth is always a good defense to libel and slander. Also, Mr. Keller, my readers would love to know the answer to the last question I have for you today."

"And that is?"

"Are you willing to open your company's art vaults and Paris storeroom to be inspected by a neutral party?"

"Of course not." He was standing to leave when he added, "Mr. Neumann, you and your university paper are far too small to take this on. I suggest, for your own good, you let this be the end of it. Good day, Mr. Neumann, Frau Ritter. I'm sorry, I didn't get your first name."

"You never asked. It's Lina."

"You're the girl in the article."

"Yes, that's me."

He hesitated, looked me over in an engaging way and then said, "I think we're through here. However, please keep discretion in mind while you are on your quest. I hope that no harm will come to either of you."

"I hope that's not a threat, Mr. Keller."

"No, Mr. Neumann. It's just that it is a cruel and dangerous world out there. Good day."

We were left standing alone. The secretary came to see us out.

"Good stuff," I said as we climbed back into the car. "But what did we accomplish?"

"They are getting nervous and reckless. They gave us a lead. Tomorrow we publish another article. Somewhere out there, somebody has a painting hidden, and they are determined for us to not find it. It's double trouble. Remember what Thomas said.

'You find the painting, you find the Nazi.'"

"So where now?" I asked.

"The lead…the lead, Lina. A little trip to Lucerne, Switzerland to see the retired art dealer Theodore Fischer."

When we returned to campus, Thomas was waiting in Pieter's office. We went over today's conversation with Wildenstein's counsel and then collaborated on what tomorrow's follow-up publication would entail.

Putting Wildenstein on the hot seat had very little downside. Because, like Pieter mentioned, they didn't want their laundry aired out in public. To art dealers, that was toxic business. Pieter let Thomas in on our pending visit to Lucerne then got back to work at his typewriter. Thomas and I walked down to his car.

"Well, things are about to settle down now, so let's get a bite to eat. Okay?"

"Sounds good to me."

We sat there in the Marktplatz, just talking over little stuff and trying to keep our relationship from being distracted by the project. Eventually Thomas said, "Lina, I've grown fond of you, but I still know very little about you."

"What's more to know? I grew up, as I said, in the abbey and just sort of made my way over to the university."

"What memories do you have of your youth?"

"Oh, not much really. I just know what I've been told. I had no reason to go back and, besides, it was right after the war. Most Germans never want to look back."

"Then, what about your future? What do you see there?"

"I don't know…intrigue?" I laughed. "Actually, adventure is what I would love to see as my future. I want to travel around the world at least once, just enough to make me want to come back home."

"And home is?"

"Oh, the abbey I guess. The abbey, the sisters, Reverend Mother, old Father Tobias at the Jesuit, they along with Erin and Helen, will always be what I consider home."

"And when you're alone?"

"Alone? Well, when I am alone, I talk to God. We have good conversations because I do all the talking." I smiled then turned the topic back to the painting. "You know, Thomas, every time I go on one of Pieter's interviews, something strange happens to me."

"Really? Like what?"

"I feel like I'm being pulled into the middle of a swift stream that's about to swallow me. I get scared and out of breath. But to get out, I realize I must swim downstream a little farther. Somehow I know that, if I do that, I will get out safely. I hope that happens."

"Lina, life is dynamic. It's always changing. And, sometimes change comes without notice. What about us? Do you think, somewhere down that river, you might find me in the picture?"

I reached across the table and took hold of his hand. "I hope so. Sincerely, Thomas, I hope so."

He leaned his forehead against mine for a while.

Like before, something pulled me away from him. I said, "I'm getting tired. It's been another long day. You heard about my bike?

"Yes, I did. I'd better drive you home."

"Thanks, but I would like to walk for a while, Thomas. It's just a mile or so. I need to be alone."

Reluctantly, he agreed. "See you in the morning?"

"Yes. I'll be at the library."

I began walking down between the shops and found my way onto the narrow residential streets. A little light was left from the summer day, but it was quickly about to disappear so I walked faster than usual. Gradually, I got a strange feeling that somebody was watching me. Quickening my steps, I tried to assure myself that I was just getting caught up in all of this. Then all of a sudden a man stepped out of the shadows and stood in my way. I screamed.

"Lina, for God's sake. It's just me, the baker!"

"The baker. I am so sorry. Good to see you. I'll be in early for my roll and coffee. Okay?" I said then hurried on.

When I finally arrived at my building, I looked up and realized that Helen must not be home yet. No lights were on. I rushed up the stairs and pulled out my key but noticed the door was already cracked open. The room was unusually dark.

Even before I flipped the switch, I knew something was wrong. When the light came on, I shuddered at what I saw. Our apartment had been completely ransacked. Ripped cloth was everywhere. In the bathroom, toothpaste was all over the floor. I rushed to my bed. The torn mattress lay off to the side. My journal? It was gone! Why would someone do that? I fell to the floor, overcome by fear and doubt, and began to sob uncontrollably.

My journal was my life, the only story I really had. Those words proved that I had been here, and now my only evidence of life had been taken away from me. Now, I would only have memories that would surely fade, be lost over time.

I reached for the phone to call Pieter. The line had been pulled from the wall. I heard footsteps approaching slowly, as if not to disturb. I moved from the floor to the back of my thrashed mattresses and buried my head to hide. A hand touched me on the shoulder, and a voice whispered, "Lina, it's me, Helen."

I looked up and cried out, "Oh, Helen! Thank God it's you! I was so scared."

"What happened here?"

"I don't know. Please go to the neighbors and call Pieter. He will know what to do."

She rushed out, and, about a half hour later, the staircase was rumbling with the noise of people rushing up to our apartment. First Pieter, then Thomas and then a mass of military people began to wander about, looking for anything that could explain what all this meant.

Later, Thomas had mattresses and a few other things brought over from the barracks, along with a whole crew of men to help in the cleanup. When they finished, Pieter, Thomas, Helen and I shared our suspicions.

Much later, after the guys left, I began to shiver. It finally hit me, and I needed to write it down. But where? Helen was in the shower when I asked, "Where is your backpack?"

She called out, "Probably outside the door. I must have dropped it when I came in."

I unlocked and opened the door. There it was. I unzipped it on my way back into the apartment, found a paper tablet and pencil, sat down and attempted to retrace the recent past. But, my hands wouldn't give up the trembling. Minutes passed. When I finally could, I wrote, Journal: *This is not about the painting. It's about me, something they want has to do with me.*

CHAPTER 13

# The Resurfacing of Dr. Lemans

"Bartolomé Esteban Murillo was a Spanish artist," whispered the voice from the shadows of the side pew, as rays of colored light streamed in through the stained glass windows, finding their way onto the altar. The odor of spent burnt wicks lingered throughout the Jesuit Church while flickering candles gave evidence of prayer and illuminated his face. This was usually a spiritual place for hope and redemption. And it was to obtain the later that he freely confessed. Not to the priest or the heavens, no that would come later. For now he confessed to us, hoping that we would somehow give him some kind of absolution.

The voice began its story. "You see, Frau Ritter, Herr Neumann, this goes back a while. There was a time when our lives were in limbo, never knowing where or what we would be doing from one moment to the next. When the Gestapo said it was your time, it was your time. But, we were the lucky ones. We were the curator of the arts. We knew things that kept us alive, so we fed this information to them piecemeal, by bits and pieces, so they would need us for one more day.

"As you've uncovered, yes, at first they took—no, stole—every piece of art from the Louvre. They reviewed, classified, then sent the paintings they thought Hitler would like up north into German warehouses, which held artwork destined for the Führermuseum. The others, the ones not 'worthy' of the museum…most were sent back to the Louvre or auctioned off in Switzerland to art buyers around the world.

"Looking for Murillo's St. Rufina and St. Justa? Well, I'm afraid that is where the trail ends. But, after all this time, so many years since the end of the war... You'd think after what they did, nobody would dare capitalize on those beautiful art pieces. Not so. Powerful, prominent families, investors and collectors continued on where the war left off, playing us like ridiculous clowns. For we all knew the true value of the pieces and the names of the rightful owners.

"I'm sorry to have misled you the other day, when you came to see me at the Louvre, but there are very powerful forces still preying around Europe, protecting their wealth and interests— some just hoping and waiting for the day they will regain power. I know my days are numbered now. I hold too many secrets they want to keep hidden. They mean nothing now to me. I just want to leave this world knowing I have attempted to wipe my slate clean. Yes, I know it will never really be clean, for the part with the Nazis."

The curator looked at us with defeated eyes and continued. "About the paintings you are after, the last time I heard of them, they had been rushed off the Louvre wall and sent under cover, maybe to Lucerne, to Theodore Fischer in Switzerland. Yes, I believe he is the person who would know where the paintings are. He knows everything that goes on in the underworld of art."

The curator gathered up a low chuckle. "The deals and the parties he has. Oh, don't worry. I am sure you will have no trouble finding him. Just pick up a phonebook and look for him under Real Estate or Art. Yes, he would love to talk freely. He is a genuine Nazi, a very proud and arrogant man. Theodore has dealt with many in the higher echelons of the Nazi organization face to face and sees no problem talking openly about his deals. He loves to brag about his ventures, how important he was to the art world and the Nazis.

"He flaunts his involvement, because he is confident he has his backside covered. There are a lot of important people and, I might add, dangerous people from all walks of life whom he protects. Politicians, bankers, investors, CEOs and priests—yes, them too. And, they all have an interest in protecting him.

"What made Theodore so invulnerable were his notorious, distinguished gallery associates. And, never forget, most all of them actually believed in the Nazis' cause, in all that superiority stuff. But, what also made him notorious was his association with other celebrated acquaintances. They were not all Germans like Rosenberg. He rubbed shoulders and did business with the likes of Henry Ford and Dr. Alexis Carrel, the geneticist who wrote the book on eugenics.

"He even befriended and advised Charles Lindbergh, the American pilot, not to buy a home because a Jew had previously owned it. Yes, that is true! He later found Lindbergh another home.

"You see, this way of thinking came about before Hitler ever dreamt of writing *Mein Kampf.* Theodore, he is the man now; he'll be happy to sit down with you, tell you about his friend Dr. Göring, the exuberant, pompous, pretentious fool. Plus, there were other friends, such as Maria Dietrich, a socialite and one of Eva Braun's chums. Maria became one of Hitler's personal art brokers. And, there were dealings with Martin Bormann, Hitler's personal assistant who acted as his banker and money launderer, while mingling about the Swiss banking cartels. Yes, Fischer will talk, and he knows things—the kind of things you're after."

Pieter madly took notes, careful not to interrupt as the curator went on. "A name you need to bring up is Kajetan Mühlmann.

Ask him if he knows his whereabouts. They say he died in a Bavarian hospital. No, never happened; he's around somewhere, under disguise, living under a dead man's name. Get Theodore to talk freely about Kajetan. He's the one who procured most of the art taken during German occupations. He created the systematic confiscation and exportation scheme and also helped the Gestapo to export the Jews to concentration camps.

"And there's Karl Haberstock. In February 1942, Haberstock, a German agent with a signed authorization from Dr. Göring, pursued a forced sale of Herbert Goldman's property. Göring was personally interested in the furnishings of the house, the tapestries, the paintings on the ceiling, the silver collection and many other pieces of art around the house. Goldman refused to cooperate with the ERR agent, so two SS officers turned up, took him into custody, telling him all was going to be good and that no harm would come to his family. They put him on a train and said they would simply be sending Herbert into exile that evening—that's all. The train was diverted. He was taken to Auschwitz, where he was tortured. When he refused to agree to a contract for the sale of his collection, he was beaten to death. His wife and daughters were sent there too. They also perished, but in the gas chamber. To men such as this, it was just about the art. It was just business."

The curator became overwhelmed with emotion as he finished. "I know, even today, heirs are trying to reclaim their art, but legality of title has come under scrutiny. So, long after the war, they are still there, along with the people who collaborated with them. There is another man. One of Kajetan's men, Adolf Ziegler, art dealer, but, more importantly, he was one of Hitler's favorite artists. Hitler trusted him, brought him into his circle of friends. He became one of the Reich's key players in art appraisals. Hitler relied on his opinion before procuring art for his museum.

"I've given you enough names now. Am I free from my shame? No? I know that. But I do feel somewhat better. So, you two leave me now. Leave me now, please, so I might pray and try to clear my conscience. You won't find me again. Like all the others, I plan to spend my last days out there… Where? Nobody will know."

We stood and left him alone there on his knees. Once out on the front steps, Pieter said, "Lina, let's talk."

"Yes. Let's."

We walked over to the Marktplatz and ordered something to eat and drink.

After we'd finished picking at the food, Pieter said, "Lina, I don't want any of this information passed on to military intelligence. I don't like the feeling of being a spy. I am not into encroaching. Let them find out what they find out. There are too many possibilities of leaks and conflicts of interest here. I've been looking over this material Thomas provided. Who are these guys?" He handed me a booklet. "Look, Lina, too many agencies, the British SIS, Israel's Mossad, America's CIA and the German BND. We know about them, don't we?"

"Yes, they harbored Klaus Barbie, the Butcher of Lyon, didn't they?"

"And the French Secret Service, the DST, known for whom they protect, certainly not whom they catch. Then there is the Russian KGB. Everything I read suggests they've infiltrated most of the other spy agencies. Some nefarious groups to say the least, huh? Anyway, what are their interests in this? All of them are relying on us to track down these war criminals. We are the ones risking it all out here on the frontlines. It's not only dangerous, we've become pawns in a bigger story. What do you think, Lina?"

"You know, Pieter, I was just thinking the same thing. And, as far as Thomas, well…Thomas, he'll find his way out of this with or without our help."

"I think you're right. And, beyond that, we don't know what's ahead. They've given us no answers, none. Not even a hint that they know what they are after. We need to hang on to each other from here on in.

"Oh, Lina, by the way, I just remembered," he said while trying to let his breath catch up with his thoughts. "Something more, we will now be publishing our reports from the Heidelberg Daily across town. Got a new contract and office."

"What? What happened at the university?"

"Well, the professor took offense to our first publication and asked —no, actually he told me—that any future articles printed in the paper must be reviewed personally. I asked why he didn't trust my judgment. He said that it wasn't that. It was the overwhelming negative responses from university sponsors and alumni; some were even threatening to withhold donations."

"How did it get to be that way? Did he let you know what he thought about the article? What did Dr. Bader say that they objected to?"

"Surprisingly, Dr. Bader empathized with some of their concerns. He explained that during the '30s, many people living in Munich and Heidelberg were strong supporters of the NASDP, and, by 1939, one-third of the university staff had been forced out of their teaching positions for racial and political reasons. The non-Aryans were sent off during the Nazi reign of terror. More than 6,000 of our local citizens were sent to work camps. He told me synagogues were burnt down. The Nazis even built the Thingstätte Amphitheatre right near here, for Nazi youths to parade around and hold rallies for their ranks.

"While he prattled on, I interrupted and asked, 'Dr. Bader

where were you when this all happened?' He looked at me, obviously stunned. You should have seen his face, Lina. It was as if God were asking him in final judgment. He wouldn't answer. I asked him again. His face turned deep red and sweat gathered on his forehead. Still no answer. I had to know, so I pushed further and asked, 'Was it because you were one of them? Isn't that right, professor? And the war was inconveniently won by the wrong side and robbed you of your dreams, right professor?'

"He fell into his seat and said, 'Enough, Pieter! We are done, you and me'. I told him that's the way it should be. We see things differently. So I gathered my things and walked out.

"The editorial section of the Daily News had already contacted me, before this. And this encounter with Dr. Bader made it all too easy for me to stop publishing at the university. It seems that national news wants to run a story, both in a German and a French syndication."

"Wow, things are going faster every day."

"Yes, they are. And, we are getting closer to finding the St. Rufina. I just know it!"

"I'm not as optimistic as you, Pieter. But I do know there are certainly a lot of people interested in every move we make."

"Tomorrow I will publish another article, recapping all that has happened since the first one. You need to go over it with me sometime today. We need to agree on everything from now on." Looking at me with a tired, distressed smile he added, "There is a bunch more letters, all over my desk. I'll send them over to your apartment so you can look at some of them. There are just too many. I'm going to need a secretary."

"Oh, I heard you had this shapely blonde, or so they say, over at the Ochsen two nights ago," I teased.

"Nothing, Lina, just a side attraction. And, besides, who told you this? Your friend Erin at the library? Believe it or not, I have other projects to work on."

"I bet you do," I joked.

"You've got me all wrong. I told you that before."

"Okay, okay, I don't want you getting all stressed about this. Geez." I laughed and continued, "I'll finish my castle tour then come by your new office."

Later, with my work finished, I rode the elevator of the Deutsche Bank building up to Pieter's floor and, much to my surprise, a secretary greeted me.

"What a plentiful distribution of beauty," I thought. If her work measures up to her presentation, Pieter had a winner.

"Frau Ritter?" she asked in a professional manner.

"Yes. Hello."

"Mr. Neumann left you an article to review along with these two large bags of mail. He wanted you to know he hasn't had time to look at them yet and for you to have a ball with them."

I laughed and added, "Funny guy, isn't he?"

"Yes, he is. He'll be fun to work for."

"Yes, he is," I mumbled under my breath with an inch of jealousy creeping in.

"Mr. Neumann said somebody will bring the letters by your apartment later. But, first, he would like you to go over the article. He has it on rush for tomorrow's edition."

"All right. Thank you, Frau...."

"Oh no, you can just call me Marcia."

"Okay then, thank you, Marcia."

Now, with my bicycle back in form, I raced across town to my apartment, ran up the stairs and was greeted by Helen.

"Lina, where have you been? I've missed you coming in and out. What's going on?"

"Nothing. Nothing you need to worry about, Helen."

"Worry about?" She laughed. "Let's see, your bike tires were slashed, someone ripped up our apartment and the baker told me to buy rolls somewhere else because he is so angry."

"With you? For what?"

"He says you screamed at him."

"No, I didn't. Well, maybe a little. But I was just scared, that's all."

"And, to top it off, we are sleeping on mattresses on the floor, and you tell me, 'nothing to worry about, Helen.' Oh, and by the way, Lieutenant Thomas Werner has been trying to get a hold of you. It sounds urgent. Here's his number. He said to call him right away. Now, I think that's something for you to worry about."

"Yeah, I think you're right. I don't think it's personal, because there's nothing urgent going on there," I said while walking over to dial the phone.

He answered with, "Hello?"

"Hello, Thomas, it's me."

"Lina! Good to hear your voice. Everything okay?"

"Sure, why?"

"Do you remember Dr. Lemans, the curator, the guy who resigned from the Louvre?"

"Yes. What about him?" I asked.

"They found him dead, hanging in a warehouse about an hour ago."

"Oh no! Are you sure? Pieter and I were with him in the Jesuit Church just about five hours ago!"

"You were?" he asked.

"Yes, it was set up by Father Tobias."

"Then we need to get together and go over this."

"When?"

"This week."

"Where?"

"I'll drive you to the barracks."

"The barracks. Why the barracks?"

"Because we now have a lot of people wanting answers."

"Okay," I said. "But it will have to wait until I get back from Lucerne."

"Lucerne, why there?" he asked.

"I will tell you about it later, when we go to the barracks."

"Okay then…I guess," Thomas said.

After we finished, I immediately called Pieter, hoping he was back at his office. When he got on the line, I blurted out, "Pieter! They found Dr. Lemans hanging dead in an old warehouse along the Neckar River."

"What? That's not possible. How do you know?"

"No, it is true. Thomas just told me, and he wants to meet with me sometime this week at the barracks."

"Campbell Barracks? Damn, they're on to something. What did you tell him?"

"Very little, but we need to get together soon."

"How was the article?" he asked.

"I don't know yet. I haven't had time to read it. What do you make of it?"

"What, the hanging?"

"Maybe suicide?" I asked.

"No, I'm afraid not. I think more like someone wanted him silenced. He knew more then he let on to us. Lock your doors and keep in touch."

I was about to hang up the phone when I said, "Guess what… two military police just arrived at my door." I called out, "Let them in, Helen."

She opened the door and politely asked them to come on in.

One said, "No ma'am. We have orders to stick around outside for the night. Just letting you know we are here if you need anything."

Still on the phone, Pieter overheard and said, "Wow, Lieutenant Werner sent them for your protection. Let me know if anything comes up. I'll be working late tonight."

After Helen closed the door, I whispered, "Helen, you must know as little as possible. Maybe it's best if you spent a few nights at the abbey, just until we've sorted things out."

"What are you talking about, Lina? We are in everything together, and it will stay that way. Your problems are mine."

"Okay, but don't ask me about what is going on. Okay? I'll tell you when the time comes for you to know."

"Okay…a pact."

"Let's eat. I need to go over some letters Pieter's sending over."

"I can help."

"No dates tonight?"

"No such luck," she answered with a grin.

As the night passed on, Helen and I peeled back envelope after envelope and read the funny ones out loud to one another. Those were a rarity in this bunch. Then, before I opened the next letter, for whatever reason, I glanced at its postmark. It was from Berlin. I quickly broke the seal, plucked out a neatly folded note, spread it open and read. It said simply, *Liesel, focus on the Rufina, and you will get your answer. Trust only me. –Sonnenschein*

I got up off my knees and looked around the room. There was still only Helen helping me out, but, for some reason, I pressed the letter to my breast, trying not to let on I had something special in my hand. It seemed to speak directly to me, but wait, *Liesel*? The letter said she would find the answer. What did that mean? I don't even know the question…what answer? What happened to the painting and why was I involved? Why my bike, why my apartment, what was next? Why not Pieter or Helen? Berlin again and Sonnenschein…was this a code…and what was this, *trust only me*? Who was this?

Thomas called me a little later, hoping we could get together for awhile before I went off to Switzerland. I was about to agree to meet him in the morning, but then I found myself wondering if he was more concerned about intelligence gathering or about my trip with Pieter. This thought made him a suspect, and I now began to push him out of the loop of my trust. And, it had a toxic effect on our budding relationship.

He felt my hesitation and said, "Hey I've got a surprise for you if you just have coffee with me in the morning. I'll guarantee you will like it."

"All right, tomorrow morning at Alex's café, just down the street from Ochsen, 8 a.m."

"Great it's all set. See you in the morning."

I still hung on to the belief that I could separate the business of the painting from our personal relationship. That possibly Thomas and I could work out something between us. But, with each passing day, outside concerns began to make that hope more and more remote.

I wrote on my tablet, acting now as a substitute for my journal and usually hidden under a kitchen floorboard: *Secrecy and hiding places are becoming excessive ploys. The dreams about St. Rufina and the mystery man were back. They both seemed to be speaking to me. I feel everything that has happened is not mere speculation and has more to do with me than with the painting. Each day I must guard my thoughts. more tightly. I only let on to what everyone already knows and keep the secrets that are meant only for me… just that, secret. Am I counting on* Sonnenschein, *for the answers… or is Sonnenschein counting on me?*

CHAPTER 14

# The Face of a Nazi

A s soon as I reached the coffee shop, Thomas waved me over to his table, already filled with sweet rolls and two large cups of hot coffee. He stood to pull out my chair and, when I sat, he got right to it.

"Wow, Lina. A lot has happened in just a few days. Can you get me caught up?"

"Let's see… As you know, Father Tobias arranged a meeting with the curator, Dr. Lemans, at the church."

"Who asked for that meeting?"

"Dr. Lemans, but he didn't give us much, except for a few names to contact. Theodore Fischer in Switzerland was the best lead. He indicated Fischer would probably be happy to talk to us. Pieter arranged a meeting with him for this afternoon. And, I'm sure you've probably already read Pieter's article in today's local paper."

"Yeah, what happened to the university paper?"

"Professor Bader fired him, or he resigned, depending, I guess, on whom you talk to."

"There was a misunderstanding?"

"No. Pieter confronted him about his past Nazis involvement, and that was that."

"So, next stop is Fischer's?"

"Yah…A little nervous about that. It seems every time we interview people, drastic things happen."

"Well, Lina, that's why we know you're on to something. Although, we haven't been able to put our finger on what, just yet. I have to admit, they do seem to be hovering around you like bees to honey. There must be more to this than meets the eye."

"What do you think is going on, Thomas?"

"Without a doubt, it is your fixation on the St. Rufina. They, meaning all the agencies, CIA, army intelligence, British SIS and the Mossad, even the insurance companies seem to think this all fits in with an ODESSA-type conspiracy. But, I don't buy it. I don't think that's it at all. Why you're getting so much attention is still a mystery. I wish I could help you out there, but it's just a lot of speculation."

"Nobody has worked it out?"

"They're all looking for something and not letting each other in on it. Especially not me."

"Why not you?"

"They probably think I'm too close to you." After a few moments of awkward silence, Thomas asked, "That reminds me, what about us?"

"Yeah, what about us?" I laughed then got serious. "Thomas, you know if we held hands walking through Old Town, there would be secret agents clicking pictures. The time for us is not now. I'm sure you agree. Hey, what about that surprise that got me down here this early?"

With a warm smile, Thomas reached over into his attaché and pulled out my journal.

"Where did you get it?"

"In the same warehouse where they discarded Lemans' body."

"But, why would they leave it there? Why not just burn it?"

"We don't know that either, but, I have to admit, you are

an important part of this. There's something about you that is quite fascinating. I thought that in Paris, and, when we left, that fascination came back with you."

"What a nice thing to say. I think."

Thomas glanced at his watch and said, "Gosh, look at the time. I've got to get back to the military barracks."

"Yeah, and me on the road."

"I'm going to have to answer a few questions on what we talked about this morning. Anything else come from those mailbags that can help us?"

"No, I don't think so."

There would be no talk about Sonnenschein and Liesel. Not now, anyway.

"Okay, then. Oh, my colonel wanted you to know that we'll be monitoring your every move. So, if you see a car shadowing you, it had better be us. See you later, and, if you come up with anything, call me first."

He started to rush off but then turned back, leaned in and placed a kiss on my cheek. His smile grew as he walked away. For me, it was on to Switzerland.

In the past, I'd spent some time researching Switzerland and could never fully understand how she always managed to stay out of the rumblings that went on around her. As the storybook goes, it's a cozy little country nestled in west central Europe, bordered on the north by France and Germany, on the east by Austria and on the south by Italy. It's been said, most likely by the Swiss, that this peace-loving country stayed out of war because she had no enemies, took no sides and proclaimed neutrality to warring parties.

In reality, her policies were a pretense—an international smokescreen for suspect dealings. As history unfolded, the rest of the world gradually discovered she was the major depository for all sorts of vile undertakings, stockpiling, archiving and flexible financing. She also fraudulently laundered, protected tax evaders and guarded tyrants' bounties as they plundered the world.

Her promised privacy and lack of transparency served to conceal those dubious, if not illegal and usually immoral, transactions. Swiss banks and government officials had their bases covered, passing elaborate legislation designed to strip Jews of legal claim to their property. The laws were so well crafted that later, when heirs attempted to make claim, it became an impossible endeavor.

Finding Swiss art transactions so extremely lucrative, the Nazis set up more than 26 dealerships and proceeded to transport tons of goods in unmarked cargo containers to Switzerland. From there, the world eagerly waited for the opportunity to buy the notoriously looted art. One of the most prodigious swindlers, shysters and enablers was a characterless man by the name of Theodore Fischer.

Like so many unscrupulous international traders, Fischer saw the happenings in Germany and France as a way to make millions. In 1939, he founded the Fischer Degenerate Art Auction House in Lucerne with all transactions financed and packaged by Swiss banks.

Pieter drove us to Fischer's home in Lucerne, approximately 220 miles from Heidelberg and a little more than three hours drive. Switzerland is about 60 percent Catholic with the rest primarily Protestant and is a throwback of Habsburg history, so the majority speak German.

Surprisingly, Fischer agreed to see us at his plush estate, just outside of Lucerne. After we identified ourselves at the security gate, it slowly swung open, revealing more than 100 yards of lush greenery. Pastel flowers flourished along the grand driveway.

Pieter said, "I bet the landscaping bill is factored into the country's GDP."

The property ended at the shoreline of Lake Lucerne. From there, you were treated to a grand view of Mt. Pilatus and, beyond that, the Swiss Alps. We continued on driving over a small hill, which I'm sure was designed specifically to hide and block public views of his palatial estate. My first impression was my last. Opulence was never discretion in its design. To call it ostentatious would underscore the pretense of his chateau. It troubled me that this was the result of attempts to suggest virtue, to placate the decadence that made all of this possible, giving clues to the character concealed inside.

We drove on until a burly man, who didn't bother to identify himself, stopped us under a covered entry. We suspected he was kindred to a security guard. He greeted us with the assurance that they had been expecting us.

We exited the car and followed him up the wide front stairs, where even he had to ring a bell. A butler eventually opened the large heavy doors and introduced us to the house. He proceeded to lead the way, passing a plethora of staircases and galleries of paintings plastered on walls, like billboards.

Following his lead, we passed a corridor where sets of books, neatly packed with art trinkets, sat atop a delicate assortment of antique tables arranged between overstuffed leather chairs. It seemed more a memorial to the man who lived here than anything else. We moved on for some time until we reached what appeared to be the other side of the house. Finally, we arrived at a comfortable room dressed by hardwood panels and floors, rough to give texture and shiny to give taste.

The room was interwoven with marble and mirrors, plus immense windows looked out over a large veranda with a spectacularly breathtaking view. It was the only room in the house that conformed with its setting. In all of nature it would have been very difficult to ever find such a sanctuary, and we both gasped at the sight.

We were quickly brought to attention by a gravelly voice coming from an enormous chair at the back of the room.

"Look around if you like."

So we strolled around, looking at personal photographs displaying this man's passions and obsessions.

"What may I offer you to drink?" the voice asked as a man stood and came closer.

"Lemonade would be nice," I answered.

"For me as well," Pieter said while turning toward the now familiar man in the photographs. "That is you at the Louvre with Hermann Göring, isn't it?" Pieter asked as he nodded toward the photo.

"Yes, that picture was taken in 1941. And here's another with Maria Dietrich, Hitler's personal art broker. And there I am with Himmler." He said proudly, "Ah, yes, Himmler, he loved paintings too…had to work with the Gestapo to get things done. There is me with Hitler."

Pieter and I stared at that one for an uncomfortable few moments.

"And, that's me with Eric Hoffer, and here is one with Rosenberg. Over here is Posse and me with the ERR officers. Yes, men of fine character. I've got most of them, except maybe Kajetan Mühlmann. He was camera shy. Sit down, there on the couch."

We did, and from there we got a clear view of all the personal mementos, as if it had all been staged for our benefit. Fischer immediately took over the conversation and rarely let it go.

"So you are the two who have decided to render a verdict on the art trade during the war?"

Pieter attempted to reply, but Fischer persisted on.

"Rosenberg introduced me to the art industry before the war. It was suffering from a case of recession, and he told me things were about to change quickly. I asked, 'how is that, Alfred?' He said, 'war, Teddy, war.' 'How does it work?' I asked.

"He said, 'Simple. Who holds title to most of the art in Europe? Jews. Jooooews! And things are going to happen. That's the way preservation works; it's genetics, Teddy.'

"You see, the Germans believed, and rightly so, that history and war is all about survival of culture and race. The wealth of a country should go to that end, providing the populace with the essentials to fight for that which is yours. War is a good thing. It is the ultimate claim, the ultimate sacrifice to your clan, your tribe."

Fischer was rambling now as he raised his hands to emphasize his point. "You see, it's just that simple…that's what we all strive for, now isn't it? The French, the Russians, the Americans, the Chinese, they all believe in their way. So war is a noble pursuit. It determines who survives. It is the final arbitrator. The communists go against the capitalists and both have the same end goal in mind, to control the wealth. The Protestants and the Catholic are the same…control the masses—all for what? To preserve their way. Hitler saw this and said they all missed the mark. What was really at stake was race. That was the determining factor, and you had to have this conflict, this competition of war, to prove who was superior and could rule their own destiny.

"Hitler started a revolution. Yes, a revolution against those liberals who thought that just by wealth alone or just by religion alone that all were the same. He knew entitlements and theology only make people weak. Germany was brought to her knees by such thinking. To become great again, she had to reject the distorted morality of the world that plundered her after WWI.

Throughout Germany, a scientific revival began. A revival of the concept of race that Darwin and Dr. Alexis Carrel propagated. You see, the inferior race could only survive if truth was distorted.

"So, what's that got to do with the art that you have come here to talk about? I can proudly say that, yes, we sold hundreds of pieces of degenerate art. Americans were our number one buyer of the art, and from whom? The Joooews! The bankers, the killers of Jesus. Even the Vatican supported our cause. They also bought our degenerate paintings, and they collect dust in Vatican vaults as I speak.

"Even more, the Jews tainted our banks, became panderers and moneychangers until they strangled our culture and brought us to the abyss of defeat. Yes, millions may have died in the chambers, so be it. But how many more good Germans died because of the cancer they spread? What is it to you?

"Officers found it their duty to expend hundreds of lives in order to save many more throughout the war. Eisenhower made those same decisions at Normandy, didn't he? What is the quality of one man's life worth to him except for the betterment of his culture, his art, his religion, his economy? Yes, it is so. Yes, we sold art taken from those...the tainted ones who said they were noble but really deceivers for their Zionist cause, denying Germans their place in history as a race; science says it is so!"

Fischer's voice hit a final high note as he plopped back down in his chair and pounded his fists on it. "Preservation is instinctive in all genetics. The highest morality is to act in accordance, to dance in war to preserve your race!"

After overcoming his tirade, Fischer calmed himself. "So, after getting a look around this room, you see, these are some of the real heroes. We fought our war with art. We helped financed the war by selling paintings. Yes, I, Theodore Fischer, and the

Americans and the British and all the other so-called peaceful countries did as well by buying them. And, we make no pretense for what we've done. In fact, we helped, by our sales, preserve the arts throughout the world. We did not banish them by destruction, but sold them and kept them alive outside of Germany. So, what are you, crusaders of the so-called looted art, after?"

It took a moment for Pieter to realize Fischer was actually waiting for an answer. "To get the art back to the rightful owners," he said. "What we are searching for is a lost painting. As I mentioned on the phone, the painting is the St. Rufina."

"Hmm, I know little about that piece. I believe she fell in the cracks. A Murillo, the Spaniard was really a classical artist. That piece would not have found its way over here to Switzerland. I would have surely known about it. Both of them, St. Rufina and St. Justa, are very valuable pieces. Look to Christie's or Sotheby's. They have been known to offer those types of pieces.

"Also, look up Kajetan Mühlmann. However, I believe he passed on a few years ago. Maybe you would have better luck trying to locate his secretary. Let's see. What was her name... aha, Astrid Klammer. She could tell you a lot about the art business under the Reich. Lots of funny goings on there. Hitler, Göring and Himmler dealt more with classical art, and some of it was stored up in the north of Germany in warehouses. Although, I doubt that you will find much traces of them now. These art pieces were cherished resources by fleeing SS officers, who were traded art to secure their physical survival from Nuremberg judgments.

"Oh, yes, that reminds me. I suspect you know, of course, about Rose Valland, the French resistance girl. She had a list of looted art, but I suspect there are others out there. People like Eric Hoffer may be holding on to something like that. That is what keeps him alive! That traitor."

"Do you have any idea where he is?"

"No, oh no. I don't give out that kind of information. It would be unethical, plus it would be just too dangerous." Fischer laughed.

We stood to leave when Pieter said, "You've certainly been obliging in helping us understand the Nazi mindset during the war and the impact of art on the German culture. I thank you for your honest dissertation—not that we agree with you. But your forthrightness was refreshing."

"Do not judge us too harshly, young man. You will see that only the victors in war define what was just and what was unjust. The next war, a new set of morals will apply. I can assure you, there will be other Hitlers and other wars."

We left as we came but were now traumatized at the bluntness and rationale imbedded in this man's mind. I would later write in my journal how disturbing it all was. Not just because of what he'd said. I'd heard some of it before but always thought such ideas could only be entertained by the insane.

This man was not insane, and his sort of logic scared me less when I assumed people who shared his beliefs were quite crazy and incoherent. Regrettably, one who has a grasp of his faculties and can express them in such a tenacious and clear presentation has a way of redeeming themselves to the masses. That may come, as he said, in other times.

CHAPTER 15

# Interrogation at Campbell Barracks

O n the way back from Lucerne, Pieter and I said very little. The time wasn't right. We both needed a chance to digest the words of this man with whom we'd sat face to face.

We'd been in the very same room with one of the world's most retched and evil of men. Though that wasn't it entirely. It was the shock that, after years of reflection, this man still believed in his depraved cause. His articulation and exuberance were chilling. And to know this happened in Germany, our homeland, and not in some other far away part of the world was overwhelming. I was familiar with those who'd lived through it with constant guilt, now appealing for redemption and forgiveness, but to consider there must be others out there like him, boasting publicly of their part in the so-called cleansing was, to say the least, disturbing.

When we returned to my apartment late that night completely exhausted, I suggested Pieter sleep on the couch.

"Helen will be out of the house by 7, and you can move into her bed when she leaves."

"Sounds good to me. Thanks."

Pieter was half asleep before I brought him an extra blanket and pillow.

After a good rest, I awoke early, rolled out of bed and walked into the kitchen to get some coffee. Helen always fixed a pot before she left. After reaching into the refrigerator for cream, I turned and was stunned by Pieter, just waking up and his eyes intent on me.

Realizing my sheer nightgown concealed very little, I stood still. My first thought was to race back into my bedroom and hide. But no, I stopped myself. I felt daring, wanting to know what his response would be. So I kept wandering about the kitchen letting his eyes glide over each curve, letting him see the woman I was.

As he sat there watching, my eyes caught him taking in the view. A blush popped up on his face. I hoped it was just too good for him not to say anything that would bring it to an end. I moved about the kitchen pouring coffee as his eyes moved along with me. With the quickening of my breath, a sensation I'd never felt before began to rouse in me. I walked over to the couch, holding out the coffee for him, thriving on the knowledge that, with each step, he could see me more clearly.

My breasts perked and tingled as they danced for him. I looked at him, but his eyes couldn't hold to mine. They passed from there down, across my stomach and rested in the dark shadow between my thighs. I could feel it all, his eyes touching me all the way. I sensed him wanting to put his hands on every inch. Then, boldly I handed him the cup, and, as I walked away, gave him a parting view.

I turned back to smile then asked, "Do you like what you see?"

Pieter, overcome by my brash behavior, was speechless — a first for him, not even a witty reply. Nonchalantly, I walked into the bathroom, shut the door, showered, dried and slipped into my bra, swinging the strap around to hook it, then moving it back, fondling each breast, enjoying their warmth. Then I pulled at the straps to secure them into their cups. I smiled into the mirror and began to put on panties, pulling them up slowly, covering me, and then slid my dress over my head. Fully dressed, I stood in front of the mirror. Now talking to my reflection, I said, "I needed that."

I needed to let someone know that I had desires and needs like everyone else, that I was not just an obsessed girl looking for a painting, not just that girl from the abbey. No, I was more, and I wondered what would come of that.

When I came out of the bathroom, Pieter was sitting at the table sipping his coffee. "Shower?" I asked.

He stumbled and blushed again. "No, no. But thanks for the show."

"Thanks for enjoying," I said with a smile.

"My pleasure," he added politely.

Realizing we were stumbling over what to say from there, we both began to laugh. He was now beginning to see me for who I was and realize that I was growing up in the world and beginning to shape it my way.

Pieter changed the subject. "Helen left you a note on the table."

I walked over, read it, then turned to Pieter. "They want me to meet with them."

"Who's 'them?'"

"I don't know. Thomas said they were part of the intelligence community, whatever that means. I read the note out loud.

"They would like an informal sit down with me at Campbell Barracks, sometime soon, meaning real soon—today, if possible. Need to compare notes."

"What, you alone?"

"I guess they don't want a journalistic eye in that room—afraid you would be compelled to publish whatever goes on."

"Do it! At least it will give us an idea of who they really are—all of the interested parties we're dealing with. Let them show their hand. And, remember who took you to the party."

"Pieter, I don't trust anybody when it comes to this. Well, you and probably Reverend Mother. I mean, you've both seen me in my birthday suit."

We both laughed again then he said, "We'll talk about that later. First, you have to be careful that Thomas isn't walking you into an ambush. There is more to this than just some painting and a few lost SS officers. I think it's about time we know more about what we are getting into."

"I'll do it," I said, and then called Thomas while Pieter listened in. The cordiality and the meeting were set. Thomas was to pick me up on the steps of the Jesuit Church at 1 p.m.

Pieter gathered up his things and said as he left, "Call me immediately when you get back and make sure you turn the tables on them. Force them to tell you what they know while closely guarding what we've discovered. Remember, good journalism."

"Yes, got it."

At precisely 1, Thomas picked me up in front of the Jesuit Church. My briefcase was packed with notes that Pieter and I'd gone over. We discretely left out most of the relevant material until, as Pieter had said, "We see who they are and whether they are friends or adversaries."

Dressed in full military attire, Thomas greeted me with a hug, and we were on our way. He spent the 30-minute ride to the barracks trying to put me at ease, attempting to get me to relax.

"It is sort of like a debriefing about what has happened these past few days. Their concern is that we keep all our facts in line."

"And, who are they Thomas?"

"They are representatives of organizations currently cooperating with U.S. military intelligence. They have a variety of interests in the case."

"Oh, it is a case now?" I asked with a hint of panic in my voice.

"Calm down, Lina. You're making too much of this."

For the rest of the ride, I detected that Thomas was being more discreet, less forthcoming than usual. He wasn't giving me any additional information than was necessary as to the type of questions that would be asked or how to answer them.

Used by the German Wehrmacht during the war, Campbell Barracks was now under U.S. command and guarded by a Marine who snapped a salute to Thomas. He returned the salutation, and we drove on through the gate. That brought me back to reality. Thomas was in the capacity of and working for the protection of the U.S. government. That fact alone gave me little assurance of what I was about to go through.

We pulled into a crowded parking lot in front of a refurbished building.

"Things have changed here since I worked as a secretary for Post Commander General Mayers."

"Really! General Mayers? You've never told me that, Lina."

"No reason to."

"He's a legend here. You know he's retired now?"

"Yes, I know."

After sliding out of the car, we walked side by side up the steps and past another security detail, this time with two military MPs positioned on both sides of the door. More salutes as they allowed us access into a long hallway. Along the walls was an assortment of military officer portraits. Thomas pointed. "See, here's General Mayers alongside General Patton."

"Good position for him. He is a decent, God-fearing man," I added.

At the end of the hallway, Thomas opened a large door and extended his arm to welcome me in. The formal setting of the chamber startled me. The room appeared to be arranged like a courtroom. A place for a panel of judges was up in front with facing tables placed just a few feet below. Something like where a defendant and his council would sit.

Thomas directed me to a prearranged seat. Seeing I'd started to become distraught, he asked if I would like something to drink.

"Yes, coffee, and make it black, please."

While Thomas left the room to fetch me a cup, thoughts raced through my mind. A debriefing…what did that mean? An informal conversation or was it something I had to give my oath to? If I varied on my answers, what then? I became apprehensive and alert.

Thomas returned with the coffee. I immediately regurgitated my worrisome thoughts.

"Thomas, I don't like this at all. What are we waiting for?"

"Umm, I think they're just going over the questions they want to ask."

"Is this a debriefing or interrogation?"

"Well, you know, in the military it's always a little of both. It will be all right, Lina. I promise."

As if on cue, the panel filed in one by one, finding their designated seats, some dressed in military uniforms and others in suits and ties. They all stood until a decorated military officer came in. Then, in unison, they followed his lead and took a seat. He opened his folder, took a few moments and said, "Good morning, Lina Ritter. Is that correct?"

"Yes, that is correct."

"We appreciate you coming here this morning. The records show you've lived in Heidelberg most of your life. Is that true?"

"Yes, it is true."

"It says here that you were orphaned from a very early age and brought up in the abbey until you went on to Heidelberg University. Is that correct?"

I nodded in agreement.

"Please speak up, Frau Ritter. Your English is exceptional," he flattered and went on. "You have found an interest in the search for a certain lost painting, this St. Rufina."

"Yes, that is correct."

"You might even say you are obsessed with finding it."

"Well, that may be a little dramatic, but yes."

"Frau Ritter, can you tell us how all this came about? This interest in this particular painting?"

"I will try to explain. You see, on a visit to Paris I ran across it there, in the Louvre."

"But hundreds of pictures are there. Why this one? What made it stand out, Frau Ritter?"

"I don't know, sir, but it did. The next day I went back to the university library, and my research confirmed that it was St. Rufina by the Spanish artist Murillo. I also discovered that that particular piece was part of the looted art from the German occupation."

"You mean the Nazi occupation, don't you?"

"No sir, the German occupation."

"You are aware, Lina, that the Heidelberg region was a great supporter of the NSDAP."

"The Nazi party? I have heard that, yes."

"Have you ever run into people whom you thought might be one of them?"

"One of them, what do you mean by that?"

"Frau Ritter, you don't know what I mean?"

"No sir, I do not. I was born toward the end of the war. Every German I know wants to forget it, for whatever reason. I don't ask them. It was not my generation! And what does this have to do with the painting?"

A black suited man from the right side of the panel spoke up. "It has to do with everything. Nazis traded looted paintings for safe passage out of the country."

Annoyed and angry at this unidentified man's tone, I shot back, to Thomas' surprise, "No. Oh, no you don't. Before I answer and cooperate with any more of your questions, I would appreciate you giving me proper respect by telling me who you are and what interest you have in the painting." I pointed now at the man on the far right. "You, yes, you. Who are you and whom do you represent?"

"My dear Frau, there is no need for you to stress. I am, well, let us just say I am here to represent Israel's interests."

I snapped back, "Mossad, that is what you are saying, isn't it?"

"Yes, somewhat."

"And you in the blue, who are you? I suspect CIA, an American? Yes, you are. The flag on your collar gave you away." I smiled as I pointed again. "And you? I suspect you are more of a businessman. Yes? Insurance.... yes insurance, and, of course, I see the U.S. military. And where are the British agents? I am certain you are here as well."

Not waiting for a reply I continued, "I know each one of you have your own interest in the looted and degenerate paintings. For the Mossad, find the paintings and find the rats. Am I right? For you, it is all about the ratlines. And you, the CIA, it doesn't matter whom you back. As long as they're anti-communist, you will help them all by trading secrets. Governments rise and fall depending on America's vital interest. Right? And, you, the insurance investor, protecting your bet, find the painting and recover the loss. And, as for the military, you are also here to protect your interest, to make sure that, when war comes, the appropriate military assets will be in place.

"Here in Germany, my generation believes the war is over. For most of you here, it is not. You need a purpose, a reason to continue the fight. The Russians, yes, maybe they will be the next battle. But gentleman, I am just a schoolgirl from Heidelberg who, for whatever reason, saw a painting. Then a curator disappeared and was found hanging in a warehouse, my apartment was ransacked, my bed torn to shreds, my bike vandalized and, to top it all off, my baker continues to refuse to sell me breakfast. My colleague, Pieter Neumann— let me spell that for you, N-e-u-m-a-n-n, yes write that down—was recently fired by the Heidelberg University newspaper. Fortunately, he now works for the Daily News. Sir, you are privy to a variety of shared resources, even the Interpol. I just have my university library. So, gentlemen, you find the answers.

"I came here hoping you knew something more. Yet all you have are accusations hidden amongst your line of questioning. Nazi sympathizer? Really? Is that a joke? It makes no sense. Why do we keep on putting out publications that are transparent in every way? Just read our articles! Every time we publish we receive threats. You tell me, Mr. Mossad Representative, is this some ODESSA plot against us? Is it real? Are they the ones who are preventing a successful search for the painting? What secrets do you hide from us? You say it is not about me. So, why are you asking these personal questions? You approached me, gentleman, because of our publicity. The world press found a new interest in this story, and we're going to keep on telling it—the truth, no matter whom it hurts, even if one of you become a target of our investigation."

The colonel abruptly interrupted. "Okay, Frau Ritter, I think we've all gotten your point, and we owe you an apology. It was not our intention to show disrespect, and I understand your objections. Yes, I agree we all need to demonstrate far more regard for you in this manner," he said while looking directly at Thomas, seeming to infer they should have been better informed about this girl's character and passion. "But, let's get the facts clear here today. We believe all of our interests, as you have so kindly described, center around you. So, of course, our natural inclination was to start with you. As to the painting, we believe that someone is looking for something, and, like you, we don't know what it is or what they are trying to protect. However, things are happening that suggest this is all very important to some underground organization. But, until we can identify them, Frau Ritter, please adhere to the confidentiality of this debriefing, if you can call it that. It is not a legal proceeding. We are simply sharing information because, if we don't know what the left hand is doing, the right can't know it either. Thank you for your open and honest response, Frau Lina. May I call you that?"

I nodded yes.

As he closed his folder, the colonel continued. "Clearly, we all have a lot of work ahead of us. And, Frau Lina, please be careful out there. Let us help whenever we can. I want you to know, to use a military term, we have your back covered, and, as you requested, we will keep you up to date on our findings. By the way, tell your partner, Pieter Neumann, he's a damn good journalist. Lieutenant Warner, we will talk later."

"Yes, sir," Thomas replied.

When he stood to leave, he turned back and said, "Oh, I almost forgot, Frau Lina, General Mayers sends you his best."

With that last warm gesture, tears came to my eyes.

On the way back, a stunned and embarrassed Thomas said very little. As he opened the door to let me out he said, "Lina, you were good today, really good. I'm sorry for putting you up against that. I hope I can find my way back with you."

"I don't blame you, Thomas. This whole thing has just become too big for the both of us. I am afraid this is about to explode into something neither one of us could have foreseen. I take comfort in the promise that God holds us in his hands. Reverend Mother always says, 'Pray for wisdom and always remember only He knows how this is going to end.'"

Thomas drove away. I was left standing alone on the church steps. A cold rain suddenly began to fall, and I let it drip down me. Soaked and exhausted, I wondered if this was an omen that I was in over my head, drowning. No, not if God had anything to do with it.

I prayed he did.

PART III

# The Journey

*Munich, Germany*

CHAPTER 16
# Retreat to The Abbey

My alarm went off at 7:30 a.m., but I was already up and ready to jump into the shower. Disappointed that Helen had left no coffee brewing, I dressed quickly and rode my bike to the bakery for coffee and breakfast rolls, then rushed over to the library. I needed to look up information about this noteworthy character, Kajetan Mühlmann. He would be our next interview, if I could find him.

We hadn't gotten very far in terms of uncovering the mystery surrounding the Rufina. Though, maybe we had gotten a little further than I thought. At least the publication had garnished a lot of interest and some unusual coincidences. So, even though we hadn't found her, it did feel like we were closing in, especially since others thought we were.

I placed my bike in the rack and began walking up the library steps. There they were, Thomas and Pieter, sitting together on the top step, deep in conversation while sipping coffee. I was a little surprised that they were so chummy. As I got closer, they both raised up their hands to offer me a cup.

Thomas said with a smile, "Neither of us thought the other was going to be here. So, we both bought you coffee."

Seeing one already in my hand, they began to laugh.

"What are we going to do with these?" Pieter asked.

"Drink them and be very alert all day. So what's with this? Neither of you have any business to do in your offices?"

"Yes, but Pieter and I thought it would be nice to come over and see how you're doing, since you've become the center of conversation around here."

"I didn't want this, and I'm uncomfortable with the thought of being the center of anything."

"Sorry, I still don't know why they are so focused on you," Pieter said.

"I've been asking myself the same question a lot lately."

"You've taught her well, Pieter," Thomas interjected. "The colonel was quite impressed. You should have seen her at Campbell Barracks yesterday. They're still talking about Lina's outburst. Instead of being the butt of the questions, she turned the thing into her own investigation."

"Because it was personal," I added.

Thomas patted me on the shoulder and said, "All right, go ahead and check out your score sheets. I've got a meeting with the colonel this morning. I'm certain he's going to ask me to sum up what I know, so can you help me out?"

"Unfortunately, you'll have to rely on your California charm for that. But, we promise to let you know when or if something new breaks."

"Hmm, why do I get the feeling you're both keeping something from me?"

Pieter and I looked down and, after a few embarrassing moments, Thomas said, "Okay then, see you later, Lina? Oops, almost forgot, official business. The colonel informed me that from now on, both of you would have a tail. The colonel says if anything happens to you, Lina, that a certain retired general will have his rank."

"What about me?" Pieter asked.

"Well, not so much affection there. Sorry about that." Thomas smiled.

"To answer your question about seeing you later, Thomas, I've got so much research to do, trying to keep ahead of you guys. After that, it's off to the abbey for me, for just for a few hours—a short respite."

"Oh, you don't need a respite."

"Yes, I do. How about I call you. Will that work?"

"Yes, that works for me."

Goodbyes were said all around, then Thomas jogged down the stairs toward his car.

Pieter and I sat back down on the steps. I caught him up on yesterday's meeting, pointing out that most everyone was there—, the CIA, British intelligence, Mossad, insurance investigators and the U.S. military—but that each had a different agenda.

"However, one group that scares me the most was not represented, the ODESSA."

"Who?"

"Remember the letters from our Rufina fans? One mentioned the ODESSA."

"Sounds familiar. Who are they?"

"Haven't you read about them?"

"What's that supposed to mean?"

"Oh, nothing. I just thought you knew everything about this kind of stuff." Pieter was not amused, so I went on. "Well, it's supposed to be this elusive Nazi underground organization."

"I remember. Something to do with Simon Wiesenthal?"

"Yes, the Nazi hunter. He says there is this clandestine organization that helps Nazis flee Germany—people like Martin Bormann, Adolf Eichmann and the Angel of Death, Dr. Josef Mengele, along with thousands of others who worked and commanded the death camps. And, those who are associated with them are not very happy with us, to say the least."

"What? What the hell have we done to make them mad?"

"I guess they're upset we've got our fishing lines crossed. Maybe while searching for the Rufina, we've gotten tangled up with some unpleasant people and secrets they do not want exposed."

"Yes, that makes sense. That's probably why groups like the Mossad are so excited. They must think the rats are starting to come out of their holes. Lina, we'd better be careful, take nothing for granted. The closer we get to Rufina, the closer we'll be to some pretty powerful organizations. So, what did you tell them yesterday?"

"Really nothing, just as you coached me. I turned it back on them and tried to find out what they knew. I think it stalled things for a while, but I'm not sure for how long."

"What about Thomas?"

"For the most part, they kept him out of the conversation. I think he's one of the good guys and seemed just as surprised as I was with all the dignitaries and formality of yesterday's meeting. Yet clearly they know something more than they've let on. I could feel it in their questions. But what, I don't know, though I'm sure they suspect something. Intimidation seemed to be their strategy, but the threat of publicity through your articles will help keep them back for a while. Although, there will be a time when we will have to deal with them."

"I know that. But, for now, I've got to get back to the office. Stay in touch, Lina. Don't go anywhere without calling me first!"

"What if I'd like to have a little romantic evening? Does that require a check in?"

"Yes, especially that. Remember, I've seen the honey you have to offer. Not too may bees can stay away from that."

"Funny way to put it. Do you use that clever line on all the girls?" I asked coyly.

"You're not going to hold that over my head, are you?"

"Yes, and don't expect to see more."

"I don't need to. I've got it all recorded to memory, right up here." He laughed while pointing to his head, somehow making me feel important. He became serious while leaving. "I mean it. Call me. Keep in touch."

"Okay, I'll be at the abbey all afternoon."

"All right, but, just to be on the safe side, remember to call before you leave."


When I entered the library, Erin greeted me with, "Good morning, celebrity."

"What do you mean 'celebrity?'"

"I saw you sitting on the steps with those two handsome, well-dressed men."

"What are you referring to Erin?" I blushed.

"Which one is it going to be, Lina?"

"Both. They're both interesting, and that's for your ears only, Erin." I leaned in with a whisper. "The jury is still out, and I am in no hurry to decide."

"Well, look at you. And I always thought it was Helen who played men."

"Nonsense, Erin. Helen and I are apples and oranges."

"But you both came from the same tree."

"Right, the abbey. Well, I've got to get to work. I need to get some film on the concentration camps. Do we have any around in the library?"

"Yes, I think a few. Are you sure you want to see that stuff?"

"I've got to. There's a reason."

"Okay, no need telling me. I will look around, then maybe

late at night, just before closing, you could view them. I don't know if we have a projector available, but I'll try to find one."

"Be careful, Erin. Don't let anybody in on this."

"All right, I'll try. You won't put my name in the paper will you?"

"Of course not, silly." I laughed. But after seeing she was serious, I assured her, "No Erin, I promise. I'll be back in the stacks... any strangers come looking for me, give me a heads up."

"You're kidding, right Lina?"

"No, I'm not."

About an hour into my research, Erin passed by and slid a note under one of the books on my desk.

*There's this overdressed man sitting in the back of the library. I think he's been watching where you pick out books. Looks like he could be following you.*

After a few minutes, I pretended to go to the bathroom, snuck around Erin's desk, grabbed the phone and called Pieter, who was over within minutes. He walked straight up to the man and announced, "I am from the Daily, may I help you?" His cover blown, the man stood and left in a hurry. A little later, Pieter walked me out to my bike, and we both looked around nervously for a few minutes.

"I think we scared him off. But let me ride with you across the bridge."

"Yes, I would like that."

Once across, we waved goodbye, and I started off on my own up the road toward the abbey.

Every time I ride that long narrow road, it's as if my personal angel is waiting for me, jumping on my shoulder and singing me a lullaby, all the way to the abbey.

I laid my bike on the front steps of the church office and,

before walking up the stairs, heard, "Lina!"

"Sister Grace, glad to see you. How is everything?"

"We have a new priest running the show."

"Really? What's he like?"

"A tough old guy. He was once head of the diocese…sent here to pasture out. But Reverend Mother is good for him. She's got him in the palm of her hand."

"I'm not surprised." I smiled.

"She's over in the garden pruning her roses. Won't let anyone with shears around them."

"I'll just wander over and surprise her."

"She is always so happy when you come to see her, more so than with the other girls. She loves you so much."

"I know, Sister, me too." I walked past the church and into the center of the garden, where on her knees was Reverend Mother, clipping away at a beautiful pink rosebush. With her back to me, she called out, "Lina!"

"Yes, how did you know, Reverend Mother?"

"I can tell your special walk."

"Could have been Helen."

"No, Helen kind of skips her way here. Much unlike her, you step carefully and directly toward where you are going."

"Is that a good thing, Reverend Mother?"

"Oh, I don't know that it is. From what I've heard lately, you could do a little more skipping." She stood, turned around and brushed off her apron. "Now you can give your Reverend Mother a hug."

She released me after a fond moment and said, "Let's go up into the office and talk, after prayer. Lina, you have prayed today, haven't you?"

"I pray every day, yet I must confess, Reverend Mother, some days more than others."

"I too, for you." She smiled.

"Well, it is good to spend a little more time with you. I pray God will give me dispensation for that."

As we climbed the stairs, Reverend Mother said, "The archdiocese needs to have an elevator for us. However, when that day comes, I suspect I'll be sent out to pasture, pruning roses all day."

We laughed together then entered her chambers. She did her usual straightening and futzing around while I plunged myself into the familiar chair at her desk. The sun radiated throughout the room as she opened windows for fresh air.

"You must have had a lovely ride here today."

"Yes, it was pretty."

We bowed our heads together for a few moments of silent prayer, and, after making the sign of the cross, she asked, "So, Lina, what is going on? Any news on this Rufina painting?"

"Well, yes and no, Reverend Mother. After several publications and one missing curator who came to…"

"Yes, Father Tobias told me about him."

"Plus our apartment was rummaged, and we met this old gentleman, if you can call him that, in Lucerne who talked more about the Nazi creed than we really ever wanted to know. Somebody thinks we're close to finding the Rufina because, just yesterday I spent time being investigated by intelligence people at Campbell Barracks."

"Yes, Lina, I've heard about that as well."

"Of course you did," I said with a smirk.

"My sources also let me know that you'd make a very good solicitor. I'm not sure why they were so surprised. Evidently they don't know you like we do. Now, how are those dreams? Are they keeping you from sleeping?"

"Sometimes they do, and the man in them…"

"Are you able to recognize him yet?"

"No, but I recognize his voice."

"His voice? What do you mean?"

"I just know I've heard it before, that's all. But when and where, I can't remember. My mind hasn't let it in." I laid my head back and closed my eyes for a moment. "Oh, Reverend Mother, it is so nice to be here. I want to stay for a while, get away from all this. But, I feel it will take only a few more interviews to make it all come together."

"What's next?"

"Kajetan Mühlmann, or, if I can't get in to see him, we'll try and locate his secretary, Astrid Klammer. Both are high society people, formally well placed in the Reich. After that, there is this Posse fellow and then Adolf Ziegler. The art dealer Theodore Fischer, the man from Lucerne I told you about, gave us leads on all these people. He believes the Rufina passed their way. It is the type of painting Hitler wanted hanging in his museum, so I hope talking to any one of them will get us one step closer.

"But, the problem is, we have to find them first. We're also getting letters in response to our publications. They haven't been very helpful, except maybe one, but it's not very clear. On top of that, for the last few days, everybody's been asking me, 'who are you?' Besides telling them I'm the girl from the abbey, I don't really have many answers. Reverend Mother, can you help me? For some reason, I'm beginning to feel this is more about me than the painting. In my dreams, Rufina tells me that I should know. I keep hearing her say it. I saw it in her eyes the first time I looked at the picture in the Louvre. Sounds pretty strange, doesn't it?"

"Oh, my child, you'll get through this. Give it time. It will all pass away."

"But really, Reverend Mother, who am I?"

"Lina, I can tell you very little about your parents, if that's what you mean. You were very young when you came to us, and the diocese never questioned why God brought someone to our doorstep, especially back then. We just trusted Him. As you know, there are rumors, Lina—remember, only rumors—that your parents became disillusioned with Hitler and the Nazis at the University of Munich, and, because of that, they were either executed or sent to death camps—like most dissenters.

"The Vatican took you in and probably changed your name for your protection. Ritter, most likely, is not your given name. But that doesn't matter now… you are Lina Ritter, our beautiful gift from God. So there you are. No better for the asking, huh?" She gave a warm smile.

I persisted. "But were they married when they died?"

"Well, of course they were. You were conceived in love, all of us see that in you. Lina, the past, well that is what it is, and, here in Germany, the past is what most Germans want to forget. It never happened, they say. Yes, that is wrong. It did. And, that is why no one cares to look back…too much shared guilt. Look forward, concentrate on the future—that is their course. So, tell me about these letters you've been getting."

"One is short and to the point. The writer tells me, 'be careful… you're on the right track. Stay focused on the painting. They know too much, and do not trust anyone except me.' "

"Does this person sign the letters?"

"Yes, it is signed, 'Sonnenschein.'"

Reverend Mother put her hands to the sides of her face, slowly bringing them down to her chin and ending with her fingers touching her lower lip. In a soft voice she asked, "Where are they posted from?"

"Berlin, Reverend Mother."

"Berlin? You said Berlin?" she echoed as she slowly stood,

pushed back her chair and walked over to the window. Looking out, as if in a trance and talking to the beautifully snowcapped mountains in the distance, she said, "Oh Berlin, you should have seen it before the war. Berlin was as beautiful as Paris, Florence or Vienna. It was one of the most charming cities in Europe, an international city where people from all over the world came to see her museums and art galleries. There were legendary concerts, lively cafés mounted at every street corner. People rode about the city, visiting soaring cathedrals and the zoo. And, on Sundays, we went out early, took the S-Bahn to St. Hedwig's Cathedral, then wandered around a flea market or lounged about on the sunny beaches of the Spree River that flowed through town, then perhaps barbecued in Tiergarten Park. Rivers and lakes for sailing and hiking were everywhere. Oh, Lina, what days they were. But that was then. Berlin, was destroyed when the war was brought home to Germany." She turned from the window and rearranged herself in the chair. "So, do you trust these young fellows, this lieutenant and Pieter, the writer?"

"Pieter, with all my heart."

"I didn't mean that, Lina."

"Nor did I, Reverend Mother. Let me try that again. Thomas is a good person, but he has a job to do. His interest is the U.S. interests. Yet, I'm certain he would never jeopardize my trust in him."

"And, Pieter?"

"He is a journalist. He's looking for the truth and, because we are on a similar journey, I'm slowly being pulled toward him. He won't violate my trust. I am sure of that. In fact, just to be on the safe side, the things I tell you, only you and Pieter know. We keep secrets that Thomas doesn't need to be in on-secrets that could possibly compromise our relationship. But, Reverend Mother, I confess I am frightened about where all this is going to take me."

"Remember what I have always taught you about God and His divine providence, Lina. Somehow it all works out in His way and His timing. He is in control. There is a rough old saying around here that sometimes we need to thank Him for unanswered prayers. And, it has always been a comfort to know God will not let you carry any burden beyond what strength He will give. Let us pray together in silence, and ask God for guidance and wisdom."

We both made the sign of the cross, and I got up to leave. As we hugged goodbye, she said, "Lina, I am concerned about the dangers that may lie ahead. Don't you think you might need to spend more time here at the abbey? We can look after you. Your old room is available. Love to have you around, even if only for the weekends."

"I just might do that from time to time. But, right now, I must go out there and find myself. Something happened that day in the Louvre, Reverend Mother. I've never had a reason to look back, but lately I can't go forward without doing so."

"Then God be with you, child."

I closed the door behind me and was gone.

CHAPTER 17
# The Eagle's Nest

**M**unich, noted for its art, architecture and classical Bavarian fashion, brought the music of Wagner and Mozart to the world and became the birthplace and hotbed of the National Socialist German Workers' Party.

Pieter and I began our 206-mile drive from Heidelberg to Munich, hoping to find another piece of the Rufina puzzle. Or, as Pieter said, "Each clue is a rung on a ladder, taking us higher. First the curator then the art dealer and now this clue to Hitler's Eagle's Nest. We're getting closer to the top."

As we traveled along, I tried to get some sleep. In between, Pieter would toss a few ideas over at me. We were working as a well-oiled machine now. I did much of the research. He would put all that data into the script, making it presentable and reader friendly. On this day, I was restless and sleeping along the way was just not happening. I looked at Pieter working something over in his mind. I smiled to myself, knowing why the ladies were so charmed by him.

He usually wore blue jeans with a colored dress shirt and tie to match, underscoring his devotion to his profession yet offering a casual flair, giving the impression his appeal was unrehearsed. His natural blond hair and blue eyes were the dream of girls, distracting them from what he was really after. With his antics he could take the oxygen out of the room. But, that wasn't what Pieter was after now. No, he was becoming the professional journalist, and that was just one of the tools in his cache. The charm would allow him in and eventually draw out the poignant information he looked for.

Dropping my trance, I said to him, "One of those dreams came to me last night. It was so real that I shrieked out loud, waking and scaring Helen half to death. She even had to slap me once."

"Oh, really? Rumor has it that a lot of people at the barracks meeting would love to get in on that." He gave a warm smile and took hold of my hand. "Lina, it was just a dream."

"Well, it certainly didn't feel like it. Helen and I got up for coffee, talked a bit then eventually went back to sleep."

"Helen knows you well."

"Ah, yes, from the beginning, at the abbey. She is a sister in my heart and will always be that to me."

"So, what have you learned from this dream, anything?"

"The man…his face is getting closer."

"What do you mean, 'closer?'"

"Lately, he seems to smile at me, or something like that, and paintings are in the background. It will come to me."

"Okay, let's get back to this Astrid," Pieter said as he looked to me for answers.

"She was secretary to Kajetan Mühlmann."

"Now, who was he?"

"The Nuremberg documents confirm…"

"Since most of that material is classified, how did you get that information?"

"I have a friend in military intelligence, remember?"

"Oh, really? I guess that's why I keep you around."

"So that's the way it is." I laughed.

"What did you think?" He smiled broadly.

"Okay, so I used a source, a friendly source, to procure this information."

"Was it Thomas?"

"No, not this time. Thomas is a good resource, but that's not his style. He's all upfront and, besides, I kind of like him. I'd never put him in that kind of a situation. No, not him. It is Helen this time. Helen's contacts are usually the kind who look good in a uniform, and she also knows an old associate from the barracks that has all kinds of connections. The lady who contacted your paper to set up this interview is Astrid Klammer. She was the personal secretary of Kajetan Mühlmann."

"What was so important about Mühlmann?"

"Remember, Fischer brought up his name. Alfred Rosenberg, who had the ear of the Der Führer, appointed Mühlmann to the ERR. His main job was to identify where the main art pieces were located prior to a Wehrmacht blitzkrieg. They would then purposely avoid bombing those locations so the ERR could swoop in and plunder the art, either by making deals or, when that failed, sending in the Gestapo. They'd usually seal the deal by relocating the unwilling parties to the camps, never to be seen again. Let me give you an assessment. Quoting from the Nuremberg records, *'Mühlmann was one of the most successful Nazi art thieves. During the 1945 trials, he had been called arguably one of the single most prodigious art plunderers in the history of human civilization. He determined which works were degenerate, those considered modern, impressionist or painted by Jews. His classification was for the purpose of either storing the art—at warehouses in Neuschwanstein for Hitler's museum— after it left the Jeu de Paume in France or sending it to Fischer's degenerate art auctions in Switzerland.'* End quote."

"Good Job, Lina. As always, I am impressed. So where is Mühlmann?"

"Well, like most good SS officers, he had a quick and timely death after the war, coincidentally from unknown causes—a dubious undertaking at best—with his funeral and grave still unknown. But, a death certificate was issued and dutifully recorded."

Pieter chuckled. "Let me take a wild guess, he is not dead and, as usual, the trail ends at the ratline. What do you know about this ratline?"

"Hold that thought, because Thomas promised me a course on European Ratlines 101. More details on that subject will have to wait until we return to Heidelberg."

"So why Astrid? What's she going to tell us?"

"The story is, she's dying and wants her part in all this somehow rectified."

"Meaning what?"

"I'm not sure, maybe simply to purge the rumors that she had something to do with the art thefts. She says she has names and places, and she can help with the current locations of the art we're looking for."

"All this in exchange for publishing a nice story about her?"

"Yes, that's basically it. That's what she's asking."

"Okay, what do you think, Lina? Are we on to something here?"

"I don't know. But, up until now, it's felt like we've been racing around in circles. With this, I believe we've fallen into something big. What about you. What do you think?"

"I think, right now we're in a learning curve. Each interview is getting us closer to the real story. But, so far, like us, they don't know what that story is either. We just need to press on, publish and keep it coming until the responses to my articles stop, then it will all end."

Silence took over the car as we ran out of things to say.

While we sped on, for the first time it crossed my mind that, with Pieter, I was willing to walk into danger and risk my life, and we both saw it as the right thing to do. I thought that going into the dark with someone aware of what is out there is one thing. But going into the dark with someone not having any idea of what fate awaits was quite another. Intuitively, we both held our cards close, simply because we feared this thing had more to do with us than any looted treasure. Afraid what we found along the way might expose something we never wanted to resurface. Maybe we had fear like the others, but we never let on. Unlike them, we held on to our honor, not giving in to hypocrisy, for that war was not our war… or was it? For now, we leaned on each other, not letting on to our discretions.

We arrived on the outskirts of Munich and then found the rest home that fit neatly into the Bavarian setting. After parking the car, we took our attachés, walked up the steps and were welcomed by one of the uniformed attendants. He led us into a lobby, where we signed in. The lady behind the desk let us know Frau Klammer was expecting us, and that the attendant would show us out to the courtyard. It was there that we got our first glance at Frau Astrid Klammer.

For some reason, I was surprised by her appearance. She looked quite sprite and well dressed, wearing a colorful summer blouse that flared around her body in such a way that gave away her flamboyant temperament. Reading glasses strung around her neck gave clues to her past secretarial position, and I could see why Herr Mühlmann kept her around.

"Sit here," she said warmly, and we found our way onto the circular lounge chairs. "Good to meet you. It's always helpful to match the face to the person you are corresponding with."

"Yes, it is. And, this is my favorite journalist, Pieter Neumann."

"Good to meet you, Herr Neumann."

"Yes, thank you for welcoming us on such short notice."

"Without wasting words and time, let us get to it," she said, and, by her stern tone, we could tell she was willing to take over the conservation.

"Now, Herr Neumann, you are aware of our arrangement for this interview?"

"Yes, of course, Frau Klammer."

"No, no. Just Astrid will do," she said with a comforting smile. "I've written down a few things to jolt my memory, so please allow me to mumble on for a minute." She pulled at her reading glasses and began to cite from the prepared script. "As you know, Al Rosenberg was the man in charge. Kaj would be on the phone each day with him."

"Kaj?"

"Yes, Kaj, that is how we referred to Kajetan. He was the boss, the man who talked directly with the Führer, Hitler himself. Kaj's job was to inventory all of the art pieces as either degenerate or classical. But, of course, you must know this by now."

"Yes, we are familiar with that, but please go on, Astrid. How did they obtain this artwork?" I asked since she seemed to be directing her conversation toward me.

"When Germany took over a country, they simply took it."

"And how was this done?"

Traversing about, not willing to be directed, she rambled on. "You must understand how Hitler ran his government. You see, he trusted no one. Therefore, he wisely set up each department with a competing department, to put a check on power. For example, you had the military, the generals who, throughout the war, would come and go. Then you had the Gestapo, the secret police, SS types under Himmler. Then there were the administrative types, like Herr Göring, kind of a crossover with the military, who was looked upon as successor to Hitler. Along with Martin Bormann, they all competed against each other. But, in the end, Hitler was the boss, and they knew it.

"As to the art, it worked the same way. Whoever got there first had the first pick. I'm sure you know Hitler had a taste for paintings. He saw himself as a master artist from his old days in Vienna. He had the final say. Kaj archived every painting—stolen, looted or whatever. He'd present them to Hitler in photo albums, and Hitler would shuffle through and pick out the ones he liked for his Führermuseum, the one proposed by Albert Speers and to be built in Linz, Austria, Hitler's hometown.

"The degenerate paintings, well, we all know what happened to them. They were placed for sale at the Louvre or sent to Switzerland to be auctioned off to unscrupulous investors from all over the world." She stopped to clear her throat. "I know I talk too much, but that is the history, as I know it. I could go on and on, but you have come to me looking for the Bartolomé Esteban Murillo Spanish Baroque paintings. Is that correct?"

"Yes," I said, leaving Pieter out of the conversation.

"Specifically the Rufina?"

"Yes."

"I believe his paintings would have been seen as classical and warehoused here in northern Germany. Yes, I faintly remember some of his pieces may have come across my desk. Although, you must know, it has been so many years ago. You see, Kaj wasn't the only one who had a list of the many paintings. As the war was presumed to be lost, these lists began to be dispersed."

"Lists?"

"Yes, lists, along with gold and diamonds; art was in great demand. You see the Swiss would exchange these types of assets. Turn them into cash to aid the SS types to escape the country, leaving few footprints."

Frustrated I asked, "Are you suggesting there is no way of tracking down these pieces of art?"

"No, Lina, I am not saying that. Just that you must look for the person who has one of the lists."

"Really? You believe there are still lists out there?"

"Yes, I do."

"Today?"

"Yes, today. And, they probably will lead you to the private buyer or investor. It's not going to be easy. You'll need to get information on their Swiss or Vatican accounts. With those account numbers, you could follow where the money is going. But, it is almost impossible. Mind you, to protect their investments, the records are anonymous. If you can penetrate these accounts, then chances will improve for you to find your painting, which I believe was taken from the Rothschild collection. Yes, it was. Now I'm starting to remember. Yes, Rothschild." Abruptly she changed the conversation and asked, "Frau Lina, may I impose on you with a personal question?"

I hesitated but answered, "Yes, you may."

"From Mr. Neumann's column, by the way Herr Pieter, you have made more than a few art dealers very nervous, I read you, Frau Lina, grew up in the Neuburg Abbey?"

"That's right."

"Do I look familiar to you?" she asked with eyes glaring, hoping to see my reaction. She continued to stare at me for a few moments, looking for something in my facial expression. I resisted answering her directly and took a short pause, as if to show her I was taking time to consider her question.

"No, Frau," I said, looking directly into her eyes. It was then that she came back with another query that felt like a punch straight to my gut. "Does the name Sonnenschein mean anything to you?"

My heart raced as I fought against myself not to give away the secret. I almost lost my composure but then disguised my reaction when I said, "No, it does not."

Yet inside, my thoughts were tumbling about. How did she know? She continued to prompt me on. I held back, not offering a clue that she'd hit a nerve. No, I would not give myself away. Calmly, at least on the outside, I answered, "No, but, why do you ask, Frau Klammer?"

"Oh, my dear, I've seen a lot of people in my time. And you somehow remind me of a situation, a person, from the past, and your passion for this particular painting, well, I've just put two and two together, but I came up with five." She shrugged off the line of questioning and went on. "Oh, but Lina…"

At that moment, she looked fatigued and, for the first time, began to show signs of possible dementia. She revealed her age as she hunched over in her chair and said desperately, "I must leave you with something, right? That is the bargain, but you must keep this just between us. You never heard it from me." She took a long deep breath then said, "Keep in mind, I came through the Reich period when no one trusted anyone. That was the Gestapo way. The list…" She whispered, "Dietrich Ziegler, his brother was Adolf Ziegler, Hitler's personal photographer, he had access. He was a fine photographer, turned dealer of art and did business with Maria Dietrich, Hitler's personal art agent, close friends with Eva Braun. He was a party badge Nazi in the beginning, however, toward the end, he became a protester. He was known to be around the Munich campus demonstrations before the crackdown. When that happened, he suddenly disappeared. Some say he was sent to Dachau. It was also reported he'd been executed by the Gestapo, along with the other protestors. His wife and children were sent off to a sub camp, which seemed almost comical since the end of the war was in sight. My how those SS men seemed to quickly disappear. They died, you know. At least that is what it says on their death certificates. Herr Dietrich Ziegler, yes I think he is the man you should find. He has a list. He must have a list!"

"Why him?"

"Why? Because, it makes sense, Frau Lina. That list can expose many people, the location of the paintings and who they were sold to." She looked around in the air, as if ghosts were about to swoop down, and fear welled up in her tired eyes. "The paintings are worth millions. They all have their own misdeeds to protect. Yes, find Dietrich. It is rumored he is out there, somewhere. I cannot say much more."

Turning to Pieter, she pleaded, "Herr Neumann, please do me justice in your column. We were just minor paper pushers. We had to go along. The gravity if we did not, the camps."

I wanted to get all we could from this sly secretary, so I asked, "So where do you think Herr Dietrich is, if he is still alive?"

"I really don't know. They all had their own escape routes, their own ratlines. But remember, Lina..." she said while pointing her finger at me, "you need to follow the money trail. Start with the Swiss, then the Vatican banks accounts. How the money is dispersed should tell you something. How you do that, I don't know. If he is still alive, I would bet he knows something about the Rufina."

"Haven't the Allied intelligence agencies tried this route?" I asked.

"Oh, I'm sure they have...so very hard to get information there. They hide dirty secrets from public view. All of them, they work together against one common enemy, not the Nazis. No, no, it is the communists that unite them now. You will see. Remember, Frau Lina, you must not trust them. You and Herr

Neumann, you have opened old wounds once again, and they will follow you until you give up on this Rufina quest or destroy you if you disclose one of their precious secrets. Many of the Nuremberg documents are still classified as confidential. Why this? I ask you, why does the U.S. government want them to remain classified? You draw your own conclusions. Look, I am just holding on here. My wars are about over. My life…it is terminal. Yet, here I am wanting to leave this world repentant. You must print me in a favorable light, so I can rest a little better for helping you get this thing straight. Thank you for coming here today. I feel better that what I have told you may help find the painting you're looking for."

As soon as we got into the car, Pieter leaned over, as if to kiss me. My eyes closed and my lips begged him on, but he slid off to offer a peck on my check. "Lina, you were amazing in there… amazing! When she threw out Sonnenschein and you didn't flinch, wow! I knew what was in your mind. What a complete surprise that she knew what only we know! And you never let on, just kept her on track."

"But how did she know?" I asked and started counting on my fingers. "Only you, me and Helen know, and Hans was there that day reading letters. No, not him. He wasn't there. It couldn't be. I've got to talk to Helen about this."

Pieter couldn't contain his excitement. "I think our dear little paper pusher, Frau Klammer knows more then she lets on, much more. There must be code names for individuals on the run, and I am sure she knows them all. We now have another name, Dietrich Ziegler. Lina, it's like you suspected. We have stumbled onto something big with a ton of issues. Now the question is, who is standing in our way?"

"And with your articles, you've let the whole world in on it, and I'm afraid that spells trouble. Somebody—make that a lot of somebodys—is going to be watching us very closely. Pieter, Dachau just jumped in my mind. It's only about 13-miles out of the way. Can we stop and spend about an hour there?"

"Of course. No problem, but why, Lina?"

"Something personal, Pieter. Please don't ask me now."

In a short time, we pulled into the parking lot and began walking through the main gate. Some of the posted information read, *Dachau was the Nazis' first concentration camp. A model camp where SS officers came to train, it was founded on the grounds of an old munitions factory and was intended to hold political prisoners. It opened in 1933 with Heinrich Himmler as chief of the Munich police. The purpose was enlarged to include forced labor, Jews, foreign nationals and common criminals. It originally held a population of more than 5,000 but over time it exceeded 12,000. More than 207,000 prisoners went through the camp and 31,951 deaths were recorded. Most were Jews and with the rest were Catholics, Russians, Polish prisoners of war, Jehovah's Witnesses and gypsies. The perimeter included housing and a crematorium. Toward the end of the war, the Germans attempted to conceal the existence of the camp by building over the crematorium, hoping to deceive the Allies. It was liberated on 29 April 1945 by the U.S. Army. Altogether there were 120 sub camps. The much larger extermination facilities were outside of Germany. Treblinka, Auschwitz and Balzac became infamous for the horrific bellicose propensity of the Nazis regime.*

As we walked through the camp, I had the feeling God must have turned his eyes away and allowed evil to wander around this place. All through this horror, I'd been in the loving arms of the abbey. Where was God when this all happened? Did he give in to the devil? For this was surely devil's work, and was it necessary to involve man in His worldly feud with Him?

"Let's leave. I've seen enough," I said.

There were too many questions without answers. I rushed us out of the gates of this hell and back into the grace of God. There was undisturbed silence as we drove home. When my thoughts took a second glance back, my heart pounded, not letting me think beyond what Astrid had said. What did she mean, had I ever seen her before? And what about her relationship with Sonnenschein? What's with this Dietrich Ziegler? The name had a ring to it. It seemed all too familiar.

Pieter broke into my silence. "Lina, we're being followed again."

"What do you mean 'again?'"

"Haven't you noticed?"

"Well, Thomas said we'd have a tail."

"Yeah, but I'd like to know if it's his guys back there. If we make it back we need to…."

Suddenly, the car trailing us put on his high beams and raced up alongside, then abruptly turned into our car, obviously attempting to run us off the road.

I screamed, "Watch out, Pieter!"

Our car skid and spun to a stop on the shoulder. The attackers punched the gas and quickly took off.

"Damn, that was close! Was that an irritated driver or a warning?"

Just then another car speed by, red lights glaring, chasing the car that almost crashed ours.

"Hope that's the good guys! Some protection!" Pieter yelled out the window.

I could hardly breathe, while Pieter continued to complain. "Geez, looks like somebody's tailing the tail. Wow, we really don't need that kind attention, now do we Lina?"

I didn't even try to answer. It was just too close, plus my knees were still knocking from the excitement and the possibilities.

Once in Heidelberg, I felt safe enough to ask Pieter to stop at the nearest telephone. One was right in front of the bakery, where I jumped out and immediately called Thomas. I told him what happened in great detail. And, when he asked if we could meet for lunch tomorrow, I said, "Thomas, why don't you look into it first, then ask me out for lunch!"

He thought that was pretty funny and laughed out loud. "Lina, now you're starting to think like a journalist. It must be Pieter's influence. I want to influence you too," he kidded.

"Do you, Thomas?"

"Of course."

"I don't need reminding. It is a disability in my situation."

"Oh, Lina, don't think of it that way."

"Okay, lunch it is…tomorrow, at the Marktplatz. See you at noon and be prepared to let me know what happened out there on the road," I yelled, feeling relieved, from what I still didn't know.

The agenda for the days ahead would be busy trying to fill in the blanks. I especially wanted to get together with Helen, and, once again, I needed the library. Hopefully Erin had turned up more stuff for me to go through. I needed her help tracking down this mystery man Dietrich. I'd decided he was the one who could lead us to the Rufina. I wasn't sure why I felt so strongly about that, but I was determined to find out.

A troubling question was infiltrating the corridors of my mind, like a song whose lyrics won't go away, taking center stage and sidetracking the search for the painting. I kept asking myself, "Why me?" again and again.

CHAPTER 18
# Heavenly

I couldn't sleep again that night. Too many things ran through my mind. So, at about 3 a.m., I finally decided to shuffle into the kitchen and warm up some leftover coffee. After snacking on a stale roll and dried-up cold cuts that went down badly, I tossed it all into the trash and poured the tasteless black liquid down the drain. I'd been away from the apartment so much lately that I couldn't tell what day of the week it was. Tired and consumed by recent events, I felt a need to escape, to let my hair down, to stop and smell the flowers. Maybe there was something to those worn out clichés. It was settled. That's what I would do—have a little fun.

First, I needed a leisurely shower. I hadn't been able to do that for several days, so I took off my summer nightgown, waited for the water to warm and then stepped in, letting the water run through my hair and find its path down my body. Oh yeah, I'd forgotten how therapeutic that sensation was. I picked up the fragrant soap and slid it over each crevice, eliciting a feeling of purification. What a comfort, being intimate, caring for and loving on myself, spoiling my body and mind. The hypnotic spell ran its course until the warm water turned cold.

My shadow reflected in the steamy mirror, I wiped it clear and smiled, remembering this was what Pieter saw that morning. I hoped I had left him wanting more. Not too bad for some lucky guy…someday.

My thoughts raced back to reality when I looked out the window to see pink fluffy clouds preparing for a beautiful sunrise. I quietly pulled on jogging pants and a sweatshirt, grabbed my purse and slipped out of the apartment and into the early morning chill. In the morning calm, every slight noise—the cat rummaging through the trash or the whistle of a bird singing to the breaking sun—seared my senses. Even the timid sounds of the breeze shifting through the trees resonated, and I embraced them. I became cautious with each step now. Lately, my life reflected a more precarious existence than ever before.

Through the chatter of sounds, I detected steps behind me coming from some unknown creature and seemingly choreographed to each action I took. When I slowed, they slowed. When I stopped, they stopped. Fear prevented me from looking back, so I quickened my cadence. It followed my lead. Should I run? No, that would give me away. I held back, allowing time to turn the corner. The smell of fresh baked bread gave relief. I was there. Now I could step from the shadowy street into the bright light of the bakery, which would harbor and free me from this pursuit. I fumbled, anxiously reaching for the door handle. When I finally pulled at it, a man passed by and said casually, "Good morning, Fräulein. What a fine day it will be."

"Yes, lovely," I responded instinctively.

I ordered some rolls from my graciously forgiving baker and carted off two cups of coffee. On my flight back to our apartment, I was relieved, and castigated myself for the fear and drama I'd created. Once inside, I displayed the wares from the bakery on the kitchen table. Looking out the window, I could see the sun cresting the mountain but not yet showing the full light of day. While walking into Helen's bedroom I announced, "Time to get up."

She moved sparingly around her bed, and a leg appeared to

have heard my plea, but, beyond that, nothing else took notice. So, in a more abrasive tone I said, "Helen, rise and shine!" That did it, and she rolled over, exposing a disgruntled sleepyhead. She fumbled to grab the clock. "It's only half past six. Lina, what is it?"

"I got some fresh rolls and hot coffee. We need to talk. I haven't seen you for a while. Now please go and take a quick shower while I warm and spread some cream cheese on the rolls."

"Okay, okay," she grumbled while pulling back the covers. Her favorite teddy bear nightshirt was tossed on the floor as she stumbled her way toward the bathroom. In a few minutes, bathrobe secured, she walked into the kitchen, still towel drying her hair.

"Umm it does smell good," she said. Looking out the window, she asked, "Is that the sun coming up?"

"Yes, of course. What else would it be? So, Helen what's new in your life?"

"What? You got me up early to ask me that?"

"No, last night on our way back from Munich, Pieter and I were run off the road."

"What? By who?"

"That's the question I hope Thomas will answer. But, truth is, things are starting to get a little crazy. So, I'm going to ask him to have someone watch you, just for a little while."

"What? Great, my social life will be shot."

I laughed. "Maybe that would be a good thing."

"You don't have to worry about that, do you, Lina?"

"Why do you say that?"

"Let me see, you've been going 24-7 with two of the most desirable and, might I add, accessible single men around Heidelberg."

"You mean Pieter and Thomas?"

"Yeah, of course I mean Pieter and Thomas. So what's with that, Lina? Huh? Three people don't make a couple."

"Now, Helen, that's not the way it is. And, besides, you know me. I'm not like you."

"And what's that supposed to mean?" Helen asked now, having fun watching me squirm to be diplomatic.

"Well, to start with, your clothes sometimes, you have to admit, are a little revealing."

"Are you saying my friends enjoy my taste in clothes?"

"I have no problem with that, Helen, but you have so many good friends who have little interest in anything except for your wardrobe selections." I smirked.

"I know what you're trying to do. You're trying to sidetrack me from talking about Thomas and Pieter."

"Okay, that's fair. Let's see, Pieter is all business, and, believe it or not, not even a kiss—well sort of a peck on the cheek, but not a real kiss."

"So it's Thomas then."

"Wrong again, Helen. He is a nice guy, but he has a life back in California. After his stint in the army, he'll go back to America, and that will be that. Enough, now let's get back to my point. I think you and I need to be very cautious. There are a lot of people out there who think we're onto something that could harm them or maybe even get them killed. I am sorry that I got you into this, but we're here and we need to be extra careful about everything. Just keep your antennas working—that's all I'm saying. And, Helen, this is important. Did you ever mention to anyone about the letters from Sonnenschein?"

"No, I didn't. Why?"

"Because, the ex-secretary we interviewed yesterday mentioned it. Her former boss was chummy with Rosenberg and

Hitler."

"Really, she brought it up?"

"Yes, so I think they know more than they're letting on. That's the scary part."

"What about Thomas? Does he know about Sonnenschein?"

"No Helen, at least not from us. So let's keep this secret to ourselves. Okay? But, what about Hans? Have you talked to him about the letter?"

"No, Lina. It can't be Hans. I haven't seen him for a while... couldn't be him."

"I think we have a person who can finally lead us to the Rufina, but it's going to take some real creative effort on our part. By the way, your connection with the army captain paid off. Sorry, but I need some more help from you, Helen."

"Of course. What?"

"Do you know anybody with connections to any of the Swiss national banks? I know it's a long shot, but..."

"As a matter of fact, I do! Eric. I met him on campus. He's also a great looking guy, although in a little trouble right now."

"Trouble? What kind of trouble?"

"He went to Switzerland to get away for a while and was working as a security guard at the Swiss National Bank, which is under some kind of investigation. While on duty late one night, he came across some of the employees working, shredding papers full of data. In their hurry to leave, they tossed a bunch of it in a trash bin, probably hoping to get to it later."

"What did he do?"

"He snatched the stuff out of the trash."

"Did he keep them?"

"No, he took copies. See, I run around with smart guys, too." She smiled and went on. "Eric and his friends decided to turn it over to this international committee that looks into that sort of stuff, hoping to eventually make a bundle of money."

"Geez, not sure I want any part of that, but I'd love to sit down and see what he has."

"I can do that. He is very fond of me, so…"

"Dear God, what have I done here?" I laughed while pulling at her hair. "Helen, you always amaze me. I love you." I stood to leave and got serious. "Whatever we talk about goes to no one. Got it?"

"Got it," she replied with a thumbs up.

"Need to talk to Erin in the library, then have lunch with Thomas."

"I knew you'd pick Thomas!"

"Helen… oh, never mind," I said, then rushed into my room, tore off my baggy sweats and put on a pretty floral blouse and skirt. "Talk to you tonight," I shouted on my way out.

While hopping onto my bike I glanced over to see a man leaning against the building across the street. His rumpled black suit and dark glasses made him look out of place. After puffing at his cigarette, he tossed it onto the ground where others had piled up. I surprised myself by walking over and saying, "I'm on my way to the library now. Where were you this morning?" He looked embarrassed. "Don't worry, I won't say a word to the colonel, and, by the way, wear something a little more casual tomorrow. You'll fit in better." I smiled then finished with, "Come along now, and please don't forget to police your cigarette butts."

I may have been smart with the guy, but I felt comfortable knowing somebody was watching my back as I pedaled away toward the library.

After squeezing my bike into the rack, I skipped up the stairs. Erin was playing with her typewriter ribbon when I greeted her cheerily, "Good morning, Erin."

"Oh, I know, Lina. More favors, huh?"

"Yes, more favors. Look, I've got some stuff I need to check out. Do you have any contacts in the University of Munich library?"

"Sure, I studied there for two years. What do you want this time?"

"Well, to start with, in 1943 they had a protest against the Nazis on campus and some students were hanged because of it. Later Himmler's Gestapo executed even more students. I'd love some back story, anything you can get about that, and, if possible, the actual names of the executed students and faculty."

"What are you looking for?"

"Just about anything,, but specifically if the names Dietrich Ziegler or his wife are mentioned…if you see those names, take a copy of it for me, please?"

"I'll try."

"Great, then…"

"By the way, Lina, I've got some film on Auschwitz in the back, and I can get a projector whenever you want to view it. But it's got to be after working hours. That kind of thing is still very touchy around here."

Thanks, Erin. I don't know how I can repay you."

"Aw, you already have. Lina, you're my best friend, especially when I really need one." She smiled gently.

I retreated back into the stacks, feeling energized now that I'd delegated some of my workload. I also felt confident we were on the right track. Like a hunter who saw signs left by his prey, I knew the painting was out there and, more than that, I was confident we were certainly getting closer to finding the Rufina.

Later, it was off to meet Thomas for lunch. My mood became upbeat, especially after arriving early and ordering myself a tall ale. I felt romantic and thought the afternoon might be tantalizing after enjoying a good meal and conversation together. Add a few more lively spirits, and we just might forget the serious business of what we were up to. It would be fun just to go about the day without any somber questions to answer.

However, I needed to clear up a few things with Thomas before we could get to that point. He arrived at the Marktplatz right on time, and I suggested a taste of wine with some cheese and cold cuts. We sat outside in the warm summer sun, fortunately not too hot to take away the comfort of the day. After hugs and hellos, Thomas said, "So you and Pieter had some problems last night coming back from Munich."

"Yes, I would say so. Scared me to death. Who were those guys?"

"Actually, all I came up with was that our guys chased for quite a while, but they gave us the slip. Got to believe they were outside our orbit."

"What does that mean?"

"Not us, not SIS nor CIA, and not Mossad. They all came up with blanks. Someone else is trying to convince you and Pieter to back off—probably afraid you're getting too close."

"Too close to what?"

"Well, even though you don't value our thoughts on this issue, at least not enough to share your intel with us, I'll tell you anyway. There are all kinds of SS types out there hoping to live out the remainder of their pitiful lives in anonymity. And, as I've said before, Pieter's publications aren't helping them feel very confident about that. So, Lina, can you let me in on what you've learned from this Astrid Klammer interview?"

"All I can say is that she is quite aware of what's going on in the alleys and backstreets of Munich. We've got some leads, names, locations and motives. But it's going to take a lot of time and effort to work them out."

"Okay, Lina. I'm not as naïve as you and Pieter think I am. I know you know more then you're telling me, and, really, I don't give a damn."

"You don't?" I laughed, but, when I tried to explain, he raised his voice.

"I don't really care Lina! I'm just a liaison for the military brass back at the barracks. I am not going to spend my life in this secret agent business. I'm just fulfilling my obligation, and it's back to the U.S. to practice law in a reputable firm. Believe me, all this cloak and dagger stuff will one day be a distant memory. So, when you want me to pass on something, okay. If not, that's okay too."

"It is not just okay, Thomas. That might be easy for you, but, for us, it is not okay. This is not some spy game. It's becoming very dangerous and real. Oh, and you can tell your superiors that they dropped the ball last night on the road back from Munich. Also, they need to start looking after Helen. I don't want her disappearing some night."

"Believe it or not, Lina, we're ahead of you on that. For the next couple of weeks, a detail will keep a close eye on her. And, between you and me, that won't be easy. She enjoys flirting with military men."

"I know that, but I promise that won't be a problem, at least not for her. And, one last thing, Thomas, I need to know about the ratline. I keep hearing about it and ODESSA."

"Oh, so now you want to know how your suspect could get out of Germany and where he might have ended up, like the other high-profile German war criminals, Adolf Eichmann, Josef Mengele, the Croat Paveli? and Walter Rauff?"

"Yes, like all the others."

"Okay, Lina, I've already told you, it's all set up. Ratline 101 is ready when you are."

"You know all about this stuff?"

He smiled. "Lina, what do you think I do back at the barracks, shine my shoes, kiss up to the brass and read *Playboy* all day? Then, when I'm bored with all that, I come across to this side of the river and make small talk with you when Pieter is out seeing to whatever it is that you two have going on?"

"Yeah, that's about what we thought." Both of us found that funny and laughed for awhile.

"Lina, sometime this week, you call the day, I'll come and take you over to the barracks. Note I didn't say *my* barracks— that would be an indecent proposal." He smirked and continued. "I'll give you a short classified lesson on the ratlines. You can even bring Pieter if it will help track down your lead. But, you must promise that when you have this lead, you'll let me in on it. I need something to take back to the colonel—that is if you want me to be able to keep seeing you."

"I'd like that, Thomas, to keep seeing you."

"What about you and me?"

"What do you mean by that?"

"You know what I mean, Lina. What are my chances with you? This business will all be over soon, everything has to end in time. You'll find your precious picture or not, but, chances are, it will end. So, what about us?" he asked flirtatiously.

"How about this, Thomas? I have a grand proposal. Mind you, I'm not making far-off plans right now, just for today and tonight, if we can evade my tail. I want to show you something, alone. Can you meet me back here at 6 tonight?"

"Sure, but what then?"

"Thomas, don't spoil the surprise. Just bring a bottle of your California wine, a sleeping bag and hiking boots, and I'll provide the rest," I said playfully.

"What? Did I hear you right?" he asked surprised.

"Yes, you do have those sorts of things in the military, don't you? And, plan on staying out all evening. Just think of it as my way of showing appreciation to foreigners. But, for now, I must get back to work in the library."

"Why do you spend so much time in that stuffy old library?"

"Why? Because, you see, that's how I keep ahead of you guys. Okay, got the plan, Thomas?"

"Yes, I got it," he said with a seductive gleam in his eye that ended in a warm smile and embrace when I stood to leave.

"Don't be late or you might just miss the train," I added while pointing over my shoulder, letting him enjoy my presence from the back. This fleeting moment made me blush and feel irresistible.

Erin greeted me with good news. Her friend from Munich had phoned, and she could get the needed information in a couple of days. Also, tomorrow, I could review those films, but again, only after hours. I thanked her and went back into the stacks to continue my search.

Sure enough, at 6 p.m. Thomas was waiting patiently at the Marktplatz. I was dressed in tan slacks, a warm yellow blouse and hiking boots, with my long blonde hair bound up tightly under a hat. Thomas looked handsome in his well-worn blue jeans with a white T-shirt under his long-sleeved flannel. His red Stanford baseball cap gave away his California roots, and, instead of hiking boots, he wore tennis shoes. With his backpack stuffed with my list of required items, he fell in alongside me when I motioned for him to follow.

I asked him to tell me all about America along the way, and he looked happy to share.

"That will be easy. What do you want to know?"

"Stanford football, the girls, the fraternity parties."

"Really? That's what interests you?"

"Yes, how are they different from here in Germany? What do they wear to class? Bikinis?" I laughed.

"No, not at Stanford! It gets cold there. Well, maybe in the summer."

"Then tell me about your family. You know, all of that stuff."

We hiked down through the middle of Old Town with our backpacks on, looking like day tourists trying to find a mountain. When we wandered through the residential area I said, "You know where I live but most nice girls in Germany don't let men in on that."

"What about Helen?" He smiled.

"Helen? No, not even her. Let's not talk about Helen. She's not here to defend herself." We laughed at that and chatted on.

Eventually we were in the forest and began traversing switchbacks up the mountain, climbing into the slowly fading sun. After about 45 minutes of steep hiking, Thomas looked around and started to ask a question when I interrupted, "Yeah, I know, most visitors take the tram. But we are locals now."

Along the way, Thomas spoke of his alma mater, his frat parties and jokes about those bikini-clad girls who wallow in the warm California sun.

"Each inch of cloth covers a lot," he said jokingly of the swimwear. "It has to, because there isn't much of it, and I've heard they are very expensive for what you get."

"Really? I've read about them in your *Life* magazine."

"The girls?"

"No, silly, about the bikinis. Mind you, we Germans have ways to expose our best sides. But laying on the beach all day— doesn't that get stale?"

"No, not really. I never thought about it that way."

We plowed on, finally arriving at a fence that read *VERTOBEN!* While climbing over I said, "Don't look so worried, Thomas. Have confidence in your guide."

We moved on until we came to a gate.

Thomas remarked, "Good I was about to think you'd gotten us lost."

Dressed in a blue security uniform, an elderly man came up and said, "Lina, good to see you. Working late?"

"No, I had to help bring this wandering tourist up." I smiled. "This is my good friend, Thomas. Thomas, say 'hi' to Paul, our keeper of the gate."

Greetings were said all around.

"Okay now, let's get going," I said.

"Lina, call me if you need anything."

"Thanks, Paul."

Although it was getting dark, Thomas realized where we were, right in the middle of the old Heidelberg Castle. I took him up three flights of stairs to a terrace overlooking the city, dropped my pack on the ground then nodded for him to do the same. I took hold of his hand, pulled him to the edge and said excitedly, "Look at it, Thomas!" The sun had almost set, and the rose-colored sky was breathtaking.

"What a beautiful place."

"Sit here, next to me. See how the city greets the night. The lights begin to twinkle on down below, and soon it will look like one grand birthday cake. It's different from the view across the river, you see?"

"Yes, very different," Thomas agreed.

And, as if prompted, the day turned into full night. We sat in relaxed silence until I asked, "Are you hungry?"

"Yes, do they have a restaurant open here at night?" he asked jokingly.

"No, only the guards, but I have brought you something. And you the wine? Yes? Good."

He tore into his backpack in anticipation. While he opened the wine, I laid out my assortment of fine cheeses with a fish spread to put on crackers. I started to dig for paper cups when Thomas pulled out two beautiful wine goblets that he'd protected with newspaper. The sleeping bags came next as the moon lit the way.

"Do you do this often?"

"Yes, when I was about 17, Helen and I would hike up here all the time. It is such a captivating place to sit, look out and sense the history that has passed by. Thousands of years have paraded by down below—two world wars and so much more. This, to me, is just next to heaven. It's timeless." We sipped on some wine then, and as I lay back on my sleeping bag, I said, "Pieter, oops sorry, Thomas."

"Bad habit?"

"No, no. Pieter and I spend a lot of time together but never up here. He has girlfriends in town, too many of them. Thomas, lie back now and get comfortable. See, just like me." When he did I said, "Now look up."

"Wow! There are thousands of them!"

"I know. It feels as though you could reach up and grab one. So many stars, it makes me think how small we really are." I stretched out my hand, and he wrapped it in his. "You see, Thomas, when I come up here, the world down there seems to disappear. All the pain and fear I give to God. And, in return, He gives me peace. Oh, if only living in this world was that easy. I would just love to talk to God and let Him talk back to me, the way I converse with you or Pieter. But he doesn't really do that. He doesn't work that way, at least not in my life. I used to pray, 'oh God, please speak to me. Just let me hear your voice once.' Reverend Mother keeps telling me to trust Him. He expects us to act on faith while making the big decisions in our lives. Here, when I look up, I can see His handy work, and that makes me believe all the evil down there is trivial compared to the goodness He offers."

I rolled over and snuggled next to Thomas, resting in his arms. I let him lean in and kiss me, tasting my lips, seeing if the warmth was returned. It was overwhelming when I returned the kiss and then kissed him again. Sensations began to take over as he caressed my body.

I gently pushed away and said, "No, Thomas. Not now. Not in this holy place."

Thomas pleaded for just one more kiss. "No, in time maybe, patience," I whispered. "For now, the world down there must play its hand out. Let us enjoy the moments we have together. No commitments, no starts, then we won't need it to end. See the stars. Lie back now, Thomas, and dream about heavenly things. We are with God, and He is up there watching."

# CHAPTER 19
# Auschwitz

After warm goodbyes, I left Thomas in the Marktplatz and arrived at my apartment around 7 in the morning to an unusual rush of attention. When I opened the door, Helen was waiting.

"Lina! Lina, where have you been? Everybody, Pieter, Father Tobias, your military tail, all of them have been looking for you. Where have you been? We thought you'd been kidnapped, left for dead or who knows what. And, even Reverend Mother called."

"No, she did not."

"Yes, she did. All of us were worried so."

"I went up to the castle."

"With who? Thomas?"

"Yes, Helen, to see the stars."

"And did you…?"

"No, Helen. Don't go there. Now, please call them all, let them know I'm still alive and well."

"And what about you and Thomas? Should I tell them?"

"Yes, of course. Nothing happened that they shouldn't know about." I smiled and assured her, "Really…just stars. And Reverend Mother, tell her I'll visit soon."

"Why me, Lina? Why don't you call her?"

"Because, Helen, she will ask all kinds of questions—you know her. Please, just tell her what I said. I will owe you okay?

And, you, maybe if you prayed a little more, you wouldn't look so stressed. Plus, work on that friend of yours at the Swiss bank. You know the smart one who copied all those documents? Right now, I've got to shower, then it's back to the library. I'm trying to get a picture of our person of interest while Pieter is getting together a follow-up publication at the Daily. Oh, by the way, you will have a guy following you around for the next few days. Thomas says he is friendly, but don't go flirting with him. He might just be the guy who nails your foot down to the floor." I laughed as I shed my rumpled clothes and stepped into the shower.

A little later, rested and ready to go, I hurried down to the bakery for breakfast. I went to the library steps, sat down and started sipping coffee. I hoped he would be there, looking for me—girlish wishful thinking, I guess.

Walking up he said, "Lina, where have you been all night?"

"Up at the castle. Did you miss me, Pieter?"

"Lina, everybody's been worried about you."

"Oh really? I heard that from Helen, too. It makes me feel good that I was missed."

"That's not funny, Lina. We were all very concerned."

"Well, I am okay, as you can see. I'm here, drinking my coffee. Sit down here, Pieter, beside me. Rest yourself, relax."

"So what were you doing at the castle all night?"

"Nothing Pieter. Just looking at the stars with Thomas."

"The stars?"

"Yes, the stars."

"So, what happened?"

"What do mean 'what happened?' Nothing happened! Well…" I said, drawing out my defense. "I can certainly guarantee, he didn't see what you saw the other day when I came out of the shower."

Pieter's face turned red. I loved doing that to him and relished in the embarrassing disposition I'd created.

"Are you blushing? That's the second time I've seen your face do that."

"Is that so?"

"Yes, Pieter, that is so. And, let me ask you this. You've never said how I looked that morning. So?"

"What?" He laughed.

"Well, compared to the rest of the girls…"

"You're making fun of me now. Right, Lina?"

"No, I want to know."

Pieter just shook his head, refusing to answer, and then he gave in. "Good."

"'Good?' That's it?" I complained. "You were so concerned about me watching the stars with Thomas, and all you can say is I looked 'good?' Pieter, get back to your precious articles, and, if you ever think something more promising will be offered, I guarantee you are terribly mistaken." I smiled smartly and went to leave then turned on my heels to say, "Good day. Oh, by the way, Thomas invited me to his barracks, Campbell Barracks that is. He's going to give me a lesson on ratlines. Do you want to come along?"

"Yeah, I might want to."

"Okay, then. You can pick me up at my apartment when I confirm the date. But, not too early. Wouldn't want to tempt you with something that you might say was just 'good.'"

"Really?"

I laughed. "Now, please tell everybody who asks that I am okay."

After skipping up the library stairs, I was greeted at the front desk by Erin.

"Lina, where have you been?" she asked.

"I know, I know. Seems everybody's worried about me. Let me tell you myself, so you can get it straight. I took Thomas up to the castle. We had a few sips of wine, ate some cold fish and cheese, nothing more—maybe a few hugs and mutual admiration of the stars. Later we fell asleep in separate sleeping bags. So, there you are. You see, nothing more. So, pass it on, Erin!"

"Okay, so no romance, just friendship. Got it. Lina, in about an hour, I'm going to close the library. I need to take an inventory for our sponsors. But first, while it is empty and my assistant is out for lunch, I will show you the Holocaust films, taken by Russian and American troops when they liberated the death camps. They were shown at the Nuremberg Trials. Are you up for it?"

"Yes, of course."

"Be warned. They are not viewer friendly. So be here around midday, and we'll go upstairs. I have the projector all ready to go."

Anticipation and the pretense of the upcoming drama drove my emotions throughout the rest of the morning. Before I rushed for an early lunch, I pulled a book about the atrocities off the stack. When I sat down alone to eat at the Marktplatz, I began to read: Auschwitz, *also known as Auschwitz-Birkenau, opened in 1940 under the direction of Heinrich Himmler and was the largest of the Nazi's 240 camps and sub camps. Located in southern Poland, Auschwitz initially served as a detention center for political prisoners. However, it evolved into a network of camps where Jewish people and other perceived enemies of the Nazi state were exterminated in gas chambers. Prisoners were also subjected to barbaric medical experiments led by Josef Mengele. During World War II, more than one million people lost their lives at Auschwitz. Later, after the war ended, Himmler was caught at a checkpoint and, while being interrogated, took a cyanide pill and died. Rudolf Hess, commander until May 1943, was hanged by April 1947 as a result of the Nuremberg Trials, but only 750 of the 7,000 staff were punished. Thousands of other SS officers, along with Dr. Mengele, escaped capture for war crimes against humanity.*

So, after suffering through to the horrors of Auschwitz on paper, I returned to the library to see it on film. Once Erin began the film, taken only moments after the camps had been liberated, my body and mind lost all control. The film rolled, showing the remains of the tortured living and the vamp of the dead. Straggling bodies were strewn all about the place, some squirming as a bug does before giving in. Limbs with no meat to them., gangly women, naked and bare, so famished their gender could hardly be determined. And it went on, the photographer's patience giving way while attempting to cover it all. The black and white scenes kept falling across the screen, showing horror after horror. Even the survivors looked to be ghosts, not aware they were still alive, walking around, going somewhere and nowhere…just fleeing from death. Like ants that smell the scent of death, thinking that if they move they might live, hoping that that bleak quest would make a difference.

Then a crescendo of madness came onto the screen—film that must have been taken by the Nazis themselves as they tossed the damned among piles of dead, burning corpses. With a scream, my heart broke for the nameless. No obituaries, no proof of life or death. This was a direct assault on humanity, a defamation of almighty God. Bodies lay in trenches carved out of the ground— mass graves to be covered. For what? A resting place for the sick, the murdered? No, that was not the purpose. It was to be a final insult to the intelligence of the advancing liberators and the world. Their defense…nothing to see here, nothing criminal, just burying the dead. In reality, it was to disguise and dispose of the evidence of treacherous crimes, with no regrets. This film would become the substance of the indictment of the Third Reich. Though, even more unsettling, it would be the legacy of the German people, who cheered along the way.

At this point, my stomach gave way to ugly grumblings at seeing death come alive, I finally had to stand up, and say, "No more, Erin! No more." I gagged and flushed out my revulsion, throwing up my lunch on the floor. Erin, in tears, turned off the projector. My thoughts were, "Oh God! Where were you? Why would you allow this to happen?" There was no righteousness in this! Was this hell here on earth? Who needs a judgment day when their deeds gave them away to God? And...why would God let this play out in His grand scheme of life?

I knew there was more at stake for me than my indigestion. It was the rocking of my soul. The fermentation of the values and morality that I had learned so well at the abbey, they were pressing me for answers.

"I am so very sorry, Erin. Please let me help you clean this up."

I needed this simple act of cleansing the floor to help my mind focus back to the present. Some time passed before those horrid visions released me.

"I tell you, Lina, it's one thing to read stale history in books, but to see the real people… The dreadfulness of it all will keep you awake for nights to come, but you needed to see it."

"Yes, yes," I said, "but never again."

I thanked Erin for sitting with me through it.

With the lights on and cleaning finished, Erin said, "That information you wanted about the University of Munich protests and this Dietrich Ziegler is in the works. Should have it here in a few days."

But, even that piece of good news couldn't take me away

from my emotions. "Why Erin?" I asked. "Why was this all hidden from us in school? The Americans know more than us."

"I think guilt and fear. At least, that is what I hear most all the time. I suspect something more. By covering it up, it keeps us from having to face it as a nation."

"Yes, but it also prevents us from looking into the eyes of our elders and having them try to explain."

"They always say they never knew."

"But they all knew. Didn't they, Erin? They knew but don't want to admit it. Some of those Jews were neighbors and friends from all around Heidelberg…yes, they knew. And, the worst of it is, they did nothing. They did very little to stop it, and their only way of dealing with it now is to pretend it never happened."

Silence was the only thing left to medicate my pain. After a few moments, I reclaimed my thoughts and my breath. "I am exhausted. See you tomorrow." I turned back at the door and said, "Thank you, Erin. You have been a good friend. Yes, a very good friend. I love that you're always there for me, helping."

"And you, Lina, for me. Go home now and rest. Tomorrow the sun will shine again. You will see."

I began my retreat back down the steps and into the fresh air. My trained body, by habit, rode my bike away.

CHAPTER 20
# Father Tobias

C ompulsion directed my bike, not toward home, for no answers were there, but to the doorstep of the Jesuit Church. I walked through the open cathedral doors. After making the sign of the cross with holy water, I found myself kneeling at the altar, pleading with God to finally talk to me. Imploring why His voice was silent when I needed Him the most, I tried to provoke a response by asking, "Are you but another fabled character who plays tricks on children—a story of wonder, a magical figure—and, like all the rest, you disappear when one comes of age, ending up a mere ritual or a rite of passage?"

In reverent quiet, I waited for God to speak. The stained glass window streamed light onto the altar, making me feel as if I were in a dream, walking in heaven's glory. But, it wasn't solemnity I was here for. No, I was trying to meet God, make it personal, as one does on the neighborhood streets. I was trying to make sense of Him and ask why He'd turned away and allowed my faith to be shaken.

I looked above the cross that hung on the wall. In torment I began to pray out loud. Asking for wisdom, as Solomon, the Son of David did, I pleaded "Make me understand your ways!"

Yet, with each attempt to ask the same question in a new way, not a word was heard from God. The solitude was broken by a simple creak and the faint sounds of footsteps shuffling their way from the vestibule.

Finally, a whisper brought me back from my lamentations.

"Lina, are you looking for answers? What is troubling you? Can I help?"

It wasn't God talking.

"Yes, Father Tobias. Yes, maybe so. No one else in here is speaking to me."

"Come, my child. Let us go into the garden, sit for a while and see what we can find together."

"Yes, Father," I said, as if hypnotized by his suggestion. I stood, genuflected then walked with Father Tobias out the side door to the courtyard. We were immediately engulfed by a garden of flowers and fruit trees. There, in the center, the statute of Mary, the mother of God, greeted us.

"Sit here, Lina," Father offered, while dusting off a wooden bench next to the trickling fountain. "Have you talked to Reverend Mother lately?"

"No, Father, I haven't."

"Oh my child, she worries so about you. So, now then, what is it that brings you here that God needs to answer for?"

I looked down and became speechless, so Father Tobias interrupted the silence. "You know, Lina, I believe there are two incontrovertible truths. There is a God, and it humbles me to know I am not Him. But, let me try to help you as best I can."

"Well, Father, while looking for the lost piece of art..."

"The Rufina?"

"Yes, Father, The Rufina. It has taken me to places far from the abbey. By far, I don't mean in distance but in ideas and dreams. It's taken me into the past, and I'm finding it hard to find God's place in it all. My faith has always been strong by simply knowing where I stand with Him. Lately, I question so much of it. I just saw films of the camps..."

"You mean the death camps?"

"Yes, Father. Now, I keep searching for the why of it all. What kind of people would do such things? And, where was God? Why did he let it happen?"

Father Tobias sat back and slowly pulled out his pipe. "Do you mind, Lina?" he asked.

"Of course not, Father."

He began the ritual of carefully pulling tobacco from a pouch in his pocket and stuffing it into his pipe. "You might not remember. Of course you don't; you were not yet born. But, before I became a priest, I was a professor at the university."

"Really?"

"Yes. I was. Back in the late 1930s not only was I a theologian, but also a man of history. So, let me try to give you an answer, and I promise to make an effort toward brevity. However, you know me. People say they'd rather see me smoking this pipe than continue with my lectures."

Smiling warmly he paused to ignite the tobacco, and the sweet smell plumed as he puffed away.

"You see, it goes back many years. Jews have always had the reputation of businessmen because of the stories given to us in the Bible. A fine example is Joseph. Remember? Betrayed and sold into slavery by his brothers, Joseph, over time, managed to become highly respected and skillful at business. His sound advice brought Egypt out of depression and prevented famine. From then on, Jews were perceived as money handlers and considered masters of usury, who manipulated the events of nations. They became bankers and financiers—sometimes selling out to the best deal appeared to be their main concern. Further justification to defame the Jewish people came because of their rejection of Jesus as the Messiah, causing them to be indicted for the crucifixion. Of course, many forgot that that was God's plan all along, for Jesus to die for our sins.

"So, here is where this German anti-Semitic sentiment had its embryonic beginnings. The Jews, as they saw them, were a nomadic, wandering group of people, unrepentant and collectively accountable for the sins of their fathers. This type of thinking has been around for thousands of years. Then came Martin Luther with Ninety-Five Theses and list of grievances. This catholic Augustine monk launched the Reformation of 1517. His ideas catered to the good and the bad of mankind.

"Not only did he conceive the Protestant mindset of the Reformation, but he also stressed the supremacy of the human conscience. He translated the Bible into German and, with the advent of the printing press, made it available to the masses. Prior to this, German peasantry was predominately illiterate. Therefore Luther's Bible was, for all practical purposes, their first primer, and it was distributed throughout the land.

"They found their literacy by reading the German Bible, creating an unimaginable impact on the future of the nation. It has been said that Luther was to the people of Germany as Moses was to the nation of Israel. But it was the tempestuous, coarseness and fanatic quality of his writings that brought out the best and the worst influences on the infant mindset of Germans.

"When denied a dialogue with Jewish leadership, Luther's intolerance turned into violent rants. As a result of their stubborn resistance to Christian conversion, he prescribed, 'their synagogues be burned, their houses destroyed, their prayer books and Talmud taken away from them' and that they 'should be set to hard labor.' In effect, his ranting flamed an anti-Judaic sentiment in Germany that had already existed years before.

"But the final blow was his support of authoritarian government. He sided with the royalty over the bewildered masses during the wars between Protestants and Catholics. You know, Lina, we have always thought of Luther in the religious context, but he also had a predisposition, a proclivity to comment in a highly abrasive way on matters of politics, culture and national pride. He never minced words when he wrote, and I quote, 'In the eyes of the Italians we Germans are merely low Teutonic swine. They exploit us like charlatans and suck the country to the marrow. Wake up Germany!'

"In time, Bismarck continued where Luther had left off and made his indelible imprint by fanning German tendencies toward nationalism, stressing duty, honor and Germans' rightful place in history. Not through the haggling of liberal ideals, no, but by the reality of military conquest. With the same fervor, other writers and philosophers emerged as apologists for war. The Great Purifier, Georg Wilhelm Friedrich Hegel would write to his German students in Berlin that war makes for the ethical health of the people, corrupted by a long peace, as the blowing of the winds preserves the sea from the foulness that would result from a prolonged calm. Nietzsche also chimed in, saying society has never regarded virtue as anything else than as a means to strength, power and order.

"Add to that H.S. Chamberlain and the Darwinian proclamation of racial superiority with the science of eugenics, and it all provided a salient solution to post-WWI Germany's economic recession. All they needed now was a leader to put the recipe together. Adolf Hitler was such a man, and Alfred Rosenberg wrote the script glorifying war, conquest, an authoritarian state, the belief in the Aryan master race and the hatred and vengeance for Jews, along with contempt for democracy and liberal communism. It captivated the German egos. And as each job was offered at the expense of the Jew and each military victory returned land in defiance of a world that had turned on them at Versailles, the Germans applauded. The new Volksdeutsche became a reality. Germans began to march in the streets to the beat of the same drum. Like tin soldiers, they came together in cadence by the thousands, holding mass rallies to hear the good news and shout, 'hail to the Führer, Adolf Hitler!'

"It wasn't until the war in the eastern front was brought back home and causalities mounted that German regret and remorse began to settle in. Then, after we'd been found out for our misdeeds, we all said we knew nothing of what the SS was doing. We distanced ourselves from the Nazis, as if we were fleeing the plague. I was there. Yes, the Jews, my friends, my family were hauled off to those camps while we, the good Germans, went about our daily lives, as if nothing had happened. Some out of fear, I am sure by now you have heard that often. But, it was true. Yes, especially at the end. Fear rode on every word. And yes, Lina, so much fear that even silence became an act of courage.

"For some, it was pure unadulterated hate, but the most despicable indictment against us was our indifference. After the war, we said we knew nothing. That is why they hide from you, but not from God. Lina, not God. You make them remember the truth, and they cannot do that without again confronting their guilt. I see that in their reluctance to talk to me, even in confession. They don't give in to me, as you do."

"But, Father, why the Vatican? Where was the Vatican when all this was going on and after it stopped?"

"Lina, the church publically denounced the anti-Semitic laws based on race, but their critique of Judaism as a theology resulted in their neutrality. This had been their position from the beginning. For the threat of a communist Russia was far more intimidating than a Nazi Germany. Their pragmatism overshadowed their morality. Oh, some brave men of cloth went to the gallows with the Jews, but others in the church, especially the Holy See, argued that to be neutral, like the Swiss, was a better course of action. But we see it was not so. They took care of their own interests first, filling up their coffers."

"But, the Jews, Father?"

"Collateral damage, just collateral damage. They justified inaction on the rationale that, in Eastern Europe, the godless Russian Bolsheviks were doing the same or worse. This had been the thinking of Popes XI and XII—that, in the grand theme of history, it had always been that way. Lina, do not let your faith give way because of this. Remember that corrupted history is not the product of God. No, it is a product of men. They use God as a pretense for their actions. As you have witnessed, we were not and many are still not godly men."

"And you, Father, why are you still here with the church?"

He paused and smiled warmly. "Because, if I were to leave, who would be here to tell you the truth? God can still use me, just as I am. Lina, as you travel on, you will uncover much and discover life is far more complex than you thought. But, do not let yourself be tainted by it. You can only do what you can do. Depend less on God's intervention. Pray more for His wisdom. Read the scriptures. He speaks to you through His word. There are choices you must make. That is why He gave you freewill.

"Now go. I have said enough, and, yes, I will see to it that Reverend Mother knows you are safe and still in God's hands. But you must visit her more often."

I nodded in agreement and said, "Thank you, Father."

In some way, when I left the church that day, I felt reassured that, in a world of thorns and torment, there would always be faint streams of light shining toward the good, giving hope for the future, a reason to believe.

Yet, it could not overtake me. Why? Who knows why. Plato's

prophetic words, not scripture echoed in my mind. "Only the dead have seen the end of war." A crucible that burdens my soul, drains my thoughts and plays on and on.

## CHAPTER 21
## Person of Interest

Pieter weaved his way around the crowded tables to my conclave in the back of the Heidelberg library. I looked up over a stack of books, and there he was.

"Good morning, Lina. Want some coffee? You look like you could use some caffeine. Bring your notes. Let's go out into the Marktplatz and see what you've come up with."

While I picked out what I thought was relevant or new information that would appeal to Pieter, he said proudly. "And, by the way, as luck would have it, a national syndication outlet contacted me this morning. They want to take this thing to the world press."

"Your story?"

"Yes."

"Make it a double latte," I said to the waitress.

"So, what good news do you have for me, Lina?"

"Not necessarily good news, but promising."

"Thomas help you?"

"Not yet, but probably soon. I'm going to be seeing him this afternoon.

"Good. Glad you are. I think it's time we let them in on what we have."

"Nothing that's concrete, Pieter. Yet I'm feeling, maybe more like wishing, we're on the right track now."

"It's just that they have the resources and worldwide

connections that we couldn't possibly match. And, for us to locate this person of interest could be like looking for a needle in a haystack. If we give them the name, the probability of successfully finding him will certainly improve. Do you agree?"

"Yes, I think you're right."

But, Lina, let's make sure they agree we get the exclusive on what they discover."

"I'll try. First, let me go over what I have on this fellow Adolf Ziegler and his younger brother, Dietrich. Both attended Berlin University and graduated with some kind of art related major. It appears they moved on to the University of Munich and received advanced art degrees. They became members 891 and 892 of the Nazi party and played a sizeable role in the movement's influence on the election of 1933. There they meet Alfred Rosenberg, who at that time was on a rampage to provide historical evidence of German culture dominance.

"The Ziegler brothers were talented painters and photographers and well educated about fine art. Rosenberg introduced them to the Reich's inner circle, and Hitler was jubilant over the two artists, especially Adolf. Adolf became Hitler's favorite painter, and Dietrich one of the Führer's personal photographers. When the German army marched into Poland, Adolf, was placed under the authority of Kajetan Mühlmann, confirming what Astrid Klammer told us. Also, the Zieglers served with the ERR and helped designate which of the looted treasures would be sent on to Linz, Austria. The Germans had a remarkable reputation when it came to documentation of their stolen treasures. As a result, much of this…"

"Do you have evidence of all this, Lina?"

"Yes, of course. It can also be confirmed by testimony given at the Nuremberg Trials."

"And, where in the world did you get this from? I don't think that's printed in any of those books you were flipping through at the library."

"Oh, let's just say I got it from a close friend, from the past. And don't press me on who it is. I cannot reveal my source," I said with a chuckle. "Pieter, you're just going to have to trust me on this. But there is one catch. It appears that some of the infamous, meticulous inventory is incomplete."

"Why is that?"

"Because, as the war was winding down, some of these guys escaped with the original documents that detailed purchases and sales. Those lists were then used to protect their escape and allowed anonymity when they sold off some of the treasure to finance their next place of residence. Now, here is where things get a little muddy while tracking down these guys. After the war, Adolf, the older brother, became a witness at the Nuremberg Trials, revealing a lot of intriguing tales to the American investigators. Those interviews, for the most part, are classified."

"Geez, everything good gets classified. Why?"

"You'll have to ask the U.S. government about that, Pieter. But, here's the lead. The younger brother, Dietrich, became an art dealer, floating around with Maria Dietrich, no relation of course. She was one of Hitler's personal art dealers that presented him catalogs full of looted art, and Hitler picked out the pieces he wanted for his private collection at his home in Innsbruck. He actually purchased a few of them."

"Some honesty in the man?" Pieter asked sarcastically.

"No, not for this sinister burlesque character. Purchased, yes, but at ridiculously undervalued prices. Now Dietrich…"

"The younger brother?"

"Yeah, the younger one, for some reason got disgruntled with the Nazis, went back to Munich in late 1943 and participated in demonstrations. The Gestapo took both him and his brother to Dachau for six weeks. But then Hitler heard about what Himmler did to his friends and gave them a reprieve. However, Dietrich Ziegler can't stay out of trouble with the SS. Back at the university, he continued to cheer the protestors on. Hermann Himmler, head of the SS, had enough and was determined to put a stop to the resistance. So, in February of 1943, he had the Gauleiter of Bavaria order the 'disgruntled males of the university to be drafted.' As for the women? He responded, 'If the females lack sufficient charm to find a male, I will assign each of them to be one of my adjutants … and I can promise her a thoroughly enjoyable experience.'

"As you can imagine, this infuriated the protesters. Led by Hans Scholl, a medical student, and his sister Sophie, they continued their demonstrations. The Gestapo responded by hauling them into the people's court and ordering them to be severely beaten before being hung by the SS. Sophie Scholl hobbled on crutches up to the hangman's noose and declared, 'You know as well as we do that the war is lost. Why are you so cowardly that you won't admit it.'

"Professor Huber, who helped organize the protests, and several other students were executed a few days later. Allegedly, Dietrich and his wife Lara were killed with the other demonstrators. However, looking at the official list of students who died there, his name is not mentioned. There is a Capt. Ernst Ziegler, but that is it. We have a death certificates for Dietrich and Laura, but that seems to be confusing as well. There is information to believe that those certificates of death appeared sometime later and were most likely tampered with. In essence, it suggests that he simply vanished. You see, Pieter, I believe he is on the run. Astrid said the Rufina was possibly a Linz selection, and we should be looking for Ziegler. So, we need to find him. I don't know why, but I feel this is our guy."

"But, Lina, that's really stretching, isn't it?"

"Well something...something just like the painting in the Louvre, is telling me it's him. What do we have to lose? It's our best shot."

"Actually, Lina, at this point it's probably our only shot."

"So, do you want to give Thomas the name?"

"Yes, why not? Like you said, 'What do we have to lose?' You trust Thomas?"

"Yes, I do. The others, not so much. Let's still hold a few things back, just in case."

"Like what, Lina?"

"Like Sonnenschein, even though we haven't heard from that person lately."

"Probably just some quack."

"No, no, Pieter. Remember, that name came into the picture just after the first publication, and Astrid mentioned it! Remember?"

"Yeah, I almost forgot. You're right. Okay, let's hold back on that when you talk to Thomas today. Now, tell me again why you trust him, Lina."

"Now, Pieter, just because we spent the night at the castle don't think I'd mix romance with intrigue. Go, get on your way or we'll become lost in all this nonsense."

I walked back into the library and thanked Erin for all her efforts to help.

"No problem, Lina. I am certain you would do the same for me. By the way, Helen came in and left you a note. On my way back to my desk I opened it.

*Good news. Got the inside info on the Swiss bank accounts. Get back to me. Helen*

I turned my eyes up and prayed. "Thank you, Lord."

"So, what's up, Lina? I hope you called for a personal reason," Thomas said as we sat down at the Ochsen.

"No, it was mostly Pieter's idea."

"Yeah, no luck here."

"No, it's not that. As you know, Pieter and I are not willing to trust any of the interested parties involved in our investigation, and for good reason, I might add."

"Hey, Lina, I know…not a problem."

"We decided…"

"You and Pieter?"

"Yes, to give you a name that we believe can lead us not only to the Rufina painting but to even more paintings, worth millions if not billions!"

"So why are you two being so charitable now? Not that I don't appreciate it. It most likely will set me up for a major promotion, but why now?"

"That's simple, Thomas. It's because you are such a righteous, trustworthy person and…" I paused to smile. "Also, to be honest, we don't have the connections, the intelligence gathering capabilities or the personnel to take this thing on. This guy could be out there anywhere in the world, and we need to track him down. You're our best chance at getting him. Mind you, Thomas, this comes not without conditions."

"Oops, I knew there would be a catch."

"No. Not a catch, only a condition. That whatever you find, we get the exclusive."

"You mean first publication?"

"Absolutely, Thomas. First publication."

"Okay, I'll see what I can do. So, what do you have, Lina, a name?"

"Yes, Dietrich Ziegler. He is the younger brother of Hitler's favorite painter, Adolf Ziegler. The record shows he was executed at Munich in 1943 after protesting policies of the German Reich. There is a belated certificate of death, but don't let that fool you. University records and Nuremberg testimony do not support this. Now, he might have been sent back to Dachau, and maybe other classified material that you have access to will show that. But, we strongly believe there are other explanations. We believe our person of interest, Dietrich Ziegler, escaped through the underground, or as you call it the ratline. And, he is still out there, alive and, in all probability, being hunted down by a lot of people. We believe he has something everybody else is looking for: A list of artwork. Art that could be worth, who knows. Let's just say tons. But, he could also be hunted by the Nazis for the very same reason, or simply out of fear that other rats might be revealed. Who knows? That's where you come in."

"Anything else?"

"Like what, Thomas?"

"Is there any other communication you'd like to let me in on?" he asked sarcastically.

"No, Thomas. Whatever do you mean?"

"Just asking."

I laughed. "You see, Thomas, you don't trust very much either."

He laughed too and stood to leave. "Okay, okay, we trust each other. Glad we got that straight. First thing tomorrow, you and Pieter come over to the barracks, and we'll talk more, after I give you my expertise on the ratline. Pick you up at 8 a.m.?"

"No, thanks. I'm sure we can find our way."

"Is the conference room okay?"

"Yes. Brass? No."

"Okay, no brass. It will be our secret. I guarantee you'll find it quite interesting. So we're done here?"

"Yes, done."

"Dinner tonight?"

"No, Thomas. Not tonight. I need some rest. It has been a long week," I said while sliding my cheek next to his.

He kissed me sweetly. "Another night?"

"Of course Thomas. Tomorrow?"

"Yes, tomorrow."

CHAPTER 22

## Ratlines

At precisely 8 a.m., Pieter and I drove up to the Campbell Barracks' gate, were quickly cleared by security, then passed on to the main office. One of Lt. Thomas Werner's adjuncts greeted us on the front steps. I wore my best crisp white blouse, gray suit and now carried my own stylish leather attaché, hoping to give a professional presence.

Pieter looked a bit disheveled sporting a rumpled dress shirt, loose tie and blue jeans, giving him the glorious presence of the passionate, consummate journalist. Today the intended target was given the impression that, Pieter was not there to put himself on display. There would be no cordiality offered.

I think that's why, inevitably, we became the best of partners in this good guy, bad guy scheme, which often rewarded us with all sorts of unintended information.

We were led into the same conference room where I'd received my grilling the other day. Already set up and obviously eager to start the presentation, Thomas greeted us then formally introduced two of his friendly adjuncts. He took over the conversation, emanating professionalism in his Class A uniform, spit-shined shoes and sparkling brass. He even sported a few extra medals, for what I didn't know. This side of him appeared foreign and made it difficult to imagine him lying next to me up at the castle. I smiled to myself thinking maybe he was trying to impress me. If that were the case, it was working.

There was no time for, "Hi guys, glad to see you." It was all business, though he asked if we'd like some coffee first. I jumped at the suggestion.

"Yes, thank you, Thomas. Make it black, please."

Pieter requested some too. After sending one of his aides off to get it, Thomas turned to say, "If you fine people of Heidelberg ever wondered what I do here, this is part of it." He pulled down the screen, and, while his aide arranged the projector, the coffee was served. A few sips later he said, "Okay, let's get started."

The first slide introduced the topic by simply stating, ODESSA/Ratlines. Thomas suggested we hold our questions until the slides were finished. He cleared his throat and clicked to the second slide. "ODESSA, according to Nazi hunter Simon Wiesenthal, was an underground group of former SS members who helped aid the escape of fellow war criminals out of Germany. The eventual destination was primarily Argentina and other Latin American countries.

In order to get there, they passed through the ratlines then reunited in other parts of the world with their fellow Nazi compatriots, longing for better times and possible rebirth. Now, ratlines are commonly known as the routes that spies, smugglers and conspirators travel. It is the way they enter a foreign country, get or pass on information, then exit safely. Of course there is a lot of secrecy in these highly dangerous clandestine capers. Some become very skillful at their trade, and financial benefits are extremely rewarding for the right information.

"After the war, these so-called ratlines, previously infrequently used backyard channels of strange suspect characters, became major highways for parties wanting to leave the vanquished and economically distressed Germany. A diverse group of people passed through them during this time period.

"So who were they? Some were war criminals, the crimes

against humanity type, like Adolf Eichmann. Others were the architect of the extermination camps, Klaus Barbie, SS Hauptsturmführer who earned the nickname the Butcher of Lyon, and Franz Stangl, Treblinka extermination camp commandant and, of course, the Angel of Death himself, Dr. Mengele from Auschwitz."

Slides rapidly clicked across the screen with sometimes remarkably clear and often colored photos of the people and places Thomas described.

"Another group was the specialized SS types. One example is Wernher von Braun. An SS Sturmbannführer, he was technical director of the Peenemünde Army Research Center, which was responsible for the development of the German V-2 missiles that, during the war, terrorized British and Dutch cities. After the war, these types of SS members were put back into service but this time for the U.S. government. Though his past was no secret to the CIA, von Braun eventually became director of what is now known as NASA, at the Marshall Space Flight Center.

"However, not only Germans passed through the ratlines. Some of them were collaborators, such as Ante Paveli? from Croatia, who managed to put 150,000 people to death. Then there were political characters, those nameless government agents, British SIS, CIA, even the KGB, not to mention French intelligence.

"The Jews also frequented the ratlines. Many found themselves boxed in, excluded and expropriated, and they saw no other choice but to use the ratlines to make their Zionist journey to Palestine, thus avoiding the wrath of the British. Many nights they were strangely imbedded in the same remote chateau as the war criminals, sleeping in the cellar while SS men slept just a few stories above. Fellow travelers passing in the fog—just going their own ways—each fleeing from a different predator."

Thomas stopped. "Did you get all that in your notes? If not, no problem. I've made copies for both of you. And, by the way, some of these long names may be familiar to you German folks, but for us they are a challenge."

As if a student, I raised my hand.

"Lina, hold your question. Let me just finish this off, then I'll let you in on what we know of this Ziegler fellow."

Pieter and I looked at each other and nodded in agreement that we would wait patiently for that enticing bit of news.

"About the routes…how did they escape? One was through the oldest and most difficult way, the ports of Hamburg and Rotterdam, but they were too risky, congested and easy to control. The primary route was to go through Innsbruck. Then it was over the well-traveled smuggling passage and early tourist route, the Brenner Pass. It's the main pass through the Alps, which connects Austria with northern Italy with Merano and Bolzano, the southern section of Tyrol, Italy. Then it was on to the ports of Genoa or Rome. There they could easily get new identifications and documentation from the Red Cross and verification by the Vatican. Both organizations took up the role of handling displaced people.

"They prepared the proper papers and equipped the fleeing Nazis with finances, allowing them to board ships to all sorts of destinations. Eventually, the word got around that Italy, meaning essentially the Vatican for the most part and southern Tyrol, was Nazi friendly, so Italy became like a sink drain. When you pulled the plug, everything swirled around and ultimately went out. That's the way it was. They came from all over Europe, Croatia, France, Austria and Germany. Even dissidents fleeing from the advancing Russians found their way to Italy.

"The Vatican hierarchy supported the Nazi flight, even using their monasteries to hide them from capture. They dressed them up as priests and, when the coast was clear, sent then to another monastery further along the ratline, eventually into Tyrol, Italy, then onto Rome. Adolf Eichmann passed through this way. Other notorious personalities, such as Dr. Mengele and even Franz Stangl, who could kill 1,500 people an hour. Yes, imagine the bizarre situation of Herr Stangl posing as a priest. When captured many years later in Latin America, he told of his escape from Germany and how he was led into a Vatican housing facility. Once there, a very close friend of the Pope, Bishop Alois Hudal, who had, by the way, written several anti-Semitic treaties, came into the waiting room. Herr Stangl recalls that the bishop held out both of his hands warmly and said, 'You must be Franz Stangl. I was expecting you.' Italy was such a pleasant place for former SS men that some stayed on for many years in southern Tyrol, while others passed on under new names to foreign countries, got new jobs and lived comfortable lives.

"Well, that's most of what we know now about the ratlines in Europe. I suspect when the U.S. government declassifies the information they've gathered from the Nuremburg Trials, years from now, we'll know more about the behind-the-scenes, cloak-and-dagger stuff—the intrigues that these secret intelligence agencies withhold from the public."

Thomas paused to take a long deep breath. "When you see so many redacted spaces and read between the lines, you become a little cynical, to say the least." Thomas sat down on the other side of the table and announced, "All right, now I'm open for questions."

Pieter jumped in first. "Why were all these people so pro-Nazi?"

"Do you really want the answer?" Thomas asked.

"Yes, of course. The issue here is why," I said.

"Okay, let's start with the Vatican. I hope I don't offend a few Catholics here." Thomas looked at me sincerely.

"Go on, Thomas," I said.

"Then, here's the way it played out. In 1929, an issue was resolved about the authority of the Vatican under the Lateran Treaty. The Vatican was allowed to, in essence, create its own nation with all the titles and rights of a sovereignty but limited to a very small area of Rome. Remember the power the Vatican held prior to that treaty? It was the political and spiritual ruler of practically all Europe. And now its influence would be limited to one square mile. At the time, it seemed almost terminal to its existence.

"To extricate itself from this predicament, the Catholic Church set up a network of dioceses throughout Europe. When the communist Bolsheviks were thrust into power in 1917, the Vatican network came under persecution in the east. Many of the priests saw firsthand the ferocity handed down by the Bolsheviks against their institution. So, when Hitler came along, the papacy, now under the leadership of a former eastern cardinal, Pope Pious XI, welcomed any alternative to the Bolsheviks. Each Nazi, scratch that, anti-communist was a welcome sight for the Vatican when Germany began to lose the war.

"The USA added the express lane to the ratlines. It simply gathered up the technical experts among the Nazi intellectuals and airlifted them to America under the code name operation 'Operation Paperclip.' And, other countries, primarily in Latin America, also had use for the expatriated Nazis. Most Latin countries were governed by repressive regimes, hoping to stay in power by force. So they used former SS men much like Hitler had. For example, it is rumored Klaus Barbie had a hand in the apprehension of the famous communist Che Guevara after he caused a nuisance in Bolivia.

"As I'm sure you've heard before, this was a period when

realpolitik, pragmatism and expedience were clearly in defiance of internationally accepted moral standards. The rational fears of a worldwide communist movement gave western Allies reason enough to justify giving the disdainful rodents passports to freedom. Sorry there, I got off script."

I interrupted, "You obviously have a passion for all this, Lieutenant."

"How can you not?" Thomas earnestly asked.

"Yes, you are right on that."

Regaining his composure, Thomas continued. "And, as for the art industry, dealers in the U.S., Britain, France and Switzerland had first pick of the art the Nazis were offloading to finance their escape. Then the rest passed on to the next echelon."

"What about the Mossad? Where do they fit in?" Pieter asked.

"Quite a different story there. Mossad came into existence in 1949 and reported directly to the Prime Minister of Israel. Their job, as far as art is concerned, is to extradite the Nazi and, if they find some art in the process, try to return it to the rightful owner, somewhat like the Monuments Men of the U.S. military. As for extraditing war criminals, the Mossad try to find a way to cut through the red tape that provides legal immunity. If that doesn't work, they apply a common sense justice. Case in point: Adolf Eichmann, the mass murderer architect of Nazi Germany; they simply kidnapped him under the nose of local government protection in Argentina, secretly moved him to Israel, prosecuted, then quickly hanged him. Righteous justice, huh?"

Thomas picked the clicker back up, and the next slide moved into position. "Here's what we have worked up for you people. Pieter, we'd like you to hold off on publishing this information until we get additional conformation. You will see why we ask that favor. However, you have the freedom to print anything you want. That's your call." Thomas waited for a response but then continued without one.

"In this slide, Hitler and Adolf Ziegler are choosing art pieces for the 1937 grand opening of Haus der Duetschen Kunst. Look in the background. Right there you'll see the faint but recognizable face of Dietrich Ziegler. The lady standing to the right is possibly either his wife or assistant. This could be your man, Lina. He was high up in the art world of the Reich. We believe his brother brought him on board to help with Mühlmann's ERR and have reason to think he is still alive. Where did we get that idea? Much of the mysterious recent events you've experienced are directly connected to your articles, Pieter. We believe you have inadvertently uncovered revealing information by way of your first publication on the Rufina. That information has led many of the diverse, interested parties to become nervous and extremely reckless.

"We believe Dietrich Ziegler falsified his death certificate and may possess not only a list of lost artwork but also a book full of sales data. Find him, and you'll probably find the Rufina. We feel we have enough to go on, but, Pieter, if you publish this right now, the turtle will probably retreat more deeply into his shell or simply move on."

"All right, Thomas. I get it. But to make this thing work, you must keep us in the loop; we need to know anything new. Okay?"

"Okay. I'll see to it myself."

"Get this guy and you might get rank," Pieter teased.

Thomas laughed. "No, no. It doesn't necessarily work that way around here. But, if it happens, I assure you I won't turn it down."

"We're done here?" I asked.

"Done."

"Good. I am famished."

"Then let's step next door into our cafeteria and chow down on some of America's finest."

"Hot dogs and hamburgers?"

"No. You'll see most days officers have a little more taste in food than that." He smiled.

Pieter looked at me, shrugged and said, "Why not? I've got about 15 minutes to burn."

We picked up a tray, selected our food then sat at a corner table. I complimented Thomas on his thorough presentation and lunch. He seemed pleased that I appreciated his efforts. Pieter brought us back to the reason we'd come.

"Thomas, I need something in writing from the colonel that we will have the first right of publication, with no American censor. My readers will see right through it."

"Don't worry, Pieter, will do."

They looked at each as if they were in a game of poker, each one feeling he had something the other needed and neither willing to let go, bet on it and play out their cards.

Then there was me. I hoped that my personal relationship with them wasn't going to mess up the lines of communication. We'd come so far, and I could feel Rufina pulling me toward her. But why? That was the taunting part I had yet to understand— the me and the why of it all. This information today meant little personally, but I feared it might eventually.

Thomas went off to talk with the colonel, and Pieter drove us back to Heidelberg. He broke the silence with, "Lina, I like the guy. Really, I do. It's just the job and the organization he works for that caution me to not let him in totally. You okay with that?"

"Yes, I feel the same. Oh, I've got something that could give us the big break."

"Helen?"

"Yes, Helen."

"One of her chummies?"

"Yes, again, one of her chummies. She has been trying to get a hold of me. We've been missing each other, going this way and that. But, you know how she has a way with them."

"Men? " He laughed. "I thought it was the other way around. Men have their way with…"

"Now, Pieter, she's just an affectionate, friendly flirt."

"And a good one at that, plus she has all the equipment to make it happen."

"I asked her if she had any friends in Switzerland who worked in a bank. She said no but has a friend who works in a security firm that had contracts with several banking data centers. I told her to look into whether he could help us. She seems excited to get a hold of me and mentioned the bank connection in her note. If we could somehow get information from the bank, understand how they work, even open an account. Remember what Astrid Klammer said? Follow the money trail…who it comes from and who it transfers to."

"Needle in the haystack again?"

"No, Pieter, think. Where did most of the fugitives do business? The Swiss and Vatican banks."

"No way can we get into the Vatican vault, but the Swiss banks, maybe with the right…" Pieter's mind was churning with the possibilities.

"The only other thing we have and Thomas doesn't is Sonnenschein."

"If that's all he doesn't know, then we're really not holding much back."

"You're right. But you never know where a lead might come from," I encouraged.

"I agree. You taught me that, among many other things," he joked.

His window was down, and he looked handsome with his blond hair moving about in the warm breeze.

"Pieter, you are always on my side, and I love you for that." I put my hand on his arm then reached across the seat and softly kissed him on the cheek.

"And that was for what again?" he asked.

"Never mind. You can't handle it," I taunted.

He stopped the car in front of my apartment and asked, "Now what is it that I might not be able to handle?"

"Come by early some morning, have some coffee and you just might surprise me as I walk out of the shower again."

"Really?"

"There is always the possibility. I have a boatload of tricks to keep you close." I smiled seductively.

"Why, Lina, I am stunned by your boldness."

I placed my hands on his. "Are you blushing, Pieter? You, the sophisticated man of the world?" I slowly opened the car door and, while making my exit, said, "Some other day."

"Promise?"

After closing the door dramatically, I smiled and said, "Nope, but it's nice to think about, isn't it? See you later."

Giving in, off he went. I walked to my building and, after looking down the street to see my protection detail, I entered and climbed up the stairs.

Part IV

# Intrigue

*Buenos Aires, Argentina*

CHAPTER 23

## Desperation Letter

T he next morning, just before sunrise, Helen shook me awake by pulling on my arm.

"Lina, I've been trying to find you, but you've been all over the place. I was called into work on a special tour at the castle yesterday, and I ran into Eric."

"A little early for guessing, but okay, Helen, I give up. Who's Eric?"

"This is the guy I told you about. Eric! He's quit his security job and is now back on campus working on something he calls database management system (DBMS). He and his friends call themselves computer geeks. They're a little weird. They sit around and read technical manuals all day long."

"Like what kind of technical manuals?"

"Let me see if I can get this right. He said they read stuff on how to communicate from here to there."

"Communicate what?"

"Like automatically keeping records of things so they can retrieve it later—faster and with more accuracy."

"That's nice, but what's it got to do with us?"

"The bank, Lina, the bank. The Swiss National Bank!"

"Really, he has a connection there?"

"Yes, wake up, Lina! Wake up! You see, the Swiss National Bank employs a lot of these geeky German guys as security guards and to also work on their computer processing systems. These new systems create what they call a data bank for savings and checking accounts. I asked my friend Eric how the Swiss banks can keep those accounts so secret. He said they're not as secret as they want you to believe. Then I asked if he could get information about past and current accounts, and he said maybe. He asked what I had in mind. When I asked if I could find out about a particular personal account, he said,' Whoa! That's against the law—prison time and financial penalties. Not sure if I want to go there.' Then I asked him if he knew anybody that might want to go there."

"Oh, I see where you're going with this. Now what?" I asked.

"The now what is 'yes.' He changed his mind, says he could do it for a price. And, listen to this. Eric has a contact who could find that kind of stuff out, but it's going to cost some money."

"How much?"

"Five thousand American dollars."

"What? For information on one account?"

"That's what I said, Lina, but he snapped back smartly, 'it's risky business.'"

I had started to gain my composure from the early wakeup call and jumped up to say, "Helen, get some coffee going while I take a quick shower to wash away my groggy brain."

After the cold water did its trick, I grabbed my robe and walked into the kitchen.

"Are you and Pieter getting anywhere on the painting?" Helen asked.

"We're working on it. Remember, Helen, say nothing about this to no one. Not even Pieter or Thomas can know that you're the one who contacted this Eric guy. No one needs to know you're involved, not even Father Tobias or Reverend Mother—no one!

It's only for your protection and my peace of mind. Believe me, this isn't just fun and games anymore. And, keep this in mind, you still have a tail watching you. So stay clear of trouble."

"What do you mean, Lina?"

"You know very well what I mean." I teased while waving my finger. "We are making progress. We're getting closer, and the interested parties out there are becoming very aggressive. Helen, go try and set up the meeting with Eric, then go about your daily routine and forget it. We'll take care of it from there. Okay? Tell Eric I'll pass on the $5,000 price tag and see what I can come up with. Heck, you and I make, what, $150 a week, tops? And, that's adding both our checks together. Anyway, tell your friend I'm working on it. Ask if he will meet with Pieter and me in the back library conference room ASAP. I'll be somewhere in the library most of the day, so you can reach me there if you find something out. When do you think you'll talk to Eric again?"

"Today. He's on campus most mornings."

"Then set it up—as soon as possible!"

"Okay, Lina. Will do."

As soon as Helen shut the door behind her, I called Pieter to tell him about our dilemma.

He said, "I'll get a hold of Thomas."

"Why Thomas?" I asked.

"Because, the Daily News won't have that kind of money for…well, maybe, but I don't want to let them in on this. Not yet, anyway—at least not until we've really got something to go on. And, Thomas, well, these spy guys have deep pockets. So let me talk to him, then I'll meet you in a few hours at the library. Let's get this thing going."

"Okay."

I put down the phone, threw on a dress, tidied up my hair and rushed down the stairs to meet a rather gray day. A cool wave of air made me wish I'd grabbed a sweater on my way out. I waved to my tail then thought, "Why not?" Strolling over to the unmarked black car, I tapped on the window. After he lowered the glass, I put out my hand as a welcome gesture.

"Hello, I'm Lina. I thought we should meet." He looked startled. "You can't tell me your name, now can you?" He looked up at me, not knowing what to say, so he said nothing. "Well, okay, then it's Mr. Tail. Follow me, but don't get too close."

He finally smiled and said, "Okay, Frau Ritter."

"I'm off to the library. Please don't come in. You'll scare off my friends."

I jumped on my bike and away I went, with Mr. Tail following. Erin greeted me with a cheerful "good morning." I motioned her over to the corner and quietly asked, "May I use one of your back rooms for a private conference?"

"For what, Lina? Sounds important."

"It is. I can't tell you what it's all about right now though."

"Don't worry, Lina. I'll make sure to look the other way."

"But it might be later tonight."

"That's okay. I haven't finished my inventory, so I'll be here late. Your friend Thomas is waiting for you in the back."

"Already?" I looked across the library and discovered him sitting calmly at a cluttered desk. When he slowly lifted his hand to say "hi," I walked over, leaned in and whispered, "hi" back.

"You got the call from Pieter?"

"Yes, $5,000!"

"That's what the contact said."

"And, who was the contact?"

"Let's keep that name out of it"

"All right. If you think that's best."

"So, Thomas, any possibilities for the money?"

"Money is not a problem. But we need more details before

we can go forward. By the way, you know this is illegal in Switzerland."

"But this is not Switzerland, and, if we can get anything on this Dietrich guy, I don't think the banks will want the public in on this conversation. Pieter's got our back here, Thomas. Who's working this out through military intelligence?" I asked.

"The colonel."

"That's good. I hope to set up a meeting tonight or tomorrow here in the library conference room."

"Do you want me there, Lina?"

"No, Thomas. Your English will only scare them off. It's better Pieter and I handle it."

He looked at me with concern. "Are you sure, Lina?"

"Of course I'm sure. You doubt me?"

"No, Lina. That little-girl-from-the-abbey disguise you once had has all but disappeared."

"Then, get back to work, Thomas. I'll call when I have it set up. Oh, and Pieter says to tell you, same rules, first publication."

"Sure, same rules. Damn that Pieter. He's always got you covered."

"It's not what you think, Thomas."

"No?"

"Only in this business."

"And that means…?"

"That means he's got me covered. And, that's the feeling a vulnerable girl like me needs right now."

Thomas stood to leave and, after leaning down to kiss me on my forehead, said, "I'd like to cover you too, Lina."


A little later in the afternoon, Helen came into the library and found me. "Okay Lina, where and when?"

"Here in the conference room. Tell him to come through the back door. It will be unlocked around 8 tonight. There will be just Pieter and me."

"Eric said another guy will be with him."

"Tell him the money is in the bag."

Helen thought that sounded funny and giggled when she snapped back, "Okay, will do."

"This is serious. When you leave here act like nothing special is happening."

"Lina, my security tail is a really cute guy."

"Good, I'm sure you'll have no problem distracting him tonight. I don't want to see you or him around. You're done with this. Okay?"

"Sure. Hope you know what you're doing, Lina."

"I don't, but it's too late for that. I just hope Pieter does. See you later. Now, get lost!"

When I walked by Erin's desk on my way out, I whispered, "It's on for tonight. Can you leave one of the back doors open?"

"It will be open."

I could tell Erin was now caught up in the intrigue of it all.

"See you around 7:30 then."

I rushed out into the Marktplatz, found my way over to the Ochsen, then asked for a phone to call Pieter and tell him to meet me.

"Give me a couple of hours. I'll be there."

Now with time to kill, I rushed home to clean up and pick up that sweater. It didn't feel like summer anymore but it also wasn't fully fall.

Back in my apartment, while rushing through lunch, I noticed a large paper bag by the front door. Helen must have let it in. I looked inside and saw it was another bundle of letters. They were all addressed to Pieter in care of the Daily News. I realized they were more responses to his articles and sat on the floor to read a few. I started to open one when intuition struck me, and I began to scramble and shuffle through them anxiously, just looking at the return addresses.

I found one then another posted from Berlin. I tore open the first and read it carefully. No, that wasn't it. My heart started pounding as I clutched the second one so tightly that, in my excitement, my fingers turned red and began to twitch. I didn't want to tear it. I reached into a kitchen drawer to find a knife and, as if it were a piece of fine art, gently managed to break the seal. I peeled it back and carefully pulled out the neatly folded letter. I held it to my breast, then went to the window to see if my protection was still parked in the street.

He was gone! Fear crept into the apartment, but I didn't know from where. I moved quickly to the door, locked then latched it. While walking back to my couch, I carefully spread open the letter. I read, *Dear Liesel.* I stopped and held my head as my mind began to buzz. It was if I'd had too much sugar, or not enough. Everything spun around my head or was my head spinning around it? I grabbed the back of the couch to hold me stable, then reintroduced myself to the letter, reading each word as if it were from a dictionary, defining them on my own terms.

In a direct declamation it said, *I knew you would find me out, not the others. Just you. Come to me, no matter what happens. I have something for you. It will keep you safe until you see their ways. Life had its way with us, but then it was never its fault but mine for wanting too much. God willing, you will find me before they do. Come to Buenos Aires, El François. There will be a messenger. I can't go back now. Loving you is all I have left.*
—*Sonnenschein*

I don't know why my eyes watered. Then, a knock on

the door...I quickly began to tear the letter into small pieces. Why? I don't know. It was the thing to do at that moment. It was like being caught naked with intimate thoughts that needed to be hidden. I rushed into the bathroom. The knocks became louder, beginning to rumble the room. I thrust the particles into the toilet then pulled the lever, and the last remaining evidence of the letter's message wisped down the drain. I recovered my composure, then ran to the door. It was about to burst. Who was this intruder? I readied myself to take him on. I unlocked the door and unhooked the latch. It opened.

"Frau Ritter, are you okay?"

I held my composure. "Yes, of course I am."

"Sorry, Frau, but I had a call from my commanding officer and was gone for a few minutes. I thought I might have missed you going out."

"No, no. No, as you can see, I'm still here. I will be here all night."

"Did I scare you?"

"Not at all. I just woke from a nap—been a long day. I will be in all night so no need to bother. Thank you for your concern."

"It's my job. Good day, Frau Ritter."

After securing the door, I peeked out the window until I saw him get back into his car. I flipped on all of the lights in the apartment and paced around for a while. With stealth-like speed, I unlatched and slid out the door, fled down to the second floor landing, opened the window that led to the back fire escape, slithered to the alley below and then vanished.

By 7 p.m. I was sitting in a back booth at the Ochsen, sipping on a warm beer and chipping away nervously on some pretzels. A little later, Pieter finally arrived and sat down next to me.

"Well, it's all set then?"

"Yes, I think so."

Pieter motioned to the waitress and said, "Please, one more." After it was served he asked, "And the money?"

"Thomas says it's not a problem. He just needs a few more details."

"And, what about the conditions?"

"I told Thomas. He said it's guaranteed. But, Pieter, we still need to protect ourselves. Let them have half the loaf and keep the rest for safety's sake."

"Sounds smart, Lina."

"No, I'm not so smart. You've just trained me well."

"Ah, but, Lina, you are very special."

I wanted to say thanks or something, except he wouldn't let me.

"No, I really mean that! You are special. There is something about you… the quality of your character, your integrity, the abbey."

I blushed a little and said, "I hope…"

"I mean that…I…you…we…" Pieter began to stumble with his words again.

I tried to rescue him by saying, "Well, it's good to know you become speechless when giving out compliments."

He tapped his fingers on the table, looked around the room, then, for no apparent reason, leaned across and kissed me. It happened so fast I couldn't have stopped him, even if I had wanted to. But, I didn't want to. He looked into my eyes, pleading with me to confirm his impulse. The longing looks lasted a few moments. Then Pieter asked with a smirk, "My apartment?"

"Certainly not mine." We both laughed loudly when I told him the details of my breakout down the fire escape and poor Mr. Tail still sitting in the street, busy guarding an empty apartment. I broke up the party with, "I got another letter from Sonnenschein."

"What?"

"Yes. I read it just a little while ago. It pleaded with Liesel to find him before they do."

"Who's Liesel?"

"I don't know. Maybe somehow he got the name wrong. But it was so personal. So personal that it was signed 'loving you is all I have left.'"

"Posted again from Berlin?"

"Yeah. The letter seems to be begging Liesel on and yet I feel this person knows me. Even more, he knows what we're doing."

"He knows what we are doing? But how?"

"I can't imagine. I've been sitting here for hours letting the letter run through my mind, over and over. Sonnenschein also says he has something for me."

"The Rufina?"

"I don't know, but, Pieter, I am so scared…for the first time really scared."

"Should we tell Thomas?"

"No, not yet. There's something we're missing here. Maybe Sonnenschein does have the Rufina. The only thing I'm certain is that we are on the right track. Not sure what's up the rails of that track, but something important definitely needs to be exposed. I think what scares me the most is that somebody is waiting for us, but who and why? Is all this happening over the painting?"

Pieter looked down at his watch. "Okay, it's time. Let's get over to the library and see if these guys show up."

"Erin will let us in, then make sure the back door is left open for Eric and his accomplice."

We walked across the Marktplatz and through the residential district to enter the campus. After tapping lightly on the library door, Erin opened it and then motioned us in. While passing the dimly lit stacks of books and empty chairs, I thought how funny that night and darkness could affect the tenor of a place. Once in the back, we entered a small conference room, sat down and waited anxiously. After about an hour—though it seemed much longer than that— we heard the heavy back door creak open and footsteps coming toward us.

"Lina?"

"Yes."

"I'm Eric," a young man said as he reached over to shake my hand. "And this is?"

"Pieter."

"Oh, yes, from the Daily newspaper."

"Right," Pieter said as he shook hands.

"Good then," Eric said nervously. He looked around the room then let his words spill out. "Helen said…"

I interrupted. "Let's not bring her into this. She's out of the picture."

"Okay, then. Let's get started. Here's what's happening. Lately, the Swiss banks have come under pressure by certain Jewish groups to disclose accounts belonging to heirs of the Holocaust victims. To try and prevent negative PR, the banks have agreed to allow full disclosure of unclaimed Jewish accounts. It is anyone's guess how much cash is involved, not to mention the art, gold and diamond trafficking between the Swiss and Vatican banks. By accident or opportunity, I noticed that late at night, after hours, bank employees were doing some extracurricular activity. Specifically, they were attempting to shred incriminating documents. I recovered a spreadsheet left behind. It listed accounts, deposits and distribution data of not only Jewish assets but of hundreds of current Nazi war criminal accounts. Some of these accounts were current, and deposits were made from time to time with requests to transfer money to certain destinations."

Pieter spoke up. "So what you're saying, from that material, you computer guys have decoded the DBMS of the Swiss Banks."

Eric looked impressed. "Pieter, you newspaper guys are good. Yes, that is precisely what we've done."

"So, if we give you a name, you can find out from where and when that person makes deposits and to whom the money is sent. Am I correct?"

"Yes."

"Incredible, so what's the $5,000 for? Is this about extortion?"

"No, Pieter, that's not it! Here's the deal. We need that money to keep us doing what we are doing, using highly advanced computers that contain large amounts of data. Look at it this way. The fish you want to catch is just one of many. We're after a lot more. In effect, we want to hold the banks accountable. When we accumulate a sizable amount of verifiable info, our guys will turn it over to responsible authorities who can then bring in the added legal and political pressures needed to expose these banks."

"How do I know you'll do what you say? What keeps you from taking hush money from the banks?" Pieter asked sincerely.

"Why do you think we have you here? For god's sake, you're the press! You and Lina have an open door to transparency. If we don't deliver, you expose us. And, we're not leaving town. Once we have this information, the banks won't be welcoming any additional exposure via your newspaper. Hopefully, it will force them to actually begin dispersing funds to the rightful heirs of disputed Holocaust claims. Yes, and, along the way, we may trip over some of the other missing treasures."

"So how does this go down? How are we guaranteed that after the money is paid, you will give us the information we want?"

"Simple, Pieter. You give us the name. We look for the person's banking transactions, give the details to you, then you pay us. Quite frankly, Pieter, we trust you—I think more than you trust us. We'll let you know where to deposit the $5,000 when it's done."

"What happens if, after getting the information, we renege and don't transfer the money?"

"Well then, no more fish for you guys!" Eric laughed. "Look, Pieter, I know you from your articles here in Heidelberg. You're one of the good guys. Just think of it as charity. That's what we do. These unscrupulous bankers must be held accountable, along with their Nazi cohorts. Justice, that's all we want. We'll make our millions later in computers. Deal? Now, what is the name of the person you want information on?"

Pieter looked at me, and I nodded in agreement. A moment of silence passed through the room, then he said, "It is Dietrich Ziegler, related to Adolf Ziegler from the Rosenberg ERR days."

The other guy with Eric spoke up for the first time. "One of the Ziegler brothers?"

"Yep, one of them."

"Okay. We will get back to you."

"When?" I asked.

"Real soon. Who's the contact person?"

Pieter answered, "Lina. We'd like to give the Daily some distance on this."

"Okay, it's Lina then."

I told him, "You can leave the information in a sealed envelope at the front desk with Erin, the librarian, addressed to Frau Lina Ritter. We will go over it and then, within three days, you will have your deposit."

"Guaranteed?"

"Yes."

Eric got up to leave, shook hands with Pieter then they quickly left through the back and into the dark night.

A chill came over me. Was it because we were about to enter into an arrangement for secrets held by devils and soon come face to face with one of them? Was this the cost for rescuing the Rufina?

Back in the safety of my apartment, the letter kept playing in my mind, like a song out of tune.

"We must keep our secrets," I thought. "Without them, we have no chance." But what sort of secrets and a chance for what?

CHAPTER 24
## Swiss Bank Account

F lipping through the library microfiche gave me a head-ache, but, just before I switched it off, an article caught my eye.

*Thousands of Jews attempted to hide themselves and their money in Switzerland. However, if they were lucky enough to make it to the Swiss borders, they were turned away. Their identification documents were easy to spot, since Swiss authorities requested that German officials affix a large capital 'J' on each Jewish passport. When German death camp deportations increased, Switzerland, along with many other countries, including the United States and Great Britain, completely closed border access to Jews.*

*Nazis stole gold, jewelry and art from the millions of Jews they murdered. They then needed to sell these stolen commodities on the open market. So, under the pretense of raising finances to help the war effort, the German Reich conspired with Swiss bankers to facilitate these financial exchanges. In essences, they conveniently held garage sales of looted treasures. Incredulously, all this time, the Swiss banks were also acquiring the interest accumulated on the unclaimed Holocaust victim accounts. The immoral actions of the Swiss bankers came into the limelight after the war, when heirs of the victims attempted to reclaim their assets. The banks refused most of the claims, using the Swiss Parliament's 1934 Secrecy Act as a defense.*

*Such chicanery is on par with the Swiss insurance companies, which continue to deny life insurance payouts to Jewish heirs because they cannot produce death certificates attesting that their relatives actually died in the Holocaust and because their premiums had not been paid while they were in the camps*

*In part because of worldwide scrutiny and possible disclosure, the Swiss banking investors turned to the one monetary entity in the world that was completely exempt from outside audits: the Vatican Bank. The Holy See was protected by its sovereignty and diplomatic immunity and was completely insulated from international scrutiny at the footstool of Christian reverence.*

I turned off the machine, pushed back my chair and closed my eyes. Rancor swelled and permeated my mind. Not of disgust, for I was beyond that with these Nazis and their sympathizers. No, it was something even more provoking.

Our attempt to penetrate bank records went beyond finding the Rufina. It had developed into a more deserving cause. We'd become small donors to the task of holding these villains accountable. Those who stood in the darkness and deemed their hideous acts as virtuous, no they wouldn't get away. We would find them and put them to shame. That would be their defeat.

My thoughts were interrupted by a voice, first in a faint whisper, then as a shout. "Lina! Lina, are you all right?"

Like coming out of a coma, I tried to focus and finally recognized Erin. I looked up at her and attempted a smile. "Of course, just day dreaming."

"Sure looked like more than that, Lina. Anyway, here it is." She placed a large white envelope on the desk. "Must be from one of your admirers. Young guy; cute but rather shy. He asked if I was Erin, the librarian who could pass this on to Lina Ritter. What am I your personal secretary now?" She teased, "If

I'm going to be a courier of secrets, I'd at least like to know something about…"

"No, Erin, you don't! Believe me, you don't want to know. That would make you a co-conspirator. So, remember, you know nothing. Telling the truth about that will help keep you safe— and legal."

"Lina, be careful. I would miss you very much if you..." I could tell she was attempting to hide her genuine concern when she casually said, "I've got to get back to work."

I fumbled with the envelope, moving my fingers around the edges, all the time imagining what could possibly be inside. Would this finally be the answer? Please, God, don't let it merely be another vague clue. I wasn't sure I could handle that at this point. Let it be the key to end this.

I slid a fingernail down to break the seal. No more pretense of control, I ripped it open and reached in to pull out a large document, much bigger than I had expected. Quickly I began to read the cover letter.

*Due to the sensitivity of the decoding process, the subject of interest will be referred to as 'DZ.' We have followed the path of DZ from its origin of bank application through each transaction that subsequently occurred. Enclosed are the deposit amounts and the destinations for each distribution, chronically sequenced. Due to the specificity of the account, we've left the analysis clearly to your own speculation. We hope you find this to be the information you are looking for. Keep us in touch by the usual channel. —E*

I browsed through the detailed transactions and paid special attention to the blacked-out identity replaced by DZ, which I assumed stood for Dietrich Ziegler. After about an hour, I rushed up to the counter and asked Erin to use the phone. Pieter was not in, so I told his secretary that it was very important that he meet me in the library as soon as possible.

Erin asked, "Anything wrong, Lina? You look emaciated, bleak and pasty, and..."

"Okay, Erin. I've got it. I look terrible. Yes, something... well, something. Let's just say this thing has taken an unusual turn of events. I need Pieter to think this out for me. Don't worry, Erin. I'll make it through the day. Today, yes, tomorrow...who knows." I tried smiling to help alleviate her worry, but I could tell she saw through it.

In about an hour and a half, Pieter walked quickly into the library. I pointed to the conference room, and we went in together. There were no hellos or other niceties as he immediately picked up my sense of urgency, if not outright despair.

"This is it," I said while handing him the cover letter. He read it silently and, as always, scribbled notes on the side. When he started flipping through the next few pages, I said, "I'll get us some coffee."

Without looking up he said, "Fine."

"Sugar?"

"Yes, same as usual," he replied as he drilled down through the document.

I returned and placed the coffee in front of him. Saying "thanks" would have only broken his concentration. I sat tapping my fingers on the table while intermittingly taking a sip. Pieter broke his silence and looked up at me.

"Wow. That's it. So, he's in Argentina! Palermo? What do you know about the place?"

"Only what I just looked up. It's a large neighborhood in Buenos Aires, and Palermo Chico and Barrio Parque are the upscale areas where the wealthy and famous reside in large homes or luxury condominiums."

Pieter read over his notes. "The bank disbursements indicate that in 1938 he opened his account, kept on making large deposits until 1944, then his transactions began to slow down. In 1946, however, they begin to pick up, probably because he moved to Argentina. That's also when a large portion of his account was transferred to the Vatican Bank, but he still left a pretty sizable balance in his Swiss account. The account name was changed to Carlo Bennet, DBA Continental Bakery Import & Exports, Buenos Aires.

"Well that's it, Lina—Palermo, Argentina. Let's get Thomas on it and see what they can come up with. These large deposits mean he might be selling other things more valuable than just cakes and cookies." He looked at me again. "Lina, what's wrong? This is the breakthrough we've been looking for! We're finally getting there. I bet he's got a corner on the tainted art world and is dealing from Argentina, right out of his Buenos Aires bakery warehouse. The Peronistas, those Nazi partisans, must love him." Noticing my unusual silence, Pieter stopped his enthusiastic pep talk. "Lina, what's the problem? You look so depressed."

Without a word, I handed him a sheet of paper on which I'd made underlines and other notes with my red pencil. He took it, read it carefully, looked up, then read it again.

"What does this mean, Lina?" he asked.

"Money was transferred bi-annually to the diocese of Heidelberg since 1944. It's a small amount, considering the rest of the transactions. I hardly picked it up. Then I looked at the next page and the next...All to the Heidelberg Catholic diocese."

"So?" Pieter asked.

"So, where do you think that money was going to? There is only one catholic school, one church and one abbey here in Heidelberg. Plus, the account is coded 'LR.'"

"What are you getting at, Lina? No way. Are you thinking

'LR' is for Lina Ritter? No, it can't mean that. "

I began to tear up when Pieter said loudly, "Lina Ritter, why do you do this to yourself?"

"I don't know. Mostly out of fear…fear of the possibilities. See, you read it the way I did!"

"No, Lina, it's just a coincidence. Come on, you're just making something out of nothing here. If it will help, talk to Father Tobias. See if he can calm your emotions and dispel your outlandish theories. Hey, let's stay on top of the story. The Rufina is what we're after, remember? I bet DZ knows we're almost there. And, just think about it. A casual visit to the Louvre, and we have one of the biggest international headlines since the execution of Adolf Eichmann. It is just a notch below the Nuremberg Trials. We'll get Thomas on this while I begin an article on this guy. As it develops, I'll see if the Associated Press will buy in." Pieter bear hugged me as he jumped up and down saying over and over, "What a story, Lina. What a story!"

His enthusiasm helped my mood, but lurking suspicions came back with a vengeance as soon as he left. There would be no time to relax. Not now. No, I was on a mission far more involved—and perhaps far more personal—than what first pulled me into this quandary. Just finding the Rufina would no longer be enough.

I ran out of the library, raced my bike to the church and blessed myself out of habit. God and my eternal salvation were the last things on my mind. Clearing my good name here on earth would serve me better at the moment. I went to the altar alone, and, in the quiet of God's earthly domain, knelt down and pretended to pray, but more for luck. I was a gambler now, denying all and holding on to probabilities, abandoning my lessons on God's providence. Earthly concerns do that more often than not.

But again, it was the good Father Tobias who saved me. He

seemed to intuitively know every time I entered this place, most likely by the particular rhythm and sound of my steps, much like Reverend Mother. He knew I was there, and there he was again.

"Lina, my child. What brings you here today?" he asked warmly.

I smiled weakly. "Father, do you know everyone by their footsteps?"

He laughed in a comforting way, as he usually does.

"Yes, you know, Lina, I think I do, at least the ones who visit the chapel as often as you. Let's take another walk into the garden. Let me share with you the last bloom of my roses before fall kicks in." He reached out his hand and added, "Come with me, my child."

We walked out to the patio and into his cherished garden. Standing next to a planter of tall roses, he took out a pair of clippers and cut one for me.

"Go ahead, Lina, smell. This is part of life. The new season will come, the petals will fall and their sweet smell will fade. Later, another will come and take its place. So it is. And, when new ones bloom, they look the same as the ones that bloomed before. Why? Who knows. He hasn't told me that," Father said with a warm smile.

And, like so many times before, my apprehensive spirit and guard was dropped by another one of his short discourses.

I said, "Father, let me tell you what brought me here today." I went on to describe the bank situation.

"What? The Swiss National Bank? Very ambitious of you, my child. You have done a very mighty thing. Who would have ever thought someone like you could get the bank of Switzerland to cough up their misdeeds?"

"That's not my concern right now, Father. God only knows

my motives on that. No, my focus is not on the bank. I'm interested in just one person's misdeeds."

"Is that what is bothering you today, Lina?"

"Yes, you see, Father, while going over this fellow's finances, I discovered his money moved to a variety of places throughout the years. But what troubled me the most was the regular payments to the Heidelberg diocese designated specifically toward 'LR.'"

"What are you getting at, Lina?"

"Money meant for LR, transferred to the diocese that supports the abbey. LR—Lina Ritter, Father! Does this mean someone has been sponsoring me all these years?"

"Now, Lina, let's rest this thing. Don't get carried away. I have Brothers who serve in the diocese, and I will look into it for you. Don't worry. I'll find out from my good friends. For now, you go in and say a prayer. God loves you, my child. This thing, it will go its way, but your home has always been the abbey. Rest there. That is where you've always found peace in the world. Now go. I'll take care of this matter for you. After you pray, find time for Reverend Mother."

Back at my apartment, I called Thomas to say I had some important information for him.

"Finally a real date? An evening out with you?"

"That would be nice, Thomas, but it's not about that. I think we know where Dietrich is."

He quickly changed his tone. "Don't talk on the phone. Tomorrow, meet me for breakfast in the Marktplatz."

"Make it later, Thomas, after lunch. There are things I have to do."

He abruptly shut down the conversation. "Okay, see you then."

The phone went to a dial tone. I imagined him running

down the hallway to the colonel's office to tell him of our good prospects. For now, it was time take a long shower, then rest. I looked out the window to see if Mr. Tail was on duty. By now, I just called him that since he refused to give a name. I took off my clothes and walked naked into the bathroom. The heat from the water and the cool of the oncoming fall air filled the bathroom with steam that floated out into our apartment. Thankfully, it began to cure my stressful pains. But, suddenly I sensed a presence somewhere in the thick mist. I pulled back the shower curtain and caught a glimpse of a figure coming toward me. I had nothing to defend myself with except a wooden bath brush. I took hold of it just as someone grabbed my arm. I screamed, then pulled back to escape.

"Lina, it's me, Helen! Clam down! It's me! Stop!" she said as I continued to fight her off. "Helen! It's Helen!"

Finally, she broke through to me. "Yes, Helen. Oh, Helen, you scared me."

"I have a male friend with me, and you forgot to close the bathroom door. Would you like me to bring him in here to meet you?" She laughed.

Relieved I said, "No, of course not. Please shut it for me."

Before leaving she turned to say, "I'm in a hurry. By the way, did it all work out with Eric?"

"Yes, it went well. Please toss me my robe before you go."

Hours later, I finally fell to sleep. The dream came again and, for the first time, I could clearly see the man's face standing beside a woman, holding onto a painting. It was the Rufina. With a tender voice, he spoke toward me. Both were smiling and enjoying each other, when all of a sudden she screamed. Startled and awake, with my heart pounding, I climbed out of bed.

I wandered the apartment for a while then finally ended up on the couch. There was no safe place for me now. I knew I'd jumped into a rushing river some time ago. I had lost control. The rapids could take me anywhere they wanted and were about to do just that. As I closed my eyes, I could hear the deafening roar of the upcoming falls.

In time, exhausted and resigned, I laid back my head and, at last, fell to sleep.

CHAPTER 25

## God of Chaos

Helen had come and gone, but thankfully she left me covered by a warm blanket. The chilly mornings were another sign fall was approaching with a vengeance. What woke me was the smell of coffee and a sweet roll that Helen must have picked up earlier. I got up, rushed across the cold floor and filled a cup to carry into the bathroom.

While the water warmed, I saw myself in the mirror and brought a hand to my face in between sipping on the hot coffee. I looked terrible. My hair mingled all about, with no apparent direction. Sleeping on the couch did little to help either. There were red creases and crisscrossed lines from cheek to forehead, a testament to sleeping face-down on the sofa.

Was I getting older, maybe, or perhaps the intensity of recent events was wearing me down? I sighed and decided there definitely was a need to take a few days to get away again, retreat back to the abbey and take pleasure in Reverend Mother's precious care.

I tipped my toe into the shower. The warm water begged me in. It seemed my world, my fears, my joy and contentment were right here, standing bare as the water messaged the stress away—such a simple, natural remedy to block out the rest of the world. Once the ritual was complete, I reluctantly pulled myself out to where life's dramas seeped back in.

Father Tobias, yes, Father Tobias promised to inquire about

the money transfers from Dietrich Ziegler's Swiss account. And then, of course, I needed to meet with Thomas to share the information we received from Eric. Unfortunately, it looked as though the retreat to the abbey might have to wait a few more days.

I began to rush about, dressing and putting my face together at a frantic pace. I needed to stay out of the library today. Every time I went there, the hours slipped by too quickly. Not today. No time for any of that luxury. There was this troublesome feeling that today everything would definitely get more personal. It was as if I were about to get the results of an important test. Hoping for the best, knowing sometimes it could be distressing, I prayed under my breath. "Please, God, let it be good news." After looking at the clock and noticing it was half past 7, I said to an empty room, "You mean I slept that long?" My heart panicked me out the door.

My bike and I knew where to go first, straight to the Jesuit Church to put an end to this wrestling that thrashed about in my head. Again, I found the church door open, as if waiting for my arrival. I dabbed at the holy water, making the sign quickly as I paced toward the altar. Seeing Jesus nailed to the cross reminded me of what little I had to bear. Somehow knowing that helped move me forward. I waited, kneeling, knowing he would come. Soon his voice said, "Lina. Lina, my child."

I could hear his familiar footsteps coming closer. I turned to reach for a hand that was searching for mine.

"Lina, here let's take a walk in the garden. I know it is a little chilly, but I love Heidelberg best when the weather is turning the page. Summer to autumn—yes, life goes on, and so must we." His hand greeted mine. "Let's go talk."

His face, his voice, the demeanor of it all…it was not a good omen, and I sensed it. But, what was it? This man of the robe, so noble, was attempting to gently let me down, to medicate my feelings before even revealing what I was suffering from—the antidote before the diagnosis.

My hand began to tremble, and he sensed it as he led me out again into his garden. Without picking a new budding rose, like he'd done the day before, he simply said, "Sit down here, Lina. I have something to tell you. Mind you, I don't know what to make of it. But it's something you should hear."

I sat down on the garden bench and stretch out my legs. After sitting down alongside me, he continued.

"Lina, I saw your concern on this matter of the money sent to the diocese, so, right after you left, I made a call. Now remember, you didn't hear this from me." He gave a slight, anguished smile.

I exhaled then attempted to breathe in fresh air, but it didn't help at all. I was anticipating the worst as Father continued in his best comforting tone, "I made the call to one of my closest friends in the diocese and prompted him to look into the matter. And, he did. It was not really so puzzling as you might imagine."

I couldn't control my emotions any longer and almost shouted, "Please, Father! Don't torment me any longer. Please just tell me what is it?"

I began to cry then sob. Why, I didn't know. I just did. Maybe it was just the sheer anticipation of it all.

He dropped his cautionary approach and jumped into it, as if he were the professor again, lecturing to his students. "The record shows in May of 1944, there was a new account opened by the person you suggested. And there was to be a discreet amount of monies placed bi-annually into that account, under the condition that a set portion would go exclusively to the abbey. Again, my friend was just following the information you gave me."

"That's it?" I thought. "Okay, I can handle that."

I was now thinking there might be some hope still. But, as soon as comfort crept into my mind, he prodded on, a relentless roller coaster assault.

"It seems there was the condition that most of the provisions were to be designated toward two individuals."

"Who were they Father?" I begged. "Helen Kohler and..."

"Helen?"

"Yes." A moment of awkward silence, then slowly, as if to soften the punch, he said, "And, Lina Ritter."

My heart stopped. Beads of water dribbled down my face. This disciple of God, poor Father Tobias, could see it in my eyes. They portrayed the truth. I looked at him, stunned out of surprise, defiled out of pride, confused by uncertainty. I sat numbed and sedated. I struggled to ask a question, but my mouth was too dry for the words to spew forth.

"No, it's not real," I thought. "This cannot be happening to me!" I shouted in the corridors of whatever cerebral substance I had left in me, hoping to make sense of it all with my intellect. That was all I had left. To revive myself, I needed a logical way out of this. I must have a reason to hang onto, something to clear up this nightmare.

I pulled away from the dear Father, breaking the stare that had locked me onto his desperate statement. I looked to the surrounding roses and let my mind settle on them. They all had meaning. But this, it didn't fit. "Where does this take me?" I thought.

I turned back to Father Tobias' prying eyes. He knew my question, before I could ask it.

"Lina, I don't know what to make of this...the connection, what it means. I can't help you there, but you are strong. Oh, I know you will wonder on about this, but God...remember the one true God is a God of reason. So, stay close to Him, let Him lead you out of this. His providence has brought you here."

I slowly slipped into a familiar reply, "Yes Father, Reverend Mother relies on that so much."

"Then, my child, you must trust that wise example. Lina, once more, we never had this conversation, now did we?"

Pulled back to earth and reality, I said, "What conversation, Father?"

His smile was infectious, and, when I stood to leave, he followed. I looked around the garden once more and said, "They are ready for a change but look so nice, so beautiful the way they are. Why Father?"

"I wish I knew, if only to give you an answer. And you, Lina, like a rose..." I could hear the compassion in his crackling voice. "Go on your way, child, and make sure to spend some quality time at the abbey."

"Thank you, Father." I turned and walked out the garden gate, feeling very alone.

I went to the library, not for research this time but to use the phone to call Helen. I checked the time and knew where she would be. After asking the castle phone operator to have Helen meet me in the Marktplatz, I added, "It is urgent. Please see if she can get away from the tour."

"Sure, Lina. I will give her the message."

I bought some snacks and a glass of beer then sat at a table in the middle of the Marktplatz. The sun had finally broken the morning chill, and the sky was clear. From there, I could take in the panoramic view of the castle, and a bit of snowcaps on the distant hills added to the beauty. It was the kind of day that made us all tourists, even Helen and me. It was a day meant to enjoy the majestic artistry of God.

I turned my thoughts to Helen. What would I say to her? All our lives this man, a Nazi and a prominent one at that....

How could I connect with her? Actually, how could we connect together, for we were both named in this indictment? For more than an hour, I tried to escape my thoughts. However, the conversation with Father Tobias continued to replay over and over in my mind. It would not leave me alone. And why would it? One way or another, Helen and I were mixed up in some kind of sham. Simply not knowing about our past would not give us a convenient alibi this time. We'd often asked about our possible relatives but were always given the same answer.

"Move on. The abbey is your family and home now," we were told. But now, as I was about to make a breakthrough in the Rufina case, I could no longer take comfort in that.

Helen walked up with a plate full of food and a soft drink and asked, "Lina, what happened?"

"Sit down here with me, Helen. There is no easy way to put this to you."

She did, with obvious concern. "I hope it's not as terrible as you look, Lina."

"Here it is, Helen. Your friend Eric provided the information we requested. There was documentation that this Nazi art dealer, who fled to Argentina, sent some of his money back here to support you and me."

"What? You're kidding!"

"No, I am not kidding. Beginning in 1944, a sum of money was distributed to the diocese here in Heidelberg. It's been verified that that money went into accounts specifically set up for Lina Ritter and Helen Kohler, by a sponsor of the abbey."

"What are you trying to tell me, Lina? What does that mean?"

"I'm not sure, maybe everything. Cleary it means somewhere in our past, a Nazi war criminal on the run was willing to support us."

"But, why?"

"Maybe, before the abbey, our families had ties with a Nazi, possibly a charitable Nazi friend by the name of Dietrich Ziegler."

Helen took a sip of soda and remained silent as she tried to wash down the overwhelming revelations.

"It all started at the Louvre. You remember the painting? Then the curator, and so on. When I look back at the meeting Pieter and I had with Astrid Klammer, she actually asked if she looked familiar to me, as if we'd met before. Then there was the Munich story about my parents' deaths, plus Sonnenschein and the letters. I kept asking myself, 'Why me? Why is all this happening to me?' How could I know then…the dreams, the voices and now the lady? You don't have them, Helen, do you?"

"No. None like that, Lina."

"And, it keeps popping up that both of us came into the abbey around the same time."

"That's right, Lina, together."

"All those clues mean something, Helen!"

We both sat in silence for a few minutes, trying to digest the information.

"And, also, Helen, I received another letter from Sonnenschein. It was addressed to Liesel and said, *God willing, you will find me before they do.*"

"Who's Liesel?"

"I don't know, but the letter appears to be talking to me. It says there is something for me. Not you. It must be me. I haven't told anyone except you and Pieter about the letters."

"Not even Thomas?"

"No, Pieter and I both agreed it was better this way. But, we did pass on the name and now the place where Dietrich Ziegler, aka Carlo Bennet, is hiding."

"To the American intel agency! Why, Lina?"

"Because they have the resources to get him. He'll probably try to make a bargain, maybe some kind of exchange of information, like all the rest of the Nazi criminals. They only divulge valuable information if it frees them from prosecution. And for us, well at least for me, I started looking for the Rufina because of compulsion, then a recurring dream. She has led me to secrets of our past. But, this is what's happening now. Ziegler knows us and sponsored us, for whatever reason. They will find him, then we will know."

"Oh God, Lina. Do you think we are relatives of a Nazi from the past? That somehow…"

"I don't know."

"It's what you're thinking, isn't it?"

"Now, let's just be calm. Think this through. I am going to give Thomas the location of Herr Ziegler, and then we'll see. But, don't let on to anyone about the letters and Sonnenschein. Please, Helen, hold this tight like before…not a word!"

"Okay! Okay, Lina."

"We need to know who's involved. This has become a chess game now, and our moves must be discreet."

"Yes, I agree."

"Go back to the castle, as if nothing has happened. I must speak to Thomas in a little while. His job is to keep tabs on me, so he'll probably be here soon."

Helen left her untouched plate of food and rode away. I dug out a pen and paper from my backpack and began writing out notes to give to Pieter—things to remember about today. I had too many questions that I didn't want to forget.

An hour later, there he was walking across the Marktplatz in his civilian clothes. I smiled at his attire because he dressed so

American and strutted like a well-trained soldier, so much so that no one in Heidelberg would ever believe his civilian disguise. He waved as he came closer and greeted me with a kiss on my cheek.

"Glass of pilsner?" I asked.

"No, nothing, thank you."

"Still at work?"

"Did I say that?"

"Yes, your intentions gave you away."

He quickly reset the conversation. "No, Lina, that's the U.S. Army's intentions."

"And your intentions, Thomas?"

"Well, let's just say I hope to spend another night with you under those stars up at the castle. Then, who knows what else could happen."

"Oh, how you dream, Thomas. You've got all of those people and I'm sure a girl or two back there in California just waiting for your return from the military. You will forever forget these summer days in Heidelberg."

"You're probably right, you know, about Heidelberg anyway. But, I won't ever forget you, Lina. I want to take you back to meet my friends and family in California."

"Sounds delightful, Thomas. And, will I get to wear a bikini in Malibu, attend parties on the beach and listen to the Beach Boys?"

"Whatever you want, Lina."

I sighed and drew back my enthusiasm. "California is your dream, Thomas. But, me, I belong here. Heidelberg is my home, not some sandy beach in some way off never land. I love you, Thomas."

"You what? Wait, hey, you say that like you were complimenting a good dinner or I was a steak entree."

I laughed. "No, it's not that way. It's the true affection I hold for you. Yet, we come from different worlds and, in the end, see things very differently. I enjoy life as it is. You aspire to greater things and places, and that doesn't necessarily work for me."

"Don't say that, Lina. I've got hope…"

"Okay, then, hope it is.

"Now, since you've dampened my heart and squelched my desires, where in the world can we find Dietrich Ziegler? At least there is some hope that I'll get a promotion from all this."

"Yes, maybe. I can tell you where he's been as recently as two weeks ago."

"Where?"

"Hold on now, Thomas. There is the issue of the $5,000."

"Yes, of course, not a problem."

"They held their end of the bargain, and don't forget you promised Pieter the right to first publication."

"Yeah, yeah, so where is he?"

"Palermo, Argentina. He does business with Deutsche Transatlantic Bank and has a separate account in the Municipal Bank of Buenos Aires. They are current and active. So, there you are. Go get him. Make sure I get to interview him. And, please, promise to keep us up to date with the investigation."

"On the Rufina?"

"Yes, the Rufina. She is the reason that we all got into this. Although, I have other concerns now."

"What are they?"

"You'll know when the time is right. I promise, Thomas, you will know."

"I hope it was all worth it. And what about you, Lina? What are you going to do now?"

"Oh, just wait. First, I'll let you show off your many talents and track down the Rufina." I smiled.

He looked deeply into my eyes for a moment then broke the silence when he asked, "Lina, why do I get the idea that you and Pieter are not letting me in on something?"

"You always think we are playing with you, Thomas. Maybe we are leaving you out to protect you. Or, maybe we just don't trust you."

"Like the others?"

"No, not like the others. Let's not go over this again." I waved him off but couldn't stop myself. "However, since you brought it up, just look at their record, Thomas! Dens of thieves, connivers, with roaches of the worst kind…complicity with the known criminals they hunt. The intelligence community would sell their righteous mother for the right intel. It wouldn't matter to them. It's all a game. A psychotic game! There are no rules… bogeymen all around. Trust in them? No, they've used that up long ago. So, let them all know we still hold a few trump cards of our own, before they do something impulsive. Because, if they do, they will never know what we know, and we will most surely publish it!"

Thomas, trying to work out a response, looked at me as if in a trance. "Remarkable, simply remarkable. How did this happen? You, the little naïve girl from the abbey…to this? Lina, you may be right about me going back to another world. Yet no bikinis, beaches or anything else will prevent me from remembering you." After a long deep breath, he smirked and said, "I just might become a monk."

I laughed. "No, Thomas, I guarantee you would not look good in a hood. It most certainly would dampen that California style."

He smiled broadly, then got up to leave. Kissing me again on the cheek, he asked, "You know where I'm going?"

"Yes, I do. Straight to the colonel."

"There will be other times, promise?"

"Sure, promise."

"We seem to promise a lot to keep this thing between us going," he said tenderly.

It had been so long since I had made an entry in my journal. Later, I would look back to what I wrote that night and realize how prophetic it was. *Today was a defining moment to end all of this, but my greatest fear is that it's only the beginning.*

CHAPTER 26
## Into The Lion's Den

B uenos Aires is advertized as a metropolitan center in the Latin American country of Argentina. The city opens its harbors to trade from around the world. Restaurants, high fashion retail markets and other businesses line its busy streets. It might appear to be the quintessential South American city, but it has a dark history of being at the epicenter of military coups and too often the hotbed of revolutionaries. One needs only to be reminded that Che Guevara, the most feared communist ideologue rebel of the '60s, found his political roots just blocks away in its Palermo district.

German is the fourth most common language spoken in Argentina due to its large regiment of German immigrants. For a variety of economic and political reasons, German defectors, Nazis and political undesirables were welcomed after WWII by Peron's repressive regime.

At 6 o'clock on October 21, in the back storage room of a Palermo bakery, owner and proprietor Carlo Bennet, along with two of his most trusted employees, hurried to box up crates for a last minute shipment to Cordoba. Distracted by the unexpected rush, they were unaware of the two trucks that slid to a stop at the bakery's front entrance. A team of heavily armed men breached the bakery's front door then swiftly moved to the rear. When the assailants came face-to-face with the men, one of the intruders shouted, "Keep calm. Do not move! Which of you is

Carlo Bennet?"

Although taken by surprised, the three bakers were prepared for such an occasion. An ensuing battle commenced. Rounds of bullets zipped through the air. An incendiary device rolled across the floor. The back door of the bakery was blown. Soon, all three employees lay dead. The assailants quickly thrashed about the bakery. Hearing sirens from the local police, they gave up the search and vanished into the city's busy streets.

Seven thousand miles away, around 1 in the morning, the dream returned. This time, the now familiar man smiled while showing a picture, and a lady with a tender voice cajoled me on, then abruptly stopped. The sounds of bullets and her screams were deafening. A man attempted to resist. I could see the blood ooze from his wounds… I woke screaming, my face contorted, my head drained of oxygen. I tried getting up but fell back when the room began to spin. I kept telling myself it was only a dream. Helen, hearing the commotion I'd caused with my desperate cry, came into my room to comfort me.

"Another dream? My god, Lina, this must come to an end. You can't take much more, and I'm turning into a wreck. Now, some coffee?"

"Yes, Helen, coffee. Let me shower while you get it going."

A few minutes later we both sat at the kitchen table talking, hoping these moments together would soften the blow of the dream and the truth we had discovered. Finally, when worn down, we went back to bed.

At 6 a.m., the phone rang. I hesitated to pick up such an early call. From my bedside, I held my hand hovering above the phone, evaluating whether I was still in a dream. Now, suddenly alert, I knew what it was about, before I answered. I lifted the receiver to my ear.

"Lina, it's Thomas." His message was short and quick.

"Something has happened…need to talk. Meet me in the Marktplatz at 7."

It took a moment to process. "No, Thomas, please make it 8."

"Okay, 8 then, but be there, Lina."

Immediately, I became aware that I had been forewarned. By the dream? Yes, I had this escalating feeling that something terrible had happened. I woke up Helen.

"Something's gone wrong!" After I said it out loud, it hit me. "Pieter? No, not Pieter! What happens if it's Pieter? What would I do then?"

"Lina, you don't know yet. Don't speculate. Call him right now…make sure."

I ran to the phone and rang him…no answer. I called his work—the same, no answer. Keeping my breath in tempo with my thoughts, I decided to do what I probably should have sooner.

"Helen, let's pray together." Kneeling, I prayed, "God, forgive us. Please don't take Pieter away. Keep him safe. Lord, there have been so many casualties from all this. Please give us a discerning heart and wisdom to do Your will."

Helen called her work, telling them she would not make it in until later. Wearing sweaters and coats, we rode together to the Marktplatz. It was a cold day, and clouds covered the sky, leaving only a speck of light showing. From time to time, the sun did peek through to show us it was day. After a short wait, Thomas finally came in view as he walked briskly toward us. When he came closer I asked, "Is it Pieter?"

"No, I don't know about Pieter, Lina."

"Thank, God," I prayed.

"But, bad news out of Argentina. Last night someone broke into Carlo Bennet's bakery and shot up the place. Our surveillance team believes him to be our man, Dietrich Ziegler. There was shooting, and Ziegler, along with his co-workers, was killed. Remember, the Argentine government has a history of being secretive and sketchy on these types of events. After the Eichmann kidnapping, they want as little news coverage as possible. So, the incident has been reported as just a robbery gone wrong."

"In a bakery? Over cakes and cookies?"

"I know, Lina. Pretty crazy, huh? There are a lot of things going on over there that the intelligence community wants to keep out of the public eye, for one reason or another."

Just then Pieter jogged toward us.

"Where have you been, Pieter?" I cried. "We've been so worried about you!"

Pieter looked at us, surprised. "Me, really?"

"Yes!" Helen and I said in unison.

"Really now, it's about time someone worried about me. I got word of the shooting from an associate news agency. I tried to get the story, but they're not really saying much. It's a hush-hush thing."

Thomas piped in. "Yeah, we've been getting the same treatment. It seems like a Mossad operation, if I had to guess, or possibly the Israeli clandestine faction Nokmim. In Hebrew it means 'avengers.' They deal out their own style of justice, like vigilantes, if you want to call them that.

"So this seems to have sealed the fate of Dietrich Ziegler, aka Carlo Bennet. Obviously there must have been something valuable there in the bakery he was trying to defend. The problem is, it leaves us with just you. Yes, Lina, now you are the key to all of this. And, I might add, the center of attention, at least in the barracks' investigation. So, the colonel's first thought was to pull you in and put the screws to you, find out what you and

Pieter know. But, I argued that that wouldn't work. And, when he asked why, I told him that all Pieter had to do was publish an article and take the whole affair public. And, that can be a very touchy situation. Nobody wants to go there.

"The colonel signed on to my reasoning, but he told me I've got 24 hours to come up with a better idea or I'll be shipped back to the states and buried in some paper copying job for the duration of my service. Now, going home is not a bad thought, mind you. But, I kind of like you people, and I'd like to see this through. Look at it at this way, Lina, if you or Pieter can't give me something to go back to the colonel with, it's over! No Rufina. No answers. No publication for Pieter. All for naught, zilch, zero. That would be an absolute waste. We are close, so close. So, please give me something! Anything. Something to give us more time."

We sat there in silence, each looking at the other, now huddled together trying to cook up a response. What would it be? Where to make our next move? To quit now was unacceptable. Thomas was right. We were really close. They needed us. The problem was, we needed them, and we needed our secrets, too. I looked at Pieter for his approval. Then I broke the silence, going rogue as I said, "Thomas, Pieter and I do have some information that, as you've suspected, we've been keeping from you."

"There's a back channel?"

"Yes, but make sure you tell the colonel no more giving away our sources and activity to other intelligence networks. We will do that when and if the time comes. We need to be speaking the same language here and need a secure arrangement with only him." I raised my finger and got up in Thomas' face. "First, you must tell him I need passage to Argentina now, today not tomorrow. Now, ASAP! I need to see the crime scene, the bakery.

"Why, what are you looking for?"

"If I told you, I would be keeping the cat out of the bag."

For the first time this morning, Thomas smiled, lightening the mood. "No, Lina. It's *letting* the cat out of the bag."

"That is what I meant," I said seriously, but, after realizing the humor, we all began to laugh.

Thomas suggested, "How about letting the toothpaste out of the container?"

"Yes, that too," I said holding back a smile.

"Okay, we are all in agreement then. But you can't give me any more information to pass on?"

"We can't, Thomas, at least not for now. And, you must make the colonel believe we have something that could potentially break this thing wide open. Pieter will stay behind and get his article ready. He knows what I know, so, if anything goes wrong in Argentina, he will get it in print. You realize national syndicates are begging for this story? He will give it to them, win the Pulitzer or whatever, while the spooks and bad guys run for cover. I don't think the colonel wants that. I'll recognize what I'm after when I see it, then hand it over, concurrent with Pieter's publication. So, if the colonel can work with those conditions, we'll have a chance. No guarantees, of course, but that's what we propose. If not, we'll work it out on our own."

Thomas turned his head back and forth then rubbed his neck as if to shake out a kink. "Okay, okay, I'll try. I'll approach the colonel with your proposal."

"Oh, and one more thing. Helen…"

"Helen?"

"Yes, Helen will be our contact, nothing more than just a contact, a messenger and that's all. And, remember, she needs you to continue her protection detail, every minute." I smiled at Helen. "No more men. At least for a week or two.

"Then that's it. Everybody approve?" I asked, while looking at Pieter. He nodded, then we all looked to Thomas. "Okay, let's all go take care of business. "Oh, and, Thomas, I need an answer by the end of the day."

"By today?"

"Don't forget, this will be good for you, too. Didn't you say the colonel gave you only 24 hours or you're shipped out, right? So hurry. I'll be packing my bags as soon as I leave here."

Once Thomas was out of sight, Pieter turned to me. "Good, Lina, but what do you have in mind?"

"In the last letter from Sonnenschein, he wrote that no matter what happens, come to me, plus there is El François, whatever that means. He said there would be something for me. I know it's little to go on, but... there is also something else I haven't told you."

Helen pulled at my arm. "No, Lina, please don't."

Pieter looked at Helen as she stared down at the ground. I took hold of her hand and said, "Pieter, we'll let you know when the time comes. It is not important to the Rufina. It's about something else."

"All right, Lina, but..." Pieter nodded for me to step away from Helen, then whispered. "Helen, Lina? I thought you wanted to keep her out of this. So, how do I know I can trust you, when you hold something from me?"

"Pieter, it's something new. It is another issue. It concerns only Helen and me. Please don't ask now. When I can answer, you will be the first to know. Trust me, Pieter, on this." I gave him my most seductive smile. "Plus, remember the shower, Pieter? Only you have seen that side of me."

He returned my smile. "You've got me there, Lina. Okay, I'll trust you with your precious secret, only if you promise to be very careful. I wouldn't want to miss out on that happening again, someday."

"Nor me, Pieter." We hugged tightly, then he left. "Helen, let's go home. I need you to help me pack."

"Are you sure about this trip, Lina?"

"What else can we do? It's you and me who hold the secret. They have no other leads. Helen, please tell me you will not give this away to anyone. If they ask, just flirt you're way out of it."

"Reverend Mother?"

"Yes, Helen, go see her. I'm sure she must have heard about our mysterious sponsor. I can't see Father Tobias holding to his vows with her. They are just too good of friends to keep something that important from each other. But tell her I will spend some quality time with her upon my return, at least a couple of days. That will make her happy. But, don't let her pry on you, Helen. I know it will be hard." I laughed.

"I know she will, Lina."

"Yes, she will try, in her own special way. But, be strong, Helen. Don't let her in on everything."

Back at the apartment, the packing began. Helen brought out a few of her dresses and offered to loan them to me.

I picked one out and held it up. "Helen, I've seen this on you. It's all cleavage. You see, you can do that. It's your style. Look how much you have to show. Me, not so much, and what for anyway?"

"Because, I've read Buenos Aires has an exciting nightlife."

"No, Helen, it's just business, all business."

"Well, take this dress just in case."

The phone rang. "Get it for me, Helen."

I heard her say, "Yes, she's here." Then, "Lina, it's Thomas."

I took the phone. He spoke quickly. "Time to get packing. Everything will be as you asked."

"I'm just about finished."

"Pretty confident aren't you?"

"No, I just knew he had little to go on except me."

"By the way, I'll be traveling with you."

"What?"

"Yes, colonel's orders. We'll be traveling by commercial airline. We need to stay under the radar. Our visas indicate we're wholesale food distributors. In fact, the Argentina Department of Commerce is in the process of setting up two business contacts for us to meet. They are trying to get you into the crime scene. We leave tomorrow. Military intel is still working on the details. Call you early tomorrow morning. Get some sleep. It will be a long flight. Bye for now."

"All set?" Helen asked.

"Apparently so," I answered, a little surprised Thomas didn't wait for me to say anything more.

Helen scampered around suggesting this and that, then returned to what was on both our minds. "Lina, any thoughts about our sponsor?"

"I'm not sure, maybe a relative or a friend of a friend, but we know he was a Nazi."

"That's what is so disturbing. How could that be?"

"Helen, whatever they did, we had no part in it."

"But, the money?"

"We had no idea, Helen. It was not under our control. We are simply abbey girls, orphans of the war. The only family we have ever known is the abbey, the Jesuit Church and the university. That will do for me. I hope it will for you.

"Though, we do need answers. Not just for you and me, Helen. But, behind all this, there is something very sinister going on, and I hope and pray going to Argentina will clear it up."

CHAPTER 27

# The Men of Argentina

The flight itinerary had us traveling Lufthansa Airlines out of Frankfurt. After flying an hour and 40 minutes, we'd arrive at England's Heathrow Airport, have a short layover, then back in the air for a 13-hour flight across the Atlantic to our final destination, Buenos Aires, Argentina.

Helen and Pieter drove with me to Frankfurt, where Thomas and I would meet up to make the trip together. Helen fell asleep in the back while Pieter and I went over our talking points— what to say and what not to, what to infer and what not. This was going to be a big cat–and–mouse thing, because, as Pieter said on the way, "Little to go on now. Just some letters from Sonnenschein posted from Berlin, and his plea for you to come to Buenos Aires. We can't get any more mileage out of this, or any additional readers, unless we can come up with something more to go on. So, pay attention to the small details. As much as I want to continue with the investigation, I still wonder if this is such a good idea. It's too risky. You know it's not Germany over there. You can't just pick up the phone and call for help."

"Pieter, what else is there to do? Quit now, after all this? You said when we started that we were going to see it through to the conclusion—find the Rufina and work things out. No, we have to finish this one way or another. After that, we can close the book and move on. And, if it means flying over there to no man's land, then that's what I have to do. Remember, whatever happens, it's not your fault…entirely."

He lightened up and joked, "What do you mean, not entirely?"

"Let's see, Pieter, I guess it's because you kind of strung me along."

"Along with what?"

"Well, you have this way of encouraging people, especially girls."

He gave out a slice of a smile. "I'll grant you that, Lina. But in this case, it's you who has done the encouraging."

"Oh really?"

"Yes. Example A: the shower. What was that all about?"

"That, Pieter, was my way of demonstrating that I could be just as desirable as those other ladies you give your attention to."

Pieter laughed. "What's that got to do with anything? I know you're bringing this up just to distract me. This line of conversation is getting us nowhere. My point is, Lina, just make it back—even if you don't come back with a good story."

"How about let's just say I'll be back with not only a good story but also the Rufina. When that happens, I'm sure my nights can be filled with different dreams."

When we arrived at the airport, Thomas stood waiting at the curb. Two other cars pulled up, one in front, the other behind. About five men stepped out, then walked over to Thomas. A few minutes later, Thomas came to open my door.

"Okay, everything is set," he said. "Pieter, you know the schedule. We should be back in four days. Don't expect any contact from us. Private communication can be hacked. So, there you go."

"I understand," Pieter said, leaning over to help me out of the car. He kissed me gently on the cheek and said, "Be careful, Lina."

Helen hugged me then grasped my hand with concern.

"Don't worry," I assured her. "I'll be okay. I'll see you in four days. Now go along and distract those security details." I smiled.

Thomas and I teamed up after they drove away. Once aboard, we were led into first class, where Thomas offered me his window seat. I was happy to take it since this was my first flight, and, quite frankly, I was a wreck. My stomach fluttered about. I've never understood how something as big as an airplane could get off the ground. Getting there in one piece was definitely pressing on my mind. Although, once we got into the air, with Thomas at my side, I quickly fell to sleep.

Later, when his hand squeezed mine, I felt comforted. "Lina, we have a layover in Heathrow, so let's get out and stretch our legs."

When we reached the terminal, I set straight for the restroom. That's when I realized the severity of the trip. Seemingly out of nowhere, two men came up to Thomas and, with serious faces, said something. He smiled at me, as if to say, "It's okay" and waved me on. Then he went into the men's room, as they followed me to the ladies' room door. After I refreshed myself, I came out and Thomas was there to meet me.

"What's this all about?"

"The two guys?"

"Yes."

"They are SIS, British intelligence. Everyone wants to keep you safe, Lina. Get used to it. That's the way it's going to be on this trip, and, believe me, I've never seen security so tight, especially for a girl from Heidelberg." He smiled.

We boarded for the long flight across the Atlantic and took off with just a few minor bumps and tremors. The pilot went on the intercom to say a few words of encouragement—at least they were encouraging to me.

"In 13 hours, we will be arriving in the beautiful country of Argentina. The weather looks good. Please allow your flight attendants to take care of your needs. The seatbelt sign will go off shortly." But then he added, "Please pay special attention to the emergency procedures our stewardess will demonstrate."

"What kind of emergency?" I asked Thomas.

He laughed. "Is this your first time, Lina?"

"Yeah, you didn't notice?"

"Okay, remember when you were in class at school and they said if the earth shakes get under your desk?"

"No, not really. Not many earthquakes in Germany. But I do remember fire drills, if that helps."

He laughed again. "Well, it's a little like that. They want to make sure you know what to do if we lose altitude or something, just as a precaution."

"For some reason, that doesn't make me feel better, Thomas."

"No need to worry. I'm here, so…"

"Do you know how to fly the plane?"

"Probably, if I needed to," he said confidently.

I slipped back into a restless sleep. Later, when I opened my eyes, Thomas was reading what looked like a report of some kind. I stole a glimpse.

"Finally awake, huh? Enjoy reading my reports?" he teased.

"Yes, trying to."

"Here, take a look," he said, handing over a few pages.

"That's the crime scene?"

"Yeah, at the bakery. It's the layout where the actual shooting took place. Also, some photos from inside and outside, the position of the bodies and type of weapons, plus possible scenarios on how the crime went down. Be careful with your stomach. The next two pages are photos of the deceased. Don't want you to drop your breakfast, at least not up here next to me."

While I looked over the documents he explained, "After the Eichmann kidnapping by the Mossad in 1960, the international press has followed Peron's open immigration policies with a little more scrutiny. Just look at this list of Nazis and collaborators who relocated to Argentina.

"You see, Lina, when we're dealing with matters that relate to the Nazis, it becomes a very sensitive topic in Argentina. They've got a lot to hide. Their PR strategy is a pretentious, blind-eye approach, letting the conflicting parties work out their own problems. If we want to continue to be allowed in, don't, in any way, embarrass the Argentine government. That's why we're flying commercial and not as official representatives of any government. We are simply business people looking to buy foodstuff to export to Germany. I know it all sounds a little foolish, because somebody will always be following us. But, remember why we're here. The colonel says it's because Dietrich Ziegler, aka Carlo Bennet, one of Hitler's art dealers has been terminated. And, he was our best lead." Thomas changed his voice as if to mimic the colonel, "And, unless Lina Ritter from the abbey, background unknown, lets us in on what she is not letting us in on, we are at a dead end.

"We intel people, prompted along by the CIA, which by the way forwarded the $5,000 to your bank informant, thank you very much. We all think you're holding some kind of ace card, a secret." Now pointing to the photo of the dead man on the floor, Thomas continued. "This situation here was possibly a preemptive strike by Mossad, a botched kidnapping attempt. It seems the demise of Carlo is of little importance. What he was doing is what's important. It's the billion dollars worth of art that he may have been dealing out the back of his quaint little bakery. We have reason to believe he was in a hurry to move his inventory when he resisted the extraction. He's dead, and you're alive. So, we've worked out a back room agreement that allows us to slip in and get a look at the crime scene."

"What about the house in Palermo, where he lived?"

"We're working on that—no guarantees. But, again, don't forget there is no secrecy about this trip. We're all playing the game. They know you're coming and that you're a key player in all this. Everybody's focusing on you. So, stay close to me. Don't talk off-script. I suspect all of our conversations, phone calls, any communication will be listened to. This has the potential of becoming an international disaster, so please don't go on with any of your dabbling attorney questions. Just observe and take mental notes. Wait to make your comments when we're safely back on the plane and in the air, not before. Now, do you understand all that, Lina?"

Amused by his overly dramatic tone, I said, "Wow, Thomas, I've never seen this side of you. You've never reacted this way toward me. Is this how you treat your subordinates and others with lower rank?"

"No. I'm just worried. Lina, you know this is a first for me too. If I fail to do this right…I don't care about rank. I care about you. Well, maybe a little about rank." He smiled.

I smiled back, knowing what he meant. "Thanks," I said, then leaned over to kiss his cheek. "It seems I'm always kissing cheeks," I added with another smile.

"That's not my fault, now is it, Lina? When we fly back let's have that talk again. Okay?"

After a soft landing, we grabbed our luggage, squeezed by the slower passengers and made it into the terminal. It was in a festive state as music boomed from a live band. People loaded into taxis, busses and private cars then went on their way. Three men met us. Two of them sported large black mustaches and one, a little younger, was obviously trying to grow one. They were dressed neatly in suits and ties and seemed out of place in the balmy, overcast weather. They took our luggage and rushed us into a waiting black limousine.

We were off to fight the chaotic afternoon traffic. After reaching an upscale hotel, we passed through the lobby and were escorted directly to the elevator. When it opened at the top floor, a group of military guards stood at attention. They led us down the hall to a large door that unlocked to reveal a beautiful suite. Another military man warmly greeted and motioned us in. He dressed as if ready to march in a parade, flaunting a barrage of medals on his uniform. Most importantly, he spoke fluent English, introducing himself as Major Durango.

"I will be your guide," said the major. "Let me show you the room."

The suite was actually two connecting rooms with a large living space in between. He explained it would be appropriate, giving some privacy for a conference, if necessary. I looked at Thomas, and he nodded in agreement.

"Thank you. This will do," I said politely.

The major added, "Now please rest, order some food. For your pleasure I've requested the hotel supply you with a bottle of Argentina's finest wine, so enjoy. In the morning, there will be a car ready for you out front. It will take you to where you want to go."

"Thank you," Thomas said as he closed the door. Left alone, we walked around the suite, then out onto the balcony. It gave a spectacular view of the metropolitan skyline and the ocean. I almost lost myself in its beauty, forgetting for a moment what we were here for.

"So this is what's waiting for all of those criminals, this is their reward and final resting place," I thought. "What a pleasant ending for such unpleasant deeds."

Sometimes you come into a country with preconceived ideas about the place. I did that with Argentina, and it would forever taint the way I saw it. All these pleasantries were just a disguise for the depravity of what really went on here.

After the long day, we found our separate rooms and easily fell to sleep.

CHAPTER 28
# Crime Scene

T he next morning came early. The major took the liberty of sending breakfast up to our room at 6 a.m. I'm sure it was more of an act of persistence rather than hospitality on his part. His job was to keep us moving, like dogs chasing their tales. When exhausted, we would be on our way home. No harm, no foul. After engulfing eggs, sausage and hash browns, along with an assortment of fresh fruit, we moved to the balcony hoping to leisurely finish our coffee and unwind.

Abruptly interrupted by a knock on the door, Thomas went to see who it could be. The peephole revealed who it was, and, when Thomas opened the door, the major announced in an overly cheerful voice, "Good morning. Are we ready for this?"

"Yes, we are," Thomas said, then called out to the balcony, "Lina, get your stuff. It's time to go."

Out of habit, I rushed in to grab a light sweater, even though the forecast indicated it would be warm.

"Oh, good idea, Frau. It will break the morning chill, and it cools down considerably in the late afternoon," the major said as he herded us toward the door.

Off we went, racing around town for about a half hour. Eventually, we arrived at a storefront at the end of a long back street in a discount business area.

"So where exactly are we?" I asked.

"About a few miles from the Buenos Aires retail outlet

district," the Major explained.

The driver found a parking space and, as if rehearsed, two additional unmarked cars pulled up alongside us. The major pointed, then the other cars sped off around the block, I assumed probably to cover the back.

Walking toward the store I glanced up to see a faded but neatly printed sign. There it was, just as reported, Carlo's Bakery.

The major motioned for a guard to open the front door and, as he held up the yellow police tape, we ducked under to enter. The hectic scene inside took me off guard. All sorts of people were doing this and that. Cameras flashed, and evidence samples lined the counter—an obvious attempt at recovering forensics. Since the incident happened a few days before and was advertized simply as a robbery gone wrong, all this activity looked suspicious, to say the least.

Distracted with a separate conversation, the major failed to take notice when Thomas and I walked toward the stairs. A policeman quickly stopped us. "Frau, I am Inspector Paredes. Please let me show you around. You see, we must not disturb the crime scene."

"What do you believe were the intentions of the assailants?" I asked while Thomas shot me an annoyed look, as if to say, "No, Lina." But, I persisted. "What do you believe was going on here, inspector?"

Happy to be asked his opinion he answered, "Oh, I think it was just another botched robbery. The owner had a weapon, and the unsuspecting robber ran into an unwilling baker."

"So, let me get this straight, inspector, what exactly were they trying to rob? The irresistible cookies and cakes displayed in the front window?"

"No, no, Fraulein. It must have been the money."

"Well then, inspector, how many marks or whatever you call

them do you suspect were in this baker's cash register?"

"Pesos, Frau. We call them pesos here in Argentina."

"Pesos then, inspector. How many pesos would have been here at the bakery?"

Becoming impatient, he condescendingly gave me a long, hard look and said dryly, "I do not know how much was taken, but I do know around 1,000 pesos are still in the cash drawer. I am not certain how much that is in German deutsche marks, but, in American dollars, somewhere around 80."

I felt Thomas squeeze my arm tightly, yet I went on. "Did the baker have a safe on the premises?"

"We don't…as yet we have not found one, Frau."

"Now, the body of the owner was found where?" I asked.

"Carlo Bennet was found in his upstairs office, and the workers in the back. One in the storage room, the other in the very back of the store."

"May I see those locations?"

"Of course, Frau." He turned sharply to take the lead.

Even though I was aware of the large population of German expatriates here in Argentina, I was annoyed at how he kept ending his sentences. All the Frau this and Frau that was a little out of the ordinary and far too patronizing.

"Which one first?" the inspector asked.

"The back storage room, please."

"As you wish, Frau," he said, then led us back to a small room with several heavy bolts on its door. Boxes of baking supplies and bags of flour were stacked along the exterior walls. I walked into the center of the empty room to get a feel for the place.

"What do you think was in here?" I asked.

"We think it must have stored some kind of chemicals for baking."

"A safe maybe?"

"Who knows. It was empty when we got here."

Seeing vents at the top and two on the side walls, I asked, "Inspector, what do you think those are for? Is there an air conditioning unit here?"

"Yes, I think so. Why do you ask?"

"Maybe to keep things cool in this room, or maybe to keep the humidity stable to protect something valuable from deteriorating?"

"Like what, Frau?"

"Oh, like possibly paintings?"

Clearly agitated he answered, "No, Frau. There were no paintings here. He was a baker, not a painter."

I tried to dodge the obvious inference by adding, "We had one installed in the abbey office just recently. It must feel good in here, especially with this hot and humid weather."

With a confused look he said, "Yes, Frau, I'm sure it does."

"Okay, let's go see where they found the body of Carlo Bennet," Thomas suggested with another distraught and agitated look directed at me.

We climbed one flight of stairs and entered the impressive room. It reminded me of an attorney's office with built-in mahogany bookshelves and a grand roll down desk. A large glass display cabinet sat in the back with more than enough comfortable chairs for a baker and a few employees. While roaming around the room, I attempted to open a desk drawer, but the inspector quickly stepped in.

"No, Frau. Nothing to see in there. Again, I must remind you this is still a crime scene—prints, you know."

"It appears this room has not been in use for quite a while. Where did the baker keep his records?" I asked.

"I suppose downstairs in the side room next to the front counter."

"Where was the body found in here?"

"Behind the desk. Let me show you the bullet marks," the inspector said eagerly as he pulled out his pencil and poked it in and out of several holes in the wall and desk.

"The body ended up on the ground next to the chair?"

"Yes, shot twice in the head."

"None on the body?" I asked, knowing we already had the crime scene photos and preliminary details.

Thomas interrupted with impatience and frustration in his voice, "Let's go back downstairs."

Admittedly, I was glad to leave. The smell of death and blood saturated the room.

Stepping down the stairs, I asked, "What kind of weapons did they use?"

"We think they were 45m handguns along with some kind of automatic weapons, but ballistics has not confirmed that yet. Is there anything else I can help you with before you leave?"

"Yes, there is one more question. Was the back storage door actually blown by an explosive device?"

"That is what we have determined."

"Wow, these common ordinary thieves took extraordinary measures. Wouldn't you agree, inspector?" His silence revealed his impulse to leave my question just that, a question. "I guess it is as you say, inspector, 'nothing here.' Well, thank you for your time."

We were met by the major outside on the street. "So, Frau, what do you think?" he asked.

"As you've stated, just a robbery. I've read about this many times back home—not as many weapons and explosives, but this is Argentina. Right?"

He laughed somewhat nervously at my attempted humor.

The major turned to an obviously relieved Thomas and

asked, "Is there anything else on your agenda?"

I answered, "Yes, one other thing. We would like to see the residence."

"What residence?"

"The baker's home in Palermo, please."

"Why is that, Frau?"

"We just want to put all our speculations about this baker to rest. I assure you, major, that will be it. We'll be finished here after that."

"Oh, very good, Frau. But let me make a call. It will take just a minute." While he walked toward his car, Thomas and I waited quietly in the warm afternoon sun. When he returned he announced, "Okay, my superior gave his approval but suggested since it's more than an hour's ride from here we should wait until tomorrow morning. I will take you back to your hotel. You can have a nice early dinner and then see the sights that Buenos Aires has to offer. "

"No, that does not work for us. You see, Mr. Werner and I have other important business we need to take care of with your embassy tomorrow. Let's get this out of the way so we can cross it off our list of things we need to do during our short stay. May we go now?"

Seeing my position wasn't going to be compromised, he took out a handkerchief to pat down the sweat from his brow then said, "First let me make another call, Frau. Then, we will see." Again he walked back to his car. A few more minutes passed then he returned, saying, "It is all right to go today."

"Now?"

"Yes, now, Fraulein. Shall we go?"

We slid into the hot car and drove on to the baker's residence. While sitting in traffic, the major asked, "Did you come up with any different ideas about the incident than we have, Frau?"

"No. Your people have it right."

The major pried for more assurance, but I held to my story. I looked over at Thomas, who looked pleased with me for a change, so I doubled down with my response. "No, nothing, poor baker. It happens in Germany as well. Someone into drugs or whatever robs an unfortunate store owner with only enough money in his register to pay the rent."

"Yes," the major agreed. "Argentina is like so many other countries in that regard—crimes for no reason. But, I can assure you Buenos Aries is a beautiful place to visit. You must see some of the magnificent resorts here. You would be amazed."

After a little less than an hour, we arrived in Palermo. While entering an upscale residential neighborhood, the major chatted like a tour guide sharing the long history of the Palermo, Chico and Barrio Parque regions. Large homes mixed with the newly constructed luxury condominiums that dotted the wide streets. As we continued, the streets narrowed, and the houses began to lose their luster, appearing spent out over the years, even though some had retained a certain curb appeal with a more sedate and traditional look. We finally slowed to a stop in the middle of the street. Now reading from a slip of paper, he told the driver to pull over. "I think this is it."

Unlike the crime scene, there was no apparent surveillance. I sensed the local authorities had no particular interest in this location or the foresight to think we would want to visit the home of Carlo the baker.

I noticed a well-manicured front yard as we walked up the front porch steps. Apparently notified of our imminent arrival, a middle-aged Latina lady opened the door before the major even knocked. Her uniform gave us a clue that she was some kind of domestic help. Without introductions, she led us into the front room. The first thing that caught my attention was the absence of furniture or personal belongings. I asked the lady, "So what was he doing? It looks so bare in here."

"I really don't know. I was called in yesterday to clean the home."

"You didn't know Senor Bennet?"

"Sorry, senorita. I am just a housekeeper."

"Who pays you then?"

"The real estate agency."

"So, the house has been up for sale?"

"Yes, I think…actually I don't know for sure."

Thomas disappeared up the stairs while the major kept a keen eye on me. "What is upstairs?"

"Two bedrooms, a bath and a small study," she answered eagerly.

There really wasn't much to see, but, remembering what Pieter said about gathering details, I continued to explore, looking for something, anything left behind. But, what? What could possibly be left in this practically empty house? He must have been on the move. I hoped that, even in his haste, there might be some clue left behind. I looked at the walls thinking this accomplished art dealer, who actually traded with Hitler himself, had to leave some sort of message behind. However, certainly not on any of these walls. There was not a blemish or faded area to divulge the past. I walked up the stairs as Thomas came down. He shook his head as if to say, "Don't bother, nothing there." But, I had to see for myself.

At the top of the stairs, I went into the bedroom. Not even drawers were available to search, just a few parcels of packing paper and travel brochures. The bathroom was next, and I began to pry open a drawer under the sink. A dead bug would have excited me by now. As I did, the vigilant major made his move.

"No, no, Frau. We must not be opening things. Forensics has

not worked this location yet."

I moved passed him to the study. Same here—nothing except for an old desk shoved in the corner. Now that was promising, unlike the large abandoned bookshelves along the walls. The major continued to watch my every move from the hallway. Trying to mislead him, I fixed my eyes on the shelves while I covertly ran my fingers along the desk. They were my eyes and ears now. I felt an ink blotter and slid my fingers under it. As luck would have it, Thomas came back up into the hallway, distracting the major just as I felt something under the blotter.

While they talked, I pulled it out. I didn't know what it was, but I grabbed hold of it anyway. It felt like glossy photo paper. Yes, like a picture. Hoping this would make the day worthwhile, I kept my hand concealed. After seeing the major turn toward me, I pretended to trip on the corner of the desk, thrusting the paper in the side of my boot as I fell dramatically to the floor. He rushed in to help.

"Are you all right, Frau?"

"Yes, thank you. I must have tripped on the desk leg." Brushing myself off, I said, "It seems as if this baker was on the move. Nothing in here."

Thomas, hearing the calamity of my fall, walked in. His face grimaced as I continued asking questions.

"What was going on here, major?"

"We don't know for certain, Frau Ritter, but it looks as though he was probably moving the business to some other location. We believe Carlo Bennet was a well-known and respected baker who catered big weddings here in Buenos Aires. Yet, he was a simple family man."

"And what about that family?"

"Again, we are not sure. They moved, maybe a month before the robbery. Those details have yet to come out."

Impatient with my questions, Thomas interrupted, "Lina, let's get back to the hotel. There is nothing more here."

I agreed, and we walked down the stairs. I took one last look in the kitchen and glanced out the window over the sink. A play set and a sand box could be seen out on the lawn. "There were children?"

"Yes, we think so."

Clearly frustrated by now, I said, "Is this the norm? Doesn't anybody around here know anything for sure? Maybe they registered to vote or got newspapers. What about forwarding mail?"

"Frau Ritter, in Argentina we have many immigrants. It is like an open door policy. We don't ask many questions about where they come from or why they came. All we care about is if they are productive for the community. That is the Peronista's current protocol. When German immigrants come to this country, they stay to themselves. Not like in Heidelberg, hey?"

"You know I'm from Heidelberg?"

"Oh, yes. We do check on people, in special cases."

"We are done here, major," Thomas said.

While walking to the car, I noticed a lady two houses down busy pruning her colorful roses. "Just a moment," I said and walked up to chat with her. "Buenos dias Senora, we are considering buying the house over there."

"Do you mean the casa Bennet?"

"Yes, that is the one."

"But, I thought it was already sold."

"Well, yes, but it's not final, so we might get the chance to buy it. Did you know him, this Senor Bennet?"

"A little. I know he was a baker, a kind man.

"Kind?"

"Yes, sometimes he would bring home leftover pastries, and

his children would give them out to the neighbors."

"So, you knew him well?"

"No, they only lived here for a short time, so unfortunately I didn't get to know them that well. But, they seemed nice."

"How about his wife?"

"I've seen her a few times. She was an ordinary-looking woman. Nothing really that stood out."

"German?"

"Maybe, and maybe Argentine I think. She would call the kids in Spanish and smiled a lot. But, again, I never really got to know her. Other than a few conversations about the children, they just went about their business."

"How old are the children?"

"His or mine?"

"His."

"They were probably a year or two older than mine." She cut a few more branches then continued. "Let's see, the youngest maybe 9 and the oldest 13. You know, in Argentina nobody asks too many questions."

"I am beginning to hear that quite often, senora. Sorry for the interruption."

"No, no. It is quite all right. Please go on."

"In the last couple of weeks did you notice anything that looked peculiar at their house or around the neighborhood?"

The lady stopped and thought for a moment. "No, not really, They were always busy, and traffic was coming and going all..." Stopping herself, she said, "Well, yes, maybe now that I think back, there was something a little unusual...a car down the street, parked down there." She pointed. "It would sit for a while, then be gone, and another would come back later...only for a few days. I never made anything out of it at the time, though."

"Nothing more than that?"

"No, just that."

"Okay, thanks for your time."

"If we're lucky, we might be neighbors," she called out.

I smiled and waved as I walked back to the car.

As we drove away the major asked, "Did you learn anything, Frau Ritter?"

"No, not much. Carlo was a generous, quiet baker who lived there for a short time. Other than a few tips on how to keep my roses healthy, she didn't know very much. Since we have so many roses at the abbey, it was quite helpful."

Quickly changing the subject he asked, "How long are you planning to stay here in my lovely city, Frau?"

"Oh, probably just a few more days. There is some additional business we must attend to. If we get that done, maybe two more days at the most."

Back at the hotel, we proceeded on up to our suite. When we stepped off the elevator, a bellhop greeted us and let us in. Thomas went right to the wet bar.

After giving me the key, the bellhop waited awkwardly for a tip. While looking into my purse for some coins, I asked, "Do you know of any good Argentine restaurants around here?"

"Yes, senorita, I know the very best."

"And what is the name of this very best restaurant?" I smiled.

"A few blocks up the boulevard is the finest in Argentina, El François."

That got my attention, and I immediately took on my impromptu disguise, trying not to expose myself. I looked into his eyes hoping they'd tell me more. He only stared back. I asked, "Are you sure it's that good?"

"Yes, you will see. You must go there. It is important that you do."

"Gracias," I said while handing over the tip, and he was quickly gone. Before I could share my news, Thomas waved from an open closet, then put a finger to his lips and motioned me in. He whispered in my ear.

"This place is bugged, even cameras. I think the only safe place is out on the patio deck. I'll check some more out there."

After finding nothing suspicious, Thomas decided the balcony was the only secure place to talk. I'd almost forgotten about the stolen picture in my boot. But now, not knowing who or what was tracking us, I decided to find a secure place to hide it until we were in flight and on our way home. Funny how Thomas picked up that I might have found something. He sensed it and began to stare at me. I returned the stare and smiled.

"What is it, Thomas?"

"You did something, didn't you, Lina?"

"What? See what this intelligence business has done to you, Thomas. You don't trust anybody, not even me," I chided.

"I didn't say that because I don't trust you, Lina, but simply because I know you."

"No, you don't. Now, I'll be back in a second—need a nature brake. I'll bring you a glass of that wine the major left. And you, Thomas, can keep going over your fact sheets or whatever you call them."

Seeing him already flipping through his charts and papers, I rushed off the patio, ran into his adjacent room, opened the closet, stepped in and shut the door behind me. In the dark I found his coat. Yes, there it was, his passport wallet. I reached down, plucked the photo from my boot and placed it behind the plastic that held his passport photo, then slipped it back safely into his coat pocket. I wisped back out to the bar and filled two wine glasses before returning to the balcony. Continuing my deception, I sat and pretended to enjoy the view.

"What are you reading so intently, Thomas?"

"Oh, government stuff." He stopped and took a long look out over the balcony. "You know, Lina, it's so beautiful…if only we were here under different circumstances." His eyes turned back to the papers.

"And what does that mean, Thomas, 'different circumstances?'"

"Come on, Lina, you know what I mean."

"Did you mean a ring, an engagement, maybe even a wedding and commitments?"

"Well, I don't know if I would go that far." He smiled sheepishly.

"Aw yes, yes. Reverend Mother told me there would be men like you out there. I think that special Stanford education forgot to teach you there is more to this than passionate kisses, long embraces and holding hands."

He smirked. "And how do you know that, Lina? Woman's intuition?"

"Yes, I know what soldiers do a long way from home."

"Oh, really?"

"Remember, at 15 I worked at the barracks under General Mayers. He warned me about lonely soldiers."

"He did, did he?"

"Yes, and we sing American songs, and we now have American taste and know your clever expressions."

"That's what the good general taught you?"

"Yes. And after Father Tobias, he was like a second *fa..th.. er...*" With the word "father," my thoughts became blurred and my heart dropped a beat. I looked up to see if Thomas noticed.

Seeing my paralysis and hearing it in my voice, he asked with genuine concern, "What is it, Lina?"

No way would I let on to my suspicion. What if it were true?

What would I ever have to offer anyone? Who would I become and where would I go to conceal my secret? Or, was this a figment of an over-ambitious fantasy? I often had stray thoughts, so why was this one so threatening? I turned to Thomas and, in a soft voice, said, "You wouldn't understand."

Feeling guilty that maybe it was his comments that caused my distress, Thomas explained, "Lina, I was joking with you. I hope I didn't…hey, I was just trying to be smart. Forgive me? Man, I don't… it's been so long since I asked a girl to forgive me. Well, to tell the truth, I never have."

I laughed. Thomas had pulled me back from my impending precipice and fortunately would never know what drove me there. I walked over and scooted his papers to the floor, allowing room for me to sit on his lap. I leaned in and placed a kiss on his lips. His willing arms wrapped around me, and I returned his embrace. I held tightly to the moment, caressed it, lined it with love to subdue the pain and the insecurity that began to build up inside. For, in there, I was truly alone.

Eventually, I stood and breathlessly said, "Enough, Thomas. No more."

He smiled back and said, "I believe that was a start to something…"

"Not now. I am really hungry. Do you think the major will allow us to go out to a decent restaurant?"

Now happy and smiling broadly, Thomas said, "Not a problem. Yes, a night on the town will…"

"No, just a restaurant," I interrupted.

Thomas got on the hotel phone. Feeling peppy, he said, "Please send up the bellboy immediately."

Within minutes, there was a knock. After checking through the peephole, Thomas opened the door and asked, "Where in this town is a good place to eat for a beautiful hungry lady?" I overheard the boy answer, "The Golden Oxen, just a few blocks downtown."

I leaned back to see the young man, but it wasn't the same bellboy who opened the door for me earlier. I came in from the balcony and asked, "Where is the other bellboy?"

"There is no other, senorita. I'm the only one on duty on this floor tonight."

"But, I talked to another just a short while ago."

"No, senorita, you must be mistaken, just me."

Thomas chimed in, "Lina, did you hear that? The Golden Oxen is just a few blocks up the street. Oh, which direction?"

"To the right, then make a left."

"Lina, we've come more than 7,000 miles from our Red Oxen, and here we have the Golden Oxen. Must be an international franchise." He laughed.

The young man looked at me and then back to Thomas, as if we were both confused, maybe by the wine. Thomas gave the boy a handful of pesos.

"Thank you. We will give it a try."

After the door closed and the boy left, I changed the plan. "No, not the Oxen. I've heard El François is the best Argentine restaurant in the city. We must try it."

"Who said?"

"A little bird told me, and it's right around the corner."

CHAPTER 29

# Passing Secrets

Thomas and I arrived at El François, found a table and began to entertain the extensive menu. A waiter welcomed us warmly then suggested we have the house special to drink. I hesitated to make the decision and said to Thomas, "Let's wait and see what we order first."

"Senorita, you must," the waiter begged. "This is courtesy of the major."

"Okay, then. Please give me your best malted beer."

"Very good, senorita. And you, senor?"

"Whatever she's having will be fine," said Thomas, clearly evading any evidence of his take-charge military purpose for tonight. He was in a sprite mood and obviously planned to make this night out in Argentina something to remember. I think it was the kiss. Actually, I hoped it was the kiss that let his hair down.

The waiter returned with the drinks, interesting appetizers and a local English newspaper. "I thought you would enjoy, senor."

"Very good of you. Thank you," Thomas said.

We began to interpret the menu, and, when we needed suggestions, the waiter moved in, pointing to a few dishes.

"Is the chicken good?" I asked.

"No, senorita, not here in Argentina. It's the beef. Possibly a good filet or prime rib and maybe the two of you would enjoy sharing one of our famous lobster tails. They're especially delicious this time of the year."

"Yes, that sounds nice. What to do you think, Thomas?"

"Yes, that's fine for me as well."

"Potatoes or rice?"

"Potatoes and a small salad will do," I responded while closing the menu, and Thomas nodded his approval." When the waiter had all that was needed and was on his way, I started to take a sip of the dark beer as Thomas buried himself in the newspaper. But, just then the maître d' came up to our table and interrupted, "Senorita Ritter?"

"Yes, that is I."

"There is a phone call for you."

I thought, "Oh no, not the major again." Well, better by phone than here at our table.

"Senorita, would you like to take the call now or have the party call back?"

"Could you ask who is calling?"

"I am sorry, senorita. That would be inappropriate."

"Yes, I guess you're right."

"Shall I have them contact you later?"

I looked over at Thomas, still catching up on the headlines. A small voice in my mind reminded me of Sonnenschein's promise, "Come and I will have something for you." I tapped my fingers as if playing a piano on the white tablecloth while I thought of what to do. Sensing this might be it, an urgent impulse set in. "No, no. I mean yes, yes, I will take the call."

"Very well, senorita. The phone is just around the corner in the lobby. Follow me. I will take you there."

"I'll be back in a minute, Thomas."

Oblivious to what was going on, he mumbled, "Okay. No problem."

I followed the maître d' around tables then out to the lobby and found the phone in a hallway a few steps down from the restrooms. He handed the receiver over then rushed off.

"Hello," I said.

A voice asked, "Is this Frau Ritter, from Heidelberg?"

"Yes."

Immediately some type of tape was slapped over my mouth, and a bag thrust over my head. Two strong arms grabbed mine then quickly moved me down the hall to an open side door.

Another voice said urgently, "Please don't resist or speak, Frau. You are among friends but in grave danger."

Surprisingly, that eased my fear a little as I now raced to the rhythm of my assailants. I heard the sound of a car door slide open with the engine running.

"Please, in Frau. We must hurry."

Instinct told me to follow their directions. I heard the van door slam shut then the sounds of screeching tires as it accelerated.

"Frau, you must keep to the floor," someone said while pushing me down.

After a brief moment, I heard cracks that sounded like gunfire.

"They are getting too close!" another voice said frantically.

By now my ears became numb as, one after another, loud bursts erupted from inside the van.

"That should slow them down!" was shouted before a loud explosion.

The van swerved, again screeching its tires as we drove on, maybe for about 20 minutes before it all stopped. Those now familiar strong arms pulled me up, lifted me out and into another waiting car.

"Please, Frau, we are your friends," was said. I became limp and gave in to their demands. Off again we went for several more minutes until it felt as if the car was descending into an underground garage and coming to a stop. Again, I was pulled out of the car, this time gingerly. "Please, Frau, just a few minutes more."

I was led into an elevator that moved upward, stopped and, when the door opened, another voice broke the silence.

"Patience, please. Not much longer."

I was led in and could hear a door close behind me. Politely a soft voice said, "Frau, please sit down."

I did, and the head cover and tape were tenderly removed. The first figure I saw was a nicely dressed tall lady. Her long flowing gown made it seem as if she'd been interrupted from an evening at the concert hall.

"Liesel? Yes, it is you, so much like your father. I can see him in your eyes and, yes, your mother; we are all friends here."

I looked around to see a small group staring back with concern. Each introduced themselves, giving only their first names. I thought how bizarre this whole abduction had been. Up until now everything had been spoken in German.

I overheard one of the ladies ask in Spanish, "Lina?" And another said, "Yes, la misma persona, Lina, Liesel—the same."

Someone asked, "May we speak English?"

"Yes, I know it well," I responded.

A deep voice, whose importance was obviously understood by all said, "I am…well, just call me Franco. I was a good friend of Herr Ziegler. All of us are here because of him. He helped us all—and others—in many ways. A dedicated man, he spoke often of you. Many of us knew of some things, but, in time, we all understood that what had been done was terribly wrong. We paid a price—some by hiding and moving about—and always worried our day would come. Like Dietrich, they would search us out for our past actions."

I closed my eyes and thought about the film Erin showed me

in the library. Individual faces were a blur, yet the straight rows of marching Nazis with arms lifted high played across my mind. The vision was void of sound, but I could imagine perverted shouts of, "Heil Hitler" and the twisted swastika banners rising high.

The apparition was broken midstream when Franco continued, "A few days before they came after Dietrich, he told me he'd sent you the message that would keep you safe, somehow. He said you were the one—the stubborn one who would find him, and he was happy for that."

I resigned myself to go along with the scenario laid out by Franco. Did they really know who I was? Liesel, they called me. By now that name had surfaced too many times. Now was the time to think more like the investigator Pieter had trained me to be and play along. Get all the information I could. Let them talk. Let them believe what I didn't…what I couldn't allow myself to.

Finally, my voice returned. "You are Dietrich's friends?"

"Yes, yes, all of us here. We loved him.

Staggered by the outpouring of affection, I asked, "What has he been doing all of these years to earn your friendship?"

One lady stepped forward and spoke up. "He was such a wonderful family baker, wanting to help…"

"But I thought he was always the artist. An art dealer, and…"

"Oh, no. Not here. He was an artist, yes, but for the weddings and…"

"The weddings?" I asked surprised.

"Yes, weddings. He created the finest and most savory foods, but it was the cakes—so many people were married with his cakes. Each made with a special thought. Such a tender and compassionate man."

"And the family? What about the family?"

Franco spoke up, "They are gone. Dietrich knew his days were short. He knew they would find him soon and sent them away weeks ago."

"Where? Do you know where?" I pleaded.

"We do not talk on such things. There are all kinds of people in this part of the world, hiding from this, planning for that and some, like your father…"

That word *father* pierced my soul, but I dared not let on they had it all wrong. "I am Lina, from the abbey," I kept telling myself. I could believe no other story. No. We were not one and the same…impossible.

"We have business to take care of," Franco said to the others as he directed them out of the room. Even the burly assailants left. "Come with me, Liesel," Franco urged while leading me into the next room. "I have something for you."

The only light came from a flickering candle sitting atop a small table. One chair was pulled up alongside it. "Sit here. You'll be able to see much better." When I did, he reached into his coat pocket to retrieve a small tattered envelope.

"Dietrich, your father, wanted this passed on to you. He said it would keep you all safe. I gave an oath that, if anything ever happened to him, I would get it to you." Franco laid it tenderly on the table. "I'll leave you alone. Do take care that you are the only one to read it. That was his request. No one but you."

After he walked away and closed the door, I slowly picked up the letter and fingered it gingerly. But, it was not for me. Could I violate this man's dying plea? Or was all this true?

I must open it. No way could my quest be taken from me simply because of the confusion over who I was to these people. It was about the Rufina, after all—not about me. I must stay focused. It was her voice that still cried out to me in the night.

I slid a finger under the fold to break the seal. My trembling hand plucked the letter out and carefully unfolded the fragile paper. I held my breath and read.

*My Dearest Liesel,*

*I knew it would be you to find me. There is no need to go on about the past. That would be fruitless, and a waste. It was my undoing, my ambition and my greed that took me there. Now you must find uncles Ernst and Johannes, where they reside. For between them, you'll find what you are looking for. If you find the star, you might also come to heaven, which looms beyond. I pray you will. But, that will be your choice. Do as your heart tells you, Liesel. Put this in your mind. Destroy the rest. All I have left is regret and love for all of you. —Sonnenschein*

When finished, I looked into the candle flame, and it occurred to me that all this had been planned. I was the prime ingredient to some kind of ancient tribal ritual. Somehow, this whole thing was to pay tribute and pass on whatever it was to pass on. It was a memorial service. That was it. That's what I had been drawn into.

I knew what I had to do to end this. I took the letter and placed it over the candle, letting the flame catch hold until my fingers felt the searing heat. Once consumed, I ran my hand over the remaining ashes. The secret was now passed on only to me.

Lina and Liesel, the same? Dietrich and Sonnenschein, the same? And my father? How could it be?

I had unwillingly become the link to his legacy, someone to make it right, an atonement of sorts. Was that it? I had no idea what the secret was. However, I'd been entrusted with a clue.

An elderly priest entered the room along with the rest of the clan. They kneeled and, instinctively, I joined in. Together we began, "Our Father who art in heaven…." And, through the fervent prayers of his friends, I began to feel the essence of this man, Dietrich Ziegler, the baker from Argentina. When we finished, it was over.

The man who called himself Franco said, "Liesel, I hope you can see why he wanted you here. He wanted you to know it was not always bad. But now, we must get you back to the hotel before you are missed. Do not worry. We have connections here in Argentina. If you have need of a safe place, we have contacts. Let's not waste time."

I followed him out to a waiting car and after warm goodbyes, was driven away.

Some time had passed as Thomas paced the hotel suite. A loud knock on the door broke his stride. Fear crept into his demeanor, and it would be the only time I would see him frail to the circumstance. His first impulse was to not respond, hoping it would pass. But, knowing at this hour of the night the knocking would soon turn to heavy pounding, he relented and walked over to answer, taking time to run his hands through his hair in order to mess it up a bit to give the impression he'd been woken up or interrupted. After peeking through the door and confirming what he thought, he paused for a few seconds, took a deep breath, then unlatched the door.

"What brings you around at this hour, major?" Thomas asked calmly.

"We are concerned about Frau Ritter."

"Why is that?"

"She was last seen walking into the restaurant. Your waiter informed us he took your dinner order and served the complimentary drinks. After a few bites of food, she was called away and never returned." The major leaned in and took a look around. "May I come in?"

"Yes, of course, please come in."

Along with two other policemen, the major barged in and, after a quick look around, went straight into my bedroom. Seeing the bed made and undisturbed, he came out and pointed for one of the other men to check the bathroom. After he emerged shaking his head, as if to say, "She's not there," the major started in on Thomas.

"What is going on here? I thought we agreed on the conditions to this visit of yours. There were conditions!" he shouted.

"You are quite correct, major. There were conditions."

"So where is Frau Ritter?"

Now running out of space to further placate them or prolong the inevitable demands, Thomas said, "That, my dear major, is of a personal matter. Some things need not be public."

"Senor Werner, I am responsible for your protection. I must know what she is up to."

"Please allow me to relieve you of your concerns, but you must remember, this is a private matter. Will you give me a promise that this will go no further than this room?"

Looking annoyed and frustrated, the major agreed, "Okay, I will play your game."

"Darling, we must show the major you're here."

I opened Thomas' bedroom door wearing only a dress shirt, revealing enough that the major got the idea.

"Lina, the major was worried he didn't see you leave the restaurant earlier tonight," Thomas explained.

I took the cue. "I appreciate your concern, major. My stomach has not adjusted to your Argentine spices, and I rushed to the restaurant restroom to relieve myself. Embarrassed my dinner was then all over my dress, I slipped out the back, came in the side door of the hotel and up the staircase. I sent a message for Thomas to go ahead without me, and that I would be here when he returned."

The major blushed and apologized. "Sorry for the intrusion," he said, then motioned for his men to leave. He was about to close the door then turned to ask, "By the way, did you hear about all the commotion a few blocks away last night? I am told there was quite a scuffle."

We both looked at each other innocently and shook our heads.

"No? Well, good night then. See you tomorrow morning."

When the door finally shut, a wave of relief came over both of us. Thomas immediately put his finger to his lips to make sure I didn't speak. He took my arm and led me into his room, and we lay down together on his bed. Playfully he reached out for me and whispered, "That was quite a performance you gave tonight. I especially liked your wardrobe choice."

I pulled back and said, "Thomas, this is not the way it's supposed to be. But, good job with the ruse. We will be going home tomorrow."

"But our plans?" he asked.

"Make the reservations. I want to be in international air space tomorrow."

In the dark, I bumped into a chair on the way back to my bedroom.

"But…"

"No buts. This trip is over," I called back.

"Oh, it feels so good," I heard him moan dramatically in the other room, acting out for the monitoring devices.

I smiled at the thought but was too tired and drained to laugh. While falling to sleep, I held onto what I'd learned that evening. Flooded with doubts and questions about the life I had known, I came to the conclusion that who I was- was not who I am.

Had I seen it in her eyes? Did Rufina call out to me to say that if I found her I would find myself? A father? At least he knew me. Yet, I was repelled by a reluctant soul, screaming in pain at the horror of the history to which I now belonged

CHAPTER 30

# Flight Back

Thomas rushed around the hotel room opening curtains to let the bright morning sun find its way in. He loudly whispered, "Lina, up, up, up. I ordered breakfast, and it will be here soon."

I gradually rolled over and rubbed my stinging eyes. I hated the humidity here in Buenos Aries. I wasn't accustomed to it. The air conditioner only made it hard to breathe, let alone sleep, so I'd left the window open and ended up sleeping with barely anything on. During Thomas' feverish attempts to wake me, that important detail slipped my mind. When I pushed back my covers, my body came into full view.

"Oh my god, Lina. For heaven's sake, not now," Thomas laughed without embarrassment.

I quickly pulled back the sheet.

"Didn't mean for you to see that."

"But, I did. Don't worry, Lina. I won't tell anyone about your sexual advances. Besides, there's no time. We've got to get out of this place quickly, so get going!"

"What's the hurry?"

He sat down beside me on the bed and talked softly. "I contacted military intel, and they've made reservations for us to fly back on British Airways this morning. It seems that the commotion of last night's explosive car chase caused a stir, and local authorities may want to detain us for questioning. Not wanting to create an international issue out of this, the state department stepped in and ordered us out, now. So eat, pack and we're off to the airport."

"What about the major?"

"The U.S. embassy called him in. They hope to keep our anxious little friend tied up with paperwork, giving us enough time to slip away. Up. Up. Up. Let's go! And, I can't believe I'm saying this, but please, Lina, put some clothes on. We'll never get through the airport with you dressed like that."

Thomas sent the bellboy down with our luggage to a waiting cab while we took the stairs, hoping to avoid the major's fledglings. Following a mad dash through the lobby, we climbed in.

"Straight and fast to the airport, por favor!" Thomas announced. To encourage speed, Thomas handed the driver a 20 dollar bill. With that, the eager cab driver took us on a Mario Andretti ride through downtown traffic, possibly violating every rule of the road—that is if there are such things in Argentina. It seemed more like survival techniques than traffic laws.

It didn't take long to arrive at the terminal, where a sky hop swooped up our bags and rushed us to the front of the check-in line. We were about to discover that, while Argentina was not a difficult country to get into, going the other way could be a challenge. Once our luggage was thoroughly searched and on its way, we headed into the waiting room.

"Damn, we still have 20 minutes before boarding. You need to get lost in the restroom for awhile," Thomas instructed.

I took extra time refreshing myself and eventually peeked out to see him motioning me toward a nearby restaurant. At the entrance, he picked up two newspapers and handed one to me. After ordering coffee, we found a quiet corner where we could hide behind our makeshift masks. Not willing to talk freely, due to our precarious circumstance, silence became the center of our conversation. I was just about to poke a hole in our disguise when I glanced out the window.

"Don't look now, Thomas, but the major has arrived with his troops. He doesn't see us yet. He's busy talking to the British official."

"Nurse your drink, Lina. We still have about five minutes to kill."

"What can we do? He's going to stay right there and wait for us to get on the plane."

"The best defense is a good offense," Thomas said.

"Oh, great. But how will that help us now?"

"When the time comes, we will walk out of here looking confident, as if everything is under control. They will search our carry-on bags..."

"My purse? For what?"

"For anything they think we have that's related to our visit, maybe tape recorders, cameras, documents or photos."

Shaken by the thought, my voiced cracked, "And then what?"

"Oh, they might try to use them as an excuse to hold us, but I don't think so. They don't want anything to disturb the charade they've played on us here."

"But, Thomas, by rushing out like this, won't they think we have something to hide? Also, those questions about that commotion last night..."

"You're right. I'm not sure the old guy bought into our response. No, he's just looking for something to protect his ass, that's all."

When the major walked away, Thomas gulped down the last of his drink. "Time to go, Lina."

My heart beat faster, but Thomas seemed calmer than usual.

Clearly, when it came to deception, he had more experience.

"Let me do the talking this time, Lina." No polite "please" was offered or necessary to convince me. "And, no more questions. Just for once, be discreet and try not to look afraid," he added.

When the voice on the loud speaker announced our flight was now ready for boarding, we stepped into the line. Thomas kept talking, "Look natural."

"About what?"

"That's good. Just like that. Keep it up—only smile every once and awhile."

When the line shortened and caught up to the counter, so did my breath. When I handed my ticket to the attendant, he paused and looked up.

"You are Lina Ritter? And you must be Mr. Werner."

"Yes. That's us," Thomas replied with a cheery lilt in his voice.

"Okay, then, please, could you wait over there? It will only be for a few minutes," he assured.

Thomas was about to protest, but the British flight attendant added calmly, "There should be no problem, Mr. Werner. I am aware of your diplomatic papers, but I am sure you, of all people, will understand we must let the locals have their way, at least for the moment. If all is in order, this flight will not leave without you."

Thomas shrugged his shoulders and ushered me over to a seat. Moments later, the major and his cadre came over. We stood, smiled and offered to shake hands with our host.

"Senor Werner and Fraulein Ritter, you did not tell me of your plans to leave town so soon. I was under the impression you had some additional business to take care of today."

"Unfortunately, our plans have changed. I phoned my office

this morning to give a report. Since I agreed with your findings, that the baker was simply the unfortunate victim of a random robbery, my commanding officer ordered me to return to more pressing issues back at our base. So, we will let others deal with the export business between our two countries."

The major knew what Thomas meant and gave a relieved smile. "All right then, but, just protocol, may I check your luggage?"

"Of course, major."

"It is just, well, how should I say this…like you, Senor Werner, I also have a boss to answer to."

"I completely understand, major. Here is our baggage ticket."

The major gave the ticket to one of his lieutenants, who took off to make his search.

"It will only be a couple of minutes, Senor Werner. Your purse, Frau Ritter?"

"Oh sorry, yes, there are no personals inside…feel free."

He handed it over to another one of his men, who carefully searched through it, then looked at the major as if to say, "Nothing there." The major took hold and handed it back, then the same with Thomas' briefcase.

"Thank you for your cooperation, allowing this to be less of an uncomfortable situation for us all."

The other officer returned from the baggage area, and the major stepped aside to receive a whisper in his ear.

"Very good. All is in order. However, there is one last inconvenience. Please, may I see both of your passports? And then I can assure, you will be on your way home."

"Of course," Thomas answered now showing signs of relief.

The major looked at me first. So, I dug around in my purse,

pulled out my passport wallet and handed it over. To my surprise, this time he methodically began searching through it himself, looking carefully behind the passport photo and inside pockets, while Thomas kept up his chatter.

"You know major, Lina and I wished we could have stayed longer in your beautiful city. Regrettably, we were not able to persuade my boss, but we would love to make plans to come back soon to…"

"No, no, Señor Werner, do not think about it," the major kicked in, not giving Thomas a chance to finish. "You have no idea how happy you've made me, now that you are leaving. The stress I have been under. Please try and stay out of this country for a while. My life will be so much easier without your inquiries."

Finished with my passport and finding nothing, he turned to Thomas. With confidence soaring, Thomas reached into his pocket to retrieve his passport wallet. I started to gasp, but, unexpectedly, the major held up his hand to stop him.

"No need, señor. It is not necessary. We have delayed you and the airline enough this morning. I am fully satisfied. You and Frau Ritter have a good flight, and, how do they say it?" he asked, while turning to the British Airway attendant. "Cheerio, is it? Yes?"

The attendant nodded his approval.

We walked quickly though the tunnel and onto the plane.

"Wow, that was close," I said after we found our seats.

"Hey, we had nothing to hide, no worry," Thomas said happily while placing his briefcase in the overhead compartment. He took off his coat, broke his tie for comfort and rested back. Not me, I was anxious to get this plane up in the air and into international air space.

Finally, the plane pulled out of its dock and inched its way over and onto the runway. The fasten safety belt light came on, as the stewardess scampered up and down the aisle to see that all of us did just that. The plane began its run, ever so slowly at first, then picking up the needed speed for takeoff. I looked out over a wing swaying, seeming to flap like a bird. At last we flew higher. Buenos Aires started to look like a tiny toy town below.

Suddenly, the overwhelming feeling that I'd left something important came over me. A part of me was down there. I was leaving this place a different person than when I had arrived. I'd come so close. Maybe if I'd come just a week sooner, then I could have asked him, was it me or Liesel that he was so fond of? Now, I'd never know for sure. Speculation, suspicion and doubt would stagnate my peace. Yet, there still was hope. Yes, hope that maybe this was only a chapter of the story. There would be more to this. Exhausted, I fell to sleep.

Soon, an annoying tug at my sleeve interrupted my restless sleep. It was Thomas. "All right, we're over international air space. Okay, Lina, tell me. Let's have it all."

"What? What are you talking about? Have what?"

"Come on, Lina. I've got to explain away this trip. You've got to give me some crumbs to go on. I have a colonel waiting back there, and he'll be greeting me, no us, at the airport. So, cough it up. Tell me, from the beginning, what you have. I know you weren't asking all those questions for nothing. You knew what you were after. Didn't you? At least give me something, Lina."

"Okay, okay! Let's go back to when we first arrived and were taken to the crime scene."

"Keep going, keep going."

"I had the idea set in my mind that the detective was holding back. That Dietrich Ziegler, also known as Carlo Bennet, was probably in the process of moving his business. I thought his art dealing from the back of the bakery must have been discovered. It appeared one employee was immediately shot when the gunman entered the front, and the other in the crossfire while loading the caché in the back. Next, the assailants entered the upstairs office and attempted to kidnap Carlo. They of course knew his real identity. The Eichmann caper taught Dietrich he was about to be taken, but he was not about to have any of that. He would not be going anywhere. In his letters, he said they were on to him. He resisted, and vengeance was put into play. After a violent exchange, he must have run out of ammo, and a gun was put to his head. Unlike a cooperative Eichmann, he refused, and they shot him."

"Letters? What letters, Lina?"

"Need not go into that, Thomas. Leave it alone. Okay? Trust me on this, please."

"Okay, for now. Go on, Lina."

"Next, I wanted to see the storage room, to see if it had an air control system. Why? Because, after the war, many of the paintings were found in chateau cellars or dry caves for the purpose of protecting the paintings from extreme weather changes. I suspected the high humidity in Argentina was not conducive to the preservation of the art pieces. And, there was the cash register. There wasn't a lot of money in there to suggest a common robbery. It made no sense, plus there was just too much of a weapon arsenal for such a small caper. So I concluded they had two objectives. One, get Dietrich Ziegler, the Nazi, and, two, find the stolen paintings. One or the other would do. Finding both, well, that would be the icing on the cake.

"I thought he was in the process of moving his assets, moving the paintings to another location. But, since the local detectives were determined to keep it quiet, there wasn't much to go on. You and I know this was a bogus investigation from the start, with the major ordered to keep his eye on us every minute. That's why I wanted to see Dietrich's home. I knew that, if he had to leave town in a hurry, his place of residence might still have some important information. And, when we asked the major to allow us that unscheduled trip, he really got edgy after making those two calls. One to get the okay. The other to stall for an agent, aka house cleaner, to clean up any evidence left behind. Even though we surprised him with the request, the major made certain that, by the time we drove to the Palermo home, there would be nothing to find. Except, there was. I found something."

"You did? What?"

"When you came up the stairs and distracted the Major with a question, under the ink blot on the desk, I discovered what I think are two photos."

"I don't believe it. Lina, you didn't?"

"Remember when I took the spill?"

"Yes."

"While you talked to him outside the library door, I took that fall on purpose. To conceal the photos, I put them inside my boot."

"What? You took evidence from the crime scene?"

"There was no scene left at that home, Thomas, just a little of this and that."

"Lina, in America that evidence would be inadmissible in a court of law."

"Argentina is not America. There is no interest in due process or justice there. And, besides, we were looking for something— the Rufina, not justice. The others are out looking to find Nazis for retribution or to intersect spook networks for politics. No, not justice."

"Lina, why so cynical?"

"Because Pieter and I told them where to find Ziegler under

the condition he would be apprehended and we would have the chance to interview him. Didn't happen that way, now did it?"

"Okay, so where are they? And by the way, how did you expect to get the pictures out of Argentina? They checked our entire luggage. Right?"

"Right, except one," I said smugly.

"What? I don't understand?"

"Lucky for us, just as I gave my passport wallet to the major, you went on and on about how you enjoyed Argentina so much and looked forward to coming back soon. The major wanted you out of the country pronto, so his worries could be over."

"So?"

"So, he never bothered to check your documents, did he? Just me, that's who they had to watch. I was their big concern."

Thomas sat back and looked at me. "You mean…"

"Exactly."

With that, Thomas got up from his seat, reached above and pulled his suit jacket down, searched the side pocket, found his passport wallet and opened it. "Where?"

"Behind your passport photo, Thomas."

His fingers pried open the tight flap and pulled out the prize. "What if they'd found it on me?"

"What was the difference? All they would have done was confiscate anything suspicious. You said so yourself. Remember, they didn't want this incident on the public radar. And, don't forget our trump card, Pieter, holding the threat of a real splash in the media."

"Impressive, Lina. Now, let's see what we've got here. See if it was worth the risk." Both of us huddled together and pulled the photographs close. "Here's our guy, I think. And, who are the other people? Must be his family."

"Maybe."

"Look, there's something in German written on the back. But, this one is torn…can't make it all out," he said handing it over to me.

I looked closer and immediately recognized him. "Yes, Thomas. That is Dietrich."

"Are you sure?"

"He looks a little younger and is wearing spectacles, but, yes, that's him."

"What about the young girl and the boy?" Thomas asked.

"Must be his family."

"Looks like a lady's arm where it's torn."

"You can see part of her dress," I said, while turning it over to read the inscription. "Let me see, it gives the date 1943, November 12. There's some names, but it is so torn I can't make them out."

I didn't tell Thomas about how they had called me Liesel last night. No reason, yet. I looked at her little face. She seemed so happy. Could that actually be me—so young, probably one or two years old? I searched for more clues in the background, but nothing revealing there. Just tall pine trees dotted the familiar landscape. Did I actually recognize something or was I trying to convince myself I did? But the lady last night said, "Lina, Liesel, the same." I looked intently as if through a microscope to ascertain some bacteria. Was I bacteria, a germ? Was I one of them? There they were, sitting tall and proud looking back at me.

Thomas broke my focus by handing over the second photo. "Here he is in all his glory and obviously in an art gallery. Dietrich is standing back among the other officers, and the Führer's leaning over and looking like he's commenting on a piece of art. Yep, that's him in the back," Thomas said, as if he'd decoded a clue.

"Yes, I see him." But the photo flashed another image to me. Was he the one that had been taunting me for all these past weeks? A man and a gallery, was that the connection? Could I let myself believe this to be true? No, not again. I must not confuse this and let it keep me from finding her, the Rufina. That's where the connection is, the compulsion to find her. That is why he appears so familiar.

Thomas jumped in again, scrambling my thoughts. "So, you smuggled these out. What does that do for us?"

"We found him, Thomas!"

"Yes, but he's dead, Lina, dead. What do we have now? Nothing. And what about last night? Tell me what happened. What did you learn?"

"I'm not certain, but I think I was taken to a memorial for Dietrich Ziegler."

"Why?"

"Because he wanted me there. And, a few bullets were expended to make sure I was there. Somebody else wanted me somewhere else."

"Who?"

I raised my hand in the air. "Who knows? I didn't ask, and there seemed no urgency to fill me in."

"Who were they?"

"I think his closest friends. They also told me his family was safe somewhere else. But, Thomas, my theory that he was dealing looted art out of the back of his bakery was severely undermined by the many testimonies of his friends. They said he simply provided the cakes, beautiful cakes for weddings."

"Weddings?"

"Yes, cakes for the city's wealthy and powerful. Apparently, he'd left all his art dealing back in Germany. And, the lady a few doors down from his house said he was a nice family man who often brought sweet pasties to share with the neighborhood kids."

"Do you really believe that, Lina? Maybe it was just a front for other shady business?"

"Actually, Thomas, right now I don't really know what to believe."

"So, we are nowhere closer to the stolen art. Is that what you are saying, Lina?"

"No. There is more, much more. To you, Thomas, this has all been about your job. Getting the facts." He started to interrupt, but I went on. "Oh, I know you're a good person, but it's still about your job. For me, it has become a personal quest. It was the Rufina and the letters that brought me here."

"So that's all you got? That's it?"

"Thomas, if I tell everything, then what secrets do Pieter and I have to bargain with? You must tell your superiors we have a lead. But that's it—just a lead. You've got to convince them to trust us and that we still need each other."

"And that means?"

"It means that I promise you, when the time is right and when we have what we are looking for in our hands, you will be the first to know."

"Really? You mean that?"

"Yes, then you can do what you want to with it. But, for now, let us make the next move."

Thomas smiled. "You're talking like this is a game and you want to move the checkers on the board first."

"I guess you could say that." I smiled back.

"Okay, I'll let you make your play. What other choice do I have? You look tired, Lina. Try to get some rest."

"Thanks, but first tell me, Thomas. How did you know to wait back at the hotel for me last night?"

"After you left, the maître d' slipped me a note that said, 'She is with friends and safe. Return to your hotel and wait.' What else could I do but go back and wait?"

"You're going to have to make up some sensible story for the colonel."

"And what do you suggest I tell him, Lina?"

"Just that we are on to something, and to sit tight."

"And, what about the $5,000?" He smirked.

"How do they say it in Vegas? That's the price to get into the game. Win or lose, at least you're in the game. I am sure the colonel has bet on one or two horses in his day."

"Well, I wouldn't know about that, Lina. From what I've heard, the colonel is fairly straight-laced."

"Try to convince him then, Thomas. Give me a little more time."

"I'll try, Lina." Now all talked out, Thomas called the stewardess and asked for two drinks.

"What would you prefer?"

"Whatever is the strongest drink you have, please."

She quickly returned with two small bottles and cups. He poured me one, then himself. We tapped our drinks together. What for? Perhaps because a deal was set, or possibly due to the enormous relief that we'd made it out of Argentina alive.

Later, while Thomas slept and I couldn't, there was a stirring inside. I looked out the window to see the dark water below and let my thoughts drift out beyond the horizon, where, at that moment, the possibilities seemed endless.

CHAPTER 31

# Ghostly Places

I woke thrashing about my seat, sheeted in perspiration. The dream had returned, griping me with fear, letting me know it wasn't finished. Thomas revived me.

"Lina, Lina, wake up. We've landed."

Impulsively I fought back.

"It's only a dream," Thomas assured the on looking passengers. "Lina, we're in Frankfurt."

Now, with coordinates to lean on, I caught my breath and resigned myself to the pent-up emotions contained since this all began. I'd spent far too much of my personal resources keeping them in control and for, the first time, I let it show how human I was. I wanted so much to go back to the abbey, find peace and hide for a while, let the world run on its own fuel. It could do without me.

But, I knew better. It would never let me go now. Maybe by passing a few more obstacles, I could find my way through and out of this terrible maze.

Pieter and Helen greeted us at the terminal, along with a large contingent of military intelligence.

"How do you feel about a debriefing session today, Lina?"

"Please, not now, Thomas. I think that's going to have to wait."

"Tomorrow?"

"Yes, tell them tomorrow. I'll be rested and hopefully a little more reflective."

"Right, see you in the morning."

"Yes, explain to the colonel we will talk then. And tell him... oh, just tell him that." I didn't want to make the mistake of giving out anything prematurely. I needed to speak with Pieter first. Get my story, my talking points in order before I gabbed on too much.

"You'll be going with them?" Thomas asked.

"Yes. And thanks, Thomas, for coming and helping me through this."

Hearing that, Pieter began to gather my luggage.

Once inside Pieter's car, I felt comfortable to speak freely. It wasn't that I distrusted Thomas. No, it was that I knew even he would be subject to the manipulation and scrutiny of his superiors. Again, what he didn't know would only be for his own good.

Relieved to get it out, I told Helen and Pieter all of it—the crime scene sham, the visit to Ziegler's residence and the photos. They were spellbound and listened intently. Eventually, I got to the restaurant kidnapping and the frightful car chase. I told them about the gathering of Dietrich's friends at the makeshift memorial and the passing of the secret. I didn't go into detail.

Pieter interrupted, "Lina, are you okay?"

In my anxiety, I lashed out, "Pieter, don't you get it? We've got to find Ernst Ziegler. That's it! I'll get Erin on it in the morning. We need to find out where he lives. The clue is all about him and Johannes."

Back at the apartment, Pieter helped with my bags, and, before leaving, he assured, "I will get on it today, Lina."

"Yes, Pieter. Find him, and we have the answer to everything. He's the key."

With Pieter gone, I took a long hot shower. It felt better than ever. I came out refreshed. Helen sat waiting on the side of my bed. "So, Lina, what do you think? Is this man actually your relative? Are you his…"

"I don't know. All I do know is, they think I am. I couldn't even get a word in. They assumed I knew. Yes, they think I'm Dietrich's daughter."

"What?"

"Yes, Helen. The lady said, 'Lina, Liesel, the same.'"

"And the photo, that's you?"

"There's a possibility that's me sitting there with the rest of the Ziegler family."

"So, how did you feel about that?

"Helen, how can I feel? Even if I am that little girl, I didn't know them. You tell me how I should you feel when you've never known someone and now you should? Thinking our families were Nazi war criminals, wanted and hunted down…how does it make you feel? With this all going so quickly, I haven't had time to consider me in all this, and now you, Helen?"

I saw she'd been stung with the news, so I put my arm around her and held tight. "Helen, I'm sorry. Please don't be upset. I know who you are, my best and beloved friend. But before you…I don't know. I hope it will make sense soon and all of this killing and conspiring will come to an end. But, let's just pray that we both will be able to deal with the worst, if it is all true. Denial, it's still on our side for now. Later, it may not be enough. But, not knowing the truth will eat us up inside. First we must find where this Uncle Ernst lives and what secret he holds. He's our mystery guy, and, unfortunately, we now have center stage. Dietrich is dead, and everything leads back to us. And, we really don't know what they are looking for yet."

"The Rufina? Is she worth that much, Lina?"

"Apparently they are willing to go to any extreme to find her.

Yet, there's more to this, Helen, more…I can feel it. I'm going to run over to the library while you go back to work at the castle."

"Yes, it's my day to give a tour."

"I'll let you know if Erin and Pieter come up with some leads on this guy."

After throwing on some sweats, I rushed over to the university library and gave Erin a short version of the events in Argentina. She was caught up in the tale with the rest of us now. I told her to look back on her research and see if Ernst Ziegler's name had come up anywhere.

"Did you say Ernst Ziegler? Lina, I think I've seen his name before."

"Really? Good, let's both get to it. Find him." I went back into the stacks and began piecing together and plotting out the intel. Then, the obvious hit me. I need to think as Liesel, not Lina. Ernst must be Dietrich's bother! If it wasn't Adolf then there must be more Zieglers, and, if so, where can I find him? Most likely, he's gone underground, and that's going to make it almost impossible. By now, he might have succumbed to the same fate as Dietrich.

Erin excitedly interrupted my speculations. "Lina, I remembered where I saw that name."

"You did? Where?"

"In the 1943 Munich protests! His name came up on the list of the deceased."

"Dead?"

"Yeah, you're right," Erin said with excitement. "I discovered his name when I went over my notes from a week ago. Ernst Ziegler was one of the executed protesters. Now, here's the kicker. After Dietrich and Adolf Ziegler were caught grumbling about the Reich, Himmler's Gestapo shipped them off to Dachau for six weeks. But, when Hitler heard about their incarceration, he admonished Himmler and ordered them set free. As far as their brother Ernst? He didn't receive the same favorable ending. Documents indicate he was executed during the Munich protest time period. We knew that, but here comes the best part. Guess where he's buried? Ehrenfriedhof Memorial Cemetery!"

"The one just south of here?"

"Yes, the same. Here is the story behind this cemetery." Erin read, "Between 1934 and 1935, the Reichsarbeitsdienst (State Labor Service) and Heidelberg University students built the huge Thingstätte Amphitheatre north of the old part of Heidelberg for NSDAP and SS events. A few months later, the inauguration of the huge Ehrenfriedhof Memorial Cemetery completed the second and last NSDAP project in Heidelberg."

"So, that's important because…"

"Lina, this cemetery is nearby, a little south of the Konigstuhl hilltop. During WWII and after, Wehrmacht soldiers were buried there.

"But, Erin, Ernst wasn't like other Wehrmacht soldiers. The situation of his death, during the protest, kind of ruled out a heroic soldier's burial, didn't it?"

"I'm thinking, due to the popularity of the Zieglers and their cordial relationship with Hitler, they may have persuaded authorities to allow their irascible, misled, impulsive brother Ernst a quiet burial in Ehrenfriedhof. Later, death certificates were filed for two other Zieglers, Dietrich and Laura. However, there are no details about where they are buried. But, again, joint investigations by the Allies indicate a strong suspicion that those deaths were, like so many other Nazi deaths at the time, fabricated. And we now know that to be true, simply because Dietrich was killed in Argentina a few days ago. Right?"

"I get it. So, Ernst must be buried in the Ehrenfriedhof Cemetery. Good job, Erin."

"I called Pieter for you. He's already trying to locate a plot map of the cemetery from the Daily's archives. Why is the location of where he's buried important, Lina?"

"Not sure yet—just following up on a hunch. That's all. Just hoping every little piece might fit in. Why or where, we don't know yet. Erin, let's keep this to ourselves again."

"Okay, got it. Pieter said after he finds the map, he'll be on his way, and you're to stay put until he arrives. But the important question I need answered, Lina, is, Pieter or Thomas?"

"Come on, Erin! I'm not even there yet."

"Well, Lina, when you get there, please let me know which one you want. I'll be happy with whatever one you leave behind." She laughed and, under her breath on her way back up to the front said, "The little girl from the abbey…right."

Pieter came in and sat down close beside me, laying a map on the table. He whispered, "I've got the plot. It was easy."

"Really, the cemetery?"

"Yes, tonight we must go and do a little excavating. Helen needs to come as a lookout."

"Why?"

"We are the only three who know anything about the message. We need her, Lina." He laughed. "Get this, she knows the cemetery's security guard."

"No way. First the bank, now this. Talk about providence. Though, I'm not sure that what she does is divine, but who knows."

He smiled.

"I guess, if we need her…"

"Okay, then at 6 o'clock I'll come by your apartment. Oh, but there's one problem—your security detail."

"How can we get rid of him?"

"I've got an idea. I'll get my secretary to help on this one.

I'll call before I come over. Let's see if we can sneak her into your apartment. Then, let her wander around your place with the lights on. That will keep them busy thinking it's you or Helen still up there in the apartment. Tell Helen not to return home. We'll pick her up at the side door of the library to meet and go over tonight's strategy."

All went as planned. Pieter's secretary was safely walking around our brightly lit apartment. The security guy had been caught napping, literally. Pieter and I picked up Helen and, all three of us huddled together at a back table of the Ochsen.

"Need to scale the cemetery wall," Pieter said while we sipped our beers and went over the map, as if posturing for the Battle of the Bulge. He handed out three small flashlights, to be used only as a last resort. If detected, we were to abort our invasion and try again another night.

We drove past the front entrance and made our way around back. For a few moments, the moon seemed to understand our mission, giving us full light, at least enough to boost each other up and over the cemetery wall. Equipped with a military trench shovel, we traversed about 800 yards to the designated area. Getting caught and disclosing our intentions was not an option. I could see the headlines now: Reporter of The Daily News Becomes Grave Robber. Also, the intel spooks would certainly require some answers as to what we were after while disturbing the dearly departed of the Ehrenfriedhof Cemetery.

We were in flight tactic mode. If someone saw us, the plan was to evade and withdraw into the night. Yet, with several hundred if not thousands of grave markers sticking up, trying to quickly flee would be, at best, a dangerous undertaking. An eerie scent filled the air, and, since our deed be less than noble, a feeling of guilt welled up inside us as we treaded upon hallowed ground. The moon caught a passing cloud, giving cover, for the moment. After sneaking around like snakes in the grass, we finally reached the targeted section of the map. But, just then a light streamed about the cemetery. Did someone detect us? Diving down behind gravestones to shield us from a small cart driving by, we waited. Without slowing, it passed out of sight, allowing us to begin the task of reading the names of the fallen, imprinted in stone. God, how so many of them died in that dreadful war, each with their own story, but here only a name, rank and a date to validate the life they lived.

Finally, there it was. Captain Ernst A. Ziegler 1912-1944.

"What now?" Helen asked.

"Now, we dig," Pieter said.

"The note said it would be near here, Pieter. 'Between them, you'll find what you are looking for,'" I added and told Helen to stand watch while we felt around the thick grass.

Helen shuddered around whispering, "Creepy stuff, hustling around a gr…ave…yard."

With that comment she tripped and fell hard. Pieter immediately jumped to put his hand over her mouth.

"It's my ankle. I think I broke it on a grave marker," she mumbled between his dirty fingers.

Again, the moon came to our rescue, just enough to read, Johannes Ziegler 1920-1943.

"Lina, look. That's it!" Pieter pointed.

All three of us stared for a few moments, then I went over to sit on the grass between the two Ziegler headstones.

"Pieter, dig here," I said.

While he worked furiously at the dirt, I crawled back to console a whimpering Helen, whispering, "Hold on."

Finding nothing, I took over, giving Pieter a rest. Another two feet down and still nothing. I suggested we move over a few feet. Pieter's ambitious shoveling outdid his endurance. So, once again, I dug some more. Probing about, finally I hit something. Now, all of us came together scratching, tearing and propelling the turf until we could see the top of a metal container. We rushed to pull it free, then checked around to make sure there wasn't anything else. We attempted to quickly replace as much soil as possible, to hide our night's handiwork, then proceeded to make our escape. With the caché safely clutched in Pieter's arms, we scrambled back up over the perimeter wall and ran to the waiting car—not an easy task with Helen limping in pain. Off we drove, stopping only for Pieter to call my apartment. His secretary was instructed to put on one on my coats and a headscarf, walk out the front, let the security guy see her and go straight to the Ochsen to have a drink or something. She was to stay there until he called again to say the coast was clear.

Surprisingly, it all worked out. We returned up the back fire escape. When his secretary walked into the apartment, I thanked her for participating in this risky business. Pieter said, "Let me get her back home. Keep the container here for now. I'll call when I get back to my place."

"Helen, lock the doors," I said.

She did, and I hurriedly tried to open the latches on the rusted metal container. I had to work at it for a while, but finally they jerked open, and something tumbled onto the floor. What looked like a big photo album fell open at my feet.

With Helen looking over my shoulder, I knelt down and slowly turned the pages. Each contained photos of paintings with what looked like the dates of purchase and prices listed underneath, along with destinations of shipments and methods of payment. I turned more pages, some with as many as 10 paintings documented, some circled in red.

Then, there it was. The St. Rufina, and next to her was St. Justa. I put my hands to my face and cried. "This is it. We found it, Helen. We found it." I fell to the floor. "She is here. Not only the Rufina but also hundreds of other paintings. And look here, Helen one was sold to Hitler, and this one to Göring." I read on, "This one was financed through the Swiss banks, and another and another."

I flipped back to the Rufina and Justa. They were both shipped to a Paris address, but the dealer's name wasn't familiar. Possibly a subsidiary of Wildenstein? Now I understood what it was all about. Dietrich had carefully detailed Nazi art transactions. He recorded what he and his brother sold, but, even more, he speculated as to the fate of other art I had no knowledge of the importance or value of most of these paintings, but it must have been in the billions. It would take years to identify them all.

That was probably why these looted paintings flourished so easily in the underground world of art, because there are so many. Who could possibly keep track? Forgotten or little known were the original owners. I began shaking, so Helen reached out to hold on.

Tomorrow would come and, with that, the question of what to do about it all. But for now, this priceless volume of the masters lay on the floor of our little fourth-story apartment. I felt an invocation enter the room, a kindling of a collective spirit, as if the reflections of mankind, held hostage, had just been set free. This truth was now my spiritual awakening.

This album, planted by Dietrich, had been waiting for someone like me to find it and tell the world about what they did. The true treachery of the Reich and its twisted ideals would once again be exposed, plus the international complicity of their co-conspirators would come to light. Hopefully, they would not now or ever again find safe haven.

After a short phone call from Pieter, I tried to rest. With emotions consuming and swirling about my mind, I'd all but forgotten the photographs. However, hours later, I was awakened by the dream again. This time I recognized the man talking to me, and the painting that hung in the back was the very same one from his photo album, the Rufina.

Awake and alone, as the world still slept, I fumbled around the apartment searching out the precious photographs I'd secretly tucked away in the side pocket of my purse. This small, simple glossy piece of paper, the image it entailed had indicted no one else…no one but me. He talked to me in those letters. But, I didn't want to know what he was saying. Ah, there it was on the closet floor. I plucked it out. The room shed little light but from a small lamp next to the couch. I held it up to look closer, see what it was trying to tell me. Was that smiling little girl in the photo me? I didn't want it to be. I loved the girl from the abbey. Oh, just to be her again. Life was clean, uncomplicated. The shelter and protection of the abbey had made me pure. It insulated my soul.

I turned it over to the inscription, Liesel—does it fit? Is that really my name? Not Lina but Liesel? If so, then who are they to me? Who was that serious-looking boy standing next to me there in the picture? And, why was the lady torn away? Was this my family?

I looked closer. So close that I now began to believe it was true. I found peace in knowing I had a family, connection. Who they were…did it matter? Just that they were there. A father, a mother and maybe brothers. I was one of them—someone with a family. Could I deny them now? Were they somewhere out there thinking of me? I will find them someday, and it will all become clear.

By accepting this, I realized I'd created something more to go on. A new journey that was now only mine. Rufina's belonged to another. Looking again into the face of Dietrich, I started to thank him for his love but hesitated, wanting to ask whether he had paid for what he had done. "Why were your last thoughts about me?" I wondered. "Was it your final attempt to get it right? Yes, that was it. You gave me the album to help make it right."

I nestled back into the couch and felt a sense of absolution, a reprieve. My new existence, would it change me? I didn't know, but I found comfort at the thought and fell back to sleep, drifting deeply into the night, dreaming now, begging him to visit and tell me more.

CHAPTER 32

# The Grand Plan

Morning came as Helen sang in the shower over and over again. *It's my party and I'll cry if I want to…cry if I want to. You would cry too if it happened to you.*

Rubbing my sleepy eyes, I looked around the room then rushed to hide the photos that still lay on the table…too late.

"Is that you in the picture, Lina?" Helen asked while walking out of the bathroom and flipping her wet hair. "Or should I call you Liesel now?"

"Oh, Helen, I wish I knew."

"Really? You don't know by now?"

"No. Yes. Maybe. There are dots, but how they connect, I'll probably never know. Perhaps that's the way life cleanses itself. Sometimes we get a new start to be able to remember only the good and not the bad."

"What are you going to do about the album?"

"Yes, the album. First we need a place to hide it, at least until we decide where it belongs. I don't think any of the intel groups are the right parties. They will either use it for profit or for whatever serves their purpose. And, the rightful owners will just become lost in the fog of snarled schemes. I need to talk with Pieter and plan this out before releasing it to the public. Once we do, it will be too hard for the banks, investors and dealers, even the Vatican, to take cover. They'll have to respond with some kind of explanation for their complicity. Helen, you know that, all along, we've tried to keep you out of this, but it just didn't happen that way."

"I know you tried. But, Lina, we've come this far; there's no way we wouldn't finish this together."

"Always remember you are family, Helen. Now, go on your way, before you make me cry again. Stay silent on this, please."

"I will," Helen promised.

"I'll be meeting Pieter today in the Marktplatz. Come by, and we'll all talk some more."

Later, after Helen went off to work, I quickly dressed then phoned Pieter. Like so many times before during this journey, the Marktplatz meeting was set. We felt safe there, in public, thinking our conversations had little chance of intrusion.

Pieter arrived, but this time we could see increased surveillance. Some rather out-of-place individuals clicked their cameras nearby. I chuckled. "For the Stars and Stripes next edition?"

"No, they wouldn't dare. That would be like shooting themselves in the foot or somewhere worse." He smiled. "Okay, so Lina, where's the album?"

"Back at my apartment. A couple of weeks ago, after the raid, I rearranged a few floorboards. For now, it's lying comfortably alongside my journal."

"I just needed to know, in case anything happens, Lina."

"I'm thinking of taking it to the abbey. At least until we determine the best way to expose what's in it."

"So, where do we go from here, Lina?"

"You're asking me?"

"Yes, Lina, I am. What's on your mind?"

"Well, I think we need to get something published, as soon as possible. My first instinct was for you to write about the album. But, then I decided that would be too dangerous. Pieter, something more vague, like announcing we have a breakthrough about the Rufina. That the Daily has reliable information to blow the case wide open and to name the private and public holders of looted Jewish art. Then, let's see, we need to pick a public place for an announcement, somewhere that will incite a network of reporters but at the same time be a safe place for us. I'm thinking we return to where all of this started."

"The Louvre?"

"Yes, Pieter, the Louvre. It's perfect, well known for its nefarious involvement in past Nazi exploits. It's a place with international appeal that will draw them in and attract attention to our cause. Give them a date, and we'll show up, make a public presentation about our findings and explain how the whole process worked. From Hitler's murdering of Jews to the confiscation of their art treasures, linking them all...the Louvre, the Swiss banks, the Fischer degenerate art sales, dealers like Wildenstein, their clients, the international community of private investors and suspect galleries that continue to display these pieces of art."

"And, don't forget the Vatican archives and the ratlines, helping make this all possible."

"Yes, that too. Even though it may be old news, many have begun to forget. Once the meeting is set, only then will I present the newly discovered and highly valued information. Sound good so far, Pieter?"

"Keep talking, Lina. I've got my ears wide open."

"We need to publicize it. The sooner, the better. Give it a special edition, if you have to."

"Do we notify them, Thomas and military intel?"

"Of course, they are the only ones who can make all of this happen. I'll talk to Thomas and tell him we will hand over our findings immediately after the presentation at the Louvre. All while making sure the Daily News reporter, Herr Pieter Neumann, will have the exclusive right of syndication."

"So there's no need to clear any of this with them? They'll just love that."

"What other choice do they have, Pieter? Sound good?"

"I guess so."

"Pieter, you must get to work today on the story. We need to publish it tomorrow if possible."

"Tomorrow...maybe. I'll try."

"And keep this under wraps. Only a few necessary employees must see it."

"Yes, yes. I get it. But, Lina, I still have some severe reservations about this."

"Why, Pieter?"

"Because, you're not considering the fact that, when we publish, all hell's going to break loose. Don't forget there are still a lot of interested parties out there who don't want this to happen and, between the news article and the Louvre presentation, I know they will be going after you."

"Well, if we include Thomas, then I think we'll get maximum protection."

"No. That's not it, Lina."

"What do you mean?"

"Lina, I mean you personally. They are going to try and discredit you."

"No, Pieter, I don't..."

"Yes, they will, Lina! They'll start looking into the background of this mysterious girl from the abbey. They'll start there, then work backward to the dioceses and the payments from Ziegler...they'll come up with something."

"What could they possibly..."

"Lina, how do you think this will read? You're the daughter of a former Nazi who turned against Hitler at the end of the war. And, your story's fabricated, made up to protect you, your family, your father or, more importantly, to save his butt from prosecution. And, Lina, they will say Dietrich played off of both sides to save himself and his family. Yes, perhaps in the process of hiding from prosecution, he turned into this nice little old baker from Argentina. But, his ace in the hole was always the album. That gave him a bargaining chip, like the Butcher Hans Barbie or the thousands of other reinvented gentile businessmen.

"And you, Lina, Liesel, whatever, will be the one to take the blunt of all of this. Why? Because they must discount your story as desperate lies, as an ulterior motive to protect your family now that you've been discovered. And the album…it will be classified as confidential and disappear into a remote government vault or some obscure warehouse. So, get ready, Lina. It will happen."

"So, Pieter, what do you think went on here?"

"I don't know. My best guess is that you and I, we followed a generation that hoped all this had never actually happened the way some said it did. We pushed away from them, even our own fathers. The brave ones died taking orders, more than not, while others went on marching with Hitler. Even after the war was lost, they still rationalized, as we Germans do, that all the abhorrent atrocities were but collateral damage in the context of war. And, when it ended, a national endemic of amnesia overcame the German population. They assured everyone who would listen that they didn't know anything about what the Nazis had been doing. At least that's what was said publicly at Nuremberg; they were just taking orders, like good German soldiers.

"Yet, privately, they knew they'd lied to themselves, out of indifference, or for a cause, an ideal. They knew it to be a fruitless attempt at a defense. Their hearts told them too late that the end is always determined by the righteousness of the means, which defines the moral nature of the deed. Oh, there were also the willing. They would die proclaiming solidarity and allegiance by heiling Hitler before they were hung.

"The next generation, ours, hoped to expel their deeds from history—pretending it never happened, censoring the truth, rewriting the books, excluding anything harmful to our national esteem until it was only Hitler and a few others who bore responsibility and blame. But, by doing so, by believing this, we became just as insensitive, indifferent and intolerant, unwilling to address the defects in our national character. That is our failing, just as it was theirs.

"Lina, I know this must be a challenge for you, knowing the rouse it will cause, revealing the malignant possibilities of your past. But it is here that we have the chance to address and rectify some of the damages of our forefathers. Yes, a small token, no doubt, placing family treasures back into the hands of rightful owners. We can't replay nor reset the past. No, just placate it with mere bandages to keep it from bleeding just that much more. But, to do that, you will be placed in the center as a sacrificial lamb. The little Nazi girl from the abbey, someone to inflict guilt upon and be banged around by all—the punching bag. Going after you will make them feel a little better about themselves. Once we publish, I fear all that will happen. And, if you think your world has come apart, wait until it really does."

"So, that's it?"

"Yes, I'm afraid that's it. I don't know if it's worth it. Do you?"

"Oh no, Pieter, I know it's worth it. For them, for me, that's my struggle. It will be as I said. Go now. Do it, Pieter. I'll put the album in the abbey, somewhere safe. I'll talk to Thomas today and try to set up the Louvre meeting and go over his dealings with the colonel. I won't let on to the publication, no need. But, I will let him think we have something very important to say to make this event possible."

"Lina, you're sure now?"

"Yes, go ahead, Pieter. Do what you do best, tell them—tell them all."

He got up to leave, took a few steps then returned and sat back down. Now looking deeply into my eyes, he asked "Did you ever think it would get this far? I didn't. I was just this university newspaper editor and you an art student and castle guide."

"No, Pieter. I didn't. How could I? But now, I do know this. For me, the good that has come from all this is you. Yes, always you. The last few weeks have seemed like years. We've walked together, haven't we, you and I? It's just that we didn't hold hands."

Pieter sighed while tapping nervously on the table, then stopped and got up, this time for good reason. He gestured for me to do the same. Holding out his hand, he pulled me close and kissed me, like he was in love. I knew I was.

"What was that for?"

"The memories from the shower." He smiled then added, "I'll call you later."

"Yes, of course," I mumbled as a tingle of sensation made my legs quiver. It lingered and how nice it felt, but I could allow it to remain only for a moment. Now it was on to Thomas.

At half past two, Thomas arrived with all kinds of news. "Lina, let me tell you, the colonel has received a lot of phone calls, all kinds of innuendo is being passed around."

"Like what, Thomas?"

"Some agents have come forward, putting together a scenario making you the center of all this. They claim that your background is the beginning of this story. The colonel demands a full investigation and wants to start by getting you back to the barracks."

"And you, Thomas, what do you think?"

"I don't know what to believe. And, quite frankly, I don't care. It's all too confusing from where I stand. Lina, they say you're a double agent!"

"What?" I laughed.

"Yes, that's what these guys are suggesting."

"And the colonel is buying it?"

"Well, let's just say he's trying to find a place to hang his hat. Because of all your secrecy, he has nothing to add or place on the table, so he just sits back and takes it all in."

"Let's not talk any more about this nonsense, Thomas. Here it is, let's see. How do I begin?"

"What are you trying to say, Lina?"

"We've uncovered some information. Information that is extremely important, valuable clues to this whole matter. You see, we believe there is a list of looted art out there."

"A list? Where?"

"In Munich, Thomas, hidden in the library, downstairs in the archives under historical art of the masters, indexed under code name Benedict. This list catalogs not only lost paintings but buyers, locations, art dealers, commissions received, dates and even the names of banks that funded each deal."

"You're kidding. Really?"

"Yes, I got this info from Argentina."

"You did?"

"Yes, I did. Where it is, we will know shortly. We have a contact working within the archives."

"Right now? In the University of Munich library?"

"Yes, that's what I said, Thomas. And hopefully we will have it by the end of the day. Tell the colonel we will deliver what we have to him, personally, after he has set up an audience with the press at the Louvre."

"In Paris?"

"Yes, Thomas, in Paris."

"When...when, Lina?"

"Soon—tomorrow or the next day. We don't want this material in our hands too long. It could be very dangerous for us. But remind him that we have..."

"I know, I know, the right of first publication," Thomas interrupted.

"Yes, that's right." I laughed.

"Damn, is that all Pieter thinks about, Lina?"

"Right, that is his concern."

"So, Lina, you hid it from me?"

"No, Thomas. I just didn't realize how reliable the information was until we got some people to research it."

"At the meeting, after they snatched you? Is that where you got it?"

"Yes."

"You played your cards cleverly, Lina," he said sadly.

"Well, like I said, it's something you need to know, and now the colonel can't accuse you of neglect over a personal relationship. You didn't know and now you do. You can honestly tell him that. Now both of you will be able to occupy a place at the intel table for awhile."

"And us, Lina? What about you and me?"

"I don't know anymore, Thomas. This thing has taken so many different directions. There doesn't seem to be much left for us."

"The kiss at the hotel?"

"That was an act of desperation, fear and insecurity."

"And love?"

"Yes, love too, but not the kind you want."

"That's it then?"

"Thomas, you don't know how this will all turn out. What if I am that spy they are talking about, a Nazi in disguise, an active participant in a cover up? Right now, I'm not sure who I am. Maybe I'm a little of all of them. I'm afraid the story might never end—a father who's dead, a mother… And then there is you, the bright young lieutenant from Stanford. Think about how this will look on your resume. There would be little chance at getting your precious promotion if we become seriously involved, now would there?"

"Now, don't sell me short, Lina."

"I know. I trust you. Tomorrow it might all change. We'll get another deal, a new hand. Maybe it will look much better then. But, for now, I've got to get back to work and you back to the colonel. If you need me, you'll find me at the abbey. I haven't spent much time with Reverend Mother lately, and I need to pray a bit more."

CHAPTER 33

## Conversation With an Angel

That familiar sense of peace overtook my spirit while riding across the Neckar Bridge. My bike curved around the bend, following alongside the Philosopher's Walk. I looked over the cascading river and became captivated by the serenity of Heidelberg, sitting as a postcard for romantic subscribers. I don't suggest to being poetic, only that it was majestic to my soul.

I was on my way home again. Oh how I resented the world on this morning for robbing me from the abbey, stealing me away because of my age, even though I'd never outgrow my life there.

I gave little concern that along with an apple, pear and some cheese, crackers and juice, my basket held a large photo album hidden under a cloth. It made for a heavier load, yet, at this moment, it didn't matter. I glanced back to see my security tail pause and stop when I turned onto the spiral road leading straight up to the abbey. The world others knew was left behind, and the one I grew up with lie in front. I loved it so.

Now, just a few feet from the abbey steps, I pulled my heavy-laden bike into the rack. Leaving my nourishment in the basket, I walked over to the chapel knowing I would find her there. It was just past lunch now, and she would never break with her routine, especially the one she had with God—not even for her roses. The sisters were not around, and that was unusual. I seemed to pass at least one every time I'm here. But, no problem, I knew my way to the chapel.

I entered to see her figure profiled against the candlelight and, as usual, kneeling in prayer. I could never creep up on her. No, she had this self-contained radar that would invariably detect anyone who came within her domain. Along with her other senses, I supposed this was given for a divine purpose, allowing her a great capacity to multitask. I walked from the back of the chapel to the front without even a flinch from her. When I was so close that my aroma gave me away, she motioned, without seeking me with her eyes, for me to kneel and pray—not necessarily to prevent disturbing her prayers but rather her way of letting me know we were in His presence. I knelt and began to pray, though it wouldn't come out. The aspirations on this day were not to God. It was Reverend Mother from whom I needed comfort.

She always cleared things up when my understanding of Him was, at best, murky. Somehow, I felt God spoke to her, expecting the message to be relayed to me. Because my prayers, though giving spiritual comfort, hardly helped explain away the discomfort I experienced after leaving the chapel and engaging in the world.

It only took a few minutes to recharge my inspirational batteries. I really didn't need a conversation with God to make that happen, for the solemnity of the church, the silence, the smell of burning candles and mosaic sunrays allowed for that. This brief moment was but a preparation for the main course. My anxiety rested as God passed on to Reverend Mother the duty of sharing what He had for me this day.

As was her way, she broke with God by making the sign of the cross while holding tightly to the crucifix around her neck, then she gestured for me to follow her out of the chapel.

Uncharacteristically, she declined to ramble on about her treasured roses. No, this time she paid little attention to them, a warning that there was much under her sleeve. I'd never experienced so much silence with her at my side climbing those endearing stairs, holding on to the rail, following behind like a trained pet following its master. It wasn't that the stairs were narrow, but they felt that way this time given the heavy mood.

We reached the second floor, where she led the way into her study, once again retreating behind her desk. Knowing my place, I lumped myself into that big comfy chair on the other side. When settled, she began, "Lina, it's been just a short time, yet it seems like an eternity."

"Yes, Reverend Mother, it does. I missed you. There isn't a minute that goes by that I don't. It's just that things have been too fast. They've carried me away."

"I know, Lina. These last few days have been trying for you. Now, tell me about your trip to Argentina."

"Well, you know the reason I went."

"Of course."

I broke a smile. "You have your sources?"

"Yes, my dear, consider that a fact." She smiled back.

"Okay, well I never met Sonnenschein. However, I went to his place of business, visited his house and was kidnapped by his friends. They took me on a wild ride, with bullets flying all around. Without your prayers, I don't think I would have made it through."

"My prayers?"

"Yes, Reverend Mother. When I'm in trouble, immediately I pray for God to place you on my shoulder."

"And that reassured you?

"It did, Reverend Mother. Thinking of you as my guardian angel makes me feel safe. It always has." I sensed her heart overflowed, knowing I thought of her that way.

Retaining her composure, she continued on with her interrogation. "What happened next?"

"Well, when the cars behind were wailing away and I could hear gunshots, the man holding me down between the seats, kept saying, 'We're friends. Just stay low. We are your friends.' And once the shooting stopped…"

She interrupted in disgust. "Lina, you must have been so frightened. I am so sorry it came to this."

"Reverend Mother, this happened so quickly. In the beginning, I had little time for fear. It wasn't until the car skidded to a stop that I began to worry. I'm not sure why, but I believed them about being friends, even while being taken away from the restaurant. Poor Thomas, he had no idea what was going on while he waited to be served his dinner.

"Next, they helped me out of the van and almost apologetically led me up into a large room. I'm not sure of its location, but, after they removed the cover over my eyes, I faced a small crowd of people who'd obviously been waiting for me. They stood before me dressed in their Sunday best. It was an odd and unsettling situation.

"Then, a formidable-looking lady greeted me warmly, calling me Liesel. I said that she must be mistaken. That Lina was my name. And then a lady spoke in Spanish, 'la misma persona, Lina, Liesel.' Somehow that made sense to the rest. Lina, Liesel, the same. They talked a little German and then agreed to speak in English.

"There was a familiarity about them, yet when I looked closer into their individual faces, I sensed a feeling of desperation. I got the nerve to ask about Dietrich and his family. A man who called himself Franco stepped forward to say the rest of Dietrich's family moved on a few weeks before and then called me Frau

Liesel when he said, 'Your father has left you a message.' He thought Dietrich was my father, but I ..."

"A message?"

"Remember Sonnenschein, Reverend Mother? Oh, you don't know what he wrote in his last letter. It explained that he was about to be discovered and, therefore, I should find him quickly. There would be a message for me, something that would help keep me safe. But I didn't know then that Dietrich was Sonnenschein. He was the one who had been writing to me all along!

"This man Franco prompted the others to wait while he led me into another room. He sat me down at a small round table with a candle, handed over a sealed envelope and then left the room, closing the door behind him. I broke the seal and took out the letter. It instructed me to find where uncles Ernst and Johannes reside and that I would find it. It also said to put his message it in my mind. I knew what that meant. So I held the letter in the candle flame and watched it burn. I still didn't know what I'm supposed to be looking for, but that was it. That was the message. Then we all joined in prayer. Kneeling together, in unison we began, 'Our Father...'"

"You prayed with them?"

"Yes, but while saying our goodbyes, unfortunately I couldn't shake the idea that these friendly, smiling faces were simply scared, entrapped Nazis on the run."

Reverend Mother sat back in her chair and encouraged me to go on. "And then, Lina?"

"We needed to get out of town now that I had what I came for."

"What about Thomas?"

"He only knows parts of the story. It's not that Pieter and I don't trust him. We felt the less he knows, the better for him."

"So, he doesn't know about the message?"

"Right, he doesn't know. Let's see, what's next. Oh, then we had to get out of Argentina but we were being watched, all the time. They'd even bugged our rooms. Thomas made arrangements for an early flight out. We did have a little excitement at the terminal." I couldn't help but smile about that. "I'd found some pictures in Dietrich's house under an ink blotter and hid them in my boot. Fortunately, I was able to get them past airport security by secretly placing them in Thomas' passport wallet."

"Pictures of what, Lina?"

"Darn, I forgot they're in my bike basket along with the album."

"Album, what album?"

"Give me a moment. I'll go get them." I rushed out the door, ran down the two flights of steps, grabbed the basket and raced back. Reverend Mother had walked over to the window and stood gazing at the mountains beyond.

I pulled the album out and placed it on her desk. "Here they are." She slowly returned to her seat to stare at it for awhile. I opened it and began pointing. "Here's what we found at the Ehrenfriedhof Cemetery. That's where their place of residence was, in the cemetery—uncles Ernst and Johannes. In the grass between their graves, we dug and found it." I became confused and surprised by my emotions and could barely speak as my voice quivered. "This was what it was all about, Reverend Mother, an album of stolen art cataloged by Dietrich Ziegler. In it, he gives the history of each piece, the buyers, the financial institutions, dates and photos of the actual paintings."

Reverend Mother nonchalantly fingered her way through the album then asked, "The Rufina, is it there?"

"Yes, here she is." I reached across the table to help turn the pages.

Reverend Mother looked at it for a second then was about to close the book when I stopped her and said, "Wait, let me show you the photos I found at Dietrich's place." I went to the last page, slid them out and handed them over. I noticed her calm and quiet spirit, and that helped put my emotions in check. Like always, she was not readily disturbed by events, and this would be no exception. I knew it was her strong conviction of God's providence that kept her unruffled. She'd often remind me to have faith in Him, follow His word. Because who were we to ask God why?

"This one is torn," I said.

"Yes, I can see that. And the other?" She turned them over and tried to read the inscriptions. "And, you, Lina? What do you make of all this?"

My feelings became apparent again as the stress caused me to stumble over my answer. Her question was blunt and to the point. Her indiscretion left me exposed. I pretended not to hear, but I did. It slammed into my ears. So much so that I felt the need for more time to answer.

But again she asked, "Lina, do you think you are this Liesel?" Then, without hesitation, she let the unspeakable out. "And, that Dietrich was your father?"

I let down my veil completely. "Oh God, oh God, I hope not. How could I live with it?"

"Remember, Lina, records don't reveal much about who you were or the circumstances that brought you here. It's not inconceivable that he was being hunted and placed his daughter here to keep her safe, to keep you safe."

"And Helen?"

"Maybe her as well. That was long ago. Lina, we are accountable for what we do in this life. You need not share his guilt. It seems as though Sonnenschein paid the ultimate price for his actions. If that were the case, he must have loved you very much. You must focus on that."

"Oh, Reverend Mother, how could I love a father I never knew? When I was on the plane and saw that torn photo for the first time, I thought about it. How can a father love a daughter he never knew? A mother, she knows the child she carried for nine months. So, how am I to relate?"

"I cannot answer that for you. But, Lina, you must deal with it. God has taken you on this journey for a reason."

"Are you sure, Reverend Mother?"

"Oh, yes. God always has a purpose. Let His reason in, and He will forgive yours. That is God's grace. Of that I am certain. Now, what will you do with the album?"

"I was hoping to keep it here, in a safe place."

"Yes, Lina. We will find a secure place, keep it out of sight."

"It won't be for long. Later, at the right time, I will give it to the proper authorities. Pieter and I feel it's important to make sure there will be the right amount of exposure. We need to publish our findings first, before handing it over to the intelligence agencies. If we do that, they will be held accountable."

"But, Lina, to do this you will surely be exposed to many uncomfortable questions about your past."

"Yes, Reverend Mother. I think that will come out."

"Are you willing to do that? Are you ready for the allegations? Regardless of the truth, you will be referred to as the daughter of a Nazis, an exploiter and murderer of Jews for profit—the worst possible motive of all. Not power, not religion or fame, but for profit. Are you ready to go through all that, Lina? Will you accept the role of Liesel? My child, that is something you must prepare for and decide if it is worth it. I cannot help you there. As your guardian angel, I must advise you to trust in God and put yourself on His path rather than insisting you can better get there by relying on your own devices. What about Pieter and Thomas? What will they think?"

"Pieter shares your concerns, Reverend Mother. He understands the risks. In fact, he told me the very thing you have. Yes, he knows. Pieter and Helen, we have a certain bond. Like many young Germans, we've been shielded from an unenviable legacy, educated by exclusion, protected from guilt and historical indictments. But, we can overcome this. Our generation must not make the same mistakes, believing in lies in order to make our beliefs possible. We must not attempt to escape what we are by going along with the indiscriminate notions of a mob. That's what Germany did, and that's where Hitler's concoction found fruit."

"Well stated, Lina. You have become what they are all saying, a strong, mature, godly compliant woman. You didn't learn that all at the university. Maybe some at the abbey?" She smiled.

"Yes, more then you know, Reverend Mother."

"So, when you decide what to do, please, Lina, this time come to me first. I don't enjoy prying it out of poor Father Tobias. He dislikes it so when I do. What are your plans now, Lina?"

"If you don't mind, I want to stay here just for a day or so."

"Of course. That would make me very happy. Your room is always open. You and Helen, what a pair. Will I see you at supper?"

"Yes."

"Fine, you know the way." She motioned toward the door. I smiled back at her, and, when I was about to leave, she said, "Oh, Lina, one more question. What about the mother?

"What?"

"Yes, your mother, what happened to her?"

"I talked to her neighbor. She said the lady was nice, and her kids often shared cookies and cakes with people on the block. Again, others thought she fled with the children about a few weeks or even a month before the incident."

"Do you ever think of her?"

"No, not really. How could I Reverend Mother? I never knew her. If that was her in the photo, she's torn away, and all I see is a very young girl with Dietrich and a boy. Her face is missing, and it looks like she's holding on to another child's hand. I don't think much about her. All I have is you, Helen, the sisters."

Reverend Mother let her emotions show in her eyes. Despite her strength, they always had a way of deceiving her.

"Enough now. I will put these pictures and the album in a safe place. You needn't worry. I know they will be around asking questions. It has been done before. Now go refresh yourself for the evening meal. The sisters will be happy to see you."

Off I went to find my room the same as when I left it four years ago. Reverend Mother never let on that somehow it was never used. No, it was ours, Helen's and mine. Nothing was ever touched. I think she told the diocese that it was for visitors. Yet, the only visitors were either Helen or myself.

Quickly, I shed my clothes and took a shower. The warm water caressed my body. I yearned to be caressed; it would happen someday. I forced myself to finally step out and put on underclothes. Then, I pulled out my habit from the dresser. I was used to wearing it here. Once it came over my head and engulfed my body, it was as if the other world didn't exist. There are pleasures that I hope to someday experience out there, but I wondered if it would ever match the peace I found here at the abbey.

At exactly 6 o'clock, I walked to the dining room to find the sisters in prayer. I sat down as Reverend Mother spoke up. "We are thankful, Lord, for the return of one of our dear children."

My tears found their way down my cheeks. I could only hope they wouldn't find a way to the table. "And also her sister in God, together with us again, Lina and Helen."

I looked up and there was Helen across the table. She'd slipped in to surprise me. She was crying too. I rushed to her as Reverend Mother ended the prayer. We held tightly together. This was a special moment. Somehow I knew it would never be the same again.

CHAPTER 34
# The Setup

A few days later, Helen came into our apartment with a bundle of letters. "I stopped by the post office and look what I found for you," she said, dropping a pile on the kitchen table.

"Oh, no. Here it goes."

"Also, Lina, while you were away I got a call. Thomas needs to see you immediately. He stressed it's important he talks with you personally. Plus, there was another call from a guy named Bryant Moyer. He wants to set up an interview, and..."

"Helen, if you get any more of those calls just tell them I'm out of town."

"Where out of town?"

"Oh, I don't care. Say I took a trip to Hawaii. Anything will do."

"What about Pieter? He wants to get together today."

"I'll call him and set something up. Right now, I'm on my way over to the library to talk to Erin. Do you think you can get out of work for a while? I want you at the meeting with Pieter. Will that be possible?"

"Today?"

"Yes, Helen, it's time to end this, and we need to finalize the plan to make that happen."

"Okay. I'll do it."

"If it's all right with you, I'd like to meet up at the Ochsen this time. I'm getting paranoid with all this stuff right now, and the Marktplatz seems too open for what we need to get done. I'll call Pieter from the library. You can reach me there if you need me. See you later," I called back while picking up my coat and rushing out the door.

After grabbing my bike, I was on my way. Riding along, I must have looked like a witch with my coattails flaring. But, I needed it. The weather was definitely getting cooler as winter approached.

I reached the library and skipped up the stairs to find Erin working with a customer. I pointed to let her know I'd be in the back stacks. She nodded and a few minutes later found me.

"Lina, a man by the name of Bryant was here looking for you. He left his card. He wants an interview for television."

"Erin, I've been at the abbey for the past few days, and I've decided it's time to end this, one way or another. Not sure how it's going to work out, but I just wanted you to know how much help you've been to me these last weeks. Without you, I couldn't have gotten this far."

"Lina, its sounds like you're going away."

"I don't know, but that's a possibility. Look, if anyone asks about me, just say I'm on a trip and you haven't seen me for a while. Okay?"

"Whatever you say."

"Gosh, Erin, I'm going to miss you. I'll get back to you when I can." I reached out and gave her a long hug. "I need to call Pieter."

"The phone? Sure."

We walked together to her office, where I called Pieter and told him the location to meet Helen and me. I also asked him to get a hold of Thomas and tell him we'd meet him after lunch.

Leaving the library, I glanced back and somehow knew it

would be the last time I would be able to sit undisturbed in the comfort and safety of the back stacks. This whole thing that started that day at the Louvre was ending, and the Rufina was about to get her justice. Now, I would be the one relentlessly hunted down.

Pieter arrived just ahead of me and already had a large pilsner sitting on the table. I sat down across from him and told the waiter, "The same, and please add something to munch on."

Pieter immediately went to his attaché and pulled out a newspaper with an AP story underlined in red. "Read it, Lina."

I grazed through the article and became sickened. "No! No! Where did they get this information?"

"I don't know, but they got it. And, they're not going to leave one stone untouched until they get the real story."

"But it says here an anonymous source has made me an accomplice to the missing Nazi looted art. How can this be, Pieter? How can they print something like that?"

"They can say just about anything they want, especially if this gets into the American press. Over there you can be accused of everything. It doesn't matter if it's untrue, as long as it gets attention and, most importantly, readers. Lina, it's happening. Just like I said it would. Somebody has leaked the story. You're being demonized. Someone's hoping to discredit whatever you divulge about the real villains involved. That's what they do, because it works."

"Well, then, we must move faster to get this album out," I said.

Helen walked in and looked around. I patted the seat next to me. "Here, Helen. Over here."

"Why so serious guys?" she asked as she sat down. I handed her the paper. "Oh my god, Lina! They're after you now."

"Yes, looks that way. I was just saying to Pieter, we must get this album out soon. So, here's what I want to do. I don't care what they say about me. Well, actually, yes, of course I do, but I can't control that. I can control when and where we release the album. If it incriminates me, so be it. Somehow the truth always seeps out, and, if that means rediscovering who I am, then I'm prepared for that. But the art, the Rufina, the story must get out, no matter what."

"And where do you propose this should take place?" Pieter asked.

"Just like we planned, back at the Louvre, only sooner. We have no other course but to tell the world the Rufina is still out there somewhere, like so many other artworks, and will most likely show up someday in an obscure gallery, maybe in France or England or the United States. These pieces will eventually be discovered hanging on the wall of some gallery. I'll bet on it. What's the point of possessing such great pieces if you can't display them?"

"Lina, the album, is it at the abbey then?"

"Yes, Pieter, it's in a safe place."

"Don't tell me you simply rode it over on your bike?"

"Of course, in my basket, under my lunch."

He laughed. "Really? With a tail following you?"

Helen wasn't laughing. "What's going to happen to you, Lina?"

"Well, I think maybe I'll need to get away for a while."

"The abbey?"

"No, not the abbey, Helen. They'll be looking for me there. Reverend Mother doesn't need that kind of attention, not now. No, somewhere else, until the story runs out. Then I'll return, when Pieter has written it all and won the Pulitzer, right?"

"No, Lina, I don't want that. You know I've always wanted what you want out of this."

He looked so sincere and concerned that my emotions ran away with me. I reached one hand across the table to take hold of his and with the other reached for Helen's. She willingly searched out to find mine and held it tight. Now holding them firmly, I said, "You both have meant so much to me. The love I have for you will always be an endearing thought. To be gone from you will be a great challenge, but I'll be back when the time is right. Like Dietrich, I'll fade away, always looking over my shoulder. But, of course in time, they too will forget. Now, with that settled, let's talk about how Thomas plays into all this." Thinking of that made me smile and chuckle a little.

"What's so funny?"

"Well, Helen, to distract the military and give us some time to get the album to a secure place, I told Thomas that, back in Argentina, I learned a list of looted art was hidden in the University of Munich's archives. I even gave him the phony code name of Benedict to help him locate it. I insisted he wait until the right time before letting it out to the colonel. I knew he couldn't wait, that he'd pass it on. I heard they had about half of their intel personnel scraping through the Munich archives yesterday. "

"What?" Pieter smiled.

"Yep. Erin said they tore the place apart."

"Funny, very funny, Lina. Great, so what to do with Thomas?" Pieter asked.

"I'm counting on him to get us a military escort for safe passage to the Louvre. Also, we'll have the album with us in your car, Pieter. Once we arrive, I will announce that a publication about the album has been released by the Daily News that morning. I will let them know we have a copy of the album, and, if there are no missteps, I'll read a statement prepared by you, Pieter—yes, you. And, then I'll turn over the album.

"I'll promise to return to my apartment and, within the week, voluntarily report to U.S. intel at Campbell Barracks to be debriefed and cooperate fully with their ongoing investigation. I'll let Thomas know it's not that we don't trust the U.S. military. It's just that previous dubious behavior on their part has created the need for us to withhold certain information. Of course, I'll remind them of the Dietrich Ziegler debacle. That said, I will also point out that the Daily has exclusive rights to any information regarding their future investigations of the lost art. Anything I haven't thought of, Pieter?"

"Damn….no, Lina. That's about it."

"If that's it, I need to get going," Helen said while standing to leave.

"Helen, please come straight home after work. We need to talk some more."

"All right, Lina." She said her goodbyes and left.

Pieter and I ordered another round and continued on.

"You know, Lina, this is the biggest…well, that's an understatement. I never dreamt of being part of such an important story. And, yet, I'm envious of you."

"Me?"

"Yes, you, Lina. Your drive, your ability to get to the core of issues and your grace.

"Grace?" I grinned.

"Yes, Lina, that too."

"Pieter, you were a good teacher. You taught me to be honest, stay with the story and follow my instincts. That was all. You keep me going. You gave me direction. Hey, that reminds me, I need to thank Erin. She turned me on to you."

"She did?"

"You don't remember?"

"What did she say?"

"She said a great looking guy that all the girls drool over was also the editor of our campus newspaper and that he was a really good journalist. I couldn't turn that down, now could I?"

"And, where do we go from here, Lina?"

"We'll find a way."

"How can you be so certain?"

"I flashed a seductive smile and Pieter leaned over, but just then Thomas walked in, looking distraught.

"Thomas, over here," I called to him. "Why the drab face?"

"Why you ask? Pieter, Lina told me there was a list of looted artwork in the Munich archives. Well, I passed that on to the colonel. He promptly sent out a whole slew of intel guys, only to be embarrassed by the museum's irate response over the accusations. I had to assure them that I would take up the miscommunication with my trusted contact." Thomas said while pointing at me.

I smiled, then quietly chuckled, holding my hand to my mouth. "Thomas, I told you to wait, didn't I?"

Finally seeing a little humor in the awkward situation, Thomas agreed, "Yes, Lina, I recall something about that, but..."

"I'm sorry it was necessary to mislead you, Thomas, especially now that I need you to trust me."

"Where have I heard that line before?"

"No, Thomas, I promise. Pieter and I have this all worked out. You see, at the meeting in Argentina, or should call it the abduction, I really was given a clue to a list of looted art, but I needed some time and space to follow up on it. We found a record of looted paintings in an album, incriminating evidence pertaining not only to the Rufina and the Rothschild collection but also many others. It's all there!"

Thomas' eyes lit up like a child getting his first bike on Christmas morning. "You're sure that's what's in it?"

"Yes. Now, calm down, Thomas. Trust me, we have it."

"Where?"

"Oh, no. Not so fast. Like I said, we need to trust each other. I will hand it over and you can give it to your intel people. Now, here are the rules. Pieter, go ahead. Tell him."

After Pieter finished laying out the plan he added, "Thomas, it's important that we have security from Heidelberg to the Louvre and, once there, we'll need a podium and some audio equipment. Lina will make a short statement then turn over the album, which I assure you'll find in order and very pleasing to your colonel. However, if there is any breach in the security arrangement, all bets are off. Don't let the gooneys scramble this one up again. Do this right, Thomas, and medals will probably be involved."

"Hey, people," Thomas interrupted. "I know you don't believe me, but I'm on your side. I've just happened to have been stuck the past two years in this uniform."

"We know that," I explained. "Yes, your country had the Monuments Men pursuing stolen art treasures for awhile. But, remember why we're so particular with the documentation. We saw what your government did with the testimonies pertaining to looted art, taken under oath from Nazis at Nuremberg. That's why we want this album to be published, so that no one can hide it behind a locked file cabinet. All will be out in the open, and the war criminals in hiding will know they will be hunted until the last piece of this art is found and returned to the rightful owners. No more legal ticks, Thomas."

"Okay, okay, I get it."

"Tell the colonel if this isn't set up the way we've asked, no deal. We will handle it our own way, and I don't think he'll take much pleasure in that. We want this to be over, just like him."

"I understand. But, Lina, what about you?"

"What about me? Thomas, did you read the article in today's news?"

"No."

"Well, here it is."

I handed it over, and he began to read. It didn't take him long to translate. "No way!"

"Look at the headline, Thomas! *Daughter of Nazi found hiding in abbey, holding Nazi secrets.*"

"Is this true, Lina?"

"No. Of course not!"

"Your father was Dietrich Ziegler?"

"Well, possibly that part, but I never knew my father or what he was."

"So, that's why you wanted to go to Argentina so badly."

"No. Again, I never knew him. I was too young. When I saw his face in the pictures on the airplane, I felt something familiar, but I didn't know him, not as my father. Now, I'll never be able to. I'll only know just what they say about him. But, I'm certain I could never have been a Nazi."

My eyes began to water, not of love or passion. No, out of rage for those who committed such atrocities and now had the audacity to implicate me. Not me. I'm willing to suffer for what I did, but not this. Seeing how my emotions had overcome me, Thomas backed off.

"Sorry, Lina. I should have known."

"No, not even I ever considered the direction this was going. I'll take care of it my own way. Thomas, this plan of ours must work. See to it, please. You will get what you're after and begin your illustrious law practice back in San Francisco. Pieter, too. He will write. The abbey will be free to go on as before, and I will become a recluse for a while."

As Thomas got up, I did too. We hugged and said our

goodbyes. After he left, I looked over at Pieter and said sadly, "If only it could have been, you and me."

He looked back at me warmly. "It's still you and me, Lina. Like you said, we'll find a way."

"Promise me that, Pieter, even if you don't mean it. I need that assurance now, more than you will ever know."

This time I leaned over and kissed him tenderly on his waiting lips and then got up, leaving him alone as I walked slowly to the door. For a brief moment, I turned and took a second look, my eyes now acting as the lens of a camera, dialing in the image. And then he was gone from view, but not from my mind.

CHAPTER 35

# The Disclosure

L ate at night, back in my apartment, I found myself opening more of the letters in response to earlier publications.
His latest editorial would go to print the next morning,
publicizing my revelation at the Louvre. As I opened them, I
began to see that not only had there been a leak of information but that the damn had clearly been breached. One letter
got right to the point, describing me as this horrible Nazi who
killed Jews, not for the sake of Germany, no, but out of my own
greed. Another expressed loyalty to Hitler and that I was a traitor to expose patriots of the German folk who would one day
rise again and find their rightful place in history. There were so
many vitriolic, bitter and even threatening letters that, when I
trashed them in my wastebasket, they spilled out onto the floor.
They had warned me. Pieter, Thomas, even Reverend Mother
and, yes, Father Tobias, all of them, in their own way, had told
me this would happen.

I went in and took a long shower, hoping to escape the
inevitable assault and wash away the ugly words. After drying off
and putting on a warm robe, I wandered into the kitchen to brew
a fresh pot of coffee. My mind couldn't let it go. Tomorrow this
whole thing would come to light at the Louvre. It wasn't just the
enormity of the event—practically the entire news media would
have a lead story to splash on their front pages—it was also the
overwhelming realization that now I would be hunted down

for what I knew about the Rufina mystery. What I found even more daunting was, as a result of what I'd disclosed about the Rufina, I had been indicted—me rather than the war criminals. It plunged me into the abyss, forcing me to answer, and for what? The prosecutor, as I saw myself, now became the prosecuted. Oh, so quickly the tables had turned, and, with that overbearing realization, my mind turned to mush.

I tried recounting when all of this had happened. Did I bring it on myself by jumping into the river too soon after seeing the Rufina? I merely tried to recover her, but she discovered me and my family. I had one, yet only for a moment. I didn't know what kind or what flavor they would be and now would never know. They were either sealed by death or had vanished out there somewhere. I thought while looking out the kitchen window, only to see my own reflection looking back with nothing to say.

I fell to sleep, hoping for a respite from it all. But then, it happened again—the dream, the voice, the paintings and the lady. Why wouldn't they leave me alone? I did what was asked of me. I found the path that would lead to her discovery. She's out there—the Rufina. Yes, she's hanging on some wall starving for love or maybe stacked in some stuffy archive, held prisoner by some wealthy prince who cherished possessions and hoarded her, keeping her hostage from the world's prying eyes. There was nothing left for me to do now. So how could I rid this from my mind? My body was overcome by the buzzing in my head.

Again, I woke as the dream faded. It was early, and the sun wasn't up. Knowing that sleep alone would not give rest, I grabbed my notebook to jot down things to add to Pieter's prepared speech for the Louvre. What was it I wanted to say? Something was missing. I could tell them about when I first met her, the Rufina. But, it would make no sense or provide compassion to redress the harm. How could it offer a resolution for the dead bodies that her search left in its wake? And, what about the face of evil that found resilience among the self-proclaimed curator of the arts, the Führer? What would free me from the quagmire that pulled me apart from inside?

I dressed and told Helen, "I'm leaving."

"Where will you go? It's too early. Stay here for a little while."

"No, Helen. I must go out and ride about the city. You get back to bed now. I'll be all right."

The sun made its early appointment on time. It was the one thing I knew for certain while slipping away unnoticed. I would ride as long as it took, until I could clear up some of the doubts and questions in my mind. I raced out into the cold morning air, again not knowing where to go. The city had yet to wake. Only the chill greeted me. I rode easily up and down through the old city, whose windows hardly blinked of light and doors were still locked shut. The street lamps flickered out one by one as the day invaded the silence of the night. Only a few faint voices and a single car could be heard.

My pedaling would eventually lead across the Neckar Bridge. Like a horse finding comfort heading to his barn, my bike knew the way. I found myself, as if walking in my sleep, wandering up the narrow road to the abbey. It was still early and, when I racked my bike, I could hear the voices of the choir beckoning me to the chapel. Such a wonderful sound, this heavenly music, sustaining me for a moment while I stood in the back.

Reverend Mother felt my presence and turned to greet me. Without disrupting a note, she gestured for me to come on in. The sisters sang while I walked toward her. When I reached her side, she handed me a hymnbook, prompting me to join in. I began to sing along, praising the Lord. I knew the words; I'd sung them so many times before.

Reverend Mother's smile widened, yet she wouldn't let her eyes fall to me. Then, when the chorus ended, we knelt together in silence, to repent and ask God to clear our hearts to receive His wisdom and to please lead us through the day with His blessings. The sisters began to file out, one by one, to breakfast. It wasn't until we passed the water and made the sign of the cross that Reverend Mother first spoke.

"What a wonderful surprise that I get to see you again this week. Lina, what brings you here so early in the morning?" Without waiting for me to answer, she continued. "By the look on your face and the time of the day, it tells me you are deeply troubled. Let's go up to my study and, with God's blessing, we'll have the wisdom to sort things out."

She put her arm around my shoulder and walked me up those creaky stairs. Eventually we found our way to her warm and inviting enclave.

"Sit, Lina."

Just then, Sister Grace stepped in to greet me. "Lina, it was so good to see you this morning in the chapel. What brings you here so early?" she asked with a broad smile.

"Isn't it wonderful? She's come to see me," Reverend Mother interjected. "Sister, would you please go to the kitchen and prepare some coffee and sweet rolls for us?"

"Yes, of course, Reverend Mother."

"And, Sister, please close the door as you leave. Lina and I will need a little privacy."

"So glad you are here, Lina."

"It's good to see you too, Sister," I said while she left, closing the door.

Reverend Mother returned to her chair. "So, what is it, Lina?" she asked while managing a faint smile.

My voice cracked, "Reverend Mother, I am so confused."

"About what?" she asked with concern.

"Dietrich Ziegler, was he my father? I'm getting dreadful letters. One side calling me a Nazi war criminal and exploiter for profit. Others telling me of their disgust, that I'm not a patriot but a traitor to the fatherland."

Clearly taken aback, Reverend Mother paused then attempted to console me with, "You must remember, Lina, we've lived through a tragic period in our lives. Emotions are not something well spent here in Germany. They're still too delicate and fragile, even to this day. Wounds have not healed. It is as if you've put alcohol to that wound. The pain is good for it, but yet you scream out, trying to find answers. You blame someone else for your suffering.

"Germany was desperate after the First World War. She was broken, with no jobs. The streets filled with dangerous thugs and gangs. Black market deals were the only way to survive. We tried to work it out by elections; that only split us down the middle. Then Hitler came. He promised to lead the way, take us back to prosperity, cut the red tape, give jobs, even more, give us back our integrity. So the nation bought into the only hope we had. And, in the beginning, he did what he said. He gave out jobs, food for our table, a sense of security and a renewed dignity. Yes, he fed the body, but at the cost of our collective soul. And then, he took us to war.

"The people, at first, were all too willing to follow. Then, the war dragged on, and our losses mounted. Stories of our defeats in Russia filtered back, and rumors about concentration death camps reached the people. They began to grumble, and German society once again began to split, each side blaming the other for its failures. That's what they're thinking when they write those letters to you. They're trying to convince themselves and you that it's not over, and they lash out. Lina, it will all pass away.

Trust me."

"Trust? No, no, Reverend Mother! I can't do that anymore. It's not enough for me! I don't understand any of this. Trust? I can't trust the church, the banks, the government. What they've justified in our generation's name has blemished my soul to the point that I can't even understand who I am anymore. And, the blood drains from my heart and rushes to my head when I'm told that I'm the daughter of a Nazi! Those vile, reprehensible men. I was one of them? I can't sleep at night because the Rufina, the man, the lady, they haunt me. They torment me, and I don't know why. Why can't all of this just go away?" I buried my head in my arms on her desk.

Seeing my anguish, Reverend Mother became visibly disturbed. I looked back up with tear-stained cheeks and, between heavy sobs, said, "You don't know what it's like. You're here in the shelter of the abbey. You don't know about the world out there!"

Now showing she could anger like the rest of us, Reverend Mother erupted. "You say I don't know what the world is like out there beyond the sanctuary of the abbey walls?" She paused to temper her response. "You think that to be so? Dear child, let me tell you a fairy tale, only this one is true."

While gathering up her thoughts, she walked to the open window, like she always did before illustrating her point. Finally, she spoke, not to me but somewhere out toward the hills. "This is a fairy tale about a young girl growing up in Berlin."

"Berlin?"

"Yes, Berlin, child." Reverend Mother turned back to me, meditating before she put her thoughts into words. "Oh, Lina, it was so lovely then, being young and believing in all sorts of wonderful things. Playing games outdoors, going to dances, spending summers on the lake and hearing the church bells that rang throughout the city, especially on Sundays. And the sweet family that welcomed you home. It would be there, in the beauty of Berlin that, in your teens, you would meet a handsome young man, full of music, full of art, plus a promising career as a photographer."

She smiled at the next memory. "He had this old camera, one of those kind that you had to set up on a tripod to keep still. Yes, standing there, taking pictures over and over until he got it just right. It would take days or weeks, it seemed, to develop them. And bless him, he would make copies for them all. Love was in the air that summer. You couldn't help but breathe in and fall in love. While living outside of Berlin, he wrote her letters, even making up songs telling how he missed her so. As time went on, he entered the University of Berlin and studied the social sciences, but his heart was always inclined toward the arts. In those brief years at the university, they got to see each other every weekend. Then the war came, clouding their bright future.

"Those were hard times. They were separated when he joined the service, but he always made time to send her daily letters. In 1918, the war finally ended. Yes, the first big war. He came home telling her that his future would be in the arts. After acceptance at the University of Munich for postgraduate studies, he asked her to come with him and to marry. She did, of course, whatever he said. She also finished her education there, but in business law. Yes, it was a novelty then, but she did it.

"Then, the Nazi youth movement became popular. It was quite fashionable to participate in government activities and politics—the thing to do in Munich and all of Bavaria. So the couple joined, along with her husband's two brothers. Adolf was a good artist and politician. Ernst was the charismatic athletic. Brother Adolf quickly moved up, spending all his free time with the Nazi elite. Hitler became captivated with his ability to paint a style of art he was fond of. And, in time, Adolf became one of the most reputable artists in Germany, even commissioned by Hitler as his favorite painter and appointed judge, along with Alfred Rosenberg, over the looted art, deciding what were the classics to be placed in the Führermuseum and which would be auctioned off. Hitler also appreciated the youngest brother's extensive knowledge of art and his ability to recognize its true value. So, Dietrich Ziegler, her husband, went along and became a respected, well-known art dealer.

Hearing her speak his name, I blinked and sat back to ask, "You knew him?"

"Yes."

"Dietrich Ziegler?"

"I did."

"And, my mother?"

"Yes."

"Laura Ziegler?"

"I knew her."

"What was she like?"

Reverend Mother raised her hand slightly. "I'll get to that. Let me carry on for a moment. They had children, two boys. The first, an athlete. Yes, a very fine athlete who almost made it to the Olympics. Oh, Lina, you should have seen Johannes run. Later came Michael. His interest was in books. Yes, he loved to read, almost anything, talking about them constantly. Then war came, again. Everyone was excited. That's the German way. Johannes enlisted and went off with his Uncle Ernst to retrieve territories taken from the fatherland. It went well for a while, but when Hitler turned north to Russia, the people saw he had something more ambitious on his mind.

"And, when the war effort went badly, at home the people

began to ask questions. But now, anyone who opposed the conduct of the war was considered an enemy of the state, to be punished, put into prison or concentration camps. Stories of Hitler, the Nazis and what they did to the Jews and others began to surface. Germans were aware of the Jewish plight. How could they not be? Their stores, homes and jobs were seized, and they were herded together, packed into trucks and sent off with few belongings. But, most Germans were lost to passion, indifference and the cause.

"Johannes was lost to the Nazis. He could not be convinced otherwise. He made his way back, but in a wooden box. When Ernst returned, he saw another way. He began to protest and joined the University of Munich resistance. In 1943, Himmler's Gestapo executed him. Yes, he's buried alongside of Johannes. It was his brother Adolf's influence that got Ernst's remains there at the Ehrenfriedhof Cemetery.

"Even Adolf and Dietrich's loyalty was called into question. Himmler had them hauled away to Dachau. When Hitler heard of this, he immediately gave them both a reprieve. But, by now, Dietrich had seen firsthand the atrocities of the concentration camps. He planned carefully for his departure from the Reich. It would not be easy. Everyone was suspicious of each other. Fears of reprisal played a large part. Each day, the Gestapo would come and take someone away. And, who knew what happened to them."

Reverend Mother kept pacing about the room. I could feel that it was not my time to ask questions. As always, she was in total control and continued, "Yes, he set out a plan, but then, she became pregnant again."

"Laura?" I jumped in.

"And, yes, Liesel was born. He called her his 'Sunshine.'" With that, Reverend Mother's tone began to flounder and squirm about. Her voice broke, attempting to nurture her heart from giving her away. "Oh, how happy he was. What joy Liesel brought. As time went on, Dietrich knew that if he didn't report and was found missing, the Gestapo and later the Allies would hunt him down. So, he carefully recorded transactions related to the looted art treasures."

"The photo album?"

"Yes, that's what they are after. He decided that, without the album as a bargaining chip, his family would never make it out of Germany alive. Dietrich had a connection at the Vatican, someone who wanted special art pieces. And, there was also his trusted Swiss accountant. So, one night, they made their planned escaped. He took his family to Innsbruck. The Vatican prepared the papers, while his family was discreetly entered into the monastery. To prevent capture by any who would come after them, he needed to deceive, to lead them off onto another trail. He did just that when reluctantly boarding a freighter bound for Argentina, knowing it would be the last time they would ever be able to see each other."

"What are you saying Reverend Mother? Into a monastery, like me?"

"Yes, my child."

"And Laura Ziegler, what about her?"

"She received a new identity and was wedded to God, as Sister Johannes Maria. She had a new life and would never go back again. To do so would place her children's lives in danger. She'd already lost one son to the Nazis and was not willing to lose another."

Stunned, speechless, unable to put a sentence together, I looked at Reverend Mother, who quickly turned toward the window to hide her tears. But, it wouldn't last long. She couldn't wait. She had to turn back to see her daughter looking at her, no longer as the Reverend Mother, but as mother. She turned around slowly. I understood her torment and could no longer hold it in.

"Mother?" I asked softly.

"Yes, Liesel."

"All these years?"

"We had no other choice, Dietrich and I. As time went on, there were many changes here. The Vatican kept moving me up. Eventually, I became Reverend Mother, and there was no way back. We've been living in the ratline, as they call it, ever since. I now rely on God and His divine providence. He knew what my heart would say. Oh yes, Liesel, we did go along with them, yes, and were willing to pay the price, but it will never be enough. We know that now. I ask God to forgive me every day for that, but I'm thankful for His mercy and blessings. He allowed me to see you grow up here, always under my wing. Yes, I felt certain that someday it would come to this. When I heard what happened that day at the Louvre... You see your father had the Rothschild collection in our home, which was really half house and half gallery. You would play all around those paintings. You'd seen it before."

"Then, why didn't you try to stop me?"

"Liesel—I love calling you that. You don't know how many times I had to check myself from saying it out loud. You see, we found ourselves in trouble because we did what we wanted. Your father and I left God out. I've promised God, this time I will be true to His will, follow and trust Him to work out the details. It was no longer about me. Just keep my babies safe, I prayed. No, I could not stop you. I had to let it take its course. I wouldn't again offend God that way."

"And the picture and the family in Argentina?"

"The picture...your father went around in a paranoid fashion, always careful not to be discovered. He tore away Michael and me from the photo, to protect us. But, you were so young, and he needed to see his sunshine's face. That made him so happy."

"And the family in Argentina?"

"That was Ana, a single mother of a good departed friend. She took care of your father, while he provided for them." Mother came over close. "Please stand up, Liesel. Let me hold you, just for a moment."

"Mother, you're crying."

"Yes, yes. Tears of joy, child, of joy." She pulled away when Sister Grace tapped at the door and stepped in.

"Reverend Mother, here are your coffee and sweet rolls."

"Thank you, Sister."

After looking at both of us she asked, "Is anything the matter?"

"Oh no, Sister. Everything is wonderful, just wonderful."

Sister Grace didn't know what to say, so she paused, then mumbled, "Well it is…if you need me, Reverend Mother. Anything else, I'll be outside."

"Thank you, Sister." She left and closed the door. I was filled with questions and eager for answers.

"The letters?"

"Yes, Sonnenschein gave it away."

"Mother, may I call you that?"

"Only behind closed doors, Liesel."

"And Helen, what about her family?"

"I don't know. She was a mystery that was kept even from me, coming to the abbey a little later than us. I don't remember. Few questions were asked back then, and much has been forgotten. However, Helen will always be family, but I don't know about her parents."

"Father Tobias, does he know?"

"Yes and no. He's a quaint old friar, knowing more then he lets on. I love him so."

"So do I, mother. And Dietrich, my father?"

"Here, come sit down again. Pull your chair up alongside of mine. I'll read you his last letter to me." I hesitated at the thought. "Please, Liesel, sit down. Share it with me." She opened the old Bible that sat on the front of her desk and retrieved a tattered piece of folded paper. "You'll see." She smiled and began to read out loud.


*Dearest Laura,*

*It seemed so long...so long ago that our lives changed this way. Oh, I've missed you, all of you. We had no other way. Life played tricks on us. Every day, as I pray to God, not seeing Him, He is there and you are there. I can't touch Him, nor you, but yet both are there within my every thought. So alive and present when I do, Laura, that I've persuaded myself there is no purpose for the past anymore, just memories. Still, it is tempting to steal time from God, to play hooky like a child again. Taking but a bit of chocolate then another, just for a fleeting moment remembering when it was all so wonderful. The clouds float back, as they always do and the passion of losing that luxury defeats me. Yet, I find you in my hopes and dreams. I thank God I can do just that. And, when spring comes each year, I delight watching lovers frolic about and meet each other, hold hands and dance. I see them and I smile pretending it is us. Just to hold your hand once again and dance. Laura, I can only cry out like this in my confessions and whisper to you in this way, never letting on, just writing out words, trying to fit in meaning. It must be that way, 'tis the secrets we must hide, such precious secrets, that you only know. We must never let on, no never. We've given*

*all we can. Oh, so much more there is to say.*
    *Love & Blessings,*
    *Dietrich*

"Read it again, mother. I've got only this one letter left to know him by."

"Liesel, there will be time for us. Not now, though."

"When?"

"My precious, Liesel, there is a world out there that wants to erase our past."

"But you, mother, you're safe here."

"No, Liesel. They will come. Since Pieter's first publication, I knew they would. There's too much at stake. I must disappear like Dietrich."

"No mother, not like father. This time both of us together. Yes, you and me together."

"And what of your young man Pieter, or Thomas?"

"Mother, Thomas will soon go back to San Francisco, forgetting about me and this."

"And, Pieter?"

"He'll find us. You will see."

"You think so?"

"Oh, yes, mother. Pieter will find us. I am certain."

"Liesel, your brother Michael, a professor is out there."

"Does he know about us?"

"No, he doesn't, but I do know, like you, that he'll ask."

"But, how could he possibly..."

"Someday, he will know. Of that I am sure." She grinned and held me tight. "You'll see. Have faith in God. He will work out the details."

CHAPTER 36

# The Meeting at the Louvre

Pieter pushed and shoved through the crowd of reporters who'd perched themselves, like vultures, in front of our apartment building, each trying to get a photo or a statement to cover space for their media outlets. I'd returned that morning from the abbey to discover new allegations swirling around.

Once inside, Pieter saw me going about the business of packing up my personal belongings. He knew I could no longer stay here in Heidelberg. I'd need some seclusion, until this thing blew over. With this on his mind, he came to console me and to hand over what he'd written for the Louvre news conference the following day.

"Well, Pieter, I guess this is the price for the press coverage we were after."

"Let them stir the pot any way they want. Tomorrow will be the last of it. Here's your speech. Let's go over it together."

I sat down with him on the sofa and read through it. "It's fine, as usual. I'll make a few changes, but, for the most part, yes, it will do."

"Okay, then, I'll pick you up early in the morning. Thomas and his crew will be around to escort us to Paris. The album?"

"Yes. I've got it. It will be with me." I stood to lead him to the door but sat back down quickly.

"You all right, Lina?"

"It's the stress, I think, or maybe a cold is coming on. I feel a bit weak and achy. I'll take some hot tea with brandy and honey. I'm sure it will make me feel better by morning. Besides, I can bundle up and sleep all the way to Paris."

"Yes, tomorrow then," Pieter said as he hugged me quickly, then grabbed his overcoat and walked to the door.

"Say something nice about me to the people out there." I smiled weakly.

"Can I get you anything?"

"No, thanks. Helen will be back in awhile with food and drink."

"Okay, then, see you in the morning."

I looked over the speech, took out a pencil and began to edit to my liking, adding and deleting lines. In a little while, a light knock on the door interrupted my work.

"Who is it?"

"It's me, Lina."

I unlocked the latch and let Helen in with two arms full of groceries. Now that the speech was finalized, I was surprised at how hungry I was. While cooking up dinner, for whatever reason, we began to share stories.

"Remember when we used to stuff our bras with toilet paper?"

Helen giggled. "Thank God we don't have to do that anymore. Don't forget the time when we put a little wine in the sisters' Christmas punch."

"Yes, they did have fun that year."

We continued to tease, sang some old songs and ended up praying together.

"Helen, you must know we couldn't find anything about your parents. I'm so sorry. That will be your quest."

"What about Reverend Mother?"

"She will be fine. That will be another surprise."

"A surprise?"

"Yes, Helen, you'll find this out in time. Whatever happens, spend more time with Father Tobias. He'll help you understand. Tomorrow is a big day. I need you for that. So, get some rest. I'll try to work a little more on the speech. Good night, Helen."

"Good night."

I sat alone on the couch thinking how my world would change after tomorrow. Would the dreams fade away? Would Rufina find someone else to prey on? Will father find his peace? I loved being Lina Ritter. Will mother allow me to be called that instead of her beloved Liesel? I suspected that that decision would be moot now. We'd get entirely new names to hide behind. Oh, what an ugly feeling to enter the ratline where other monsters lurked. I prayed God would allow me to see the sun through the clouds once in a while, if only for just for a few brief moments— just to let me know it was still there. I would also summit myself to His will, as mother did…Amen.


Early next morning all preparations were complete. Pieter called and Helen answered.

"The motorcade is on its way," he said. "Is Lina all right? Is she feeling better?"

"Not really, but I'll bundle her up, and you should try to let her sleep on the way. She didn't get much last night."

"Can I get her some cold medicine at the pharmacy?"

"No, thanks, Pieter. I took care of that. She took some a little while ago and feels drowsy now."

"Do you think she might want to postpone this for another day?"

"Oh, no. She wants to get this behind her. No, she plans to

stretch out on the back seat of your car."

"Okay then. I'll be by in about 45 minutes."

"She'll be ready."

On time, Pieter turned down the street to see her standing by the curb, hiding just out of sight from the news crowd. She was ready and waiting in the chill of the morning, all bundled up in a winter coat with a scarf tied over her head, holding the attaché case tightly to her chest. Pieter rushed her through a chorus of onlookers.

"Lina, get in the back seat quickly, out of the cold and lie down...rest."

With a scratchy voice she answered, "Okay."

After climbing into the driver's seat Pieter called back, "You sound awful."

"Let's go. Let's go."

"You don't need to talk, Lina, but I hope you liked the speech I wrote." Pieter looked into his rearview mirror to see a raised hand giving him a thumbs up, as if to say, "Yes, it is good."

Off they went for Paris, with a black unmarked car leading in front and one following behind. Pieter brandished some sort of walkie-talkie that allowed for a running conversation with Thomas in the lead car. They spoke mostly about the procedures in place at the Louvre. There would be a podium with a sound system, and an area for media had been sectioned off. Security arrangements were to be tight.

Thomas explained, "When we get near the Louvre, your car will take the lead and then be directed to a pre-arranged parking spot. Lina will be rushed to the podium immediately to make her statement to the intel community and the press. There will also be a live television feed for the international news outlets."

Pieter had copies of his advance lead story from today's Heidelberg Daily News. Upon arrival in Paris, he would circulate it to syndicated news organizations.

The cars sped toward the French border. The intensity built as each mile ticked away. Pieter spoke nervously with Thomas, saying little, just passing time. Hours later, when they reached the outskirts of Paris, the chatter began to pick up. Thomas began directing Pieter through the busy traffic of Paris, finally arriving at the Louvre's back parking lot. Seeing her still asleep in the back, Pieter said, "Lina, it's time. We're here."

"Bathroom please," she said softly.

"I'll find you one." Pieter got out of the car and told security to stay close. In a few minutes he was back. "There's one right behind the podium."

When she stepped from the car, for the first time, she appeared to embrace the moment. It had been just a few months since she'd first left here with the Rufina dangling about her mind, incoherent of what had taken place there in the Louvre and how it would lead to today's events.

Still covered by her trench coat and scarf, she noticed the sun still persisted. Her dark glasses now served a purpose beyond a disguise, deflecting the cameras' prying eyes. The restroom was a welcome chance to freshen up. Pieter waited outside. When she came out, he asked, "Ready to go?"

She nodded yes.

Pieter and Thomas led her up to the podium. A media spokesman gave a short introduction.

"We've come here today to shed some light on an important historical issue. Lina Ritter, referred to in the press as the 'girl from the abbey,' along with Pieter Neumann, writer for the Heidelberg Daily News, have kindly come here to brief us on their extensive research relating to looted art and to give their thoughts on the location of not only the St. Rufina and St. Justa paintings, but others as well. So, without any more speculation, let me introduce to you Lina Ritter, who I am told has a prepared statement. She will release important documentation to support her conclusions but under the condition that she take questions later at Campbell Barracks in Heidelberg, sometime next week. Please welcome this remarkable young lady from the abbey, Lina Ritter."

There was an awkward quiet as she stepped up to the podium, still wrapped in her scarf to fend off a chill. She pulled out a paper and unfolded it. Pieter and Thomas moved off to the side of the riser and looked out at the attentive crowd of reporters ready to take their notes. In a clear, resonant and audible voice that filled the air, she began.

"My name is Lina Ritter. Yes, I am the girl from the abbey who stumbled into the Louvre and found an enchanted painting, the St. Rufina. It was on display right here in the gallery, alongside the Mona Lisa. For some mysterious reason, she haunted me. She pleaded with me to discover her secret. It became an obsession. She called to me in my dreams. I didn't know why it was happening. But it drove me to find out more about her. During that search, I learned about the Nazis' art looting. "

Pieter sensed there was something dramatically wrong. That wasn't his speech at all. That wasn't what he had given her yesterday. He turned to Thomas and said under his breath, "That's not it."

"What?"

"The speech I gave her." Pieter and Thomas looked at each other bewilderingly as she continued on. They listened closely, trying to detect clues as to what was happening before their eyes, paying more attention now to the pronunciation of each word she spoke.

"Germans, along with French collaborators and profiteers, sold art looted during German occupation and taken from the dead of the Holocaust, right here in the Louvre and also later in Switzerland at undervalued prices at the Fischer art auctions. At Nuremberg, for their horrific actions, many of these reputable art dealers were indicted for crimes against humanity. However, this didn't stop the international art traders from profiting from the plundered art. Among them were the British, the Americans, the French and the most perverted violator of them all, the Holy See. The Vatican later tried to wash its hands—much as Pontius Pilate once had—in a futile attempt to distance themselves from their complicity with the Nazis' rape of humanity. Yes, people bought the art, knowing from where it came. It is a false world we live in when expedience overrides a sense of morality, is it not? The history books suggest this happened only in Germany. Only Germany! No, of course not. In modern, enlightened times shouldn't we welcome the challenge to do better? For to do less, we are destined to trod down the same perditious road.

"I come here with the knowledge that I cannot rectify the past by what I do today. No. Finding her, the Rufina, and other treasures can do little more than convenience the rightful heirs, even though that is a big part of it. No, there's far more to it than that. We must demonstrate that there is a better side to mankind. My hope is that we can raise the moral bar closer to heavenly virtues."

Pieter turned to Thomas again, "That's not her!"

"Who is it?"

"Helen! Yes, it's Helen!" While she continued, they moved closer to get a better look, to confirm their suspicions.

"So in that effort, I'm giving the international community a portion of an album, a glossary of art paintings accumulated by my father, Dietrich Ziegler, detailing items purchased, dates, buyers and dealers, all of which took place during that dark period of history. Now it's up to you, the international community, not to exploit the matter to your interest, but to find those who now are in possession of this art, with either forged or imposed legal claim. Shame them, if you must, but for the noble purpose of getting the art back into the hands of the rightful owners.

"As for me, in this world I will suffer for the sins of my father, and that is just. For wasn't the Führer's dream for all of Germany and its future generations? Was it only due to her defeat that we are here today? I ask you, what would the world be like if that were not so? Heil to Hitler? A very different world, of that I am certain. And, there are those today who still long for it! May God save us from them."

The crowd waited in stunned silence then began to wildly applaud. While cameras lit up the early evening sky, Pieter began to laugh. Jubilantly he announced in Thomas' ear, "She did it. Yes, it's Helen, and that's not my speech."

Almost screaming over the noise, Thomas asked, "Was it as good as yours?"

"No, no. It was better. Oh, so much better."

Pieter and Thomas escorted her through the crushing crowd, evading the cameras by quickly slipping her into the waiting car. A beaming Helen waved back as it whisked her away.

CHAPTER 37

# Hail Marys

By the time they returned, I was gone. There were only a few remnants left behind of the girl from the abbey. I said my regards and apologies in notes that Helen gave to Thomas and Pieter. I explained to Thomas that life gave us certain starting points, and his was quite different from mine. As for the love we may have entertained, we'd been caught up in a whirlwind, and, like all whirlwinds, ours eventually dissipated. Yet, it was a grand interlude a fantasy of our own making, and it was fun to play my part in it. I think we both knew it must end. He would go back home to California, marry, become a senior partner in his father's firm, run for office, become a mayor and never look back.

"Pieter, what did you say to him?" the priest asked.

"Not very much. No, he didn't need words. Pieter already knew in his heart where I was, and his life was just beginning. He would go on to win many awards for his journalistic achievements. On his way, he would find me. I knew that, and so did he. Our lives would never be just a start up. Little did we know that, when we first met here at the Ochsen, it would be like a marriage, a commitment that endured the times."

Eager for more and full of questions, the priest went on. "What of Reverend Mother?"

"She slipped away from the abbey and the title she carried, like day when night comes."

"Sister Johannes Maria?"

"If she were here, she'd say that the disguise was not necessary any more. It wasn't a costume for a special event. No, it was real. But life was bleeding out of her. There would be more accounting to do, but it wasn't her place anymore."

"What of God's providence, Lina?"

"Yes, Father….." Several attempts to answer him were disrupted by my faltering voice. "Father, please excuse me. I need to catch my breath. It's been so long since I've been called by that name. It carried me through my protected youth. Oh, I loved it so. It served me well."

"And God's providence?" he asked again.

"Oh, yes, Father. Mother said that is the story of our lives. She believed He had His hand in it all of it. He was in control and still is."

"And you and the church?"

"Me? Well, I am here. Still asking forgiveness, still at the altar, but not of the church. It might seem hypocritical, but I believe the church is not of God, but of people. It gives us the solemnity to pray and feel His presence. Jesus searched out the Mount of Olives to talk with God. So too for me. But, Father, I haven't left out hope. Each day I knock at God's door in faith, hoping He will answer me, not in some mystical fashion, but like He did with the saints, appearing and talking to them, like I am with you. I still cry out, waiting for Him to do just that with me some day."

"What about Helen, Lina?"

"After awhile they forgot about her, realizing she knew nothing more. Eventually, yes, she found her way, but it was so much harder for her. I'd found a family that was truly mine. With all its frailties, it was my family. She never knew that joy in her life, so she started her own. Oh, Father Tobias, what became of him? Do you remember him?" I asked.

He whispered into the cloth that divided us,, "I do."

I smiled, remembering. "What a delightful man he was."

"Yes. He brought me into the church. Soon after, he told me he'd lost heart with this life and that it was time to move on. Then the old friar did just that."

"Was it a nice memorial service for him, here in Heidelberg's cathedral?"

"Yes, Lina, it was," he said sincerely.

A flood of emotions came over me as I thought of my time with him.

"So, where will you go from here?"

"Oh, I will keep on going forward. Like mother, I have more accounting to do."

Attempting to console me, he said, "Lina, it wasn't your world that let you down."

"Oh, yes, it was. Father's, mine, yours and the next generations'. We all share the same history, don't we? You cannot pick and choose from it. Life is not like a restaurant, where you get to select from a menu, only choosing what is pleasant and discarding the rest, that which is distasteful. No, life is not like that. It will catch up with you, sooner than you think. Father, we don't come into this place with clean baggage, do we? Yet, we must carry on. That is our legacy, our heritage, good or bad. It is ours, and we must play it out, for the better. It is our history, and we can't afford to resent it or say it never happened, when we know it did. Or, God forbid, it will all happen again, and this time right in front of our eyes. Father, I thank God every day that He gave us another chance at the cross. We have to take it from there knowing that, in the end, we will be judged for how well we do with that gift."

"Will you be back this way again, Lina?"

"Maybe, but Father, if I do, it will not be my choice but His."

Finally he asked, "Lina is there anything else you need to leave at his feet?"

"No, Father, there is not."

"Then, say the Rosary five times, my child."

"So many?"

"It's been a long time, Lina. The Hail Marys, please say them slowly. Remember Notre Dame, our Lady, our Mother, she will understand and guide you. Pray to her. Now, let us pray together, in silence."

After a few minutes in prayer, the good Father waited for my reply. It never came. He prayed on in silence but, still, it never came. By then, he must have pondered, "Was this a ghost I'd been talking to?" Eventually, he put down his rosary, opened the confessional door and walked around to the other side. Reaching the open door, he leaned in and found it empty.

By then, I'd left, fleeing back from where I came. After his eyes searched around the church, he returned and noticed an album. In it were the treasures they had been looking for. I had no need for them now. I was safe. Inside was a brief note.

*Dear Father, I trust you will give this album to Pieter Neumann. He will know what to do with it.*

Like before, winter came, then spring and summer, again and again. So many times, so many places and names. Who could keep count?

Part V

# Providence

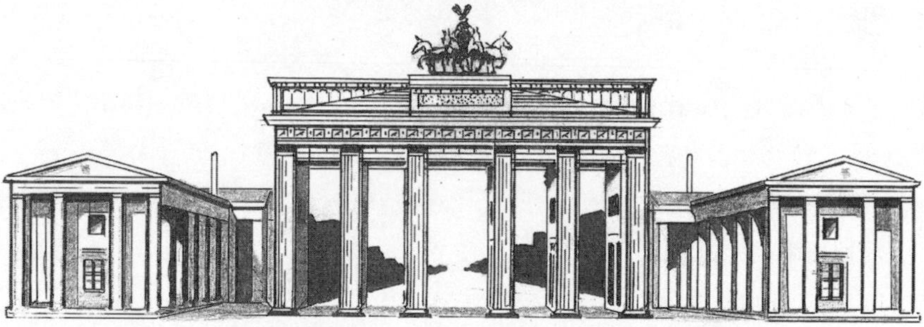

*Brandenburg Gate, Berlin Germany*

CHAPTER 38

# Berlin in Spring

It was springtime in Berlin, and gardens were alive with an abundance of illuminated colors. A few reminders of the harsh winter lay in patches under the shade of large oak trees, but the landscape was definitely in transition. The city began to come out of hibernation. People bustled about the streets, excited to take in the sights and sounds of the new season while strolling around parks and lakes on a Sunday afternoon.

At Humboldt University of Berlin, this time of year had special meaning. School was about to recess. However, lectures and tests were still underway. The mighty professors of this astute and prestigious university were putting the last-minute touches on the subject they'd scrutinized over the last quarter—attempting to pull it all together in a meaningful way,.

So it was with Dr. Becker, as he preached the sermons of the great German philosophers, explaining the purpose for their exposés. Anyone who could forestall their own personal drama for an hour could drop by to hear these lectures and find delight in doing so. Some merely indulged themselves in classroom doorways, listening for a while as spectators to entertaining ramblings. Others participated, frantically taking notes, as expedient students do, knowing full well this material would show up on their finals.

However, Marlene, one of the good professor's teaching assistants, had a special interest in today. Not only had she spent countless hours correcting his students' term papers and editing his new book, she'd also served as an apprentice under his tutelage for the past two years while working on her own doctorate degree. Fond of him and reluctant to see him go, she listened intently to his last lecture at the university. Expertise and notoriety gave him the opportunity to dismiss himself from the rigors of campus life and enter the radio media arena as a political analyst. An advancement, was the thinking of the lot, but he would be missed, certainly by his assistant, whose love for him in these past few years was evident.

She melted into a worn yet comfortable seat in the back of the overflowing lecture hall and listened intently as he made his summary statement.

"Throughout this course, you have focused on worldly philosophers and their impact on German contemporary political thought, starting with the Roman empire, describing the First Reich, then passing on to their successors, those icons of political consequence."

He paused for dramatic effect, then brashly continued. "It was the ideas from the great thinkers! Some, of course, were German philosophers, theologians and political thinkers whose reasoning made the mind fertile for modern civility. It gave the populace a purpose and rationale for action, gave legitimate claim to leadership for kings, dictators, democrats and leaders of religions. But, caution here, my dear students, let's be reminded that but by the slight of the tongue and the turn of the pencil, some men of reason have also been credited for leading us to decay and destruction in the 20th century.

"So who were these thieves of thought who rambled about with ideas and so freely provided foundations for future generations? They were the likes of Luther and his explicable theology. It freed the medieval mind to search for himself through the dynamics of scripture, and led to a personal relationship with God."

After giving descriptive passages from Leibnitz, Kant, Herder, Schiller, Hegel, Treitschke and ending with Nietzsche, he then acquitted himself. "Yes, well that is the end of this course and my love affair with this fine university. Although, please allow me to add, at this juncture, life is still an infant. Hopefully you will lead the way."

For the past two years, at each closing, Marlene made the most of it, joining in with students to give an enthusiastic applause—this time lasting much longer due to the professor's eminent retirement. They retreated together back to his office and, while walking, he reminisced on how special his last few years at the university had been. Finding the office door, he opened it and, while stepping past his secretary, said, "Hold my phone calls please, and cancel any appointments I've made."

By the wave of his hand, he gestured for Marlene to come into his cluttered room. "Sit here," he said, offering the chair across from his desk.

She thought how much he'd changed in these past few years. Oh, he still was attractive, always pleasantly dressed in a suit and tie. He still had that charming smile and proud posture, ever the gallant gentlemen. But, it was how much whiter his hair had become.

He reached into his desk drawer and pulled out a bottle of cognac and two glasses. "Yes, Marlene, it's time you had one with me." He poured and passed a glass. After holding his up, he announced, "Here's to us." Seeing he'd allowed it down his throat with one gulp, Marlene followed his example. "Strong stuff, huh?" He laughed. Agreeing with him, she tried to blow out the effect of it.

"You know, Marlene, I've been strained by your loyalty to

me over these past years." Seeing concern on her face, he added, "No, no, I don't mean it in a bad way. It's just…well, I'll figure that out one day. So, what are you going to do when I'm gone from here?"

"I'm not sure, Dr. Becker. Finish my doctorate, maybe go into journalism."

"What has infected you to want to do such a dastardly thing?" he asked with a broad smile.

"I've always had an interest in that, being a journalist and traveling about."

"You have? Where would you like to go?"

"Maybe to Heidelberg."

"Heidelberg? That doesn't seem like a worldly mission."

"Yes, you are right about that, Doctor. But, it's quiet. I think I'll like the life there."

"Oh you would? You've been there?"

"Yes, once, while passing through. And, I've read a lot about it in a magazine."

"Well, Marlene, there's a little left. Have another?"

"No, thank you, Doctor. I must be on my way. I need to get to the hospital this afternoon."

"Are you all right?"

"No, no, it's not me. It's my mother. She's very ill and needs my care from time to time."

"So sorry. Will I see you tonight at my going away party?"

"Maybe. I just need to see how mother is doing."

She stood to leave.

"Wait a minute, Marlene. Is your mother that nice lady who sometimes sits in the back of the auditorium when I'm lecturing? The one who picks up after the students? Is that her?"

"Yes, but because of her health, she hasn't been able to visit for a while."

"Yes, I remember her. I've missed her friendly smile. Well then, get on your way. I've got to start packing up here. My plane leaves tomorrow. Then, I'm off to Munich to meet with the radio producer."

As she was about to close the door behind her, he said, "Marlene, please try to come tonight. I don't know what I'd do without seeing you before I leave."

"I'll try, Doctor. It's just that mother...just mother."

At 7 o'clock, I hurried from the apartment, grabbed a trolley to Waisenstrabe, then up the street to the Zur Letzten Instanz. It was my first time at the legendary restaurant. When I entered, the consigliore greeted and asked, "Dinner?"

"Dr. Becker's gathering?"

"Yes, let me take you there."

The grand dining room was packed with the party well on its way. I made my way around and was offered champagne by a nice looking gentleman.

"Aren't you Dr. Becker's assistant?"

"Yes, I am."

"Marlene, isn't it?"

"Right again."

"He speaks very highly of you."

"I am very fond of him as well."

"Have you known him long?"

"Oh, yes, a long time."

"How nice. We will miss him around here."

"Me too."

Just then, across the room, Dr. Becker caught sight of me and rushed across while attempting to balance a glass in his hand.

"Marlene, glad you could make it! How's your mother doing?"

"Not well."

"Sorry to hear that. Please come and sit with me and my family." A very attractive, well-dressed lady stood to greet me warmly.

"Hello, I am Sigrid Becker, der professor's wife," she said with a pleasant smile. "And you must be Marlene."

"Yes. We met briefly at the department's last Christmas party."

"Oh, of course. I've heard so much about you from Michael. All good, I might add. Although, I have to admit, I've been a little jealous of the time he spends with you."

"I'm flattered then, I think."

Sigrid kept up her beautiful smile when she said, "Join us, please. Here, sit next to me. Let's get you something to eat." She motioned to the waiter, and he understood. "So, Marlene, how long have you lived here in Berlin?"

"Three years come September."

"Really? And where were you born?"

Maybe it was the glass of champagne or her sincerity, I'm not sure, but I let down my guard while answering, "Heidelberg."

"Heidelberg?"

Just then Dr. Becker sat down with us. "What's this about Heidelberg?"

"Marlene just told me she was born in Heidelberg."

He looked confused. "Really? What a wonderful place, romantic, quaint and such beautiful scenery."

"Yes, it is," I said, hoping the subject would change. But the Doctor went on. "Beautiful churches, especially the Jesuit Catholic Church and the abbey. Have you ever visited the abbey, Marlene?" Without letting me answer, he added, "They have the most beautiful rose gardens there."

I jumped in. "You've been there? To Heidelberg?"

"Yes."

"To the abbey?" I asked, trying to hold back my emotions.

"A couple of times. Yes, while on vacation I attended mass, and this old monk began chatting with us." He turned to his wife. "Sigrid, remember the old friar we spoke with back in Heidelberg?"

"Yes, of course."

He turned back to me. "Well, he suggested that if we had the time, besides seeing the old castle, to make sure we ventured across the river Neckar and visit the abbey."

"Was his name Father Tobias?"

"Yes, yes, that was his name. "You knew him, Marlene?"

"Yes, I did. He heard my confession many times."

"But, you told me…"

I had to quickly remove myself from the conversation, so I turned to Sigrid. "Are you excited to go to Munich?"

"Yes and no. We'll see in a month or two, when we finally get settled. That part of Germany is so different from Berlin. We'll see." A lady waved to her. "Please excuse me for a minute, Marlene. I've got to say goodbye to someone."

When she got up to leave, the waiter brought a plate of food. Even though it looked delicious, I was on a mission now as I turned to Dr. Becker. He'd just finished talking to the university chancellor, so I took the opportunity to ask, "Are you going to be in the office tomorrow?"

"Yes, I need to finish packing."

"May I see you tomorrow, Doctor?"

"Of course, Marlene."

"It's my mother. She asked if she could come by, if she's well enough, to pay her regards for you helping me with my studies these past few years. Would that be possible?"

"Of course, Marlene. You needn't have asked."

"Then, let me say good night."

"But, you haven't touched your food."

"Sorry, I'm worried about my mother. So, I must rush off now. She needs my care. Please say goodbye to your lovely wife for me. I know my mother would have loved her."

I rushed out of the restaurant, but, when I turned up the street, I pulled myself into the wall and began to sob. My emotions gave me up completely. Sometimes life could be so cruel. I took a few moments for me to regain control of my tears, wiping them down with my sleeve. I made my way over to the trolley that took me back to the hospital. I found her lying quietly, alone in the room. "Mother, can you make it with me tomorrow?"

"Yes. I can make it tomorrow. God will show us the way to our family. Didn't I tell you to wait on God? Providence, God's perfect timing. Now, please go home tonight. I'm especially tired. I'll get some rest here. I promise."

"No, mother. I won't leave you, not tonight. I'll just sleep here on the couch." I lay down and tried to rest, but I was too tired for that.

"Is he happy?"

"Yes, mother, he is so happy."

"And his wife?"

"Yes, her too. You'd like her."

"Would God like her?"

"Yes, mother. God would like her too."

She whispered, "I loved all of you so..." Then she went silent.


It was simple, but crowded. Friends came from all over Germany. Most of them I never knew. I never told them. There were so many. One paid for all of it. Roses were everywhere. Eventually, one by one, they reluctantly began to go their separate ways. It was as if they'd buried their hopes with her. After mass finished, I sat alone in the church with her. I couldn't leave her this way. Then, as if by design, I heard footsteps. They caused me to cry out. Oh, how I wished for it to be the old friar, Father Tobias, coming from heaven with reassurance and peace that mother was all right. Tears fell from my face as I pleaded with God. Then, a familiar hand touched my shoulder. Moments later, kneeling next to me, holding me close, he finally broke the silence and his cover with a trembling yet distinct voice. "Liesel?"

I echoed back. "Liesel, yes, yes." I turned to look up into his swollen eyes. "Michael, yes, it's always been me."

"And our mother?"

"Oh, she loved you, Michael. It was her last words before God took her home. She so loved us all, father, Johannes, you and me. We were her world. The others, did you see? They all came."

"Yes, they did, Liesel. She was loved."

That day, kneeling, wrapped in Michael's arms in front of mother, I looked up into the brightly lit stained glass and, for the first time, God spoke to me.

CHAPTER 39
# The Good Harvest

fter the Berlin Wall went down in 1989 and Cold War tensions began to fade, the East German government released documents that were previously classified, not only by them but also by the Russians. Those documents implicated the U.S., French and Belgians, along with Great Britain, for complicity with the Nazis after World War II. Their defense for such activity was the necessity to confront the expanding fear of communism and upcoming Cold War. The byproduct of the declassified documents produced a wealth of material, hidden from the public by the Allies, stocked as confidential in archives that would now, some 45 years later, resurface and detail many of the post WWII activities in Germany.

A great amount of time has been spent since then to bring Nazi war criminals to justice. Life expectancy has clearly become a major obstacle. In order to obtain criminal prosecutions, mortality issues have quietly challenged their captors. However, an exception must be made for the recovery of the arts. Most likely, they will be with us until eternity. Therefore, the reclamation of the arts is a categorical imperative.

A few related stories have recently surfaced and made headlines in major media outlets. From the Dallas Observer, October 23, 2009 headline Nazi Looted Paintings Discovered At Southern Methodist University reads as follows:

"Robert Edsel, from the Monuments Men Foundation that scours the globe for the millions of pieces of art stolen by Hitler and the Nazis, found two such items on the campus of his alma mater, Southern Methodist University. Specifically, they were discovered in the Meadows Museum. They are: "a pair of famous paintings on display at SMU's Meadows Museum created by Spanish master Bartolomé Esteban Murillo (1618-1682) of Seville's patron saints, Justa and Rufina. Estimated to be worth more than $10 million, they are believed to have been stolen from the Rothschild family in Paris in 1941. The Nazi ERR (Einsatzstab Reichsleiter Rosenberg) code evidencing Rothschild ownership is still visible on the stretcher bar of one of the paintings; it appears to have been rubbed off the other."

Responding to the discovery, Patti LaSalle, exec director in SMU's Office of Public Affairs, sent a statement from Mark Roglán, Director
Adjunct professor, Meadows School of the Arts
Southern Methodist University concerning Edsel's
announcement:

"Everyone has always known these were pieces confiscated by the Nazis. And as part of its commitment to share information about its collections, the Meadows Museum has posted on its website the provenance, or ownership history, of the 143 paintings in its collection, notes their ownership by the Rothschild Family Collection in Paris and their confiscation by the Nazis. The paintings were purchased for the Meadows Museum from a gallery in New York City in 1972. Since that time the paintings have been widely published, exhibited at museums throughout the world, and studied by numerous scholars.

The posted information includes a reference to the research of Robert Edsel and a note of appreciation. However, neither Mr. Edsel nor his associates has ever presented SMU with any evidence that would question whether the paintings were properly restituted. In researching and compiling provenance for works in the collection, the Meadows Museum has followed guidelines issued by the American Association of Museums and the Association of Art Museum Directors."

Another update covering the Nazi looted art was added:
From The Vile Plutocrat July 16, 2011:

"New York based billionaire art dealer Guy Wildenstein, has been charged with possession of stolen goods and breach of trust in relation to 30 stolen or otherwise missing artworks that were discovered in the Wildenstein Institute's Paris storeroom."

Just about every week similar Nazi looted pieces have been popping into the news and the probability of such artwork showing up in major museum's galleries and advertised for sale by art dealers is extremely high.

These articles were included, not for the purpose of implicating individuals or organizations but to shed a light on the nuance of the world art industry. For the most part those in possession of such artwork are quite aware of their nefarious past. Why not post that infamous history along side of the artwork displayed in galleries. If there's no shame in it, let the public be aware and decide. It's time to pull back the curtain. It's ludicrous to suggest in a featured story that the findings are inexplicable discoveries. Does the art industry know more then what they profess? It appears to be a very complex and dubious web the industry has spun to deceive the public. But why do that? I believe simply because the value of these art pieces has increased incrementally. So, if you factor the cost of litigation, insurance implications, and the uncertainty of title, it creates reluctant investors, most likely cumulating in the destabilization of the entire art world market.

It highly begs one to suggest, that this is all a ruse to deflect the real business of the art world, one that unfortunately thrives at the cost of thousands of Jewish lives that vanished in German Nazi crematoriums. Now, is that just business as usual? It seems that way, for in order to fight the profiteers over title, the claimant is required to assume the cost of litigation while shouldering the burden of proof as they wait then hope for a 'fair and equitable resolution'.

It is time to handle this issue differently than just a series of white-collar crimes that allows economics and political considerations to overwhelm moral and ethical implications. Historically, not doing so has had the lethal affect of demoting civic values to a set of incomprehensible babble, a murky precipice for a declining civilization.

-Syndicated Columnist, Pieter Neumann

# $\mathcal{G}$IL LEFEBVRE

A man for all seasons, Gil Lefebvre is a veteran, a former professional athlete and an educator who has also worked in politics and law.

Now an accomplished writer, Lefebvre launched this new phase of his life and career penning commentaries, essays and poetry. His most prominent published works are four novels. The first, *Unto Caesar Unto God,* assesses the merits of religious activism. The second, *Not Too Far To Have Never Been,* delves into the challenges that defined the Vietnam generation, examining them through the lens of romance and suspense.

*Catalina Summer,* his third novel, is a romp through a wondrously exotic and historic island setting, á la Huckleberry Finn. With his newest and fourth release, *Obsessing Rufina,* Lefebvre captures the hurt and deception of post-World War II Germany as seen through the eyes of an intrepid college student. Stumbling upon art crimes perpetuated by the Nazis and their cohorts, the novel's heroine refuses to turn a blind eye to the sins. She dares to investigate and expose, with help from two intriguing yet wholly dissimilar romantic interests, a sordid past that others would just as soon forget.

Currently, Lefebvre is working on another historical novel. *The Regal Sons of Douglas* is a true tale of individual triumph on the gridiron of the University of Southern California (USC) campus in the early 1900s – a story with as much heart as Notre Dame's beloved Rudy's.